Tim LaHaye is a noted author, minister, and nationally recognized speaker on Bible prophecy. He is founder and president of Tim LaHaye Ministries and a cofounder of the Pre-Trib Research Center. A pastor for thirty-nine years, Dr. LaHaye has written more than fifty nonfiction books and coauthored the Left Behind series, the most successful Christian fiction venture in publishing history, with Jerry Jenkins. LaHaye and his wife, Beverly, who have been married for more than sixty years, live in Southern California. You can visit his website at www.TimLaHaye.com.

Jerry B. Jenkins, former vice president for publishing and current chairman of the board of trustees for the Moody Bible Institute of Chicago, is the author of more than 175 books, including the Left Behind series with Tim LaHaye. Dr. Jenkins's writing has appeared in *Time, Reader's Digest, Parade, Guideposts,* and dozens of other Christian periodicals. He owns Jenkins Entertainment, a filmmaking company based in Los Angeles, as well as the Christian Writers Guild, which aims to train tomorrow's professional Christian writers. He is also a contributing editor to *Writer's Digest* magazine. A sought-after marriage and family speaker, Jenkins lives with his wife, Dianna, in Colorado Springs. You can visit his website at www.JerryJenkins.com.

BOOKS IN THE JESUS CHRONICLES

John's Story: The Last Eyewitness

Mark's Story: The Gospel According to Peter

Luke's Story: By Faith Alone

THE JESUS CHRONICLES

Book Three

LUKE'S STORY

BY FAITH ALONE

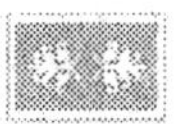

TIM LAHAYE *and* JERRY B. JENKINS

BERKLEY PRAISE, NEW YORK

BERKLEY PRAISE
Published by The Berkley Publishing Group
A Division of Penguin Group (USA) Inc.
375 Hudson Street, New York, New York 10014, USA
Penguin Group (Canada), 90 Eglinton Avenue East, Suite 700, Toronto, Ontario M4P 2Y3, Canada
(a division of Pearson Penguin Canada Inc.)
Penguin Books Ltd., 80 Strand, London WC2R 0RL, England
Penguin Group Ireland, 25 St. Stephen's Green, Dublin 2, Ireland (a division of Penguin Books Ltd.)
Penguin Group (Australia), 250 Camberwell Road, Camberwell, Victoria 3124, Australia
(a division of Pearson Australia Group Pty. Ltd.)
Penguin Books India Pvt. Ltd., 11 Community Centre, Panchsheel Park, New Delhi—110 017, India
Penguin Group (NZ), 67 Apollo Drive, Rosedale, North Shore 0632, New Zealand
(a division of Pearson New Zealand Ltd.)
Penguin Books (South Africa) (Pty.) Ltd., 24 Sturdee Avenue, Rosebank, Johannesburg 2196,
South Africa

Penguin Books Ltd., Registered Offices: 80 Strand, London WC2R 0RL, England

PRINTING HISTORY
Putnam Praise hardcover edition / February 2009
Berkley Praise trade paperback edition / February 2010

Berkley trade paperback ISBN: 978-0-425-23219-4

The Library of Congress has cataloged the Putnam Praise hardcover edition as follows:

LaHaye, Tim F.
Luke's story / by Tim LaHaye and Jerry B Jenkins.
p.   cm.
ISBN 978-0-399-15523-9
1. Luke, Saint—Fiction. 2. Bible. N.T.—History of Biblical events—Fiction. I. Jenkins, Jerry B. II. Title.
PS3562.A3151L85   2009   2008040377
813'.54—dc22

This is a work of fiction based on characters and events depicted in the Bible. The publisher does not have any control over and does not assume any responsibility for author or third-party websites or their content.

NEW KING JAMES VERSION®
Build Your Life On It.™

146119709

To

Frank LaHaye and Harry Jenkins,

who await us at the Eastern Gate

Mercy there was great,
and grace was free . . .
at Calvary.

Part One

THE SLAVE

ONE

Syrian Antioch, A.D. *20*

Having just turned fifteen, Loukon was not even required on the errand that would shape the rest of his life.

As the son of slaves under the charge of Theophilus, he could just as easily have remained tending the animals at the master's vast estate in Daphne, near the outskirts of the city.

But, as usual, Loukon's insatiable curiosity had gotten the better of him. That same sense of wonder that had spurred him to learn to read as a child and beg scrolls from the master's house staff made him sprint to the flatbed wood wagon as the thick driver secured the horses to it.

"Where to this morning, Lippio?" he said, as adult slaves climbed aboard, rimming the back, legs dangling.

"Through the city to the river, lad. Picking up a shipment of marble."

"Marble! No wonder so many men. Last time you brought papyrus by yourself."

"I must make haste, Loukon," Lippio said, settling behind the horses.

"I've never been all the way into Antioch. Let me come?"

"You know that's not up to me, and I don't have time to wait till you get permission."

"One minute! Please!"

"One."

Loukon raced to ask his father, tilling the gardens with his mother and others.

"If you'll help us upon your return," his father said.

"Of course!" he said over his shoulder. "Lippio! Wait!"

"You're not coming to watch, Luke," Lippio said as the boy mounted the wagon and sat next to him. "We'll need every pair of hands."

"I hoped you would say that. May I drive the horses?"

"No! Now, just sit still until we reach the Orontes."

Sitting still was no small task on the heavy rig. The wagon bounced and jostled, its wood and iron wheels rattling through ruts until the dirt road led to stone streets that would take them into the city proper. Loukon held on, feeling the pressure in his thighs as he pressed his sandals to the floorboard. Inches away, Lippio's hairy arms strained to keep the horses moving slow and steady.

The only slave his age who could read, Loukon had been studying the history of this very area and badgering adults with questions about it. Now he took to instructing Lippio, who gave him a look as if he needed no teaching.

"This is the center of the Imperial Province of Syria!" Loukon exulted.

"And you can thank Caesar Augustus for that," Lippio said, "*Quiescat in place.*"

"Yes, may he rest in peace. What? You don't think I know Latin too?"

Lippio shook his head. "It shouldn't surprise me, but that is all *I* know in Latin. I'd wager you are fluent."

"Not quite, but someday."

"You realize how privileged you are, Luke."

"I'm learning."

It was true. Loukon had been slow to recognize that the slaves under Theophilus were treated unlike anyone else's. But a trip like this made that even more obvious.

Antioch was militarily strategic to Rome, located at the foot of a mountain range. It also served the trade routes into Egypt and India and Parthia. And of course the Orontes River led to the Mediterranean. Lippio steered them through the Eastern Gate, decorated with a statue of a wolf nursing Romulus and Remus.

"Do you believe in the gods?" Loukon said.

Lippio gave him a look.

"What?" the young man said. "Are you not religious?" Loukon pretended to be teasing, but such things intrigued him. Some of his fellow slaves worshiped the God of the Jews, but most either believed in the Roman gods or none at all.

"You know better than to discuss such things," Lippio said. "Especially with your elders."

"You're saying it's none of my concern?"

"Of course it isn't! It's personal. And there are enough other things to be thinking and talking about."

"Such as?"

"You're the educated one. Aren't you interested in all the cultures that come together in this city?"

Loukon saw people of seemingly every race bustling about. The slaves were obvious. Many were branded and marked, even shackled.

All went about their work quickly, eyes cast down, followed by masters with sticks and whips. No wonder strangers who learned that Loukon was the son of slaves seemed to wince or even grimace, as if discovering he had been stricken by some plague.

"I've never seen our master treat his slaves like that," Loukon said.

"And you won't," Lippio said, pulling into a line that included velvet-draped carriages bearing dignitaries, covered trailers laden with who knew what kinds of imported goods, and pedestrians. "Theophilus is most excellent in that regard. What other master would allow the likes of us such freedom?"

"Why does he?"

Lippio kept his eyes on the vehicle ahead and pulled the reins. "It has to do with his Stoicism. Don't ask me to explain it, because unlike you I do not deem it polite to discuss it with him. But I believe he sees all men as equals, even though clearly we are not. Yet isn't it nice to be treated that way?"

The broad expanse of stone pavement extended nearly 30 feet across and was lined on either side by tiled roofed porticoes 20 feet high and 30 feet thick. Hundreds milled beneath these, sheltering themselves from the sun. Loukon stared at the decorations of marble and mosaics, along with the statues under the colonnades, as the wagon slowly and noisily made its way past temples. One was gold-paneled, and there was a circus, Roman baths, and several theaters. The majesty of the city finally began to give way to plainness and eventually squalor. This Loukon found fascinating.

"Look at all the soldiers, Lippio. You know the Roman legion commander here is second in power to only the emperor himself."

"Well, he has his hands full in this district, doesn't he?"

Lippio made a clicking noise and yanked the horses until they sidled into a narrow side street, lined with five-story buildings pressed close together. Each had row upon row of shuttered windows, behind which, Loukon knew, the poorest of the population lived.

Not far from the river they rumbled past a synagogue. As the wagon slowed to a crawl and Lippio navigated yet another tight turn, Loukon overheard men praying.

One thanked God he had not been born "a Greek, a slave, or a woman."

"Why would he say that?" Loukon said.

"Don't ask me," Lippio said. "Like you, I was born two of those three, but I would rather be a slave under Theophilus than live here a freeman, wouldn't you?"

Loukon nodded. "I *am* grateful I was not born a woman, though."

Lippio laughed. "Me too, Luke. That would be too great a burden."

When finally they reached the Orontes, Loukon saw small craft laden with oil and wine and cloth and spices and grain and nuts. These would be transported to larger ships at the harbor on the Mediterranean for trade around the world.

Lippio steered the wagon toward a man standing in the sand by huge pallets stacked with marble slabs. The man looked relieved. "I let the ship sail on with the rest of its cargo," he said, "praying you would arrive and I would not be left here guarding this all day while finding no other buyer."

"Do not fret, friend," Lippio said. "My master is trustworthy."

While Lippio was completing the transaction, the slaves clambered down and began loading the marble onto the wagon. Loukon helped the best he could, but the loads were so heavy, he knew he wasn't making much of a difference.

Presently Lippio joined them and lent his weight and his back to the task, moving the loads about until all but two stacks had been secured. "These will be the biggest challenge, men," he said. "Make sure each stays level as we put them atop. If they shift, there will be no righting them, and don't try to be a hero. If the load tips, just clear out or you will be crushed."

"But the marble will surely break," Loukon said.

"Much of it would, yes. But I'd rather return to the master with all my men and less of the marble than the other way around."

The agent who had sold the goods was clearly no slave and obviously not about to help. He seemed to watch dispassionately as the crew painstakingly maneuvered the several-hundred-pound loads into position. They had the second-to-last pallet in place to be lifted above their shoulders and slid onto the top when Lippio instructed them to pause and inhale.

"Together now!" he said.

Luke helped lift, but when the load was raised beyond his reach, he moved out of the way, only to watch in horror as the pallet tilted. The men strained to keep it steady, sweating in the sun. With a sickening scrape, the top slab of marble began to slowly slide.

"We're good!" Lippio called out. "We're good! Let it go!"

As the men ducked, still trying to keep the rest of the weight level, the slab slipped free and slid directly toward Lippio. Loukon could see that if the man merely followed his own advice he could have leapt out of the way, which, of course, would have caused the entire load to fall.

But there he stood, glistening muscled arms shaking with the effort, and the corner of the slab ripped into his right biceps, tearing a huge gash all the way to the bone. As he screamed and fell, the rest of the men were somehow able to wrestle the load to the ground and save the rest.

Lippio writhed, blood shooting from his riven arm with each beat of his heart. Loukon quickly knelt next to him and tore a strip of the hem off his own garment. He tied tight above the wound.

"I'm going to die!" Lippio cried.

"You're not!" Loukon said, turning to the men, who looked pale and frozen in place. "Help me get him up! He must sit with his arm raised! Now! You and you, help him up! I'll drive the horses." He turned to the marble agent. "You guard the rest of this until we return."

"I'm not responsible! I have other duties!"

"You'll deal directly with my master if any of this is lost!"

The men loaded Lippio into the seat next to Loukon, and the lad told one to squeeze in beside him and make sure the man kept his arm elevated. "It will keep him from losing more blood!"

Loukon wrangled the horses through the deep sand and back onto the street, the going slower than ever now with thousands of pounds of marble on board.

"Don't let me die, Luke!" Lippio said, his eyes wide, voice thin.

Luke finally got the wagon moving at a steady clip, pushing through the narrow streets and back onto the wide thoroughfare. There he passed curious traffic where people at first scowled and shouted and shook their fists, then fell silent as they saw the injured man and gave way.

The worst part of the journey was the last mile of rutted dirt road, where Loukon was forced to slow to keep Lippio from pitching off his perch and the marble from shifting and falling. A couple of hundred yards from the estate, Loukon enlisted one of the men in the back to take over the driving. Then he leaped down and ran all the way, quickly outdistancing the wagon.

Loukon flew into the main house, apologizing to one and all and demanding to know where the physician was. Someone pointed him to the parlor, where the elderly man was teaching the master's grandchildren.

"Lippio has been seriously injured and will be here shortly!"

The physician, who had evolved into more instructor than doctor over the last few years, hobbled behind Loukon, breathlessly asking the details. As soon as the wagon breached the gate, three men carried Lippio in, his arm still raised.

The mistresses of the house gathered the children as the physician ordered the men to deliver Lippio directly to his own chambers and called for water to be heated and aides to attend him.

"If this man survives, Loukon," the physician said, "you will have saved him."

TWO

Loukon spent much of the day waiting outside the physician's quarters, venturing back out to his duties only after learning that Lippio would indeed survive.

"He's going to be very sore for a long time," the old physician said, "and I don't know if the arm will ever return to full strength, but your quick thinking and action spared him."

"You taught me well."

"I recall advising you only on the care of the occasional lame animal."

Loukon shrugged. "I didn't know what else to do."

THAT EVENING, as he sat in a tiny hovel with his parents over a meal of bread and bean soup, Loukon regaled them with the events of the day.

His mother remained silent as his father shook his head. "That was risky, Luke. What if you had caused him more harm?"

"No one else was doing anything, Father! It didn't seem right to let him lie there and bleed."

"I suppose not. But did you have any idea what you were doing?"

"All I knew was that doing nothing would have been wrong, and I had to act fast. You can imagine how scared I was."

"But how did you know to bind him above the wound and keep his arm raised?"

"It just made sense. Men of medicine believe blood originates from the heart, and all of his would have been spilt through the wound if I had not stopped it."

"I should be proud of you," his father said, "but it sure seems your eagerness gets you into situations where you don't belong."

A knock came at the door and Loukon's father nodded to his mother. She quickly rose and opened it to a young maiden.

"Your son's presence is requested by the master," she said.

"The master?" Loukon's mother said.

"Theophilus himself," the girl said, hurrying away.

Loukon's father raised his brows. "Go with haste," he said. "And tell the truth."

THEOPHILUS WAS a robust man in his late forties, white-haired and dressed in brightly colored garments. He remained seated near a fireplace as Loukon was ushered in by an aide. Theophilus seemed to study him, finally gesturing toward a chair.

Loukon bowed and sat.

"I'm told I should be bowing to you, young man," Theophilus said.

"Oh, no, sir."

"You had adults doing your bidding during the emergency. You even cowed the marble seller! He had the rest of the lot delivered!"

"I hope I didn't offend anyone."

"You certainly didn't offend *me*."

Loukon felt self-conscious as the man gazed at him. He wondered if he was expected to reply.

"Your parents have been with me since before they were married, when I moved here as a young man. I remember when you were born. May I call you Luke?"

Loukon forced himself to merely nod rather than to gush, "You can call me whatever you please."

"You know why you're here. I am thanking you for the valuable service you performed for me today. I have been told the details, but only secondhand. I shall procure the story from the victim himself when he is up to it, but I would like your account."

"My account?"

"Tell me exactly what happened."

A few minutes later, Loukon concluded with, "And then you sent for me. I must say, Lippio nearly gave his life trying to protect your property."

Theophilus, who had sat smiling through much of the story, now gazed seriously at the young man. "I understand that, but we are talking about you just now. You are aware, I suppose, that many slave owners would restrict offspring from the many opportunities you have been afforded."

"Oh, yes, sir, I know. No one else I know, in my station I mean, is able to learn and to read and—if I may say—to be involved in so much that goes on around here."

Theophilus leaned forward and rested his elbows on his knees. "There are those who think I give you too much rein. I myself have wondered at times, seeing you cavort, dashing about here and there and involving yourself in so many activities. But it has seemed to profit me, especially today."

"Well, sir, I know that when I am of age, I will be required to toil as my parents do, and so perhaps I have taken advantage of your good graces and enjoyed freedom that most slaves do not."

"You are not the typical child of indentured servants."

"Sir?"

"My people tell me of your curiosity, your eagerness to learn, your proficiency in language. Even an interest in history?"

"That might be my favorite pursuit," Loukon said. "That and medicine."

"If you were to choose a field, which would it be?"

"Probably the bean field, sir."

Theophilus threw his head back and laughed heartily. "And a sense of humor as well! Very good!" He crossed his legs and leaned back, his visage serious again. "Now, truly, if you were not limited to a slave's future, what field of study would you most prefer?"

Not limited to a slave's future? Loukon had never even considered such.

"I don't understand."

"Come, come, Luke. Allow yourself to conjecture. Say when you are of age you are sent to the university at Tarsus. What would you study?"

"Everything! Isn't that what *university* means?"

"Yes, yes, but eventually serious students focus on one area. What would be yours?"

"I'd have to think about that. But as I say, it would be between history and medicine."

"How much do you love history?"

"A lot."

"Medicine more?"

Loukon shrugged, wondering if he should do that in front of his master. "Perhaps, but not much more."

"I want you to think about something. Consider this offer. Between now and when you are university age, you no longer tend the animals or work the fields but rather study under my tutors, my physician, and the others."

"Seriously?"

"Of course. You have been pestering them at odd hours for years anyway, haven't you?"

Loukon felt himself redden. He nodded.

"And then," Theophilus said, "let's say I sponsor you to attend the university in Tarsus."

Loukon was wide-eyed. "I'm finding this hard to believe."

"And you may have heard stories of students so poor that they share a garment between them. One stays in bed studying while the other attends the lecture hall, and then they change places."

"Actually, I have heard that, but I never thought it would have any bearing on me."

"But what if it did?"

"I would be grateful for two garments."

Theophilus laughed again. "Here is my caveat, Luke. I prefer that you lean toward medicine, a more practical pursuit. Do not abandon history, of course. But you would be more useful to me as a physician. My own is aged, as you know. In seven years or so, when you have graduated, you could return as my house physician."

Loukon was still having trouble taking it all in, and it must have showed.

"There's more," Theophilus said.

"More?"

"Should you succeed, while I would require your services for a few years, I would grant you your freedom so that eventually you could practice medicine wherever and however you pleased."

Loukon was starting to get the picture. "I've always thought being a ship's doctor looked like fun."

"You'd have to attend to your own seasickness, I fear," Theophilus said, smiling. "But there's even more."

"I don't dare ask."

"I would also grant your parents' freedom."

Loukon let his shoulders slump and he fell back in his chair, unable to move. So many questions, but the words stuck in his throat. He gestured and shook his head.

"They have been most faithful," Theophilus said, as if that explained everything.

"But they, but you—I just—"

"Mind your posture, son. Sit up. The mind works better that way."

"Sorry, it's just that I don't understand. I mean, I've seen that you are not the typical master, but what would make you—how can you—?"

"Am I not free to do as I please?"

"Of course, but who are we that—"

"You are an unusually bright young man, and your father—your mother too—have proved most diligent and faithful to me."

"But haven't many?"

"Hear me, Luke. Yes, many of my servants are worthy, but few are able. Most are better off with my providing their food and shelter right here. Granted their freedom, I fear they would flounder. You see?"

"My father would succeed. He can do anything."

"I agree. He might need counsel, even a loan for a time. But he strikes me as a man of character and initiative."

"He is! He will be so thrilled!"

"Oh, son, now I have entrusted you with a confidence that must not be broken. You cannot breathe a word of this, even to your parents.

Imagine if it got around to the others. Or if you did not uphold your end of the bargain. Remember, you must study diligently to be able to qualify for the university, and then you must succeed there, returning to me as a qualified physician. Only then does all the rest fall into place."

Loukon felt as if the secret would make him burst. "I understand."

"Do you? This will remain a solemn agreement between us?"

"How will I explain being a student here in the meantime, rather than a worker?"

"Leave that to me."

"Master, I cannot tell you how grateful I am. It is as if my whole life has changed in an instant."

"Well, let us just say that it could. Your future is in your hands. Now, go, before your father finds it hard to believe my expression of thanks lasted this long."

Loukon stood. "Thank you, sir."

Theophilus waved him off, but Loukon hesitated.

"Surely, you're not having second thoughts already, Luke."

"No, but—"

"I've explained everything."

"Begging your pardon, master, but actually you have not. I'm curious."

"Of course you are. That's your trademark. But I don't know how else to make it plain. You have an active mind, and—"

"Forgive me, sir, but I understand that and appreciate it. What I am curious about is you. You are a different kind of master than any other I have ever heard of. Why?"

Theophilus rose and approached, placing a hand on Loukon's shoulder. "Something you will learn as you mature is that it is generally not prudent for a man to talk about himself. I have always been uncomfortable with it and do not appreciate it in others. Also, I am a firm believer in the restorative powers of sleep, and I like to rise early too—as you know. It is time for me to retire, and I daresay, past time when you should too."

Loukon was again at a loss for words, but he was desperate to not let this go. "Sir, please. I admire that you are different from other men. It is the very reason your servants are so devoted to you. I must know what makes you different. I promise not to tell anyone."

Theophilus sighed. "Very well, but all in good time. Prove yourself worthy of my trust in assigning my tutors and physician to you, and I will discuss philosophy with you. For in the end, it is the philosophy of life I have embraced that makes me who I am, whatever that is."

"Someone told me today that you are a Stoic. Is that true?"

Theophilus cocked his head. "As a matter of fact it is. Who told you that?"

"Lippio."

"Indeed? And what did he say of it?"

"Very little. Said he couldn't explain it but believed it made you the master you are. In truth he felt it imprudent of me to discuss religion."

Theophilus guided Loukon out. "Well, as I say, it is a philosophy—it is not religion. But I keep my word. On the morrow you shall be assigned courses of study. Apply yourself to the task, and when good reports come to me, you and I will discuss Stoicism. Fair enough?"

"Thank you, sir."

"Now, let me check in on our patient and then hope I am not the last one here to fall asleep."

THREE

Syrian Antioch, A.D. *21*

It had taken months for Lippio to be up and about again, but it became quickly evident that his injury was debilitating and that his arm would never be the same. Despite a host of treatments and remedies and much physical therapy, the injured muscle atrophied. And while the man could force the limb into position and use his fingers in limited fashion to help him drive a team of horses, he had otherwise become effectively left-handed.

Luke gave much thought to Lippio's dangling arm and what might be done to somehow restore it. But in all his studies with the house physician, nothing they came up with made a difference. To his credit, Theophilus directed that Lippio's duties be adjusted to work around the malady. He became an overseer, supervising teams of slaves, mainly in caring for the animals and for deliveries and pickups of exports and imports.

Although he was unable to help Lippio regain use of his arm, Loukon spent time with the man, encouraging him and keeping his spirits up. His compassion for Lippio was apparently reported to Theophilus, for again the young man was summoned to him.

"I am hearing good things," the master said. "It is clear you care about people, especially those who have suffered. That trait should serve you well in the field of medicine."

"I'm learning so much."

"I understand that too. I am eager that you become an enthusiastic student at the university in two years."

"I wish I could go now."

Theophilus smiled. "All in good time. I want that you be versed in Stoicism before you leave. That philosophy pervades the university, as you can imagine."

"And you yourself will tutor me in it?"

"No, no. I wish I had the time and the ability."

"But you have clearly embraced it, sir."

"Yet I don't pretend to be a teacher. I promised we will discuss it, and we shall, but only from a personal standpoint. You learn its history and its various disciplines, and as it applies we can talk about how I try to practice it."

"Its history?"

"Oh, yes. Stoicism is more than three centuries old already."

"I have much to learn."

"Maintain that attitude, Luke. I worried that praising you for your intellect might result in narcissism."

"Oh, I hope not, master. It seems to me humility is the hallmark of true learning."

"Well said. Perhaps the day will come when you and I can discuss the—how shall I say it—vanity or the futility of self-improvement through philosophy."

Loukon scowled. "But you, sir, seem to have made of yourself—"

"Don't make me regret being so self-revelatory, son. Yes, I try to practice Stoicism and hope it has made me a kinder man, one who views all men as brothers. And as you really study it, you will become aware of its lofty goals for self-betterment. And yet I can testify to the constant struggle against my own passions."

Loukon was taken aback. Perhaps his master had already been more forthcoming than he should have been, especially before one of his own slaves—and a young one at that. And yet if the man was willing to be so transparent, Loukon wanted to know everything. Did even one so revered as Theophilus struggle to tame his own desires and weaknesses? Loukon couldn't imagine it, but the man had opened the door.

"You, sir?"

Theophilus smiled. "Let it be our secret that I am not perfect. And how about you, son? Do you not battle jealousy, sloth, lust?"

Loukon's face burned. If he expected the man to be so open, he himself was obligated to be open as well, especially given their relative stations. How had Theophilus hit on the very vices that so frustrated Loukon? He raged with envy when anyone received more attention from the master than he. He strived to appear humble and selfless, yet found himself hoping everyone noticed. And lust? The fair maidens his age and even several of the beautiful mistresses of the household had become such objects of desire for him that he could often barely think of anything else.

"Yes, master, I would like to be able to control myself so that I might one day grow to be a man like you."

Theophilus chuckled. "You nearly said 'an old man,' didn't you?"

"You're not old."

"Again, your compassion comes to the fore. I confess I look forward to the day when we might become friends, rather than master and servant."

"I cannot imagine ever being worthy, sir, but your promise beckons me from a distant horizon, and I feel I am on a quest to capture such a prize. But the journey seems long."

"It will be. But I am proud of you for your first steps. Just another two years of diligent study here, and then you will discover what education is really all about. At the university, I daresay you may not stand out. I hope you will. I desire that you show well and honor me thus, but mostly I want excellence to be your brand, so that when you return you will prove my trust well founded."

Theophilus always seemed to have the right words to spur Loukon to even greater enthusiasm for his pursuits. Keeping from his father and mother his master's long-term plans was no easy task. All Theophilus had done to clear the way for Loukon to study rather than to work was to have his father's overseer tell him, "The master believes your son's brain is stronger than his back. He would like him to study rather than to toil in the sun in the hope that he might become an indoor servant one day."

At first Loukon's father had been suspicious. "It does not make sense to me. It's your good fortune, of course, but there is value in learning to work."

"I know how to work, Father. And I am willing. You know I do whatever chores you assign me."

"Yes, you do. But you spend the daylight hours with the tutors. Does Theophilus see you as a member of his family now and not of mine?"

"I barely see him, let alone talk with him. But he has never expressed such. He merely sees a future for me serving him in a different capacity."

Loukon thought his mother—quiet, as usual—appeared thrilled

for him. Proud. But how he wished he could tell her and his father the truth: that their own freedom rested in his diligent study.

THAT THEOPHILUS WAS PRIMARILY an importer of fine goods also benefited Loukon. Daily he was able to take notes using the best quills and ink and papyrus available. These he stored in his parents' tiny home, amid the quarters of all the other slaves. Many were the nights when—his mind racing and sleep hard to come by—he would creep into the kitchen and light a lamp, poring over his manuscripts. He was learning so much, all the while wondering if his mind had a limit. Where would all this learning and knowledge go when his head was full?

Loukon most enjoyed working on improving his handwriting, especially when writing in different languages. He had promised the master that he would make medicine his focus at the university, but part of him looked forward to the mastery of history just as much.

One late night his mother padded out. "Luke, you need your rest."

"I know. But I feel privileged. And studying has become my life."

"Don't let it become your death. Now, to bed with you."

FOUR

Loukon lay on his back in the darkness wondering what about his mother had seemed different. She was much younger than his father, yet she seemed to have aged overnight. Many of the older slaves slowed over the years until they seemed to sleepwalk through their chores. They ought to be grateful, Loukon thought, that they had a master such as Theophilus. He knew many slaves under other owners died before their time because of beatings and other forms of punishment when their productivity slipped.

Loukon's mother had always had a lightness in her step, despite the fact that her eyes bore a weary sadness. Neither of his parents had ever mentioned it, but the old physician had confided to Loukon that his mother had borne three children besides himself, none of whom had survived.

"Two preceded you, Luke," the old man said, as he was teaching Loukon about childbirth. "Born dead. The other lived about a week and died when you were a year old. Some women are just not destined to bear many living children. In the case of your mother, it was for the best."

"For the best? Why?"

"They were all female offspring."

Loukon nodded. He would have enjoyed having a brother, even a sister. When he interacted with the young maidens on the property, he sometimes imagined them as sisters. Other times he imagined them as potential wives, of course. But the doctor was right: it was probably just as well his sisters had not lived. The world was no place for a woman.

The joke around the place was that slaves had slaves too—their wives. While Loukon's mother was most industrious and seemed to take pride in managing the tiny household—besides her all-day work in Theophilus's gardens—her husband made all the decisions. Loukon had heard her counsel him and discuss things with him, and perhaps at times he listened to her and even deferred to her. Yet always the last word was his.

"I'm sorry," the physician said. "I assumed you knew. Please, let's keep this between us."

Loukon nodded, afraid to ask if any of his sisters had merely been left to die. The more he learned, the more capricious seemed the nature of such decisions. Husbands were expected to pick up and hold a newborn as a ritual of accepting it into the family. Even slave husbands often merely looked at a newborn daughter and walked away, in essence sentencing her to death. If she was not welcomed by him, she was to be left outside, exposed to the elements, often to become prey. Mothers wailed, siblings sobbed, fathers bore the brunt of their anger, yet still men ruled their homes without question and held sway over life and death.

Something deep within Loukon rebelled at this, though he could not imagine a thing he could do about it. He'd heard of deformed male babies and perfectly whole female babies left in the streets of Antioch. Might he someday organize other compassionate people and rescue these babies, raising them to be productive members of society? Oh, there were already those who scooped up these unfortunates and invested in them, feeding and clothing and housing them, even teaching them the rudiments of work. But they became mere chattel, tradable commodities.

Loukon hated nights like this when his mind remained engaged and he argued within himself about the inequities of the world. If he did not get his full complement of rest, study became difficult the next day. But what was he to do with the war within himself? On the one hand he was praised for being compassionate and told that this was one of the hallmarks of the physician. On the other, he was expected to merely accept that women and most slaves—except those fortunate enough to belong to the rare benevolent master like Theophilus—were of no more value than a healthy animal.

Loukon's father seemed compassionate enough toward his wife, yet it was clear he accepted his role as head of the family and expected to exercise his authority. As a slave, it was only behind these doors that he enjoyed such a role, so Loukon could hardly blame him.

But lately his mother had plainly slowed. Her color had changed. Loukon feared it was more than fatigue or even melancholy over being one of few women her age with only one child. And yet his father had not seemed to notice.

Loukon wished he could talk with her, ask her about herself, see if she would discuss the memories of her losses. But he had pledged to the old physician that he would not break his confidence.

Loukon knew he must sleep. He must. His tutors had been very encouraging and had passed along to the master more reports of his academic excellence. Something deep within him told him that this was no time to be presumptuous, to assume that he was going to be automatically accepted at university. He wanted to continue to learn, to maintain rigorous study habits. But that required rest, and getting his mind to slow and drift was not easy.

He crept outside and moseyed among the slaves' quarters. The night was cool and the sky clear. As Loukon studied the expanse of stars, he somehow understood how some could believe in a creator God. His intellect told him that the idea of monotheism was far-fetched, but was it not possible that a supreme being was behind all this and existed far beyond the stars?

As the lad returned to his bed, just when he believed he was getting drowsy, he heard coughing from his parents' room. Then a sigh, and a moan. To Loukon's amazement, the sounds of distress were coming not from his mother but from his father. Soon he heard him rise and rush from the house, vomiting. When Loukon rose to see if he could help, he met his mother at the door. She was bearing a lamp.

"I will tend him," she said. "Get your rest."

"Give him some of the soothing root extract," Loukon said. "But not too much."

"I could use some too," she said.

"Truly? How long has your stomach been sour?"

"Since this morning. Both of us."

"Has anyone else complained?"

She nodded. "It wouldn't surprise me if others were suffering. Many seemed slower today. But few said anything."

Loukon's father dragged back in, scowling. "I'm fine," he said. "Perhaps just something I ate."

"Luke thinks we should take some—"

"I said I'm fine. Suit yourself if you need something, but I need quiet. The night is now short."

As his father scuffed back to bed, Loukon's mother found the extract. "Just a sip," Loukon told her, "and take some with you. Father may need it after all."

Within half an hour Loukon heard both of them moaning, then his father rushed outside yet again. When his mother soon followed, Loukon heard them arguing. His father was insisting that he didn't need her help or any tonic, and she assured him she was not out there to help him but was ill herself. Loukon wanted to go out and urge them to be quiet and to take whatever medicine they needed, but he knew his father would find him impudent for presuming to parent his parents.

LOUKON FINALLY DRIFTED into a fitful sleep, frequently interrupted by his parents' moans. By morning his father was unable to rise, though his mother forced herself to the gardens. As soon as Loukon arrived at the main house for his mathematics lesson, he learned that the physician had been up most of the night, tending to other slaves.

"Nine are confined to their quarters, Luke," he said. "I may need you to assist me if this spreads further. It's at times like this I wish your master was less suspicious of magic and more amenable to appeasing the gods."

Loukon laughed. "You would try to appease the gods and cast spells? Surely not."

"I would rule out nothing, lad. If we don't discover what is sweeping this place, we may need to get the master and his family to the seaside."

That afternoon Loukon's lesson with the physician was canceled so the old man could nap. He was reportedly exhausted from so much activity during the night. But the old man was roused and Loukon himself pressed into service when word came that a woman had collapsed in the fields.

Of course Loukon's first concern was his own mother. She should not have tried to work that day after the night she'd endured. But they said "fields," not "gardens," and there was a difference. Sadly, the report was inaccurate and the stricken woman proved to be his mother after all. The physician enlisted two men to carry her back to her hovel, where she was put to bed next to her husband. He did not even stir.

The old doctor checked their heart rates, and Loukon told him of their travails the night before and what they had taken. "They are both quite feverish," the man said. "We may have to bleed them. Make haste and fetch my equipment."

The doctor sent one of the other slaves to inform the master that he should begin preparations to move his family to their Mediterranean retreat.

The full import of what was going on hit Loukon upon his return to his own family's quarters with the physician's bowls and blades and ointments. All over the vast compound, people scurried about, tending to the sick and gossiping about who had been stricken. Whatever plague had struck this place, it was going to tax everyone to the limit.

Loukon delivered the tools to the bedroom, then dragged in a heavy wood bench, where the doctor laid everything out. He quickly washed Loukon's mother's forearm and draped it off the side of the bed, placing a bowl below it. After scrubbing her wrist with a concoction he said would dull the pain, he deftly sliced into her veins.

"Help me," the doctor whispered urgently as she cried out and began to thrash. Loukon sat on the bed and held her down, assuring his mother that they were taking care of her. He was alarmed, however, when she grew ashen and her lips turned blue.

"Is she dying?" Loukon said, alarmed at the whine in his own voice.

"She will without this. Tell me when the bowl is half full."

And the doctor moved to the other side of the bed and did the same to Loukon's father. The man grimaced and hissed when the incision was made, but he did not wake.

The old man sat on the bed with his back to Loukon, and the boy saw him lower his chin to his chest and heard him sigh heavily. "I may have to seek counsel from colleagues in the city," he said. "I don't know what else to do. We may have to bleed everyone and hope we can eliminate whatever foul invasion has taken over these people."

Loukon found himself silently frantic. Dare he pray to the God of the Jews? He had heard fellow slaves talk of beseeching their Lord for favor and help. But that would be so hypocritical. He did not believe. He only hoped there might be such a creator at this time of dire need.

Urgent rapping at the door was followed by a young boy entering. "Doctor, come quickly. Several others have fallen."

"I cannot leave these," the physician said. "I must soon stanch the bleeding and close the wounds. Loukon, go and see if you can help. I'll be along when I can."

"Me?"

"Who else?"

"But I cannot leave my own—"

"Do you know how to stop the flow and bind the wounds?"

"No, but—"

"Then go! I will tend to them, and I will count on your report of how the others are doing when I arrive."

Leaving his parents, bleeding and—he believed—dying, was the hardest thing Loukon had ever done. But as he followed the young boy down the row of slaves' quarters, he forced himself to concentrate on the task at hand. People lay everywhere, tended by frenzied family. Some vomited, others lay moaning. All seemed to suffer the stomach ailments and fevers his parents had.

If bleeding out whatever poison had gripped them was the right course, there would be much of that going on the rest of the day. The question was, how contagious was this? Would anyone be spared? For now, Loukon took some small comfort in that he had not seen anyone his age or younger stricken.

Already he could see healthy slaves quickly packing necessities for the master and loading his family into carriages. Loukon told the young boy who had summoned help to gather more bowls and told him where he could find the physician's blades. "Get help and bring as much of this as you can to me. Now, hurry."

The boy ran off as Loukon began making the rounds, checking on people. All had speeding heartbeats and their faces and heads were hot. He assured them all that the doctor would get to them soon, and that in the meantime they should take small doses of stomach-soothing extract and retire to their beds, anticipating a bleeding.

The boy soon returned, laden with bowls and blades. But as Loukon led him to his own home, the boy said, "The master has need of you."

"Right now?"

"He said immediately. That it was urgent."

"Tell the physician I will be back as soon as I can."

FIVE

Loukon found Theophilus surrounded by aides and healthy slaves. His family had been loaded into carriages, and the entourage appeared ready to pull out.

"What are you doing?" Loukon said, immediately regretting it when he saw the shocked looks, especially his master's.

"*I* sent for *you*, Luke. You have a question for me?"

Loukon couldn't help himself. "Where are you going?"

"I have been urged to temporarily relocate to our place—"

"I know. I heard. But how does this look to everyone?"

When Theophilus hesitated, one of his top advisers stepped forward. "It looks like what it is, young man. It is the height of prudence that the man on whom this estate depends should be spirited away from the danger. We all agree."

"I don't," Loukon muttered.

"You have no say, let alone any standing," the man said, but Theophilus raised a hand.

"Luke, I summoned you because I want you to come with us."

"Me?"

"All my tutors except the physician are going. We might need your expertise, but more important, you would be able to continue your studies with us."

"Sir, my parents lie near death. I could never leave them!"

"If they are indeed near death, Luke, no good can come of your attending to them. You risk your own life even considering it."

"How should I feel if I abandon them and get news of their deaths? I would never forgive myself."

"Let him stay and die," the adviser said. "Such impudence!"

"Silence," Theophilus said. "Luke, listen to me. If I thought anything would be gained by my staying, I would stay. Whatever this is, I am powerless against it and must protect my family."

"And yourself," the adviser said.

Theophilus sighed and, to Loukon, appeared disgusted. "My friend," he said to the adviser, "go and check on Loukon's parents and bring me a report."

The man looked horrified at the thought, but Theophilus gave him a look that sent him off. "Luke, I promise we will return as soon as we know it is safe. I admire your loyalty and your passion. It is what gives me such confidence about your future. But you must trust me. The greater good is served by our preserving you, along with the rest of us. Do not make me order you to come. Simply comply."

"You would make me?"

"I would."

Loukon wanted to lash out, to spit that the master was proving he was anything but the Greek ideal of the perfect man. What would happen if he simply returned to his parents' hovel? Would it be the end of his status with the master, the end of his dream and his future?

An adult slave moved near him and whispered, "Do what he says, son. He could have you put to death."

Theophilus? Never. Legally, yes, it was his prerogative to do as he pleased with his own slaves, but Loukon could not imagine he had ever acted upon it.

The adviser returned and whispered to the master.

"Oh, no," Theophilus said. "We must go. Loukon, gather your papyrus. Anything else you need, we will provide at the seashore."

"Wait! What is happening? Are my parents all right?"

"They are grave, son, but the physician himself has fallen ill."

"Then I *must* stay! I cannot go! Who else will look after the people?"

"You would be supervising a mass burial, Luke. Now I must insist that you ride with us."

"I want to stay."

"Enough," Theophilus said, not unkindly. "I have spoken. You will thank me one day. Now get your things and do not delay."

Loukon knew he had no options. At least gathering up his stuff would take him home, if only briefly. He could peek in on his parents. He ran to the row of slave quarters, aware of more people writhing, much wailing and groaning.

"Do not come near me!" the physician called out as Loukon looked in while gathering his schoolwork. He grabbed an extra tunic, but it was all he could do to not get near his doctor/mentor. The man looked terrible, slumped on the bench next to the bed where Loukon's parents lay, now deathly pale and motionless.

"I want to stay and help," Loukon said. "But the master—"

"Do as he says, Luke," the physician said. "Nothing can be done for any of us. We will all be gone by tomorrow at this time."

"I must say goodbye to them," Loukon said. "How can I leave without—"

"Luke, hear me. I do not expect them to survive, but I do anticipate that they will regain consciousness before their final crisis. I will tell them whatever you wish."

"Forgive me, doctor, but you are older and frail."

"If you're worried I'll be gone before they are, write a message. I will be sure someone reads it to them."

Loukon immediately sat and began to scratch with a quill at a small roll of papyrus. He was desperate to communicate love and gratitude and assurances that he would make them proud. A lump invaded his throat and his eyes filled. Meanwhile a messenger appeared in the doorway with word that the master demanded his immediate presence at the gate.

With tears streaming, Loukon reached the message in to the physician, who was looking worse by the minute. Loukon's last view of his parents was of them lying side by side. And still.

His father and mother, like the rest of the adult slaves, could not read. Who but the dying physician himself could be entrusted with reading his message to them?

"SIT WITH ME, LUKE," Theophilus said. The lad hesitated, but the master patted the seat and he reluctantly climbed in and plopped down. "You don't have to speak. I know you're angry with me, and grieving. I pledge we will memorialize all we have lost, your parents and my physician primarily. Trust me, while you will find it difficult to believe, this is also an ordeal for me. I do not want to leave any more than you do, but when you realize you have been spared for a reason, we'll look back on this as the right thing."

Loukon sat shaking his head. "Logic tells me you are right, but I cannot stand the thought that I am so powerless to help. And that I have abandoned my parents on their deathbed, something neither would ever have done to me."

"If the worst happens, son, and you will allow me, I would be honored to serve as your surrogate father."

Loukon knew Theophilus meant well, but that was the last thing he wanted to hear. The man was strangely clumsy in his attempts to encourage and console. Loukon decided to remain silent and deal with his master only as events dictated. He just hoped he would not be expected to jump right into his studies as soon as they settled in at the seaside retreat.

Loukon attempted to keep his mind off the impending tragedy of his losses by trying to anticipate the compound he had never seen. He had heard other slaves tell of the place, all wishing they could be assigned there permanently. But visits to the Mediterranean by the master and his family were rare, and the privilege of accompanying them was passed around.

It was little consolation to the distressed young scholar that he would be at a beautiful spot when the awful news reached him.

"You must not allow this to make you fall behind in your academic pursuits, Luke," Theophilus said.

The poor man was trying so hard. Loukon again wanted to lash back at him, to tell him he would be entirely unable to concentrate on anything for some time.

Despite all, when—late in the day—Theophilus's home away from home finally came into view, Loukon was stunned. The setting sun shone off the sea, and the beautiful landscaping made the setting idyllic. The property was much smaller than the Daphne estate, but the house was every bit as large.

Loukon was grateful for something to do and immediately inserted himself into the cadre of slaves unloading the family's goods and moving them into the house. It made no sense, he knew, but he told himself that if he kept busy, that would somehow keep bad tidings at bay.

Such hope was dashed within an hour when a courier, who had to have left Daphne not long after the family did, arrived with a report. Several crowded around the master, hoping to hear when he did. But Theophilus took the man into a private room, emerging moments later, looking sad.

"Luke," he said, and the boy found himself deeply grateful to be summoned. He followed the master into the room. "Would you care to sit?"

"No, thank you."

The master looked as if he wanted to touch Loukon, but the boy was glad he refrained. He simply wanted the news and to then be left alone.

"We have lost eleven already, Luke. Your mother, the physician, and Lippio are among them." He reached for papyrus on a desktop. "A list of the others."

Loukon was surprised he was able to find his voice. "My father remains?"

Theophilus nodded. "But there is little hope. I was not aware Lippio had even been affected, were you?"

It seemed a strange question in light of Loukon's having just been informed of his mother's death. He shook his head.

"Would you like some time for yourself?"

He nodded, and Theophilus excused him to his quarters. Loukon felt guilty as soon as he entered and sat on the bed, his meager belongings piled in a corner. No slave quarters for him here; these were the nicest accommodations he had ever enjoyed. His parents had never even seen such a comfortable place, let alone been allowed to use it.

Loukon lay on his stomach and hid his face in his hands. He was full of questions. Was his father conscious, aware he had lost his wife? Had either been read Loukon's farewell? Was his father suffering? It was not unlikely he was gone already.

Some of the names of the dead had included people of faith, those who believe in whom they referred to as the one true God. So where was He now?

Memories flooded the boy's mind. Now that he knew how most slave children were raised, he realized how good his own childhood had been. He had long been aware who he and his parents were and who they were not, but he had never suffered.

Until now.

As Loukon's breathing became steady and deep, he realized how bone-weary he was. His sleep had been fitful and, as his father had said, the night short. Then his day had been as strenuous as he could remember. And the very idea of arguing with his master—especially in front of his family and advisers and even other slaves—humiliated the boy. He would have to apologize when the time was right.

WHEN LOUKON AWOKE three hours later, he was aware of voices in the great room. He quietly made his way out to where he could hear without being noticed. Theophilus was surrounded by advisers who seemed to be maneuvering for position in the conversation. The consensus was that the master should remain where he was until authorities had determined that the estate was safe for return. That could have been weeks. No one knew how many more might be affected or how long it would take to bury the dead and cleanse the place. It was unlikely that the cause of the killing plague would be determined or that it could be contained. But until experts believed the hazard had been eliminated, no one believed Theophilus should risk a return.

"And when," one asked, "will you tell the boy about his father?"

"I'll not be able to keep it from him, nor would I choose to. He'll want to know as soon as he wakes. I just hope he gets a little rest."

"I'm awake," Loukon said, stepping into view.

Theophilus immediately rose and approached him. "I'm sorry," he said.

"Thank you. Of course I knew it was inevitable."

"Don't worry about any duties for the time being. Let my people know if you need anything."

"I am your people, sir."

"Consider yourself part of my family now. And as I promised, we will honor your parents, and all we have lost. I can't say when that will be, but I guarantee it will be appropriate and meaningful. I very much respected your parents, Luke. I will miss them."

SIX

The estimates of how long it would take for Theophilus and his family to return to Daphne proved woefully inaccurate. The master seemed out of sorts for weeks as he directed—from the Mediterranean retreat—mass burials and the torching of the slaves' quarters. Frequent visits from provincial authorities and even representatives from Rome resulted in heated meetings and much turmoil.

Theophilus dispatched trusted aides to Antioch and Tarsus to procure more slaves, but even this effort was stalled when he was informed that he would have to house these people elsewhere until the rebuilding at Daphne had been completed. There was not enough room, or work for the slaves, on the Mediterranean.

At first grateful to take the master up on his offer of no study until he was ready, after weeks of moping about, Loukon found himself eager for anything to occupy his mind. He hated to bother Theophilus, with all that had to be on his agenda, but when he got a moment's audience with him, Loukon said, "I believe I am ready to take up my studies again."

Theophilus seemed to weigh him with his eyes. "I have a task for you first."

"Anything, sir. Thank you."

"I pledged an appropriate memorial to your parents and the others. I would like you to take charge of that."

"Take charge? I would be unable to host it or to speak."

"Oh, no," Theophilus said. "I myself would be expected to serve as host and eulogizer. What I require of you is to gather all pertinent information on the deceased: names, birth records, duties, any personal stories I might be able to relate. And then I would like you to suggest an appropriate memorial, something that would remain after we have orally honored these."

"When will this be, sir?"

"Upon our return to Daphne. I considered doing it here, but that seems so impersonal. It strikes me that we should do this within a respectable distance of where they have been entombed."

Grieved and hurting as he was, Loukon found himself desperate for just this sort of exercise, and he threw himself into it. He spent an entire evening reminiscing on papyrus about his own parents. Then the next morning he shortened it to its essence so Theophilus would have time to include a few sentences about each of the dead.

Loukon spent several days carefully interviewing several at the retreat about anyone they had lost. He wept with them and shared his own memories, finding it all quite melancholy and yet satisfying and healing.

To his abject dismay, however, Loukon sensed pride creeping into him for the very fact that the master had asked him to take charge of this. His parents had been in the ground only a short time, and his wound remained sharp and deep. And yet the baser part of his nature was looking forward to the day when Theophilus would thank him publicly for his efforts in staging the memorial. What was wrong with him?

Finally the day came when he was allowed to visit Daphne for the first time. Many of the surviving slaves had been working on the rebuilding of their quarters and purging the rest of the estate in anticipation of the master's return, and only they could relate stories of their lost family members.

In all, more than thirty had perished and twice that many had endured long recoveries from whatever it was that had swept the place.

"I get daily reports, of course," Theophilus had told him, "but bring me back a detailed account. Consider it part of your studies, an assignment in constructing a thorough evaluation. I want to know how the new place is shaping up, and I'd like an honest forecast of when you think we might be able to return."

"Master, I want to thank you for this task. I can't say that I'm enjoying it actually, but I am grateful for the activity."

"Do you still regret having left?"

"Of course. Don't you?"

"I try not to dwell on it," Theophilus said. "The guilt for selfishness crouches at the door of my mind, but I try to combat it with logic. I remind myself that there was nothing I could have done, and that I have been spared to continue to do right by my fellow man. Now, where is your thinking on a permanent memorial?"

"It might prove costly."

"Let me worry about that, Luke."

"What would you think of a sculpture or some sort of depiction that would honor the dead?"

"Tell me more."

"I envision either statues or a great iron seal, something that would allow you to etch the dates of the plague and the number dead, and show perhaps a family—a father, a mother, and children—with their tools."

Theophilus's voice was thick and he covered his mouth with his hand as he spoke softly. "That is a magnificent idea, Luke. I think a sculpture would be just right, and we could place it in an open area in front of the new servants' quarters. I'll enlist the services of an artist immediately."

Loukon left the meeting grateful that the master had appreciated his idea, but still he battled himself within. Was there no depth to his shameful pride? Was he, as Theophilus had once teased him, guilty of narcissism? It was a trait he despised in others. And in himself.

THE SLAVE ASSIGNED to transport Loukon back to Daphne was in his mid-twenties and nothing like the gruff but gregarious Lippio. He was quiet much of the way, and when Loukon tried to draw him out, he proved surly.

"I suppose you see yourself as the master's son now," he said.

"I don't, but he has offered me that role."

"You don't say. Be careful how you respond, because to the rest of us, you will always be what you are now."

"I don't presume anything else, sir."

"You can save the 'sir' business for the master. I'm a slave who drives horses and breaks his back in the sun all day. Unlike you."

"I'm willing to do that."

"I'll just bet you are."

"What is your name?"

"What's it to you? That you have lived near me all your life and don't know it confirms everything I have thought about you."

"Forgive me. I was just trying to make conversation. The fact is, I do know your name and those of your brothers and sisters and parents. I also know that you lost them all, and I want you to know how sorry I am."

"You know all our names? Prove it."

"Yours is Diabolos," and Loukon quickly listed the rest.

"Don't expect us to become friends just because you knew that. For all I know, someone you interviewed told you."

"I didn't need anyone to tell me. Your eldest brother tended the animals with me. Two of your sisters worked the gardens with my parents, and your other sister worked in the field with you."

Diabolos fell silent.

"It's okay to be angry," Loukon added finally. "I feel the same way. When you feel up to it, I would like to ask you about your family so the master can talk about them at the memorial."

"Perhaps. But do you realize that if you had still been tending animals, you would probably be dead now too? How do you get such privileges—getting to read and study and stay out of the sun most of the day?"

"I feel fortunate. The master noticed my interest in such things, is all I can say. I am as surprised as anyone else that he has allowed this."

"It's not fair."

"Would you like to do what I do?"

"Who wouldn't?"

"Why not tell him?"

"Theophilus? He would laugh me out the door. I can't read and wouldn't know where to begin."

"But you're interested in science, mathematics, rhetoric, art, history, medicine?"

Diabolos laughed aloud. "Hardly! I am interested in remaining inside all day and doing nothing, like you."

"If you think what I do is nothing, you are mistaken."

"Well, just in case you're unaware of it, the rest of us resent your privileges."

"And what am I to do about that? Refuse the master's kindnesses so I don't separate myself from my people?"

"That's what I would have done."

Loukan found himself not only offended and resentful, but also angry. He wished he were bigger so he could challenge Diabolos to a fight. He imagined bloodying the man's face, knocking him to the ground, and kicking him to within an inch of his life. And here he had been trying to convince the man that he was just a fortunate, humble servant.

What am I really?

LOUKON SPENT NEARLY the entire day interviewing survivors of the plague about their loved ones. He found it strange to wander where he and his parents had lived and to see nothing but dirt. The new quarters were in the same area but several yards away. And they were nice, roomier, and Theophilus had apparently approved an engineering project that directed a stream of water through the complex that would greatly aid with sanitation.

Just before it was time to head back to the Mediterranean, Loukon made his way to the rough-hewn tombs where his parents and the others had been interred. He repeated aloud from memory what he had written his parents weeks before. When he got back to the estate, Diabolos was standing by the wagon and horses.

"Ready?" he said.

"I need to gather my things," Loukon said. "But I would like to ask you about your family first, if you're up to it. Come inside where I can write."

"Can't we do it back at the retreat?"

"We might not have as much time. What if you are assigned other duties?"

"Or am not allowed in the house like you."

"Come in, Diabolos. Please." The young man followed him. "You know, of course, that I know what you're going through. Don't forget that my parents were among the first to die. I even understand the guilt of being the only survivor."

"But you had a reason!" Diabolos said, sitting across from Loukon. "I was out in the workplace with everyone else. I wasn't lounging inside doing nothing!"

"I am sorry, Diabolos. I truly am. Now, would you tell me about them?"

All the while Loukon was taking notes, he was resenting Diabolos and wanted to strike back at his meanness. He somehow forced himself to dredge up some compassion for this sad, sad man. If Loukon felt the slave was being unfair, he could only imagine how Diabolos felt about him. But of course he didn't have to imagine it; Diabolos was nothing if not forthright.

LOUKON ALLOWED HIMSELF to hope that by the time he and Diabolos had reached the Mediterranean retreat again, they might have forged some sort of a relationship, if not an uneasy friendship. Even a truce would have been better than the distance he felt from the man.

But no. While he thanked Diabolos effusively, Loukon got only a nod, and when he came upon him around the grounds during the ensuing days, his greetings were barely acknowledged. It was as if they had not spent the better part of a day together.

Loukon spent most of the next two weeks daily working on the eulogy for Theophilus to read at the memorial. A target date had been set for the return to Daphne, and Loukon found himself eager to get back. Would he be assigned his own chambers in the servants' quarters, or would he have a place in the main house? After the encounter with Diabolos, he wasn't sure which he would rather have. Slave quarters would be fine with him. In truth, he'd rather stay in relative luxury, but he wanted his peers to think he was required to stay in the main house.

It was time to endure the memorial. *Endure* was the right word, for as sweet and meaningful as Theophilus would make it, it would be an ordeal for the grieving. Maddeningly, part of him still hoped the master would acknowledge his part in the preparations.

Once it was over, Loukon could get back to his studies. He hoped he hadn't fallen hopelessly behind. With university looming on the horizon, he believed he could focus and find within himself renewed enthusiasm for the task of conducting the memorial. He desperately wanted to honor the memory of his parents while also proving himself worthy of his master's trust.

Loukon had come to the difficult decision that if Theophilus again raised the matter of his becoming an adopted son, even in just a symbolic way, he was going to decline. As much as he respected the man and appreciated the sentiment, he had the deep feeling that he would be dishonoring his own father to accede to the request.

Anyway, his dream was to one day be considered a colleague of Theophilus. And that would never happen if he was forever seen as a son. Would turning down such an overture cause a breach in the relationship? He couldn't risk that. Loukon would count on the innate goodness of the man, his Stoicism. There was no way he could survive in the world without the man's patronage.

Most exciting to Loukon at this stage of his studies was that once he was back into the routine, the study of Stoicism—including the master's personal embracing of it—was next in his program. He could hardly wait. His competition at the university would probably arrive steeped in the philosophy, and if they weren't, the institution would soon remedy that.

SEVEN

Late the evening before Theophilus and his family—and everyone else attending him at the Mediterranean home—were scheduled to return to Daphne, all were assembled in the courtyard. One of the master's aides outlined the schedule for the next morning. He listed all the slaves who would rise before dawn and get everything packed, leaving no later than sunrise so that all would be in place when Theophilus and his family arrived late in the afternoon.

Loukon was alarmed to find that he was not listed among those going first. As soon as the meeting ended, he sought out the master.

"Allow me to go with the first group," he said. "I have much to do there and want to work alongside the rest."

"Oh, no, I thought you would appreciate being spared that, Luke. We have wholly refurbished the physician's quarters in the main house, and my thought was that you would reside there. I would not give you his title or anywhere close to his duties yet—all that comes with your graduation from university—but I want people to begin seeing you in the role you will eventually inherit."

Loukon shook his head. "I need a favor, sir. I would really rather stay in the slave quarters. Is there room?"

"Of course there's room. We built it for growth. But I wouldn't have you going back to—"

"To where my parents so honored you with their diligence? Sir, I sincerely want to be thought of as a brother to the rest of the slaves. I believe I can be of more help to them that way, especially when I come back as their physician. Please. It would mean so much to me."

"Let's sit," Theophilus said, and Loukon felt bad for extending the man's evening with the big day coming. "Son, as you know, I try to treat my servants better than any other slave owner treats his. But I am also aware that a certain distance must exist between the classes. When you return from the university, you will be an educated man, soon to be free, and you should carry yourself that way."

"I respectfully disagree, sir. I have reason to believe that many of my own already resent me."

"I have heard the same, but you know they resent me too, regardless of how well I treat them."

"They are simply jealous, master. I need not give them more reason to envy me. They know I am not a person of means and probably never will be. Just allow me to live among them. I will spend my days in the physician's quarters anyway, but I believe they appreciate and trust me more this way."

Theophilus ran a hand through his hair and squinted at Loukon. "You are one strange young man, but in this I sense you may be wise. Find out from the overseer which of the chambers have not been assigned, and select whichever you want. Do let the slaves move your things in."

"I am still a slave, sir. And while I may have gone soft without manual labor for so long, I am happy to move myself in. And I have so little that it will give me time to help get the main house in order for you too."

"You are determined to remain a slave, aren't you?"

In fact, Loukon was deeply troubled. He had done the right thing, he knew. But in his heart of hearts, he'd rather the master had forbade it.

In the predawn darkness Loukon loaded his stuff onto the wagon he knew Diabolos would be driving, then helped pack assorted items from the house. When it came time to pull out, slaves crowding every available inch of the wagons, Loukon climbed up next to Diabolos.

"Big day ahead," he said.

"Are you going to be jabbering the whole way? This is the middle of my night."

"Sorry."

"What are you doing here anyway? I would have thought you would have been awarded a purple robe and allowed to accompany the master himself. Fall out of his good graces? Don't tell me he has relegated you back to slave quarters and slave status!"

"That has always been the case."

"Oh, spare me! You have been found out! You proved slothful or sassy, didn't you?"

Loukon fought to stay silent and to not even shake his head. Lowering himself to gain back some respect or trust was clearly not going to work with someone like Diabolos.

"You're right," he said. "I've been eliminated from the inner circle."

Diabolos threw an arm around Loukon's shoulder and roughly pulled him close. "Well, don't cry over it, man! I'll show you the ropes!

It'll all come back to you. Did you get assigned my wagon? Because you know the driver is the overseer for the day, so you'll have to do what I say when I say it."

"Well, first I have to get moved in. And then I thought I would—"

"No, no. You'll move in last. Your quarters won't be going anywhere, will they? And then *you* don't decide what you'll do. *I'll* let you know."

"But I told the master I would help with the main house . . ."

"The main house has plenty of men assigned. I'll use you where you will be of the most help."

Maybe this returning to slave status wasn't such a good idea after all. Part of Loukon wanted to take advantage of his relationship with the master and simply tell Diabolos off and do what he pleased. But no. He would serve the hurting man. And if that didn't soften him, that was not Loukon's problem.

When finally the caravan rumbled through the gates of the newly built estate at Daphne, the drivers as one silently guided their rigs into a semicircle around a massive sculpture that stood before the slave quarters. It was a magnificent bronze thing, gleaming in the sun and depicting a man and a woman and a boy and a girl toiling in the gardens.

No one spoke, but slowly they climbed down from the wagons and approached, staring, gasping, whistling. It was clear this was the perfect gift from the master.

"This is where the memorial will be held tomorr—"

But Diabolos grabbed Loukon. "Tell me and I'll tell them. You are not in charge here."

"The memorial service will be conducted here at dawn tomorrow. The master will eulogize the dead."

Diabolos grandly announced it to the rest of the slaves. "Now, let's get to work!"

. . .

At the end of the day Loukon was finally free to move his own meager belongings into a slave's chamber. He had been assigned to carry things everywhere but to the main house, and Diabolos seemed to gloat the whole time. Loukon was determined not to let it show that he was being humiliated, so he smiled often and worked quickly, though he was soon exhausted. The truth was, it had been too long since he had done manual labor. But he forced himself to keep pushing, hoping to prove that Diabolos could not get to him, let alone defeat him. In reality, however, he was seething and none too proud of himself for it.

Loukon was arranging the last of his study materials and putting his second tunic away when he heard the master's family's conveyances come through the gate. He took one last look at the spartan but more than adequate room that would be his until he left for university, then hurried out to welcome them.

Excited as he was about the future, this had been mostly a sad day for the majority of the slaves. They were clearly impressed with the statue and the lengths to which their master had gone to rebuild and make more comfortable their own accommodations. But returning to this place, even reuniting with family and friends, had to bring back the hard memories of their loss. It certainly did to Loukon.

Theophilus stood high in his carriage and merely thanked everyone for their help, reminding them to meet in front of the statue at dawn.

Loukon hurried back to his new quarters and had just dropped onto the bed when he was summoned to the main house.

"I thought you might want to see what we've done with the physician's area," Theophilus said.

Loukon was certain his surprise showed. "I would love to, but what made you think I had not already seen it?"

"I have eyes and ears everywhere, Luke. I am fully aware of how you were treated today, and how you responded. I am not a proponent of corporal punishment except in the most egregious circumstances, but all it would take is one word from you and I'd have that overseer flogged."

"Oh, no. Thank you, sir, but it was not that bad. And I can only imagine what is weighing on his mind."

"Jealousy, I daresay."

"More grief, probably," Loukon said. "I believe he lost more family members than anyone else."

"You're a better man than I am," Theophilus said.

If only that were true. The revenge Theophilus suggested sounded delicious. But how would Loukon have lived with himself if he had taken advantage of it? And what kind of a man was he to think he was honorable in declining it when down deep he longed for vengeance?

IN THE MORNING Theophilus was at his best, Loukon thought, striking just the right tone of care and bereavement along with kind words about all who had served him and had fallen to the disease. He was particularly effusive about Lippio, "who had already sacrificed a limb in faithful service," the physician, "who served me into old age and will be difficult to replace," and Loukon's parents.

But when the master left out any mention of Loukon and his contribution to the memorial, the lad was deeply disappointed.

The rest of the people seemed moved by Theophilus's encouragement and consolation, especially when he gave them the remainder of the day off and urged them to visit the tombs where their loved ones lay. After the memorial he invited Loukon to join him in the house.

When they were seated, Theophilus said, "I want to be sure we are in agreement now about what comes next in your development. The tutors tell me you are coming into the most advanced areas of study with which they can challenge you. Their recommendation, and mine, will be crucial for your acceptance into the university at Tarsus. My main concern is that you are thoroughly engaged in this pursuit, that you have not changed your mind or, worse, become overconfident about succeeding. This is no small task."

"I am ready and eager, sir," Loukon said. "We are, however, long overdue on your pledge to impart personal information to me about Stoicism."

"I know. But the tutors tell me—and I am inclined to agree—that you need the rudimentary grounding in it first. And then, the closer you are to leaving for the university when we talk it through, the more it will stay with you when you need it. You are at the top levels of all your subjects, but remember that at the same time, none can be taken for granted, so do your best with all they teach you."

"I am committed, sir."

"And finally, Loukon, I want to thank you for all you have done for me and for my people. My belief in your compassion and care have been borne out, and I am eager to see you here in the role of full-time physician. I am sorry that I was not able to grant your parents their freedom in time for them to enjoy it."

"Me too."

"I only hope you will someday find it within yourself to forgive me for not allowing you to stay with the dying. I know how hard it was, because it was for me too. But I did not want to deprive the future of what you have to offer. Do you understand?"

"You don't need my forgiveness, master. Though I may still disagree and feel like a deserter, I know your intentions were pure and you had my best interests—and others'—at heart."

"May you always be this wise and understanding, especially when I am not."

That made Loukon feel only worse for his resentment of not being recognized at the memorial. He wondered whether he would ever gain maturity in his mind.

LOUKON TOOK to his bed that night as exhausted as he could ever remember being, but again he had trouble turning off his swirling thoughts. A truth he was desperate not to admit to anyone, at least not yet, was that as excited as he was about attending the university and taking advantage of all it had to offer—against so many odds, considering he was born a slave—he was also terrified at the prospect.

All his life he had enjoyed a small, tightly knit community of people who knew him and, for the most part, liked him. In fact, while he knew there had to be many who resented his obvious closeness to the master, only Diabolos had been forthright enough to express himself. The others were too polite or worried about their own standing with Theophilus, allowing Loukon to just assume they were fine with him and what was in his future.

But what would it be like at university? Hundreds, thousands of strangers? And all would be as bright and accomplished as he—and probably more so. What if he was just nimble of mind enough to get in but not able to perform at a level where he could stick with it and succeed? He would not be able to face anyone, let alone the other slaves—and certainly not Theophilus—if he failed and had to return.

EIGHT

Loukon could have gotten his tutor into trouble with the master. His name was Zeno, and he bragged of having been named after the man who had introduced the very idea of Stoicism to the world some three centuries before. But this Zeno, Loukon's teacher, acted one way around Theophilus and another when only his students were present.

As soon as the man—tall, clean-shaven, and short-haired—caught sight or sound of the master, his posture changed, his tone became earnest. He became more professorial, humbler. He seemed to bow and scrape in Theophilus's presence. *Obsequious* was the word for it, Loukon knew, but he also sensed that the master was on to Zeno. He seemed to ignore all the fawning. That was one reason Loukon chose to keep to himself his misgivings over the man.

As soon as Zeno was alone with his students again, he slouched, spoke in a haughty, bored tone, and seemed to see himself as one of the world's great intellects. No question he was brilliant and widely read, but that he himself was a Stoic and named after the philosophy's founder proved the height of irony to Loukon. For this man exhibited every character trait Stoicism was supposed to counter.

Zeno studied his fingernails or gazed out the window as he held forth on the pillars of Stoic thought. His namesake—Zeno of Citium—had taught three centuries before in Athens at the renowned Stoa Poikile (painted porch), whence came the name of his philosophy.

"We Stoics believe," Loukon's tutor droned, "that self-control is the key to mastering damaging emotions."

Like conceit? Loukon wanted to ask, but he was already dabbling at practicing Stoicism and was able to rein himself in.

"To understand the universe, one must become a true thinker. Imagine the spiritual sense of well-being you can achieve this way."

"You have gained this?" Loukon said.

"I have. Peace has visited me, as practicing virtue and reason has allowed me to grasp natural law and shut out the noise of the world. Men who are slaves to their passions do not understand truth and that it is virtuous to pursue it."

Recalling what Theophilus had once said about still struggling with certain vices, Loukon said, "So this belief, this practice, has rid you of immorality?"

Zeno allowed his eyes to drift from the window to Loukon's face. With what the student assessed as a condescending look, he said, "Well, I can confidently say I am no longer bound to taboos, superstition, belief in myths, worship of gods, and the like. And I can detach myself from hurtful experiences, largely through loving all other beings."

"You love all others?"

"Let me put it this way, lad: Stoicism presents a picture of the world as unified. Logic, ethics, physics, all play a part. The key is to focus on living in harmony with the universe, over which we hold no sway."

"Otherwise we're victims of fate?"

"We are anyway. As I say, the secret is to harmonize with all these influences by living a life of self-control based on wisdom. Clear judgment allows us to free ourselves from negative reactions to suffering and rather accept it passively."

Strangely, despite that Zeno seemed so vain, the philosophy itself was reaching Loukon's core. He believed that if he could somehow understand it at its deepest levels, he could avoid being a boor like Zeno and become a respected man of honor like Theophilus.

"You see," Zeno said, "we want to move past mere logic to true understanding of the universal reason inherent in everything."

"And this will gain us what?"

"The ability to live in harmony, seeing value in everyone, and understanding the order of the universe. Sadness and bad conduct are traits of the ignorant."

"So if a person was cruel, it would be because . . . ?"

"Because he is ignorant of his own cosmic purpose. We must examine ourselves to be sure we have not strayed from the universal reason of nature."

Loukon was more than intrigued. Though he doubted that Stoicism had cured Zeno of anything, he sensed there might be something in the philosophy for him. It resonated deep within him and seemed to complement his compassion and care for others, particularly the ill or oppressed. Stoics made much of being humanistic and not religious, and yet these character traits seemed the same goals as those held by people who worshiped several gods or even just one.

"Is this, then, something we study and learn and master?"

"Oh, no. It's a matter of living it out, working at it, practicing it. We must have constant dialogue with ourselves to be sure we are living the way we should. Socrates, of course, long predated Stoicism, but even he asserted that he was neither Athenian nor Greek but rather a citizen of the world."

It was time to break, but Loukon sensed Zeno was eager to continue answering his questions.

"Is it Stoicism that makes Theophilus such a good master?"

"Completely," Zeno said. "He actually believes that wealth and class should make little difference in the interactions of men."

"Is that realistic?"

"Perhaps not, but if brotherhood and equality are the hallmarks of one's philosophy of life, it has to influence how one lives and acts."

"Is it a conflict for a Stoic to be a slave owner?"

"It would be for me," Zeno said. "But I would not venture to speak for Theophilus."

SEVERAL MONTHS LATER, Loukon was finally granted another audience with his master. For the first time, Theophilus appeared uneasy during the conversation, as if he regretted having agreed to speak personally about his own philosophy of life.

"I am very curious," Loukon said, "about how Stoicism works. It is one thing to study it, and another to live it, is it not?"

"That is true," Theophilus said slowly. "Your tutor is a Stoic, as you know, and yet I am not sure I see the evidence of it in his personality."

It was all Loukon could do to remain silent. How he wanted to enthusiastically agree.

Theophilus seemed to want to lead the conversation, as if to keep personal questions at bay. But Loukon had decided he would not be denied.

"Tell me what you have learned, Luke. As I told you, it will benefit you to be versed in this by the time you enter the university."

Loukon quickly rehearsed everything he could remember, which led him to more questions. "This brotherhood of man and universal love for all beings of course makes me wonder how you have dealt with the issue of owning slaves."

Theophilus leaned forward and pressed a palm over his mouth. Finally pulling it away, he said, "I thought it might make you wonder. You are aware, I am sure, that there are many Stoics who urge clemency for slaves and find slavery itself wholly incompatible with the philosophy."

"But you clearly do not."

"Oh, it's not all that clear, Luke. You must see the conflict within me played out every day in the way I treat those who serve me. Naturally there is distance, a gulf fixed between owner and slave. And yet if I say I truly believe that all men are equal in the sight of the universe, how can I lord my rank over them? They depend on me for their very lives, their shelter, their food, their existence. And yet I would exhibit the height of hypocrisy to treat them as if they were of less value than I. Already there are disparities in our accommodations and food. I suppose a true Stoic would allow his charges to live in his home and eat from his table. I must ask, Luke, what prompts your grin?"

"Oh, I apologize, sir. I do not intend to be rude."

"No, no. Speak."

"Well, it's just that I was thinking that a true Stoic would free his slaves."

Theophilus's face clouded and he nodded. "We touched on this once before. Freedom would not be profitable for every slave under my charge. Freeing them might do them more harm than good. Short of that, I want that my life be governed by my philosophy."

"If I may pose one more question . . ."

"More than one, if you wish."

"Thank you. I gather from my study that one of the chief aims of Stoicism is some higher plane of behavior. Am I being presumptuous in that?"

Theophilus rose and beckoned Loukon to walk with him. The lad followed him out of the house and into the twilight of the courtyard. "You're wondering if I have made any progress in my attempts at controlling my own passions. How about you? Have you?"

"No, but neither have I formally adopted Stoicism as my own. Will you be requiring that of me?"

"I considered that, but I see many wonderful qualities in you anyway, as I have said. No, I believe I'll leave such a decision up to you. Your education, your employment, your freedom will not hinge on such. What I desire for you in the long run—say, when you reach my age—is peace of mind. I wish that my philosophy would grant me that."

"You do not have peace? You seem to."

"I fear I am confiding too much, Luke, but I trust you."

"I hope I have proven myself trustworthy."

"So far. The fact is, that while I believe in the divine nature of the universe, I do not believe in God or the gods *per se*. The very idea seems to war against Stoicism."

"Then what do you mean by *divine* nature?"

"Just that there seems to be a grand, overall logic to the universe. Things seem to make some sort of spiritual sense. And yet, though I live my life with all this in mind, working at self-control and virtue and logical thought, I have never seemed to master my own passions. I still seek my good over others', I crave attention, I can be petty and jealous. And while I have been more than fortunate, enough never seems enough for me. You see what I'm saying?"

Loukon found a bench and requested permission to sit. "I understand, but if you do not worry about offending the gods and you foster a reputation of fairness and goodness, why no peace of mind? Only because you are not pleasing yourself, not living up to your own standards?" Luke dared not admit that he faced these very same struggles.

Theophilus spread his palms and shrugged. "I don't know, Luke. I just don't know. I had hoped Stoicism would make me a better man, put me on the journey of the Greek ideal. I have studied other pursuits, but Stoicism is as close as I have come to finding an acceptable way of living. The best I can say for myself is that I am striving."

"Perhaps there is nothing more that can be said."

"Perhaps, but you see how sad that is? I want to be truly worthy of my reputation as a good and decent man, not to simply be grateful that people think so. I know the real me, and I am not satisfied."

"And thus you continue pursuing the noble path."

"I have been doing that for too long to still be judging myself so inadequate."

"Maybe you are being too hard on yourself."

"I would like to think so, but even conceding that does not bring me the sense of satisfaction I long for. I can tell myself I am doing the best I can, but when it is not good enough to persuade even me that I am achieving the character I long for, it wears on me. I am no longer a young man. I see little hope."

"You are despairing more than I realized."

"And you wonder why I see so much hope in you?"

"Often, yes."

"I am desperate that you become what I have not. You seem to have a natural virtue, a concern for others, an eager, inquisitive mind. So go off to the university committed to spend yourself for the benefit of others. Be the man I wish I were. If my only legacy is sponsoring a man for the world who will prove that altruism is attainable, maybe that will be enough."

Loukon rose and laughed. "Forgive me, but you have laid on my shoulders a great weight of responsibility. What if it turns out that I am every bit as human as you, or even more so? If I fail, then what? All is lost?"

"You will not fail, Luke. You will achieve. You will make me proud."

"I will give it my all. But as I told you long ago, I battle my own desires and passions as well."

"But you're young! That is part of maturing. I want to believe that if you understand what you're striving for, you will be able to avoid the pitfalls I suffered. You can focus on the denial of your passions and the embracing of selflessness and service to mankind."

Loukon rose and they walked back toward the main house. Loukon said, "Do you mean to lay on me the burden of all your disappointments and broken dreams?"

"No. And I apologize if it appears that way. Rather, I want you to know that I believe in you."

Part Two

THE STUDENT

NINE

For such a bright and successful man, Theophilus seemed naive to Loukon when it came to understanding human nature. On the one hand he was a thriving businessman and generally kind to everyone. On the other, he threw a farewell party for Loukon that he clearly thought would thrill all the slaves. One of their own had been chosen for favor, for privilege, and Theophilus addressed them as if they would be proud and happy for Loukon.

Theophilus's own family beamed and smiled and clapped as the master bestowed upon Loukon a wardrobe, university supplies, and even a package of delicacies from the kitchen for the ride to the harbor and the voyage across the Mediterranean inlet to the west, where ground transportation had been arranged to complete the ninety-mile journey from Antioch to Tarsus.

But the slaves who crowded the main house—many inside for the first time in their lives—appeared at once agape over the surroundings but not so impressed by all the attention lavished on Loukon. The irony in this was that most had always seemed to like and appreciate him. He had begun tending to their physical needs—in limited fashion, of course, for he had yet to be formally trained in medicine. And he lived with them, was one of them, had suffered loss like many of them.

And yet he had long enjoyed privileges they had not. Loukon was perceptive enough to know when people were excited for him and when they were just paying him lip service. He stole glances at them from his prime seat—next to Theophilus at the head table—and save for a few of his parents' friends, most bore smiles that were plainly pasted on.

Loukon was being treated like Theophilus's own son, and rather than endear him to the other slaves, the master was merely widening the gap between them. While they were eating, Theophilus threw his arm around Loukon and drew him close. "I will miss you but look forward to your holiday visits and your eventual return in my employ."

"Thank you, sir. I appreciate all of this more than I can say."

"You look embarrassed."

"Mortified, actually," but when Loukon saw how crestfallen the man appeared, he decided to not get into why.

"I plan to close the festivities with musicians and dancers," Theophilus said. "Then I will announce that your reward upon finishing at the university will be a position on my staff—as physician, of course—and your freedom."

"Oh, sir, please don't! The physician part is all right, if you feel compelled. But you must understand that telling slaves of another's freedom will engender only resentment and envy."

"Truly?" Theophilus looked astounded.

"If you trust my judgment at all, please accede to my wishes on this."

"If you insist."

. . .

WHEN THE EVENING CONCLUDED, Theophilus had Loukon stand with him at the door as all filed out. Again it was evident to Loukon which of the slaves were truly happy for him and grateful to the master—very few, in truth—and which were forcing themselves to shake his hand and thank Theophilus. Loukon feared this was all lost on the man.

EXCITED AS HE WAS and eager to get under way, Loukon had everything packed and stacked and ready to go when he retired that night. Sleep was nearly impossible. He was exhausted and yet longed for dawn when he would ride—with the master himself—all the way to the harbor.

Slumber finally overtook him, and he was stunned awake at a rooster's crow. Loukon ran to bathe in a shallow pool, then dressed in one of his new sets of clothes and sandals, grabbed one of his boxes, and met the master at his covered carriage.

"Set that crate down," Theophilus said. "No manual labor for you today. Diabolos, please load Loukon's things."

Diabolos gave Loukon a look and bowed to the master. "With pleasure, sir."

When the driver had loaded everything, Diabolos leaped aboard and reached to help Theophilus up. As the master settled in back, Loukon boarded, but when he reached for Diabolos's helping hand, the slave pulled it away.

As Loukon pulled back the curtain and found his place beside Theophilus, Diabolos grandly bowed low in an exaggerated manner that was not lost on the lad.

"Proceed," Theophilus said, as Diabolos closed them in. The master whispered, "You can see how happy he is for you, treating you like a freeman."

"Indeed," Loukon said.

As the carriage jostled to the harbor, Loukon found himself strangely melancholy. His eager anticipation was quickly becoming dread of the unknown and longing for the comforts of his own home and daily routine. And there would be no turning back. He could not show these emotions before the very man who had bestowed all this upon him. Yet at the same time he knew this was a boundless opportunity, the first step on his journey to an entirely new life.

But a lump rose in his throat, and it was all he could do to dam his tears. As Theophilus spoke of opportunity and possibilities, Loukon pressed his lips together and nodded, grateful he was not required to speak.

At the harbor he and the master stood chatting as Diabolos loaded his stuff onto the ship. When Theophilus thanked Diabolos, he again bowed deeply and smiled—deviously, Loukon was sure—acting as if this chance to serve the master's pet was his highest privilege.

Finally Loukon and Theophilus embraced. "I know you will apply yourself with all diligence," the master said. "Safe travels."

"I cannot thank you enough," Loukon said, the tears finally coming. He was embarrassed until he saw Theophilus also weeping. How had he earned this man's love?

"Thank me by doing me a favor," the man said, his voice thick.

"Anything."

"Drop your formal Greek name, at least among your new mates. Introduce yourself as Luke."

"You don't think they will take me less seriously?"

"Your scholarship will speak for itself. And it will be no secret that you are a sponsored slave. I worry that you not appear to be putting on airs."

"I certainly don't want to do that."

"Then do as I say, and I daresay you will quickly endear yourself."

LOUKON WAVED as the ship set sail, then sobbed as Antioch faded into the distance. By the time he disembarked at Tarsus, he had gathered himself, and he quickly found his prearranged transport to the university.

If Loukon had found Antioch impressive, Tarsus was nearly overwhelming. A seaport more than ten miles north of the Mediterranean via the Cydnus River, the quarter-million-population city boasted a well-fortified harbor, surrounded by rock. When he was met at the university gate by students who helped move him into his quarters, Loukon introduced himself as Luke and would think of himself by that name from then on.

His discomfort at his new surroundings quickly gave way to excitement, as everyone seemed to be smiling. Luke had barely gotten his stuff moved into his sleeping quarters—a cramped room with eight cots in a massive pillared building—when he was summoned with other new students to "an important orientation meeting" at the Roman baths on the other end of the campus.

"Should I bring papyrus?" he said, only to be assured that he would need nothing but an open mind.

When he and a half-dozen others were herded by older students to the ornate bathhouse, Luke quickly recognized the ruse and joined in the laughter and fun. One by one the plebes were escorted inside, where they were summarily tossed into the steaming water fully clothed, then expected to make their way back to their chambers, drenched and chilly in the open air.

Luke was smart enough to decline the upperclassmen's offer of purchasing protection against library fines, but he saw other young students dutifully forking over their ducats.

The bona fide orientation meeting was announced for a couple of hours later, and students were urged to begin socializing and getting to know one another. Luke chose to wander the great campus alone, but he was soon joined by a short, sharp-nosed man with nearly black eyes, dressed in Orthodox pharisaical garb.

"New student?" he said, pumping Luke's hand and introducing himself. "Saul. I'm a local."

Luke told him who he was and where he was from, surprised to find that despite his direct gaze and manner, Saul too was new to the campus.

"But not new to education. I began studying the Pentateuch at age five and the Mishnah at ten, and I have just returned from Jerusalem, where I have been studying at the Hillel rabbinical school since I was thirteen."

"My, my," Luke said. "What do you plan to do with all that education? Teach?"

"Perhaps. Or become a rabbi. Some in the synagogue are uncomfortable with my even associating with Gentiles—"

"Like me."

"You seem harmless enough," Saul said, smiling. "But many of my superiors are more suspicious of the Greek influences on my studies."

"My people have much to teach."

"Oh, I agree, despite that we oppose much Hellenistic thought. But I oppose nothing that might be of use in serving the God of Israel."

"You speak of Him as you would speak of an actual person."

Saul grinned. "Is it any wonder my elders are so wary of you Greeks? Of course He is an actual person. He is not like you and me, needless to say, thus we do not even spell out His name when we write about Him. And in speech we refer to Him as Yahweh."

"And how do you serve Him, as you say?"

"By knowing His history, loving His laws, following His statutes."

"I have heard of the laws. Just out of curiosity, do they leave any time for other things?"

"Such as?"

"Recreation."

"Do you mean to ask if I have any fun?"

Luke laughed. "That's what I'm asking, yes."

"Stick with me, Luke, and you'll have as much fun as you want. I know every street and alleyway in Tarsus. And I fancy myself an athlete. One of the first things we are to study in history here is the Battle of Marathon five centuries ago and the man who ran all that way to tell of the victory and then died of exhaustion. I am organizing a run just like it, not to or from Marathon, of course, but I have devised a path that is about the same length."

"And who is to run this?"

"I will, and many of my new friends. Join us! It will be, as you say, fun."

"It doesn't sound like fun to me. Isn't that more than twenty-five miles?"

"It is. But what better way to learn? We're doing it tomorrow, after morning classes."

"Won't it take hours?"

"It will for me," Saul said, "but you plainly have longer legs and look more fit. You'll probably be waiting for the rest of us when we arrive back here."

Luke had never run a mile, let alone more than twenty-five. But what better way to start getting to know other students? As he was considering it, Saul excused himself and ran to help another new student carrying his belongings into the dormitory.

As he prepared for the orientation meeting, Luke could not get Saul, or his running challenge, off his mind. He was going to do it, he had decided. But what was with the intensity of that young man? He was articulate and direct, and his eyes had seemed to bore into Luke's.

But was Saul of Tarsus a potential friend? His very energy and ideas might exhaust Luke. On the other hand, wasn't that what university life was all about—expanding his world, learning new ideas, considering new thoughts, meeting new people?

No way could Luke live a life satisfying to a devout Jew, but Saul seemed an open-minded sort. Perhaps his education abroad and his receptiveness to gleaning what he could even from philosophies opposed to his own would make him a valuable acquaintance.

TEN

As Luke was leaving the orientation meeting that evening, struck by the mass of students overrunning the campus, Saul approached from a distance. The dark, wiry man was waving, and when he came fully into view, it was clear he had been injured.

"What happened to your eye, Saul?"

"Oh, this? It's nothing. I challenged an older student to a fistfight, and he took me seriously. I mean, I wanted the challenge, but he thought we had to be angry with each other and not just sporting. Before I realized I had to really fight back, he had landed a good blow."

"What were you fighting about?"

"Nothing! I just like to box. And he was much bigger, so I wanted to give it a go. People seem to misunderstand me, though I try to be clear. Do you find me hard to understand?"

Luke laughed. "I don't understand why you'd want to take on an older, bigger student just for sport, or run more than twenty-five miles, but I don't have any trouble comprehending what you're saying."

"Well, that's a relief. And you are running with us tomorrow, right?"

"I'll give it a try."

"Oh, but you must finish. You don't have to win, but finishing is everything."

"Fair enough. I promise to finish. Probably at the back of the pack, but I will finish."

"That's the spirit, Luke."

"Now, what have you done for that eye? It's nearly swollen shut."

"I applied a poultice of heated mud and leaves."

"No wonder it's swollen! Are you not familiar with the new approach to such injuries? Cold is the way to go, not hot. Heat causes more fluid to come into the affected area. Come with me."

Luke led him to a small stream, where he formed a mudpack and cooled it in the water, then pressed it gently over the eye. Saul winced but then admitted that it felt better already. "Will this keep it from turning purple?"

"Probably not," Luke said, "and it may ache if you still try to run tomorrow."

"Nothing will stop me from that. He didn't injure my legs. By the way, he got the worst of our fight."

"He did?"

"Oh, yes. I may have broken his nose, and I know I split his lip. He was none too happy, but I thought we had a rousing battle."

Luke studied Saul. The man seemed to embrace life with gusto. "I plan to stay on your good side," he said.

Saul laughed. "So how about this university? Even I was unaware how prestigious it was. Can you believe all the top educators they have brought in from all over the world? What are you studying?"

That was easy. Luke had memorized his subjects weeks before, when word had come of his acceptance. He rattled them off: "Medicine, botany, astronomy, rhetoric, philosophy, and geography. How about you?"

"Nearly the same, but neither medicine nor botany. I am also studying law and mathematics. What is your interest in medicine? You've proved proficient in it with me already."

Luke told him his plans.

"You seem to have the aptitude for it. And if I keep picking fights, I may need to keep you close."

THE NEXT DAY Luke nearly changed his mind about the big run. Saul had rounded up more than a dozen others who looked just as reluctant. The problem—besides the folly of trying something for which he had trained not at all—was that Luke had already found his first classes daunting. The professors seemed gleeful about sharing that they had no plan to ease into rigorous study. In his first three classes, Luke was assigned more reading for one night than he had done in a week in Antioch.

But he had promised not only to run, but to also finish, and somehow Saul's earnestness made him want to impress the young man with his own fortitude. He would force himself to somehow complete the long run, then he would retire to the library and read as long and as fast as was necessary to complete his assignments.

Luke was struck to find that Saul had erected a beautiful black tent at the spot where the run was to begin and end. It was outfitted with chairs and cots, pitchers of water, and other necessities. "I had no idea this was such a formal affair. Where does one come up with a structure like this on short notice?"

"Not a problem," Saul said. "Tentmaking is my family's business.

And they all look just like this, fashioned from cilicium, a strong cloth woven from the black hair of the goats in the Tarsus Mountains. While other merchants mine those mountains for lumber and minerals, my father has made a small fortune in the tent business, and he is not alone. Here, feel this material. Other craftsmen use it to make floor coverings, partitions for houses, cloaks, even bags to transport bodies."

"Have you learned the trade?"

"Oh, yes! I made this tent myself, and I brought more cilicium with me. If I have the time, or the need, I can support myself with this."

"Your classes must not be as rigorous as mine, then. I don't know when I'll have time to sleep."

"Sleep? I didn't come here to sleep! There is too much else to do!"

"You exaggerate."

"Only a bit. I do not need much sleep, Luke. A few hours a night is all. I love to read and to write, to use my hands, to be active. Frankly, I'm looking for others who enjoy talking, especially late at night. There is nothing I enjoy more."

"Well, I need more sleep than that, but I may seek you out when my mind does not allow me to slumber. A good discussion may be just what I need."

"Discussion? Arguments are better! You take one side, I another, and we plead our cases until morning."

"And then sleep through our lectures," Luke said. He enjoyed making Saul laugh.

Saul gathered the other men around. "My only counsel is to not start too fast," he said. "I have never done this either, but I have watched athletes race in the coliseum, and often the ones who start out too quickly soon tire and finish last. Pace yourselves and enjoy the view."

He explained the simple twenty-five-plus-mile loop that would take them "through all the different parts of one of the world's greatest cities. Stay on my course and you will not get lost. And though you may tire, don't miss all the sights. No matter where you're from, it's unlikely you've ever seen a larger trade center on the Mediterranean coast. I'm proud to say our merchants are known throughout the empire, and they have poured much of their profits back into the city. It has good roads and much ornate beauty. Don't miss it. Don't run with your eyes cast down, no matter how tired you become."

Saul began running in place. "Get the body loosened up, and we will soon be off."

To Luke's great amusement, Saul was the first to violate his own advice. As soon as he had called out, "Ready? Let's go!" the young Pharisee lit out at nearly top speed, teasing the others to try to keep up. Many tried, including Luke, but after a mere quarter of a mile, they slowed.

Luke was winded and attempted to settle into a steady gait, trying to ignore that the speedy Saul was fast moving out of sight. As they left the campus and began a gradual slope down into the city, Luke tried to take in the surroundings, but his lack of physical activity for so long quickly caught up with him, and after he had slowed to a jog and covered little more than a mile, he was ready to quit.

He stopped and rested his hands on his hips, bending at the waist and gasping. "Done already?" some said as they passed him, and he didn't even have the energy to respond. Two stragglers sidled up next to him and said, "This is ridiculous. We're heading back too."

"I'm not heading back," Luke said. "I said I would finish, and I will."

"You've barely begun, man! Give it up."

They turned and began trudging back up to the university, but as soon as Luke caught his breath, he broke into a trot again, only to find that the strap on his right sandal was already digging into his flesh and raising a red spot. Dare he run barefoot? Surely not for the whole race. He soldiered on, soon trailing the rest by half a mile.

It wasn't long before Luke had to find a place to sit and study the blister forming on his right foot. Checking his left, he found an irritation beginning at the back of his heel too. Maybe this *was* ridiculous. How important was his pledge to Saul that he would finish? He would soon have to slow to a walk, and his goal to be back to the campus before sunset would be hopeless.

As the day wore on, Luke began to wonder how far behind he was, only to surprisingly overtake a few of his schoolmates sitting and enjoying refreshments with town folk.

"Still at it?" they called out. "We're done! Let Saul run himself into the ground. We had no idea . . ."

Luke just waved and kept walking. Occasionally he would jog a few steps, but he soon realized that even walking the whole way was going to tax him to his limits. Along the route he continued to come upon others sitting off to the side, not one with any intention of continuing.

By very late in the afternoon he reached the halfway point and believed he had caught and passed everyone but Saul.

Famished, thirsty, aching, blistered, and sore, Luke stopped after sundown and begged fruit off a street vendor, vowing to pay the next day. The sustenance awakened him a bit but did nothing to heal his broken-down body, and now he lumbered on, only because there was nowhere else to go.

To his astonishment, as Luke finally began the incline that would take him back to the campus more than eight hours after he had begun, he saw a small figure in the distance, laboring to lean into and go up the hill. Saul.

The little man was limping badly, and Luke quickened his pace, just enough to know that he would be able to reach Saul before they finished. They would be the only two to complete the course. What a foolish idea this had been, and yet Luke anticipated a sense of accomplishment to go along with his ailments and the likelihood that he would not come close to finishing his reading that night.

When he drew close enough, Luke hollered out for Saul, who slowly turned and smiled wearily, extending his arms. "Luke! Is it you alone?"

"It is!"

Saul beckoned for him, but Luke had no more in him. He just shuffled along. Saul would have to wait.

When Luke finally reached him, Saul embraced him and they continued. "I'm proud of you," Saul said. "I confess that after halfway I knew I had offended all these by goading them to run, and had I not been the one who instigated this, I myself would have quit long ago. But frankly, if anyone else were to finish, I did not expect it to be you."

"Well, thanks for that. I looked that weak, did I?"

"No, I just underestimated your will, Luke. I am impressed. More than impressed. I have learned much about you from this."

They entered the gate with a couple of hundred yards to go to reach the tent. Luke's eyes met Saul's and they shook their heads. "Can't believe it's almost over?" Saul said.

"The tent seems to move farther the closer we get!"

"I am about to learn even more about you, Luke."

"More about me?"

But before the question was out of Luke's mouth, from somewhere Saul had mustered the strength to break into a run. He was certainly not sprinting, loping was more like it, but he quickly pulled away from Luke, even though the lad instinctively started running too. Was it possible to catch Saul, despite his surprise head start?

Just a hundred yards to go now, and Saul was half that distance ahead. It was hopeless, but still Luke wanted to finish well, so he forced himself to maintain his pace. Little would be gained by slowing now, and he was going to be wholly spent either way.

And as he continued, feeling the strain in every fiber of his body, he looked up to see Saul slow to a stop five yards from the finish and reach out, waiting for him. "We must tie!" Saul said.

Luke grabbed his hand and they staggered across the line together, collapsing in the tent and finding water pitchers. They doused themselves and fell onto cots on either side of the tent.

"I may never rise again," Luke said, "let alone walk."

And his new friend chuckled as he panted.

ELEVEN

None of the other participants in the run returned to the tent. They apparently found their way back to their quarters by other routes. Luke and Saul made the mistake of lying inert for too long after so much grueling activity, and when they finally rose, neither could move without much strain.

"I promised to remove this tent tonight," Saul said, and Luke immediately offered to help. He estimated it took them twice as long as it might have, had it not been for their pain and fatigue.

When they reached Saul's chambers, which he shared with three other students, Luke spent another hour trying to attend to his and Saul's respective ailments. Both had terribly blistered feet, aching joints and muscles in their legs, sharp pains in their shins, and a general malaise that made them want to merely lie around.

"You seem to be a physician already," Saul said, his roommates agreeing.

"This is working?" Luke said, as he applied both warm and cold compresses to his and Saul's legs. "I feel no better. The cleansing of our feet is probably the best I have done."

"I didn't say I felt better," Saul said. "I just meant that you seem expert. I fear I have damaged myself beyond repair."

"You might need more than a few hours' sleep tonight."

"I'm sleeping already. I'll be reading in my sleep."

Despite their commiseration, Luke and Saul dragged themselves off to the library, where they tried to read by torchlight and candlelight, often nodding off in the wee hours.

The next day Luke felt even worse, limping to lectures and apologizing for having fallen behind on his very first day. "You will be wise to catch up quickly if you plan to remain here," one professor told him. "I understand you were one of the victims of Saul's Folly."

Luke and Saul roared about that later, but both plunged headlong into their academic pursuits and spent much time together over the next several weeks, studying, reading, telling each other about their families and histories, quickly forging a friendship Luke hoped would last.

But there was something troubling about Saul. While he was quick of mind and was generally of good humor, he bore not an ounce of diplomacy. Regardless the issue or topic, he spoke his mind forcefully. And though he was also quick to listen and to see the other sides of arguments, he was unable to change his tone, even when it came to personal matters.

Luke noticed—and could tell that Saul did not—that Saul's own roommates had taken to merely tolerating him. They never met his eye, made faces behind his back, and in general had stopped engaging him. They merely listened to his opinionated comments on every aspect of the university, the world, and life in general. Often he groused about what he considered the pagan behavior of almost everyone but himself.

One late afternoon a few months into the school year, Luke and Saul finished their evening meal and strolled to the library as the sunlight faded. As they sat near torches and lit reading candles, Saul said, "You know, there are those among my elders, those who are carefully monitoring my progress here, who believe it is unlawful for me to dine with you, Luke."

"Because I am a Greek? But are you not also a Roman citizen? If you can be a Jew and a Roman, can I not be just a citizen of the world, a being in the universe like you? Why must our differences come between us?"

"Ah, I see the Stoics have reached you, Luke. I too embrace much of what they teach, except where it violates the ancient Scriptures."

"And I know enough about those texts to know that if you as a Pharisee intend to honor the letter of the law, you *are* transgressing to dine with a Gentile. Even to sit with me, to converse with me, study with me."

"True, and I don't know what that will mean for me, for us, in the future, should I become a leader in the synagogue."

"Are you serious, Saul? Do you feel guilty about associating with me?"

"I do."

"Do you despise me so much that I am a heathen to you?"

"There is the dilemma, Luke. You know I do not despise you. I love you like a brother. But you *are*, after all, a heathen."

"I am no more heathen than you, friend. Neither of us partakes of strong drink, neither is a carouser—though it's probably fair to say I might prefer to be one. I find you honorable in your speech and behavior. You have not shown a cheater's heart or a braggart's or thief's. You are blunt, I will say that. And if you have a vice it is that you are judgmental."

Saul looked genuinely surprised. "I am aware that I am forthright, Luke. But is it a judgment call to say a man is heathen who does not acknowledge God?"

"I take *heathen* to imply one who engages in debauchery and violation of his fellow man. Is that how you view me?"

"No, I merely see you as a well-intentioned Gentile."

"One with whom you are restricted from associating."

"Technically, yes."

"Do I cause you to stumble, then, in the practice of your religion?"

"No more than all the other Gentiles here. I don't know how I am to function on this campus if I am to separate myself from all of you. Almost every educator here is a Gentile and a Stoic besides. I am conflicted, and as I say, the day may come when I might find myself in a position of authority and required to follow the mandates of the law."

"And then we would no longer be friends?"

For the first time since they had met, Luke noticed Saul hesitate. But his response was chilling. "Then we would no longer be friends."

Luke rose and strode to a window. "You make me bold enough to speak my mind, because you always do."

"Yes, please."

"I'm just wondering. Are we really friends now? Or am I merely a novelty you are tolerating for a season? Can we ever truly be friends if you see me as beneath you?"

Again Saul hesitated, as if he wanted to dispute that. But Luke continued. "Don't deny it. A Greek, a Gentile, is not worthy of the devout Jew, especially the Pharisee. You see yourselves as not only strict followers of biblical law, but also the final arbiters of it. For the sake of this argument, I am striving to not take that personally. Just acknowledge the truth of it. I am a second-class citizen to you and always will be."

Saul smiled. "And yet you are so engaging."

"Do you not see how patronizing that is? To you I am a dog, a pet. You would not consider one human, though you would feed it and scratch behind its ears."

"Is that what you would wish from me, Luke?"

"You're still making light of this?"

"Only because I am warmed to see you take so enthusiastically to the discussion."

"But this has gone from discussion to argument, and now it threatens our very relationship."

"Then let's not allow it to, Luke. Let's enjoy this season at university."

"As a sort of break from reality?"

"Exactly."

Luke was not as good at this as Saul was. He was at a loss and could only rush outside into the cool air of the evening, feeling as if he had already lost a friend he had only recently gained. The work at the university was both invigorating and exhausting. He was homesick and missed his master, his friends, his tutors. But getting to know Saul and being fascinated by his personality—and character—had made things easier.

But what now? His misgivings, which he had only recently allowed into his consciousness, were being confirmed. He was merely tolerated by Saul. He served as recreation, distraction, a mildly interesting curiosity, in the end unworthy of true friendship.

To Luke's great relief, here came Saul, seeking him out. "This is not the Luke I know," he said. "You have not struck me as one who backs away from a discussion, even an argument."

"Put yourself in my place, Saul. What if you were the one considered heathen, unworthy?"

To Luke's deep dismay, Saul was apparently unable to hide his dumbfounded look. Clearly he had never allowed himself to even consider himself subservient to any non-Jew. Saul was among the chosen, gifted with a remarkable mind, blessed to have been raised in wealth and taught anything and everything he needed.

"Luke," Saul cooed, parentally, "you yourself have told me you were born of slaves, raised a slave. Legally you are not even a full-fledged Roman citizen. Would you expect to be the equal of a freeman, a Roman, even if I were not a Pharisee?"

So that was it. He had been presumptuous. He could serve as Saul's attendant, his sidekick, but never his equal. "Let me say this," Luke said, "I will not play the sycophant. I can admire you, but I will not worship you."

Saul fell silent and looked serious. Finally he said, "I do not seek worship. I would that you would worship God."

"But as a beginning practitioner of Stoicism, I do not believe in myths or gods."

"I am not speaking of Roman or Greek gods," Saul said. "I am speaking of Yahweh, God of gods, Lord of lords, maker of heaven and earth, the God of my fathers Abraham, Isaac, and Jacob."

Luke shook his head and returned to the library to gather up his things. Saul followed. "What?"

Luke turned on him. "You might as well be speaking a foreign language."

"I know several. Would you like me to try another?"

"This is not humorous. I can see that you are not just a student of Jewish history, but that you are also a believer."

"I am more than a believer. I am a Jew."

"Fine. I am a Stoic."

"Don't you see, Luke? You chose a philosophy of life. That's admirable. But I was born a Jew."

"And that makes you better than I?"

"I did not say that, but I will say this: God makes us what we are. If you are a true Stoic, you will passively accept the logic that you are who you are and I am what I am."

Laden with his study materials, Luke strode from the library, strangely warmed to find that Saul seemed to still be pursuing him. Maddeningly, he realized that Saul could only fear losing an admirer.

Luke took a somber tone. "Saul, do you have any idea how insulting and demeaning your view is?"

Saul hurried along beside him back to the dormitories. "And your view is that we should be equals."

"That's what friends are."

"No, I aver that that is what a Stoic believes all men are. The sad fact is that it simply isn't true. My question for you is, can you abide it?"

"Abide what? A pretend friendship with a man who sees himself as my superior?"

"No, the privilege of a season of friendship with a man you would not qualify to engage in any other context."

Luke stopped and stared. "You truly believe this, don't you?"

"Truth is what it is. It does not change based on how we view it."

"Then I suppose you think I am stuck."

"I know you are," Saul said. "If you fully embrace Stoicism, you must believe I am your brother. I can condescend to you as I wish or cast you aside based on the laws that bind me, but you must tolerate even this seeming boorishness."

"Seeming?" Luke said.

And he rushed off into the night.

TWELVE

Luke could not bring himself to seek Saul out, to meet at their prearranged spots, to dine together, to study together, to discuss and argue until late into each night as they had done for so long. How he missed the man and his mind and the exercise of interacting with him! And yet Saul had been as clear as anyone could be. He was a man of God, a chosen one, and while he may have been amused, even impressed, by Luke, to him Luke was subhuman.

He saw Saul around, of course. The man was hard to miss. Despite being a first-year student, he had already become one of the most recognizable faces, and voices, on the campus. He inserted himself into student government, held forth on Tarsus politics, commented on religion, sin, and any issue of the day. He debated one and all on their responses to Roman decrees, defended Tarsus' right to remain a free city, not taxed by Rome despite being under its jurisdiction.

Saul continued to organize athletic contests, though nothing near as foolish as his beginners' marathon. He seemed to be everywhere, and when he was not given an audience, he created one. Nearly every week Luke came upon him standing atop a crate or a rock and forcefully railing against some real or imagined ill on the campus. If the crowd thinned, Saul would shout some bold claim against some nearly sacred tenet of Stoicism, such as that it was impossible for a man to achieve either peace or virtue aside from the acknowledgment of God. And before Luke knew it, Saul would be surrounded by more students and even faculty.

Strangely, this breach in a friendship that had barely been born had a positive influence on Luke in one important respect. It seemed to him he had only two things on his mind every waking moment. He missed what he thought he had had with Saul. And he became obsessive about his studies.

Not spending hours interacting with Saul allowed Luke uninterrupted time for his reading. And while he often discussed texts and academic pursuits with other students, he did not allow himself to become as invested as he had with Saul. Yes, he was aware he was afraid of being disappointed or cast aside again. And Luke also had to admit to himself that no one else argued in quite the same maddeningly cogent manner Saul did.

That didn't mean Saul was always right, but he was certainly hard to argue with—and that had made it all the more invigorating.

Luke found himself becoming a loner, which he eventually decided was good for his studies. He could not, would not, lower himself to whatever position Saul needed to place him in for a relationship to work. On the rare occasions when he would personally run into the man or catch his eye, Luke thought he detected regret and even sadness in Saul. Was it possible he missed their interaction too?

Perhaps, but the man could not have been clearer that Luke had to know and understand and, as a Stoic, accept and keep his place. And that place? Luke was a pagan, a heathen, a slave, a Greek. Worse, he was a Gentile. Compared with Saul, yes, Luke was all those things. And while, as Saul said, Saul was born what he was while Luke chose his own philosophy of life (despite being born a slave), Luke decided that Stoicism surely seemed more humane than Judaism and certainly Pharisaism.

The only way to reengage with Saul without accepting a thoroughly subservient role, Luke knew, was to play Saul's game—to confront him, challenge him, argue with him, dispute his claim of superiority. The problem was that while Luke could not accept Saul's lofty image of himself—especially from a moral and religious standpoint—neither could he deny that the man's intellect far outstripped his own.

At times Luke felt so lonely and so missed the stimulation of arguing with Saul that he considered stepping out of character and tangling with him. But it just wasn't in him. Confrontation just for the sake of interaction was not part of his makeup. Luke enjoyed being known as a compassionate, caring, listening sort. It suited him, confirmed his own view of himself. His parents had not been of a station that would allow them to be anything but subservient, and yet even among their peers, they had never been confrontational. His father had never hesitated to tell Luke or his mother what he thought, but otherwise he was polite and gentle, a hard worker and diligent. Luke was grateful for that example. But if he had to credit his own gentler personality traits to anyone, Luke looked to Theophilus. The man, though at times naive regarding how his own slaves viewed him, was nonetheless unwaveringly fair and kind and generous.

THE EVENING before a holiday that would see him return to Antioch for the first time, Luke put quill to papyrus and wrote Theophilus. His plan was to tell his master just how much more he valued him and regarded him after half a year at university, and in the event the words would not come when they were face to face, the scroll would have to suffice.

In previous missives he had described the campus, the city, the marathon run, his classmates, and his studies. Now he fully described all that had transpired with Saul and his resultant loneliness. "Do not fret over this," he concluded, "as I have discovered the benefits of it for my studies, which remain my top priority here. My goal remains to make you proud and to affirm your faith in me. As I write this I await our reunion with eager anticipation and you have my every good wish that all is well there, including your health and that of your family and servants."

To Luke's great distress, and yet it should hardly have been a surprise, none other than Diabolos showed up to retrieve him from the harbor. Fortunately the trip was a short one, because the driver had been directed to take Luke to the Mediterranean retreat rather than to the main estate in Daphne.

"No trouble, I hope," Luke said, as he helped Diabolos load the carriage.

"Trouble for who?"

"Sickness I mean, in Daphne. The master is not trying to avoid another plague or anything . . ."

"Oh, no, your majesty. This is all for your benefit so you don't have to rub shoulders with the likes of us."

"Oh, don't Diabolos. I *am* the likes of you, and I looked forward to enjoying my own bed in my own quarters, among my friends."

"You don't have any friends in Daphne anymore, Loukon."

"Please, call me Luke."

"Oh, you've given up your name now too? Well, *Luke,* the rest of Theophilus's slaves are quite aware of the difference between us and you by now. You're to spend your entire holiday with only the master and his family here, living in their house, eating at their table, watching their sunsets. And guess who has been awarded the unspeakable privilege of getting to live in the servants' quarters and attend to your every need?"

"No one, I hope. I need no such aide, and I prefer—"

"Oh, no, no, it's not up to you, exalted one. And it wasn't up to me either or I might have declined."

"You? Oh, I'm so sorry, Diabolos. I will talk with the master and—"

"You'll do nothing of the sort. I assured him that if he had not assigned me, I would have volunteered."

"But I thought you said you would have declined."

"How like you to not listen. I said it wasn't up to me. Unlike for you, nothing is up to me."

"Why do you torment yourself that way? Do you look for opportunities to betray me somehow, make my life miserable?"

"I wish I had the power, but no. I'm merely trying to play the game, *Luke.* I need to be in the master's good graces to get any privileges around here. I did myself no good by being so obvious against you last time."

"I did not inform the master."

"Someone did. He lectured me and told me that you asked for mercy because of my grief."

"And that does not persuade you that I am not your enemy?"

Diabolos looked into the distance and shook his head. "You simply don't understand, do you?"

Luke examined himself. Was he somehow becoming as naive as Theophilus? "I guess I don't, Diabolos. Tell me."

"You really want to know?"

"I do! Please."

"Let me get your stuff into your quarters so I don't get into trouble.

The master awaits you on the back veranda. If you have time to talk, you know where I'll be."

Luke found it strange to enter the house alone, merely nodding to aides who greeted him and pointed him to the back. He could not fathom a reason Theophilus would not have been out front to welcome him. Indeed, he would not have been surprised if the master had met him at the ship.

When he emerged onto the balcony that overlooked the Mediterranean, the sun was setting, and he wished he could simply drink in the view, but his eyes found Theophilus and his wife, a couple of longtime advisers, and what appeared to be a wealthy married couple he did not recognize.

Theophilus immediately rose and rushed to Luke. "Here is the man of the hour now!"

The others rose too, and he was introduced to the couple. But before anything more could be said, Theophilus apologized to one and all and said he had an urgent matter to discuss with Luke briefly. He pulled the lad into the house.

"Luke! I'm as embarrassed as you must be! I shall have that driver flogged for forgetting to wash your feet."

Luke looked down. He had been so engaged with Diabolos that he had entirely forgotten, and clearly, so had Diabolos.

"Oh, please, master, don't take it out on him. We got to talking, and neither of us even thought of it. Let me do it myself."

"Nonsense! You are our guest, and this reflects on me! I can only hope our visitors did not notice, and that if they did they think less of my hospitality than they do of you."

"Please, sir, just show me to a basin and—"

"Luke, this is Diabolos's job, the reason he is here."

"But will we not appear more rude the longer we wait?"

"True enough."

Theophilus ordered a maiden in the kitchen to quickly wash Luke's feet, which humiliated him. Meanwhile, he heard the master call for an aide, instructing him to send Diabolos back to Daphne to be replaced. Luke wanted to intervene, to argue, to plead with Theophilus to reconsider and hear him out, but there was no time. The concern now was for the honored guests, whoever they were and whatever their interest in Luke.

He followed the master out again, noting that Theophilus was still red-faced and distracted. Luke wished he could get a message to Diabolos and decided he would somehow find a way to Daphne during the week under the pretense of wanting to reunite with friends, but primarily intending to clear the air with the slave.

The handsome couple on the veranda turned out to be associates of Theophilus and his wife, apparently invited to meet Luke with the intention of eventually introducing him to their daughter. Luke was stricken dumb at the thought. This, he had heard, was how marriages were arranged, but surely not for a slave. Slave marriages were arranged too, but only among those of their own kind. He had no business talking with these people about such an idea.

Luke quickly tried to assess the situation. The mother beamed at him from behind her husband. She was beautiful with a knowing smile and seemed to like what she saw in Luke. If the daughter looked anything like her, Luke would be a fool not to want to meet her.

The husband bore a more serious visage as he clearly studied Luke from head to toe. Meanwhile, Theophilus seemed to be going through some trauma. He sat off to the side, out of their vision but fully in Luke's, and seemed to be trying to communicate something to him with dancing eyebrows, winks, pursed lips, and the like. Luke was tempted to just say, "What is it, master? What do you want me to say or not say and why didn't you just advise me when we were in the kitchen?"

"So you are an adopted son of this father of many daughters," the man said.

Luke glanced at Theophilus, who nodded vigorously. It didn't seem right to lie, so Luke said, "Well, yes, sort of unofficially, yes. I lost my parents to a plague and—"

"That's so awful," the woman said. "It must have been terrible for you."

"It was. In many ways it still is."

"And what was your father's business?" the husband said.

"He was a tiller, sir. He tended the gardens, alongside my mother."

The couple seemed to freeze in place, their expressions locked. The man cleared his throat. "Tell me, Luke, are you a Roman citizen?"

"Ah, no, not yet. I look forward to that very much upon completion of my university training."

"In medicine."

"Correct."

The man turned to Theophilus, who looked apoplectic. "You intend to free this man then, I presume."

"Yes," Theophilus said, his voice squeaking. "He will serve as our physician for a time, then be free to pursue his own goals."

"One of which," Luke said, "is to perhaps be a ship's doctor, which would jeopardize my candidacy for husbandhood, would it not?"

The woman scowled. "If you're looking for a reason not to meet our daughter, look no further. You are the son of slaves?"

"And a proud one."

"Theophilus," the man said, a whine in his voice, "you could have told us."

"He'll be a freeman soon enough," Theophilus said, "and he will make someone a fine husband."

"Someone, perhaps. But not our daughter."

They rose to leave, ignoring Luke. Theophilus's aides shook their heads at Luke as the master escorted the couple out, and of course he soon returned and dismissed everyone but Luke.

Theophilus sat heavily and pressed his lips together. Then, "Luke, I expected more circumspection."

"Lies, you mean? Why didn't you say so?"

"Of course I didn't want you to lie. I didn't lie. I just thought you'd be able to assess the situation and—"

"Sir, forgive me, but you lied by omission. Are you ashamed to have become the patron of a slave? Is that why you have pledged to free me? Would it embarrass you to have a slave as a physician?"

"You're bordering on impudence, son."

"I apologize. I don't mean to. But frankly, your actions here disappoint me too."

Theophilus turned and gazed out to the sea, now dark, as the sun was disappearing. "I know. I'm sorry. I don't know what I was thinking. It's just that I have met the young woman, and she is a treasure."

"Does she share her parents' view of those beneath her station?"

"Oh, they don't really feel that way, Luke. They too are Stoics."

"As it suits them. They certainly don't embrace the view of the equality and brotherhood of man, do they? Did you see the looks on their faces?"

Theophilus slumped. "I did find that disconcerting. I pray I never come across that way."

"Only when you try to pass me off as something other than what I am."

Theophilus stood. "I'm embarrassed," he said. "Forgive me for this clumsy effort."

"I assume you meant well."

"You do wish to marry one day, do you not?"

Luke shrugged. "Perhaps. But I expect my life will be hard, even when I am free. Medicine is no pursuit for someone who covets wealth, and any woman's father will know that."

"You will wait until you become free though, correct? You would marry a free woman."

Luke leveled his eyes at his master. "Because then I will be too good for a slave?"

Theophilus sat again and covered his face with his hands. "You see how difficult this is, Luke, and why I have said you are a better man than I?"

Luke didn't know what to say. How could he counsel his own master, owner, patron? True, the man needed somehow to meld his philosophy with real life. But Luke was coming at this from an entirely different place. He was the slave. Naturally this all looked unfair and bigoted to him, but how would it look from Theophilus's view? And how would it look to Luke when he did become free? Would he in fact still be open to marrying a slave, and would he set about freeing her?

Luke was grateful he didn't have to think about it yet. There was so much he needed to accomplish first. He was in only his first year of university, and the last thing he needed was the distraction of worrying about marriage.

He sighed. "I know you mean well, sir."

"I want to do more than mean well, Luke. I want to be the kind of a man I should be."

"If you mean that—"

"I do!"

"Then grant me this one request. Allow me to deal personally with Diabolos."

"And how will you do that?"

"I'll go to Daphne and seek him out, and we will work through it."

"You will see that he is disciplined?"

"I have no standing to do that."

"Of course you do. I will grant you full authority."

"That is the opposite of what I intend. I need to assure him that I have cleared his name with you."

"Cleared his name?"

"This was as much my fault as his. His motives are not pristine, I know that. But this was a mere oversight and must be treated that way."

"I want that young man to know his place and his responsibilities."

"And I want him to know I share his place and want to see him succeed and stay out of trouble."

"I do not understand you, Luke."

"I'm just trying to be a good Stoic, sir."

"But you have been this way since long before you were taught Stoicism, and I have been attempting to practice it since before you were born. Surely your compassion must come from within."

THIRTEEN

Theophilus gave permission for Luke to ride back to Daphne with whoever came to replace Diabolos. "But," he said, "he is not likely to be here until late, so delay your journey until daybreak. Rome has had to change its courier schedules and we have had to change our import and export runs because of increased bandit activity after dark."

"Are you not then worried about Diabolos or his replacement traveling now?"

"Neither will be bearing any goods, and they carry no cash. If they are accosted, I doubt they'll be in danger unless they do something foolish. If the new man is not here in due time, then we can worry."

The time seemed right for Luke to express himself to Theophilus, but knowing the scroll he had written was in his pack somehow caused him to take the easy way out. He didn't know what had gotten into him, as he had never had trouble communicating with Theophilus, at least not in years. When the master began yawning and mentioning the late hour, Luke asked if he could leave his written message with him.

"Certainly. What is it?"

"Just something I felt more comfortable putting in writing."

"Not bad news, I hope."

"Hardly."

Luke fetched the scroll from his room and gave it to the master before retiring. He had just settled in when he heard a soft knock at his door. It was Theophilus, clearly moved. "Thank you, Luke," he said, hurrying away.

Luke guessed it was about midnight when he heard voices outside and crept to the window. There stood Theophilus in a billowing dressing gown and with matted hair, speaking urgently to two aides and two slaves. "No word at all?"

"Nothing. We have no idea whether Diabolos made Daphne, was accosted, or has fled."

"He had no reason to flee. I could have had him flogged for how he treated Luke, but I merely sent him back and told him to send a replacement."

"Perhaps he feared what was to come," an aide said.

"He'd better now," Theophilus said.

"Now, sir, we don't know that he is being willful. He could be in trouble."

"We'll know that soon enough." The master turned to the slaves. "Get torches and take two of our most rested steeds, and arm yourselves. Cover the route between here and Daphne as fast as is feasible, and send Balasi back with a wagon. He will attend to Luke while we try to locate Diabolos."

Luke wanted to go with the two slaves, but he was not proficient at riding, and he knew Theophilus would never hear of it. He worried about Diabolos and hoped they would find him neither having been attacked nor trying to escape. But Luke couldn't imagine another option. The master had shown great trust in Diabolos, especially under the circumstances, allowing him to get himself back to Daphne.

It would be great to have Balasi around. The old slave had been a friend of Luke's parents and of Lippio. He was quiet and some thought a bit shy, but he had always been obviously fond of Luke. By dawn he should arrive, along with whatever news there might be about Diabolos.

As Luke lay trying to drift off, he couldn't quit worrying and wondering if he was just too eager to be understood. It niggled at his brain that there were those who thought he was lording his privileges over them and would forget that he too was a slave.

Luke was of the opinion that Diabolos's larger problem was frustration over his own life and the awful loss of his parents and siblings. Luke's grief had been sharp and debilitating. He could only imagine what it must have been like to lose so many more family members.

But that didn't excuse Diabolos's treatment of Luke, and he had been a disagreeable sort since long before the plague. Luke had always seen the young man as lazy and contentious. Why did it seem so important to him now to, in essence, win Diabolos over? And why hadn't Luke's refusal to inform the master of Diabolos's previous offenses won him any favor? The fellow seemed even more put out that Luke had pleaded with Theophilus to be lenient with him.

Tormenting Luke, however, was knowing that at the heart of the matter, Diabolos was right. For all of Luke's efforts to appear a humble slave like all the rest, the fact was he was not and would never be again. And he enjoyed his position, even his image among his former peers—at least the ones he was still able to fool—as a man of true humility.

Still Luke hoped Diabolos had done nothing so foolish as try to escape. Theophilus's reputation as a benevolent master was so widely known that slaves under other owners asked to be traded to him. The only slave who had ever abandoned Theophilus ran off when Luke was a child, and when he was discovered and apprehended, the master sold him in Antioch. To this day, Luke didn't know how much of the story was legend and how much was true, but rumor had it that the man was no more loyal to his new master and suffered much physical punishment. The lesson, of course, was that slaves under Theophilus had it as good as they would ever see it and would be insane to seek a better situation.

Surely even Diabolos wasn't angry enough or stupid enough to run, was he? Unfortunately, his failure to send someone back—if he had reached Daphne—made the master and his advisers fear he had not made it at all. If that was true, and he was not on the run, it was possible he had been the victim of foul play.

Sleep eluded Luke as he tried to force his mind to come down on one side or other of the two possibilities. He was suddenly roused from his bed by loud hoofbeats and the sentry at the gate demanding the rider identify himself.

It turned out to be one of the slaves who had gone in search of Diabolos, and he shouted that he had news for the master. By the time he reached the house and dismounted, Luke was at the window and Theophilus was padding out.

"What news?" the master said.

"We found the wagon upended off the road and Diabolos with his throat cut!"

"No! Dead?"

"He still stirs, but we dared not try to get him on one of our mounts, and we could not right the wagon. He is fading, master, and we need help."

"I'll go!" Luke called out. "And we must not delay!"

He threw on his tunic and sandals and grabbed a satchel from the physician's chamber. As he raced from the house he asked the slave, "How far?"

"Not three miles."

"Let me arrange a wagon or carriage, Luke," Theophilus said.

"Send one after us," Luke said. "There's no time to waste."

As he leapt onto the horse behind the rider, Luke found himself back of the saddle on the steed's bare flanks. He reached around the rider and dropped his satchel in the man's lap, then wrapped his arms around the man's waist.

As the horse was urged to gallop out the gate and onto the main road, Luke worried he would be pitched off, and he held on as tight as he could.

NOT TEN MINUTES LATER, Luke was kneeling next to Diabolos in a ditch off the side of the road. The wagon was deep in the culvert on its side, and one would have had to be searching for it to see it.

Diabolos's breathing was shallow. Luke motioned the two slaves closer with their torches and could see that the young man had lost much blood. But was quickly able to determine that the wound, he assumed from a knife, need not be fatal if he acted fast, as it had missed the major vein.

Diabolos looked pale and terrified. He wrapped one of Luke's wrists in a death grip and rasped, "Bandits. I tried to outrun them, but the wagon was too heavy. They forced me off the road."

"But why, Diabolos? You had nothing of value to them. You should have just stopped and shown them."

"I didn't want to give them the satisfaction. Anyway, you know I'm a fighter."

"Yes, and look what it's cost you. Any other injuries?"

"Just scrapes and bruises, I think. Am I going to die?"

"Not if I can stop the bleeding." Luke rummaged in his satchel for absorbent cloths. He had seen the old physician actually sew up wounds like this, but he had never done it. Needle and thread were among his supplies, but he hoped he wouldn't have to use them.

No such luck. It seemed the more he tried to pack cloth into the gaping hole, the more bleeding he caused. Trouble was, he had none of the ointment the late physician had said made the stitching of flesh more bearable. "Hear me, Diabolos. I must draw your flesh together and bind it. You must lie as still as possible."

"You aim to sew my flesh like cloth? No!"

"Or you can lie here and bleed out to your death."

"How am I to hold still if you pierce me yet more?"

"These men will hold you still."

The slaves planted their torches in the ground, and each took one of Diabolos's arms. To keep the injured man from further thrashing about, Luke planted a knee on either side of his chest and bent low for the best view of the wound. The jagged opening was perhaps a bit longer than two inches and extended from the left of Diabolos's neck to the middle. Luke used a mixture of water and ointment to cleanse it the best he could, causing Diabolos to shake his head from side to side and cry out.

"You must not move now," Luke said. "Trust me that this is the best course of action."

Diabolos nodded and appeared to set his jaw.

"Think of something else. Imagine yourself anywhere else you would rather be."

And to Luke's astonishment, this caused Diabolos to chuckle.

"What?"

Smiling through clenched teeth, he managed, "Wait, wait. I will dream of thrashing you to within an inch of your life, and it will be right in your own comfortable chamber there in the master's house."

Luke shook his head. This was certainly no time to argue with the man, but he was nonplussed.

"You're wondering why," Diabolos rasped.

"Later," Luke said.

"No, I'll tell you. You think defending me to the master makes everything all right. It just makes it worse. You think I want a fellow slave speaking up for me?"

"You'd rather be flogged?"

"Yes! Now, make it so one day I will be strong enough to do to you what I imagine!"

"Hush," Luke said, settling himself to keep Diabolos as still as possible. "You know if I save your life tonight, you'll owe me yours."

"Oh, anything but that."

Despite the impossibilities of the situation, Luke detected some humor in his rival. Were they bantering like brothers? He hoped so. How could Diabolos still hate him, resent him when he was throwing himself into saving the man?

"Now press the back of your head into the ground as firmly as possible, and do everything you can to remain perfectly still. I'm new at this and must be careful not to make things worse."

"Don't tell me that!"

"I will be honest, if nothing else."

"Just get on with it!" Diabolos said, setting himself.

Luke threaded the needle in the flickering light and leaned in to get the full scope of the damaged area. With his free hand, Luke grasped either side of the opening and found it slippery with trickling blood.

As soon as he tried to pinch the ragged ends together so he could sew, Diabolos suddenly drew his knees up and into Luke's back, knocking him forward and making him press his hands to the ground to keep from toppling onto the man's face.

"Sorry!" Diabolos cried out.

"You must control yourself," Luke said, now having to cleanse his own hands before continuing.

He finally realized that if he let the blood on his fingers dry a bit, it gave him a better grip on the otherwise slippery gash. That allowed him to quickly draw it together and hold it as he forced the needle in. Somehow Diabolos was able to keep from thrashing, though he hissed and whined until Luke had completed six large loops and tied them off.

Luke and the other two slaves were together able to right the wagon, though its rear axle had been damaged and they had to wait until Theophilus sent another to slowly rumble and lurch the whole slow way back to the compound.

Over the next several days, Luke monitored Diabolos, stationing him in his own bed and having a cot set outside the door for himself. Though it quickly became clear that Diabolos was out of danger, his healing wound turned fiery red and painful, so Luke had to tend to it every few hours.

Theophilus expressed concern every day that Luke's vacation from school was being spoiled this way, and he sent for Balasi anyway to serve him. Luke felt strange, a slave in effect employing a slave. But the old friend of his family proved most helpful, though Luke was careful to never ask him to do anything he could do for himself.

Balasi seemed older and slower than Luke had remembered. He loved to talk, though, and that was a nice diversion. He privately assured Luke that while, yes, there were those among the slaves who were jealous of Luke, they did not seem to resent him and many, many more were happy for him.

"They look forward to when you come back and become their doctor," the old man said.

Luke was napping on the cot outside his room one afternoon when he roused enough to be aware that Balasi had delivered his midday meal and was also taking a tray in to Diabolos. When he didn't return immediately, Luke sat up, aware of an earnest conversation behind the door.

"Your dad and me was friends, you know," Balasi was saying. "And I owe it to him to speak my mind. Now it looks like you're going to be okay in time, and you know you owe it to that boy out there."

"He's little more boy than I am, old man. We're close to the same age, but there's nothing else the same about us."

"There could be, except that you're nasty to him and to everybody else. We all lost somebody, you know, son, Loukon included."

"But look what he's got now. He might as well be a freeman already."

"He deserves it if anybody does, and you know it."

"Make me the master's pet and let me sleep in his house and study under his tutors and I'd deserve it too."

"Aw, go on, Diabolos. You and I wouldn't know what to do with all that learning. It was obvious Loukon was bright before he could hardly speak."

"Yeah, but you can tell how much he loves being over everybody else."

"I don't see that in him at all. You only see it that way 'cause you're jealous."

"Well, who wouldn't be?"

"You shouldn't be. He saved your life. And word is he kept you from a flogging too. You ought to be glad the master listens to him."

"How am I supposed to feel, a slave just like me defending me to the master?"

"How are you supposed to feel? Grateful. Your parents would be ashamed."

"Don't be talking about them."

"Why not? Can't you remember how good they were? I'll bet they were proud of Loukon."

A long pause made Luke wonder what was going on. When Diabolos spoke again, the pain and anger were obvious.

"They were!" he spat. "He was all they could talk about. It was like they wished he was their son and not me!"

Balasi's tone suddenly changed from scolding to sympathy. "We all go through that, Diabolos. My parents always compared me with my brother and sister. It was wrong and it was hurtful, but they were just trying to make me a better man."

"It didn't work."

Balasi laughed. "I know. But they tried. You want to know what your father used to tell me about you?"

"What?"

"You don't think he talked about you? He talked about all his children."

"What did he say?"

"He said you could do anything you put your mind to. Said you were more than just a big, strong boy, but that you had a good mind too."

"I can't even read."

"Neither can I. But you know as well as I do that there is a lot more to being smart than being able to read. We don't all have to be geniuses like Luke."

"My father really said that?"

"Why would I lie? He said you being a slave was a waste, that you would make a good freeman."

"You'd better not be just saying this."

Balasi's tone went soft again. "You know I'm not. And you also know you owe Loukon two things."

"What?"

"Prove to me you have the mind your father thought you had. What two things do you owe Loukon?"

"I don't know. I guess thanks for saving my life."

"Of course. And what else?"

"Keeping me from getting punished?"

"Thanks for those two things and then something else."

"You're going to have to tell me."

"No I'm not. How have you treated Loukon?"

"Pretty bad, I guess."

"Then besides thanks, what do you owe him?"

"I know."

"Tell me."

"An apology. But I have to tell you, Balasi, thanks is going to be a lot easier for me than an apology. I haven't apologized for years, and only when my father made me apologize to my mother."

"You need me to make you do this?"

"You can't."

"I know, and I wouldn't want to, because then you wouldn't mean it. You can thank Loukon for what he's done for you, because there's no question about that. But don't you dare apologize for the way you've treated him until you can really mean it."

BY THE TIME Luke was to be taken back to the harbor for the voyage to Tarsus, Diabolos had been up and about for a few days. He was timid, shy, quiet around Luke, answering only his medical questions. Luke urged him not to do anything strenuous for another couple of weeks and had to refuse when he offered to help load Balasi's wagon for the ride to the harbor.

Balasi did the work, with Luke's assistance, then helped Diabolos into the seat so he could ride along. The trip was awkward, because Luke kept expecting Diabolos to say something. Balasi wound up making small talk about the weather, the route, the ship, and the master's new restrictions against anyone under his charge being out on the road after dark, alone or otherwise.

Finally they unloaded and got Luke's stuff aboard, and Luke said his goodbyes to the old man. Balasi climbed back onto the wagon, but Diabolos remained with Luke, still silent.

"Well, take care of yourself," Luke said. "I've told the mistresses of the house how to change that bandage, but don't exert yourself for a while."

"Yeah, okay. Listen, I wanted to thank you for what you did for me."

"Don't mention it."

"Of course I'm mentioning it. You saved my life, and before that you kept me from getting into too much trouble with the master. You didn't have to do that."

"You're welcome."

"I mean, I got myself in enough trouble anyway, but you tried to help."

"Okay, then. Maybe I'll see you next time I come back."

"Yeah."

Diabolos pawed at the ground with his sandal, and Luke was glad there seemed no urgency on the part of the ship's crew. Others were boarding and cargo was being loaded on.

"You looking forward to getting back to Daphne?" Luke tried.

"Yeah, not too many friends here, of course. Just Balasi, but he'll be taking me back."

"Um-hm."

"Listen, Loukon, I got to apologize to you."

"You do?"

"Yeah, I do. I've been pretty mean to you, and I got no excuse. I mean, I thought I had my reasons, but I don't."

"Well, thanks. Apology accepted."

"We okay then?" Diabolos thrust out his hand.

"We're okay." Luke shook it.

Diabolos looked terribly uncomfortable and could not meet his eye.

Luke pulled away to board. Now if he could only have a similar conversation with Saul.

FOURTEEN

From that first visit to Syria until the time he graduated from the university with honors, Luke poured his entire being into his studies. It seemed to him that the pain of the loss of his parents was beginning to dull. The reconciliation with Diabolos, the reassurances from Balasi, and most of all his ability to save a man's life had allowed the rest of his own life to come into focus.

He considered himself a full-fledged Stoic by now, in both intention and practice. Luke decided that the only weakness in the philosophy exposed itself when adherents made the mistake of thinking it would put them on the path of achieving perfection in all areas of their lives. Every day he became more aware of the reason behind Theophilus's frustration over his reputation not matching what he knew of himself deep inside.

The same was true of Luke. While he seemed to have no enemies—except for the ubiquitous Saul—the affection he felt on the part of other students and faculty often made him feel guilty. People told him they liked his personality and character, as if they were one and the same. Luke knew better. His personality was what people saw and knew of him. They liked his smile and made it clear they assumed it meant he was at perfect peace with himself and the world. His elders, especially, often mentioned his kindness and compassion to all, regardless of their social or economic standing.

But deep in his soul, Luke was alarmed at his true character. He did not like what he saw. He would not apologize, even to himself, for trying to do good, to live at peace with all men, to see everyone as a brother, an equal in the universe. But what about his motives? Did he do this from some altruistic core of perfection?

No, that hated inner man craved attention, yearned for praise, and—ironically—deeply longed to be known for his humility. In the privacy of his own room—a luxury afforded only to upperclassmen—he felt overwhelmed by the darkness in his soul. Working, studying, achieving, impressing, smiling, doing for others—it was all wonderful and made him almost immeasurably popular. But he found himself quietly jealous of anyone who achieved in any other area and gained attention from it. Though he might be the first to lift the flag and honor the man, he also secretly wished some ugly truth would be revealed about this rival for his place at the center of the stage.

Just when he grew tired of the invading thoughts putting him in a sour mood—which he hid behind a constant public smile—some modicum of attention would be directed another's way, and his attitude would be swept into an abyss where the sun was not to be found.

This private awfulness became Luke's overwhelming secret, and he desperately feared being found out. If he had ever been devoted to mastering Stoicism, it was now. He would start afresh, determined to do all in his power to be a better man, inside and out.

. . .

WITH ABOUT A YEAR to go before the completion of his matriculation, Luke had almost talked himself into a new outlook. He told himself that he must do more than simply act happy for someone else who was being lauded, he must also be truly pleased with and for them. He left his chambers for class that day determined that he would reach to his highest ideals at the next opportunity.

As if the stars or the gods or the fates or the muses—or any number of other ethereal myths he didn't believe in—had conspired against him, who should the next center of attention be but Saul of Tarsus.

Saul had been the talk of the campus since the day he had arrived, but Luke had taken secret delight in the fact that the man's fame came with caveats. No one denied that Saul was brilliant and indefatigable. But all saw him as odd, even annoying.

That was the trouble with religious people, Luke decided. They were judgmental, all-knowing, condescending, and worst of all, noisy. Hardly a day went by when Saul did not somehow make himself the center of attention. He had an opinion on everything and was never content to keep it to himself. He held forth on every aspect of life on the campus, deigning to criticize every Greek and Gentile student and member of the faculty—which of course made up the vast majority of the university population. Shortly after their personal falling-out during the first half of their first year, Saul had taken to dining only with other Jewish students.

The further he advanced in the polity of the local synagogue, the more he dressed to reflect his stature. He had quickly become one of the youngest elders in the congregation and announced his qualifications to anyone within earshot.

If Saul was the most visible and famous student on the campus,

Luke seemed everyone's favorite. That pleased Luke to no end, though he never admitted this to anyone else.

But just when he had committed to forcing himself to find some genuine pleasure in another student's glory, whoever it turned out to be, who was lauded but Saul himself?

Luke was leaving his favorite lecture—history (yes, he enjoyed it even more than his medical pursuits)—when he heard everyone talking about Saul. "What's he done now?" he said with a smile.

Luke was told that Saul had outshone all other rhetoric and composition students. A friend told Luke, "The two professors agreed to work together on the assigning of a project. Students were to choose some opinion or argument about which they felt passionate, then craft a composition and also present it orally. Saul chose to write and speak about why everyone at this university should wish they were Jewish and should acknowledge that his Lord was the one and only God."

"And that succeeded at this Stoic institution?" Luke said, shaking his head.

"Yes. Imagine. Both professors allowed that when they had heard of his intentions, they were prepared to judge him harshly. Even though the opinion was offensive and unlikely to persuade anyone—which turned out to be the case—both professors agreed it was one of the best-written compositions of a strikingly cogent argument they had ever read, even by scholars much Saul's senior. And when he delivered the message rhetorically, entirely from memory, it was greeted with a standing ovation."

"Well," Luke said, "bravo and good for him!"

"He's an amazing man with a brilliant mind."

"That he is," Luke said.

He followed his friend to the dining commons, privately seething. This wasn't working. He could feign all the praise he wanted, and yet this news had been too much to take. Luke had been as impressed with

Saul as anyone, but he enjoyed his own place as people's favorite. Saul didn't need this glory on top of everything else.

Worse, Luke's reaction only shone a light on the darkness of his own heart and soul. He hated himself for this pettiness and selfishness. Why couldn't his Stoic philosophy, as Theophilus said, make him a better man? Why could he not rein in his envy, his anger, his self-centeredness?

Maybe if he made himself congratulate Saul, his actions would lead to true feelings of benevolence and admiration for his rival. He peered about the commons, only to espy Saul surrounded by his Jewish friends. They seemed to be enjoying more merriment than ever, as if celebrating his achievement.

Saul, of course, was at the center of the group, holding forth on something or other, and every few moments those with him exploded in raucous laughter. Luke was becoming more repulsed by the minute, knowing full well his feelings were due to jealousy. Now would be the perfect time to make his foray.

He approached Saul from behind, and a few of his friends noticed and nudged Saul, nodding at Luke.

"Well, hello, Luke!" Saul said, rising and shaking his hand. "Tell me you've heard the good news and have come to congratulate me!"

So full of himself!

"Actually, I just wondered if you had time for a brief discussion later today."

"Why, yes! It's been ages since we've talked. I'd enjoy that very much."

"But of course I would not be permitted to dine with you."

Saul laughed aloud. "True enough, but I am not restricted from conversing with you. But you really haven't heard the news?"

"What news?"

Saul told him exactly what he had just been told.

"Isn't that wonderful," Luke said, shaking his hand again. "You must be so proud. It's a privilege to know you."

"It is, isn't it?" Saul said, and although he had a twinkle in his eye, Luke believed he meant it. "And what a Stoic thing to say."

This made his mates laugh.

Luke merely nodded and smiled, unable to think of a rejoinder.

"I'll meet you in the greater courtyard at sunset, then," Saul said. "How's that?"

"Perfect," Luke said, retreating.

Now he had compounded his envy with deceit. What was wrong with him? Throughout the rest of the day, he resolved to be honest with Saul that evening.

SAUL APPEARED DISTRACTED and eager to get on with it that evening when Luke approached. "Do you have another commitment?" Luke said. "Should we do this another time?"

"No, this is fine, but yes, of course, I have other commitments tonight. There are precious few breaks in my day, which I assume is true with you too."

"It seems I study all the time."

"I study too, but I also speak, write, engage in athletics. And I love to debate. Is that what we're going to do now?"

"I hadn't planned to."

"Then what?"

"I have just a few questions for you. About Judaism."

"You have come to the right person, as I assume you know."

"I knew you would think so." It was out before Luke could corral it. "I am just trying to be funny, Saul."

"I know, but in humor resides the truth. Not only am I the right person to ask about the one true God, but yes, I also know I am. In my mind, it is not conceit when it is true. If I thought I were an authority on Judaism and was not, I would be guilty of foolish pride. But I doubt you could raise an issue about my religion about which I am not versed. Try me."

"I am a Stoic, as you know."

Saul nodded.

Luke hesitated, not wanting to admit to this man that he had found the philosophy wanting, especially when it came to personal piety.

"But you miss God," Saul said. "Do you not?"

"You know Stoics believe in logic and reason, that which can be seen and felt and studied."

"Don't tell me God cannot be studied, Luke. I have been studying Him and His ways and statutes for as long as I can remember. I began studying the Scriptures when—"

"You were five, yes, I'm aware. Deeper stuff at ten, and off to rabbinical school at thirteen."

"You have a good memory."

"You generally don't let people forget." Again Luke had allowed his bitterness to come through, and he hated himself for it.

"When I talk about myself, I mean to talk about God," Saul said. "The true student of Scripture should reflect the Author."

Luke wanted to tell this self-possessed man that he was a poor representative of God, if there was a God. But rather he said, "Just as an academic pursuit, I'm curious: Does the practice of your faith make a difference in your personal life?"

"Who I really am, you mean? In private, behind a closed door?"

"Precisely. Are you able to control your passions, to keep out the things of the world that would distract you?"

"Let's sit," Saul said, unusual for him. Luke had rarely seen him sit except for a meal or a lecture. He joined the man on a stone bench.

"My pursuit of God *is* my passion," he said. "I do not plan to marry, if that is what you're aiming at. My entire life will be sacrificed to the Lord for His service and for obedience to His law."

"So pride, jealousy, anger, sloth . . . none of these things invade?"

Saul fell silent a moment, another rarity. He rubbed his hands together and seemed to study the darkening sky. "Not for a long time. Though these are the things that come to mind when we celebrate a feast of atonement."

"Atonement for sins?"

"What else?"

"I don't know. It's just—well, I—I just have never seen these things manifest in you."

"Nor I in you, Luke, but I daresay that is not due to your Stoicism."

"Why?"

"Your philosophy, as I understand it—and believe me, the longer I study here, the more I know of it—is not about laws and statutes. I rarely need to atone for sins, because I am focused on following God's laws. It is my life."

Now Luke had something else to envy, though he was no less put off by the man.

"Interesting," was all he could muster.

"That's it? That's all that was on your mind?"

If he only knew.

INTERVAL

Fifteen years bridged Luke's life from the time he graduated from the university in Tarsus until an encounter with an old acquaintance would change his life and make his one of the most recognizable names in the annals of history.

The talk of the campus the day he left was that the irascible Saul of Tarsus was on his way to Jerusalem to work in the temple, with designs on one day becoming the youngest member of the Sanhedrin. "And he'll probably do it," was the general consensus, even by those who could barely stand to be in the man's presence.

Luke had to admit he would be glad to be out of earshot of Saul and wondered if the three hundred miles between Syrian Antioch and Jerusalem were enough. He had long since resigned himself to the fact that one of his major issues with Saul was jealousy. He didn't want the man's reputation—for he was widely considered obnoxious and annoying—but to Luke it seemed unfair that his own good qualities were not worthy of such fame.

For his part, Luke headed back to Theophilus's estate to serve as the family and business physician. Luke pleaded with the master to not welcome him with the same type of fete he had hosted when sending Luke off to university.

"Sorry," Theophilus said, "but the meat and fruit have already been ordered."

"Please tell me the slaves have not yet been invited."

"They haven't, but no doubt they expect to be and are eager to come."

"Trust me, they are not. If you value my opinion in the least, accede to my wish that this be a private party, perhaps just your paid staff and the family."

Theophilus scowled. "If you insist."

"I do."

"Here's my thinking on your freedom, Luke. I would like to ask you to serve me here for five years. At the end of that time, if you wished to stay on, we could talk about compensation. Otherwise, you would be free to pursue any employment avenue you wish."

"Thank you, sir. And I have one more request. I would like to live in the same chambers I stayed in before I left."

"In the slave quarters? Wouldn't it be easier for you and more comfortable right here in the house?"

"Of course, but I fear it would separate me too much from my people. And I would always be just moments away if you needed me in the night."

"If you're sure."

"I am."

"But once you are a freeman, if you were employed here, I would insist—"

"That would be fine."

. . .

BUT IT NEVER CAME to that. During the five years Luke served as Theophilus's physician, his work often took him into Antioch for supplies and consultation with other doctors. He enjoyed his role in Daphne and occasionally at the Mediterranean retreat and seemed to endear himself to the entire population of the compound, but the squalor of the worst parts of the city seemed to plant something deep in his heart.

Every time he saw abandoned children or poverty-stricken families suffering all manner of ailments and diseases, the images stayed with him for days and often interrupted his sleep. Luke began to wonder if he was investing his life in the best possible way for the good of mankind, as his Stoic philosophy urged.

With a few months to go on his commitment to Theophilus, he thought it only fair to give the master notice of his plans. When the time was right and he had a few minutes alone with Theophilus, he told him he wanted to talk about the future.

"I would like that," the master said. "And I suppose you're wondering about my plans for your freedom."

"I have no doubt you will have everything in order."

Theophilus nodded. "The documents have been drafted and everything will fall into place precisely when we planned. And I am hosting a feast for my family, my staff, my slaves, and many of your colleagues, and don't give me that look or even start with your protestations. I will not be dissuaded this time, and I have even taken the liberty of discussing it with a few of the slaves. My sense is that there will be no resentment, that in fact they are thrilled to see what you have become and what will become of you as a freeman. I daresay you are an inspiration to all, especially many of the young who would like to work toward the same goal someday."

"I will attend with gratitude, sir."

"We would have the festival even without you!" Theophilus said, laughing. "Now, what is on your mind? Do you wish to know my plans for your employment?"

"No, I wish to inform you of mine."

Theophilus clouded over. "You're moving on, then?"

"Not far. I plan to set up a headquarters in Antioch with two of my colleagues there. We will take turns serving as cargo ship physicians to support ourselves, and while one is at sea, the other two will run a free medical center for those who could otherwise not afford care."

Theophilus sat back and slapped his thighs. "Luke, I could not be more proud of you. What a wonderful idea! Allow me to help the cause with a small monthly stipend for supplies."

"I wouldn't have dreamt to ask, sir. Thank you!"

"And don't become a stranger. I'll be hiring a new physician, of course, and would want your counsel in selecting the right one. Perhaps even some help in his training. We could get started on that straightaway."

"My hope would be to visit often, though I expect my schedule will be unlike anything I've grown accustomed to. Frankly, I'm excited about being at sea for short periods. There is much need there, though the pay is small. But friends tell me the best gossip, or I should say news, comes from the ships' crews that pass through Seleucia Pieria."

"No doubt," Theophilus said. "When I was more personally involved in the day-to-day work of importing and exporting, I kept up with happenings all over the world by interacting with ships' captains.

I miss that. Everything is secondhand now. Do promise to keep me up to date on what you hear."

"I will."

"Starting with all the hubbub in Judea."

"I'm not aware."

"Really? My aides tell me a working man from Nazareth is causing a commotion, traveling about, speaking to great crowds about the kingdom of God."

"Indeed?" Luke said, laughing. "And is he planning to usher it in?"

"I don't know, but they say many believe he has healed people."

That gave Luke pause. Had he not, in spite of his devotion to Stoicism, found himself longing to be known as a great physician, one of the best in the land? "Healed them? Healed them of what? And how?"

"The blind, the lame. He heals them with a touch or a word. Rumor has it he raised a man who had been dead and in the tomb four days."

Luke shook his head. This had better not be true. And how could it be? "People will believe anything. Surely no one with a brain is accepting this. Is Rome aware of it?"

"If not, it soon will be, unless the novelty of it wears off or until he is exposed as a charlatan. I should think the Jewish leaders would be most upset, as he apparently has no authority to be expounding on these matters. Others have arisen to draw great crowds, only to fade into obscurity. But if you hear any more out of there, let me know."

As Luke lay trying to sleep that night, he couldn't help but smile at the prospect of his old friend Saul responding to this obscure teacher arousing such interest from the people. Woe to the poor man if he was forced into a debate with Saul!

By the time Luke had enjoyed his festive send-off—and Theophilus was right that many of his fellow slaves seemed genuinely happy for him (including Diabolos)—and gotten started on his new career, he didn't have to venture to the harbor for news from Judea. The fame of the carpenter named Jesus was spreading. Even some visiting the free clinic had stories and opinions about the controversy.

A woman told Luke, to his uproarious amusement, that the teacher had fed thousands of people with just a couple of fish and a few loaves of bread.

"And I suppose you've heard of all the healings too," Luke said, still chuckling. "A blind man? A bleeding woman?"

"Oh, more than that," she said. "I heard that more than once he healed everyone gathered to listen to him."

"Everyone? All of them? How many?"

"Hundreds at least," she said. "That's why some think he's of God."

"Of God? Do people really believe this?"

"Some believe he could be the Messiah."

"Indeed?" But Luke could see that his merriment was offending the woman. He managed a serious look. "And you? What do you make of it, ma'am?"

She seemed to think a moment. "I would like to believe it," she said. "I wish he would come here. Then I wouldn't have to come to you and only hope I improve."

Luke winced. He had never claimed to have magical healing powers, and frankly he resented that someone hundreds of miles away was doing just that and having his legend reach this far.

"I didn't mean to offend you, sir. But you must admit it would be wonderful if a true healer came here and blessed us."

Luke nodded but was distracted as he finished his examination and treatment. When the woman left, he sat resenting a man he had never seen. He found himself hoping Saul *would* be assigned by the Jerusalem synagogue to investigate the miracle man. Yes, he allowed himself to wish he had the time and resources to make the trek to Israel and check this out. The very idea of someone drawing so much attention to himself, especially under the guise of helping people, flew in the face of every Stoic principle.

Luke did not believe in myths, gods, miracles, magic, or healing outside the bounds of medicine. And raising someone from the dead? He didn't know how the trick was accomplished or whether it might have just been a tall tale that became more believable the more it was told, but Luke could not imagine rational people being swayed by any of this.

Over the next few years, the stories from Judea overwhelmed all other news. Aboard ship the occasional story of a trading scandal or even an episode of piracy kept Luke entertained. But always the gossip turned to Israel and the miracle worker. Some crew members clearly exaggerated everything they'd heard, eyes bright as they piled tale upon tale.

But then came the voyage where a ship's cook claimed to have been an eyewitness.

"Wait," Luke said. "You saw this man, this Jesus?"

"Saw him and heard him."

"Did he perform any miracles?"

"No, but he seemed like the kind of a guy who could."

"Really? And you deduced that from what?"

"I what?"

"What made you think that, just from listening to him?"

The man shrugged. "He just sounded like he knew what he was talking about. You know, I didn't even understand it all. He was telling stories, and I didn't understand them. But he was telling what the kingdom of God was like."

"So he claims some divinity?"

"He what?"

"Some say he could be the Messiah."

"I don't even know what that is," the man said, "but when he told stories about people losing things and finding them and said that was what the kingdom of God was like, even though I didn't understand why, it was plain that he did. Sounded like he knew, that's all. And he talked nice, like you wanted to keep listening to him. And children? They flocked around him, loved him. And he seemed delighted by them."

Luke believed none of this, and yet it was clear that many did. More than many. It seemed all anyone could talk about. Something was happening in Israel, but what? And why did he so revile a man he had never met?

A few months later a crew that had sailed from Joppa was abuzz about Jesus. "The Jews are exercised about him and the Romans are aware," the captain said. "Whatever is going on with him can't last. It's as if he and his disciples have disappeared. They only show up here and there without notice, then seem to vanish again."

"The Jews' problem with him, how does that manifest itself?"

"The scribes and the Pharisees seek him out, argue with him, try to charge him with offenses. I saw them try to capture him near the temple, and he disappeared right out of their midst."

"How did he do that?"

"I don't know. He was there one minute and gone the next."

"Just poof, into thin air?"

"I don't know about that. It looked like it, but it could have been the crowds."

"These scribes and Pharisees, did you hear any of their names?"

"No."

"Did you get a look at them? Was one of them younger, like my age, short, thin, dark?"

"Didn't notice. I was looking at the teacher. He called them snakes."

"He did?"

The man nodded. "That's why I say his time is short. He won't get away with that for long."

"What will they do to him?"

"Who knows? I was just an observer. But this man seems to be afraid of no one. And that does not bode well for him. There are people it is wise to fear, especially in Jerusalem. Crowds seem to adore him—worship him, even. And if he speaks out against the authorities for long, they will be forced to act. That will be the end of him."

Saul of Tarsus had to be acutely aware of this so-called healer. Luke began plotting how he might save enough money to look for his old university mate. A former enemy could be an ally in getting to the bottom of all this hubbub.

Part Three

THE BELIEVER

FIFTEEN

A.D. 42

At thirty-seven, Luke felt in the prime of his life. But despite having gained his freedom ten years before, he had certainly reached no level of social status in Antioch. He lived in one cramped room above the tiny clinic where he worked from dawn to sundown nearly every day he was not at sea.

His one pastime, which occupied him by candlelight most evenings, was writing a history of Antioch, not about the city itself but rather its people—its lower class, the ones he encountered every day. Luke had learned that people were ashamed to have to come to a free clinic, and so to put them at ease, he chatted casually with them, getting them to open up. Then he would ply them with questions about their pasts, their families, and all the influences that brought them to where they were that day.

By carefully rationing Theophilus's small monthly stipend and his own income from serving as ship's doctor on Mediterranean vessels coming into and going out of Seleucia Pieria at the mouth of the

Orontes, Luke was able to keep a stock of good papyrus and quills. He had no designs on ever seeing any of his writings distributed or even seen by others. He simply enjoyed the exercise and relished especially the interviewing.

On his occasional day off he might visit Daphne or even venture to Theophilus's Mediterranean retreat to chat with his aging patron. His former master had a new physician, and so Luke was spared having to delve into that area. The old friends could merely bring each other up to date, talk politics, and discuss the growth of Stoicism and what the new religion that had come out of Israel might mean for Syria.

As had been predicted and as Luke expected, Jesus of Nazareth had come to a violent end. The Jews, his own people, had enlisted Rome to help squelch him, and he had been put to death in the most heinous way. What proved a marvel to both Luke and Theophilus, however, was that the man's fame had not died with him.

They were at first amused, then bemused, when his disciples and many followers claimed he had risen from the dead, appearing to many of them before ascending into heaven. That the body had never been produced by the authorities caused both the Jews and the Romans no end of grief. Still, Luke and Theophilus were certain that normal people would eventually come to their senses. But there was no estimating the capacity for the human mind to believe what it wanted, rational or not.

The so-called miracle worker's disciples seemed devout. Members of ships' crews who had encountered them preaching and teaching here and there said they spoke of the risen Jesus as the Christ, Messiah come in the flesh, having ushered in the kingdom of God. Others said these men themselves performed the same types of miracles the carpenter had. Believers had begun to gather in homes, sending out pairs and teams of preachers to spread what they called the truth.

Rome and the Sanhedrin had not stood long for this either, and well-known leaders among this new religion had been arrested and imprisoned, and some had even been martyred for the cause. Rumor said that Saul of Tarsus had been involved in ferreting out these rebels and rabble-rousers and seeing they were punished. Luke heard Saul had been present when one of the most beloved of the young stalwarts was stoned to death.

One of Luke's medical voyages aboard a trading vessel arrived at dawn in Joppa, where a two-day layover allowed him time to get to Jerusalem. Leaving the ship through piles of cargo, he negotiated with donkey drivers, rented a healthy but skittish ride, and began the day-long journey into the hills of Judea. The acres and acres of olive trees and grapevines reminded him of some of Syria's fertile plains, especially near the Mediterranean coast, but Israel seemed to have more livestock, especially goats and sheep.

The ship's captain had told him where the trading company's agents housed the traders and told him to use his name to try to secure a room. A few hours from where he would first catch a glimpse of Jerusalem, Luke was welcomed to a small inn, where his feet were washed and he was able to buy a cheap meal of bread, olives, cheese, and grapes.

Luke slept soundly through the crisp night and rose early, hoping to find Saul at the temple in Jerusalem by noon the next day. The City of David had few similarities to Antioch, for while Roman soldiers were everywhere, the government had not dominated the metropolis with its designs and statuary. This was primarily a Jewish city, allowed to practice its religion.

Yet, like Antioch, the city was full of people of all nationalities and languages, and as Luke threaded his way through the narrow, winding streets, he rubbed shoulders with peasants, animal herders, merchants, and tax collectors.

Luke found the Upper and Lower Markets fascinating, rimmed by craftsmen busy producing what they would sell in the storefronts. An intoxicating blend of odors that included fresh fish, cheese, spice, and fruit hit him, but he was sobered to also pass through the square where slaves were bought and sold.

Intriguing as he found the old city and as much as he would have enjoyed taking the time to jot some notes, Luke was on a mission: to reconnect with his old classmate Saul. Perhaps the man had matured and would be less obnoxious. And maybe Luke had grown up too and could interact with Saul without judging him. Whatever Saul had become—and however high the stature he had reached in his profession, it would not surprise Luke—Luke himself was widely known as a compassionate and even beloved man. He did not have to hang his head in the presence of any man, and certainly not Saul of Tarsus.

But when Luke mounted the steps of the temple and began asking for him, he was met with troubling responses.

"I am a Sadducee and do not keep track of Pharisees, one rabbi said. "What do I care what has become of him?"

"I studied the differences at university," Luke said, "but remind me of the basic schism."

The man looked bored. "We would be of a higher class," he droned. "We're landowners, merchants, and the like. We are not so opposed to Rome, or to Greek influence."

"But religiously . . ."

"We accept only the Torah as authoritative."

"And the Pharisees?"

"Add much oral tradition."

"And how did you differ on your responses to Jesus of Nazareth?"

The man waved dismissively. "I haven't seen him for years, have you? Oh, yes, he was to have risen from the dead! But still I don't see him. The Pharisees worry more about him and his followers than we do, because they believe in resurrection, immortality—even angels, if you can imagine. They criticized him for breaking all our laws, working on the Sabbath, associating with sinners, and the like."

"Do you and the Pharisees agree on anything?"

"Yes. Even those middle-class doctors of the law ascribe to the truth that the Lord our God is one God."

"And whom should I ask about Saul of Tarsus?"

The rabbi waved toward a wide opening behind him. "I haven't seen him for a long time either, sir. But one of his own ought to know where he has gone."

Luke found his encounter with the Pharisees just as unproductive. When he mentioned Saul's name, the elders looked at one another and hesitated. "What is your business with him?" one said.

"We attended university together, in Tarsus."

"You might look for him there."

"In his hometown? Is he no longer a leader here? Is he back making tents?"

An older rabbi shrugged and chuckled. "He was no leader here, though he carried himself as if he were."

"Come now, Iseabail," another said. "We certainly cannot fault him for his zeal. He was no sloth, that is sure. He was clearly the most strident among us against the Nazarene and the other blasphemers."

"Nonsense! He merely watched the cloaks of those who executed one of them."

"But he made up for that, leading his own team to ferret out the secret meeting places and bringing the insurgents to justice."

"And sometimes death."

"But where is he now?"

"That's my question," Luke said. "What, he simply disappeared?"

The men eyed one another again. Finally Iseabail spoke. "We don't know where he is, but there are rumors. A few years ago, Saul was actually rising within the synagogue—"

"With clear ambitions to become the youngest member of the Sanhedrin one day," another said.

"Oh, that is not all bad," Iseabail said. "At least he had focus. Saul was leading the effort against these many cells still meeting furtively, despite the admonitions of the temple and the king and even Rome, and he had seen countless numbers of them brought before the authorities. The last we knew, he was on his way to Damascus to conduct similar activities—with our authority. He never returned."

Luke stood waiting for more, but was met with silence. He opened his palms to them. "That's it? You didn't go after him, ask about him, try to find him? What if he came to a bad end?"

"Of course we went looking. Or someone did. I don't recall who just now. But the report we got was that he had left the synagogue and perhaps even left the faith."

"Oh, surely not," Luke said. "I never knew a more devout Jew."

Iseabail approached and spoke lowly. "Rumor has it that Saul may have actually become a traitor."

"A traitor?"

"To Judaism itself. He may have turned and joined the opposition."

"I can't believe it."

"We'll probably never know. Strange stories arose in Damascus and other outlying areas, but no one has seen him or heard from him in years. For all we know, he could be back in Tarsus."

LUKE FOUND that easy enough to determine. The next time his business took him to Tarsus, he asked after Saul at the university, where no one knew anything. Then he made his way to the family tentmaking operation, where he was told simply that Saul was occasionally in touch with them, so they knew he was alive and well.

"But is it true that he is no longer involved in the activities of the temple?"

"That is what we understand."

"Has he left the faith itself, as the Pharisees in Jerusalem fear?"

"We do not speak for him," Luke was told. "That is something you would need to discuss personally with him, if you ever find him."

Luke found himself overwhelmed with curiosity, while knowing he had neither the time nor the means to be tracking down an old acquaintance. On every voyage he listened for any mention of Saul, and on occasion he asked if anyone had ever heard of the man. Once in a while someone would recall the zealous Pharisee of Jerusalem, but no one had any recent knowledge of him.

Luke had begun simply curious as to Saul's take on the new religion that had sprung up and even spread as far as Antioch. Then he became vexed at the mystery of what had become of Saul. He would be the last person in the world Luke would expect to defect from one side of this controversy to the other.

And finally he realized that it was probably only fate that would ever reunite them.

SIXTEEN

Rumor had it that one of the many small groups of believers in the resurrected Jesus was meeting within two streets of Luke's clinic. He wondered if they welcomed outsiders, skeptics. Mostly he was intrigued with whatever might make otherwise rational people believe something like this. He was also curious about whether they might have heard of Saul of Tarsus and if it could be true he had somehow joined their ranks.

Luke did not find the time to inquire further or see if he could attend one of the Sunday meetings. These people said the first day of the week became their holy day because it was the day they believed Jesus had risen from the grave. Needless to say, this vexed the Jewish leaders and population, who announced they were keeping an eye on these people.

Meanwhile, Luke had become a creature of habit and routine. He largely enjoyed his life and activities and had the feeling he was helping people, if only physically. Though his education and freedom and occupation had elevated him from peasant status—but not much further—Luke found himself identifying with a general malaise he detected on the part of nearly all his patients. Regardless of what he suggested or what treatment he effected, and regardless of whether he and the patients saw some improvement in their conditions, life remained hard. People seemed burdened by the daily grind of life. Just like Luke. There were those moments, he had to admit, when believing in some holy man actually sounded attractive. But he was admitting this only to himself.

Every once in a while a patient would identify himself or herself as a believer in Jesus and would ask if Luke also believed. He always asked why they might think so.

"You just seem the type," he heard often.

"I'm afraid I am not. I believe in what can be seen and touched and studied. I think it is healthier for the mind to trust in the material world and not things that cannot be proven."

"Oh, that Jesus rose from the dead is no longer just a story, sir," people would say. "We have been visited by those who saw Him after He was crucified."

Luke fought to not show his skepticism, let alone his contempt. Well, he decided, perhaps it wasn't really contempt. What he felt was more pity that these people had to have this myth to hang on to. Or was it envy of their passion and their faith? And he had to admit, if any of his patients smiled or at least seemed content with their lot in life—despite their poverty—it was these people, these believers in Jesus.

Maybe the day would come when he would try to visit one of these house meetings. When word finally got around that several of these small groups were banding together to meet in a larger facility, Luke decided he would try to slip in unnoticed. Just as a historian.

. . .

After a particularly busy and harried week at the clinic, Luke packed his seafaring bag and made his way to the Orontes for the trip to the harbor. He was to serve as ship's physician on a trading vessel coming in from Tarsus and then heading to Joppa and finally to Alexandria. His last two voyages had been uneventful, and he had been able to catch up on some much-needed sleep. He hoped that might be the case this time as well.

As Luke waited ashore, the vessel docked and the passengers began off-loading while the crew dealt with the cargo. Luke always made it a point to wait to board until the last minute, so he would stay out of the way of those disembarking and the unloading and loading of cargo.

He was idly watching the passengers make their way down the gangplank and begin to search through the baggage for their belongings when he spotted a familiar figure accompanied by a young man. It had been years, but it had to be him!

"Saul?" Luke called out. "Saul of Tarsus?"

It was clear he had startled the man, who shot him a double take, then looked around to see who else might have heard.

"It's me," Luke said. "Luke from Antioch!"

Saul rushed to him, the young man trailing. Age had not changed Saul much. Maybe there was an extra line or two in his face, more thickness to his middle, a more chiseled look to his features, but Luke would have recognized him anywhere. Still small and wiry, he seemed to have the same energy he had always had.

"Dr. Luke!" he exulted, first pumping Luke's hand, then embracing him. "What are you doing here, old friend?"

"I could ask you the same. I have heard all kinds of rumors about you."

"I'll confirm or deny them all if we get time. Are you coming or going?"

Luke told him his schedule, and Saul grew suddenly serious. "Please," he said, beckoning the young man and introducing him as his traveling companion. "Barnabas came from here to fetch me. He and I studied under Gamaliel in Jerusalem years ago, but he has been ministering here, not just to Jews but also to Greeks, for some time and now needs my help. Barnabas, Luke was a fellow student of mine at university. Listen, ask the captain if there might be room for me to stay aboard until their stop at Joppa, then I'll catch another vessel coming this way. If there is, see to getting my things back on ship. You can proceed into town to meet with the brethren."

Ministering? The brethren? Could it be true that Saul had aligned with his former enemies? And had this Barnabas been working near Luke in Antioch?

As Barnabas hurried off, Saul said, "I should have asked first whether I would be welcome to sail with you."

"The Saul I knew would never have asked," Luke said, smiling. He was alarmed when Saul did not appear amused.

Saul threw his arm around Luke and drew him close. "First, my name is Paul now. Can you get used to that?"

"I'll try, but—"

"Before we converse a moment more, I must beg your forgiveness."

"My—?"

"Hear, me, Luke, please. I have prayed for the chance to one day plead abjectly for your pardon for how boorish I was to you at university."

"Oh, we were both young men, and—"

"No, now please. Your memory is as good as mine, and I have been haunted by every proud word and action. I am more than willing to kneel right here in the sand until you—"

"There's no need for that, Saul—Paul. Of course I accept your apology and forgive you. Let's put it behind us. But you must also know that I harbored envy and jealousy too, toward you."

"I was wholly unaware, Luke. Of course, I really considered no one else back then. How could I?"

"Forgive me."

"Of course!"

Luke was plainly overwhelmed. What had happened to this man? The Saul he knew may not have asked permission for anything, but certainly he would never have apologized or asked anyone's forgiveness for anything! Luke's curiosity about Saul's opinion of the Nazarene was now crowded from his brain by his intrigue over the new Saul.

Barnabas returned with news from the captain—including the fare—and Paul fished several coins from a leather bag and sent him back with them. "When you're not tending to the crew, Luke, I'll steal as much of your time as you'll allow. I have so much to tell you."

LUKE COULD NOT BELIEVE his luck. As soon as he was aboard he reported to the captain and was informed of only one medical need, a crew member who had torn a finger open on a hook line and had had it rudimentarily bandaged. Before they even set sail, Luke carefully took off the soiled wrap, which stuck to the man's wound. As the sailor winced and flinched, Luke cleansed the area, noting that the flesh had been ripped to the bone. He gently applied ointments, rewrapping the finger tightly with clean cloth.

"Had I been here when this happened," he told the man, "I might have sewn it closed. But I believe this might work now, though healing could take longer."

With no other ailments or injuries reported, Luke had uninterrupted time with Paul amidships, until the waves seemed to grow and they moved to the stern. The sailing was smoother there, and as they sat and watched the shoreline recede, Paul began one of the most amazing stories Luke had ever heard.

"First, let me tell you from the beginning that not only have I changed my name, but I am also an entirely different person from the one you knew. Whatever rumors you heard about me, if they indicated that I have wholly switched allegiances, they are true. I have gone from being a man dedicated to destroying everyone I believed was opposed to the truth, to one who believes with all his heart that they were right and I was wrong."

"But how, Paul? Forgive me, but the man I knew could not be told anything that contradicted his views. What could change your mind when your whole life and being seemed given over to practicing your faith?"

"No one believed the change, Luke. But let me tell you how it happened. Years ago I was in Jerusalem, making a name for myself in the synagogue and among the Sanhedrin as a young man with a future. I was the first one there every morning and the last one there every night. No task was beneath me. I learned every ritual and discipline, and while I had virtually memorized more of the holy texts than even the most learned and elderly rabbis, I was also eager to serve, to clean, to do what no one else would do.

"And when this sect arose that believed in Jesus as a miracle worker and even the Son of God, I involved myself enthusiastically in its persecution. You know that what we believed was blasphemy was punishable by death. We killed many of them, Luke, and those we did not kill we arrested and had imprisoned."

"Is it true you were present for the stoning of one of the believers?"

"I watched the cloaks of those who hurled the stones, Luke, and I believed so strongly in our cause that I am just as guilty as those whose rocks found their marks. The shame of it still haunts me, but worse, I cannot forget the superiority and the righteousness I felt that day. I sincerely believed we were doing the will of God."

"Why? I too was amused and bemused by what I heard of these myth-believers, but they seemed harmless enough."

Paul shook his head and looked down. "To me there was nothing innocent or amusing about them. I took their affronts personally, as did my allies. To my mind they believed in a dead man who had claimed to be of God, to be the Messiah Himself. It was the height of blasphemy. This young man, Stephen, held forth about our own history and how it meshed with Jesus, and when we countered him and jeered him, he called us stiff-necked and uncircumcised in both our hearts and our ears. He said, 'You always resist the Holy Spirit, just as your fathers did.'

"Well, now he was talking about our revered ancestors. He continued, 'Which of the prophets did your fathers not persecute?' He said they had killed those who foretold the coming of the Just One—and by this he meant the Messiah, 'of whom you now have become the betrayers and murderers.' He accused us of having received the law of God from the angels but having not kept it."

Paul appeared as if he could barely go on.

"I can see why that would upset you, Paul."

"Upset us? It cut us to the heart! We rushed him as one, cursing him, baring our teeth at him. I was sure we would scare him to death and make him run off, but he just raised his face and gazed into the skies. He said, 'Look! I see the heavens opened and the Son of Man standing at the right hand of God!'"

Luke was struck that Paul looked as if he were back at the scene. The veins in his neck protruded and pulsed, and his face darkened. "We put our hands over our ears and cried out, continuing to run at him. We drove him out of the city into a rocky place, and I was asked to guard the garments of those who slid out of their cloaks and took rocks in hand. To my deep regret I shouted encouragement as they hurled stones at Stephen."

Paul's voice grew thick with emotion as he recounted the scene. "All the while they stoned him, Stephen was praying, calling out to God, saying, 'Lord Jesus, receive my spirit.' As the blows knocked him to his knees, he cried out, 'Lord, do not charge them with this sin!' Soon he lay dead.

"Luke, I exulted in this! I was thrilled with what we had accomplished. I stood over the body, shaking my fist and screaming that he had gotten what he deserved and woe to others who dared attempt the same.

"I returned to the synagogue excited, committed to our work and our cause as never before. I truly believed that God would have us eliminate this blasphemous sect, eradicating them from the face of the earth. My zeal was noticed, I assure you, and if you thought I was devout at university, you would have hardly believed how staunch I had become now. I sought and received authority to lead bands of others in ferreting out these believers in Jesus. We raided house meetings, we received reports from witnesses, we knocked on doors at all hours of the day and night. For a few years following the crucifixion of the Man they believed in, I became the leading persecutor of these heretics. Every arrest, every judgment, every sentence only emboldened me more."

Paul fell silent and Luke studied the darkening sky, something troubling him deep within. Truth was, this was all too unsettling, and Luke was afraid to face what he was really feeling. "Were these people really a threat to your religion, Paul? What were you afraid of?"

"I wasn't afraid! At least not at first. I was angry, insulted, offended for the name of God. But I confess that the more we tried to make life miserable for them, the more they multiplied. I could not understand it. Why could they not see that their hero was dead and gone and was not returning? Many new believers claimed they were convinced by miracles. I had not seen any of these personally and, of course, did not believe they were real."

"That would have been my view, Paul. It still is. To a scientist, a man of history and of medicine, it would take God himself speaking to me to make me believe."

"Or a miracle?"

"Or a miracle."

"What do you think changed my mind?"

"You saw a miracle with your own eyes, something that could not be explained, something you know without doubt was not a magician's trick?"

"Come, come, Luke. You knew me better than that."

"I suppose I did. I'm listening."

That he was listening was an understatement. Luke was aghast, and had it been anyone but Paul telling this story, he might have dismissed it out of hand. That the most dynamic personality he had ever encountered could become so radically different made him listen all right—with his entire being.

SEVENTEEN

When it came time for the evening meal, Luke and Paul made their way down into the galley and, despite the crowd, were able to sit where they could be heard by only each other. Luke noticed that in the corner of the noisy, steamy room, the man whose finger he had bandaged sat with crewmates and gingerly favored his wounded hand.

Luke excused himself and headed over, sidling between benches, to ask the man how he was doing.

"I can feel every beat of my heart," the mate said.

"Is it turning red?" Luke said.

"I haven't dared check."

"May I?"

"Sure."

As Luke knelt to carefully unwrap the bandage, the others at the table peered over his shoulder. He turned to look at them, hoping to shame them into giving the man a modicum of privacy, but the man said, "It's all right. They saw it happen."

Sure enough, the wound was bright red at the edges, yellowing farther out. "I have other ointments and tonics that may help," Luke said. "Come find me after the meal."

When he returned to his table, he told Paul he feared something had invaded the deep wound.

"I'd like to meet the young man," Paul said.

"You may. I'll be seeing him later. But continue, please."

Paul thrust a chunk of bread into a thick stew of seafood, tucked a bite into one cheek, and said, "Well, all during that time I led a great persecution against the believers in Jerusalem. The ones we could catch were either in hiding—like their leaders, apostles who had known Jesus personally—or scattered throughout Judea and Samaria. Some of the bravest and most devout of them carried Stephen to his grave, and we heard of much lamenting over him.

"I tell you, Luke," Paul said, gulping from a cup, "my goal was to make havoc of this sect, and I accomplished this by entering every suspect house and dragging off men and women, committing them to prison. Maddeningly, I soon learned that those who were scattered went everywhere spreading their doctrine."

"So on the one hand you were succeeding, and on the other you were failing."

"It seemed that the more I did, the more I encouraged them! All I could think of was threatening and murdering the disciples of Jesus. I begged an audience with the high priest and felt good about myself when he not only agreed to see me but also complimented me on my efforts. I told him I had heard that some of the heretics had fled to Damascus and asked if he would provide letters for me from him to the synagogues of that city, so that if I found any who were of The Way—which is what they had come to be known, whether men or women—I might bind them and haul them back to Jerusalem."

Besides his own personal intrigue, the historian in Luke also loved this story and wished he were writing it down. "And he gave you this authority?"

"He did. He praised me again, provided the documents, told me he was proud of me, and wished me Godspeed. I confess, Luke, I was as proud of myself as I could be. Not only had this been my idea, but I had also clearly already impressed the high priest, and I just knew that if I succeeded on this mission, my future as a Jewish leader in Jerusalem would be guaranteed."

"So you were doing this as much for yourself as for God?"

"Oh, certainly! I didn't see it then, of course, but it's quite clear to me now. Then I truly believed God would be pleased with me as well. And there is no better feeling."

"For one who believes in these sorts of things, I suppose." What had been so ingrained in Luke that he found it so difficult to think unconventionally? Dare he believe in something beyond himself, as so many of his patients now did? As Paul clearly always had? As Saul, his old acquaintance had seemed miserable. But Luke's believing patients exhibited an inner peace he could not understand. And now Paul seemed so different.

Paul rubbed a sleeve across his mouth and grinned. "So said by one to whom God Himself would have to speak, or before whom some miracle would have to be performed in order for him to believe."

"I'm afraid so," Luke said. "I've seen too many misguided people put their trust in the immaterial and wind up none the better for it." He was lying. While he had long been a skeptic, he could not deny the difference he saw in his believing patients.

"So how do you assess the experience of someone like me, Luke? I am not an uneducated man."

"Of course not. But you yourself told me that your religious studies began at age five. You never had a choice. And now, if I may be bold, you have simply, for some reason, traded one ethereal belief for another."

"But what would cause that?"

"I assume you'll tell me."

"That I will."

They finished their meal, and Luke followed Paul topside again. A crisp, cloudless night made the moon and stars appear brighter, and their reflections danced on the waves as the vessel sailed southwest toward Egypt. The sea was calm and the boat steady, but both men wrapped their heads and shoulders in their cloaks as they leaned against the side.

"I arranged quite a little party for the sojourn to Damascus, Luke. This was a well-traveled route, and I knew it would accommodate many men and animals. We started out at dawn one day, and I carried the documents in my own satchel, bursting with anticipation to see the looks on the faces of the rabbis in Damascus when they read them. My plan was to have my associates get us set up in an inn and inform the local authorities that we might need their help in apprehending the heretics. I envisioned leading a long band of bound and shackled men and women all the way back to the temple in Jerusalem and enjoying every accolade that would come my way.

"I had traveled this route many times, and as we journeyed to where I knew the city would come into view over the next rise, I imagined freshening myself at a well and changing into my most appropriate attire for meeting with temple leaders.

"Suddenly a light shone around me from heaven."

Luke squinted at him and held up a hand. "Heaven? How did you know it was from heaven and not just the sun appearing from behind a cloud?"

Paul laughed. "Sometimes, my friend, one simply knows. This was unlike any light I had ever seen, including a bolt of lightning once in the middle of the night. No, this light was so bright it knocked me to the ground, and as I lay there, I heard a voice say, 'Saul, Saul, why are you persecuting Me?'

"I said, 'Who are You, Lord?'"

"If you didn't know who it was, why did you address him as Lord?"

Paul chuckled. "Whoever it was, he was superior to me at that moment, I can tell you. Then the Lord said, 'I am Jesus, whom you are persecuting. It is hard for you to kick against the goads.'"

"You believe Jesus himself was speaking to you."

"Without question."

"And what did he mean, kicking against the goads?"

"I had no idea, but I immediately had the feeling I had been fighting against an unconquerable enemy. I was trembling and astonished, and could say only, 'Lord, what do You want me to do?' "

"You immediately surrendered?"

"Luke, I had no choice. Jesus was speaking to me from heaven, and I knew He could have killed me on the spot."

"And what did he tell you to do?"

"He said, 'Arise and go into the city, and you will be told what you must do.'"

"What did your traveling companions make of all this?"

"They stood speechless, telling me later that they had heard a voice but saw no one. When I arose I opened my eyes and could see nothing. My men led me by the hand and brought me into Damascus to the house of a man named Judas on a street called Straight. For three days I could see nothing, and I had lost my appetite. I neither ate nor drank all that time. I simply prayed the entire time. And during my prayer, the Lord gave me a vision. In my mind's eye I saw a man named Ananias coming to lay his hand on me that I might receive my sight.

"Now soon, Luke, as God is my witness, a man arrived and introduced himself as Ananias. He said, 'The Lord spoke to me in a vision, and told me to arise and go to the street called Straight and inquire at the house of Judas for one called Saul of Tarsus, for behold, he is praying and in a vision has seen a man named Ananias coming in and putting his hand on him, so that he might receive his sight.'

"Ananias told me that he told the Lord he had heard from many about me and how much harm I had done to the saints in Jerusalem. He had even heard I had authority from the chief priests to bind all who call on Jesus' name. But still the Lord told him to go and said to him, 'for he is a chosen vessel of Mine to bear My name before Gentiles, kings, and the children of Israel. For I will show him how many things he must suffer for My name's sake.'"

Luke found himself actually envying Paul's passion, though this was all too much to fathom. "Gentiles, kings, and your own people? Did that make any sense to you?"

"Luke, really, what makes sense to a man in my condition? I can tell you I had no doubt God was working in me somehow. That was all I knew. Ananias laid his hands on me and said, 'Brother Saul, the Lord Jesus, who appeared to you on the road as you came, has sent me that you may receive your sight and be filled with the Holy Spirit.'"

"What did that mean?"

"Well, I didn't know either until immediately there fell from my eyes something like scales, and I received my sight at once. I arose and was baptized. When I had eaten, I felt strengthened. Then I spent several days with the disciples of Jesus at Damascus."

"And all of a sudden you had gone from being their enemy to being one of them?"

"Immediately. And God gave me utterance. I preached in the synagogues that Jesus is the Christ, the Son of God. All who heard were amazed, and said, 'Is this not he who destroyed those who called on this name in Jerusalem, and has come here for that purpose, so that he might bring them bound to the chief priests?'

"But I increased all the more in strength, and confounded the Jews who dwelt in Damascus, proving that Jesus is the Christ."

"Proving it how?"

"From the Scriptures, which I knew almost by heart. And by performing miracles."

"You? You performed miracles?"

Paul nodded.

"Show me."

"Show you? The miracles that Jesus and His disciples performed are not for entertainment, Luke. They are done to show the power of God unto salvation. When men see them, they believe and come to repentance."

"Repentance?"

"Of sin. I have come to believe that Jesus is who He claimed to be, the holy and righteous Son of God who came to seek and to save those who are lost. He bore their sins in His own body on the cross, sacrificing His blood and His life for the remission of sin."

Sin. The concept sounded so earthy, so crass, and yet it resonated with Luke. Sinful was how he felt about his pride, jealousy, conceit, lust, boastfulness. Sin was what his master Theophilus and he rued when they talked about trying to take control of their own passions and how wanting Stoicism was in this regard. They had never called it sin, of course, preferring other terms. Was it possible he could be forgiven, repent, and not be controlled by his own desires?

EIGHTEEN

I'm intrigued by how your own people responded to this change in you, Paul. You had been making a name for yourself. Your defection must have been noisy."

"Oh, it was! In fact, after many days I became aware that the Jews were plotting to kill me. I naturally wanted to return to Jerusalem, though I feared I faced the same fate there. My hope was to persuade the disciples of Jesus that my conversion was real and to see if I could come alongside and help them in any way. But I dared not travel back out of Damascus the way I had come, for word was that the Jews were watching the gates day and night, and they would not be merely arresting or imprisoning me. The disciples of Damascus took me by night and let me down through the wall in a large basket, far from any gate, and I was able to steal away."

"So you got to Jerusalem?"

"In truth for several years I lived in seclusion, studying, praying, and preparing myself for ministry. Partly I felt I needed to wean myself from my old ways and prepare myself for the new. But I confess that it was too dangerous for me to return to Jerusalem, once the leaders of the synagogue there had heard what had become of me. And I knew the disciples of Jesus would be wary of me also.

"It was seven years after the resurrection of Jesus that I finally stole into Jerusalem. But my hopes were almost immediately dashed. I put out the word quietly that I wished to talk with the leaders of Jesus' disciples. I had heard they were camped in an upper room at a private home, but messages came back to me that they had no reason to believe I was being sincere. So many of their number had suffered at my hands that they naturally feared this was a trick to infiltrate them.

"My only recourse was to seek out my old friend Joses, with whom I had studied under Gamaliel as a youngster."

"You and Barnabas knew this Joses?"

"Oh, no, sorry. They are one and the same. Joses was how I knew him, but when he became a believer in Jesus and began aiding the disciples, they renamed him Barnabas, which means 'encourager.' Believe me, he lives up to his name."

"And he was able to gain you an audience with Jesus' disciples?"

"It wasn't easy, but they trusted him. Their trust of me took longer. I shall never forget sitting awkwardly before Peter and James in that upper room, their arms folded, their visages stony. I could not blame them, of course. I represented the worst of their enemies. And yet, do you know, the lad of that household told me privately that Peter had once urged him to pray for me."

"For your demise, no doubt."

"I did not get that impression. It had to do with Jesus' teaching that they should pray for their enemies and do good to those who despitefully used them. No one fit that description better than I."

"But though they had prayed for you, they did not immediately welcome you?"

"Of course not, and why should they? They bade me sit, but neither welcomed me warmly nor offered even the hint of a smile. They had had someone wash my feet and offer me drink, so I thanked them for their hospitality. The response was simply that James said, 'You were an accomplice to the stoning of our friend.'

"I knew of whom he spoke, of course. Stephen. I felt compelled to be wholly transparent with them, and so I said, 'And many more you know not of, to my abject shame.' "

"Did they forgive you?"

"Oh, no, not then. They clearly still distrusted me and suspected my motives, and again, I could not blame them. Peter merely asked what business had brought me to them. Barnabas, bless his heart, immediately interrupted and, while he called me learned and eloquent and perfectly capable of speaking for myself, averred that I was there under his personal sponsorship and pleaded with them to hear from my own mouth the story of my encounter with God.

"Peter said, 'We see you as the enemy of God.' What could I say? I admitted I had been the chiefest of sinners but I said that I was now begging their indulgence. When Peter nodded, I plunged into the account I told you."

Paul stopped, as if waiting for some response. Luke said, "But, of course, unlike me, these men wanted to believe you. You were a prize for them."

Paul pressed his lips together and leaned forward, speaking quietly but with his usual earnestness. "Luke, let me tell you what I told them, because I can only imagine your skepticism. I was one who once had confidence in the flesh, and if anyone else thinks he may have confidence in the flesh, I more so: circumcised the eighth day, of the stock of Israel, of the tribe of Benjamin, a Hebrew of the Hebrews; concerning the law, a Pharisee; concerning zeal, persecuting the church; concerning the righteousness that is in the law, blameless.

"But what things were gain to me, these I have counted as loss for Christ. Yet indeed I also count all things loss for the excellence of the knowledge of Christ Jesus my Lord, for whom I have suffered the loss of all things, and count them as rubbish, that I may gain Christ and be found in Him, not having my own righteousness, which is from the law, but that which is through faith in Christ, the righteousness that is from God by faith; that I may know Him and the power of His resurrection, and the fellowship of His sufferings, being conformed to His death, if, by any means, I may attain to the resurrection from the dead.

"Not that I have already attained it, or am already perfected; but I press on, that I may lay hold of that for which Christ Jesus has also laid hold of me. Luke, I do not count myself to have apprehended; but one thing I do, forgetting those things that are behind and reaching forward to those things that are ahead, I press toward the goal for the prize of the upward call of God in Christ Jesus.

"I pleaded with those disciples to be like-minded with me, because I believe that our citizenship is in heaven, from which we also eagerly wait for the Savior, the Lord Jesus Christ, who will transform our lowly body that it may be conformed to His glorious body, according to the working by which He is able even to subdue all things to Himself.

"I implored them that they would see me as one of them, a coworker in the kingdom of God through Christ."

"You were asking a lot," Luke said.

"Indeed I was. Peter and James sat silent, trading glances, but soon Peter stood and reached for me, calling me his brother and embracing me, welcoming me to their work. I nearly wept with joy."

"But despite their acceptance, was it safe for you to do your work there in Jerusalem?"

"Nothing is safe for me anymore, Luke, and probably nothing ever will be. I spoke boldly there in the name of the Lord Jesus, amazing everyone, especially the rulers and the Hellenists—the very ones the martyr Stephen had debated. I soon became their target, of course, but when the disciples found out, they took me to Caesarea and sent me back to my hometown for my own protection."

"So you *were* in Tarsus. Would you believe I asked about you there once?"

"You did? What for?"

"I had sought you out in Jerusalem after you had left for Damascus, and that's where I first heard the rumors. I couldn't believe it, of course, but your family covered for you."

"Many watch out for me," Paul said. "Else I would already be in heaven."

"How did your movement reach Antioch?"

"The churches throughout all Judea, Galilee, and Samaria began walking in the fear of the Lord and in the comfort of the Holy Spirit, and so they multiplied."

"That's the second time you have mentioned the Holy Spirit. You can only imagine how that sounds to this Stoic's ears."

Paul chuckled and apologized. "The disciples told me of Jesus promising them a comforter when he departed for heaven, and how the Holy Spirit had come upon them as tongues of fire and allowed them to be understood in other languages. Now, don't look at me that way, Luke. You too are going to come to faith in Christ, and then your eyes and ears will be opened and you will understand."

Luke smiled, hoping it didn't appear as fake as it was. "Not likely. But continue with how the sect has spread as far as my own city."

"This was all started by those who were scattered after the persecution that arose over the stoning of Stephen. They traveled as far as Phoenicia, Cyprus, and Antioch, preaching to no one but the Jews. But some of them were men from Cyprus and Cyrene, who, when they had come to Antioch, spoke to the Hellenists, preaching the Lord Jesus. I believe the hand of the Lord was with them, and a great number believed and turned to the Lord.

"When news of this reached the church in Jerusalem, they sent out Barnabas to go as far as Antioch. When he got there and saw how far the grace of God had spread, he was glad, and encouraged them all to continue with the Lord in great purpose of heart. When we get back, Luke, you will find him a good man, full of the Holy Spirit and of faith."

"And by then you believe I will understand the Holy Spirit."

"By then you will be filled with the Holy Spirit and able to heal more than you ever dreamed as a mere physician."

"We shall see," Luke said, longing for just such an occurrence but still battling his skepticism. "Now bring me up to today. What were you doing disembarking in Antioch?"

"That was all because of Barnabas. He came to Tarsus to seek me and bring me back, telling me the work was growing and that he needed my help. I believed this was of the Lord, and I plan to stay there as long as necessary to assemble with the believers and teach a great many people."

"You know what you're getting into?"

"Of course not! I take each day as it comes and trust the Lord to give me wisdom and strength."

"Has Barnabas told you what your critics in Antioch call the believers?"

"Oh, yes. Christians. They say it derisively, but I like it. We are what we are."

NINETEEN

Luke had been genuinely intrigued to see Saul after so many years and so many stories, but he frankly wasn't sure now what he thought of the Paul version of the man. In many ways, this was the same fearless, intense, opinionated, and tireless character he had known at university. But hadn't he simply traded one tall tale for another? There certainly would be no dissuading Paul from his beliefs, but nothing said Luke had to agree with him. Still, he was more than curious. This sect of the so-called resurrected miracle worker was indeed sweeping the world, and if the growing body of believers in Antioch was any indication, there seemed no stopping it.

That didn't make it genuine or true, of course. Romans and Greeks had been worshiping mythological gods for centuries, and Luke knew better than to assume that made them any more real. But had there been verifiable miracles? And could there be some cure for the worst inner characteristics of men, whether or not Luke was yet ready to call those sins or call himself a sinner?

Either way, his curious, history-scholar side wanted to understand the entire scope of the developing movement. Regardless what became of it, history would contain some record of it, its various episodes, and any residual effects it might engender.

"I'd love to tell you more, Luke," Paul said. "I want to persuade you that it's true and that you—"

"Forgive me, Paul, but I need some time alone. Perhaps we can continue this in the morning."

Paul seemed to study him. "I will be praying for you."

"I have no doubt that you will. Pray that I'll be able to sleep, despite all the thoughts rattling in my head."

Paul grinned. "I'll pray the opposite. I'll pray God troubles your spirit until you rouse me from my own slumber for more of this truth."

ONE LUXURY AFFORDED a ship's physician, even a part-time one like Luke, was that he was not required to share lodging with the crew. Lodging was too kind a term for it, of course, as the dozens of men merely shared a common area below where they hung wet sandals and salty garments on nails and slept in swaying cots made of braided rope attached to the rafters.

On the occasional voyage on a lesser ship, Luke had been assigned one of these rudimentary hammocks and found sleep nearly impossible among the snoring and ill—usually from drink—men. He appreciated a bit of privacy and quiet, though his chambers were cramped and had no window. The sounds of the water and the wind and the sails and the creaking of the boards usually served to lull him to sleep, as long as his own hanging cot did not sway excessively because of high seas.

This night was relatively calm, yet still Luke found himself unable to doze. Was Paul really praying that Luke would not be able to sleep? His quarters were pitch-black and he was as comfortable as could be expected, but the way his mind raced reminded him of his childhood. Back then he had had to quietly steal into the kitchen and light a small lamp so he could read until drowsy. Was it mere fate or destiny that he had been born with such a brain? He was grateful for how it had benefited him—favor with his master; an eagerness, yea a hunger, to read and learn. He knew he owed his very freedom to his intellect, but his own adopted Stoic philosophy fought against believing in coincidence or chance. He did agree with Stoicism's idea that men were powerless in the face of nature, so he had to attribute his scholarly curiosity and abilities to that.

His old friend, having paid for the privilege of private quarters, surely believed that whatever Luke enjoyed in this life was a gift from God, the creator of the universe. Could it be? What made Paul's god anything more than the mythological beings so many Romans and Greeks revered?

Paul's story had been dramatic and fascinating. And despite all the skepticism Luke had borne over Paul's religion—back when Paul was young and known as Saul—he had never suspected the man of exaggerating. At worst, he believed Saul had been steered to his firm convictions by having all of this forced into his mind as a youngster. He had always seemed honest to a fault, direct, blunt, a realist. While he clearly truly believed his god was the one true god, maker of heaven and earth, the only seemingly fanciful stories he espoused were ones contained in the ancient texts of his religion.

But what of all this new stuff? Healing the sick, giving sight to the blind, raising a man and even a young girl from the dead, and even the resurrection of the miracle worker himself. A bright light from heaven, the crucified Jesus speaking to Saul from the sky, visions, Saul's own healing from blindness, his complete change—not of personality or character but of his life's purpose.

It was all so much to take in.

After another hour of thrashing in the darkness, unable to rest, let alone sleep, Luke thought it only fair that Paul share his distress. He dressed and made his way to Paul's quarters and lightly rapped on his door.

"Coming, Luke," Paul said, laughter in his voice. Could he see through doors now too?

When Paul emerged, his hair mussed from sleep, Luke said, "How did you know it was me? Did God Himself tell you?"

"He could have," Paul said. "But the fact is, no one but the captain knows me on this ship, and this is his sleep shift."

Luke shook his head.

"So I assume you have more questions?"

Again they climbed topside. They sat near the bow, and Paul resumed his story. Luke was so enraptured by the account and its ramifications that he was startled when the injured seaman interrupted with apologies.

"It's really starting to vex me," the young man said, holding out his hand. "I can barely stand the pain and must hold it aloft for any relief."

"Wait right here and I'll get something that should help. Introduce yourself to my friend Saul, er, Paul."

Luke hurried back to his quarters, where he mixed a potion he hoped would be effective. But when he returned, Paul was alone. Before he could even ask after the crew member, Paul said, "I prayed for him. I think he'll be all right."

"But he needs this medicine."

"You'll be able to determine that when you see him again. Now, shall I continue?"

"Well, sure, but first, did you say you prayed for him? You think praying for a man with a deep wound that is turning is all he needs?"

"It seemed all he needed. I did tell him about the Christ first, however."

"And how did he respond to that?"

"He seemed interested. I kept it simple. I merely told him that God had sent His only son into the world, that He lived a sinless life so He could qualify to be our sacrificial lamb. He died for our sins, was buried, and arose again the third day, now sitting on the right hand of God in heaven. I told him if he believed this, he could be saved from his sin, and that if he had faith, he could also be healed of his wound."

Luke cocked his head. Paul had really lost all connection with reality. "And did he have this faith?"

"Frankly, Luke, he appeared to."

"And so you healed him?"

"I didn't say that. I said I prayed with him and for him. He expressed faith in Jesus, and I expressed faith that *God* could heal him."

"You'll forgive me if I add this tonic to his wound so that we might *help* God heal him, if necessary."

"Though I gather from your tone that you are making sport of what I have been telling you, I beg you to keep an open mind."

"Oh, of that you may be certain. And regardless of whether I accept all this, I am confident that you believe it, and that makes me want to hear the rest of it. But for right now, I must find my patient."

"You'll probably find him resting comfortably. Which I also plan to do, if it's all right with you. I'll see you in the morning, unless you need me before that."

Luke and Paul ventured into the bowels of the ship, Paul heading to his room while Luke followed the sounds of snoring and groaning and peered into the communal sleeping quarters. An old crewmate in a cot near the door asked who he was looking for.

"The wounded man," Luke whispered.

"That's his bed," the man said, pointing. "But he's not there."

Luke moved into the room and someone else asked what he wanted. He pointed to the empty cot.

"That boy's on duty," another said.

"Oh, surely not," Luke said. "He shouldn't be working."

The man shrugged, so Luke headed up. He watched as a crew of six scampered about the masts, trimming the sails. "You there!" he called out, pointing at the young man. "You're not to be working!"

"Be right down," the man said, securing a rigging.

Soon he came clambering down a rope ladder and landed in front of the physician. He held up his injured hand. "Keeping it wrapped just to be safe."

"Let me see that," Luke said. "How's the pain?"

"Gone!"

Luke led the man to a bench along the side and set his lamp where it would illuminate the area. He pulled the man's hand close and slowly unwrapped the bandage. Not only did he find no discoloration, but he also found no wound! Luke lifted the lamp to where the flame was just inches from a thin, pink scar.

"What's happened?" he said. "Tissue and bone were exposed earlier."

"Your friend told me if I would believe in Jesus, He could heal me. And I did. And He did."

Luke settled the lamp between his knees and held the man's hand in both of his, pulling it even closer to the flame. No bruising, no swelling, no opening, just the scar, as if the deep wound had healed months before. Luke pressed his thumb against it. "Any soreness?"

"None! Jesus healed me, and I'm telling everybody! You think I can leave the bandage off?"

Luke was nearly speechless, his heart racing. "I don't see why not," he managed.

He let the young man get back to work, but the prospect of returning to his own dark bed held no appeal. For the next couple of hours he paced every inch of the ship, letting the chilly winds blow through his hair, studying the starry skies, shaken to his core. Everything he had ever known and believed was now in question.

He had told Paul, and meant it, that it would take a miracle to make him believe, not just stories and accounts. Well, what was this but a miracle? It was not secondhand. And he was no amateur. He knew a serious wound when he saw it, and this man had an injury that could have cost him his whole hand.

Could he believe his own eyes? Hanging in the balance was everything he had ever been taught and accepted. Paul had told him that miracles were not performed simply for someone to show off. They occurred in order that people might believe and come to repentance.

What would his fellow slaves say? What would his colleagues think? What would Theophilus make of it?

Luke walked and walked, and every time he espied the injured sailor he watched in awe as the man used both hands on the heavy ropes.

Luke had never been so overcome. All this talk, all these accounts, Paul's own story, and now this. This was evidence. This was proof. And it demanded a response. He could not sleep, could not awaken to another day without doing something about what he now knew.

The physician felt as if he were teetering on a precipice, fully aware that life as he once knew it was over. And for the first time in his life, he prayed.

Hardly knowing how to start, he whispered, "God of the universe, if You are there, would you please make Yourself plain to me?"

Almost immediately, though he did not hear this audibly, it was as if God Himself spoke directly to Luke's soul. He said, "You need more?"

Luke stopped and gripped the side of the ship with both hands. Letting go, he slowly slid to his knees. "No," he said aloud. "What more should I need? Can you forgive me for my unbelief, change my inner self, free me from my passions?"

He wanted to hear God say yes or at least impress that upon his heart. Luke *felt* forgiven, had a sense of peace as if a great weight had rolled off his shoulders. But could a grown man move from a life of science to a life of faith in an instant? He had told Paul he would need God to speak to him *or* show him a miracle before he would believe, and now he had experienced both. What other conclusion could he come to?

He wanted to shout, to leap for joy, to tell someone. He raced again to Paul's room, only to find the door open and Paul sitting on his cot. Luke gushed what had happened. "I need you to explain it all to me, and right now. What has happened to me?"

"Do you believe?"

"I do!"

"Then you are saved! Praise God."

"Saved from what?"

"Saved from your sin. Come, let's go back up where we can sit."

They returned to the very bench where Luke had examined the healed man's hand. "Listen to me now, Luke," Paul said, "and let me make plain to you the gospel I told you about, which now you have received and in which you can stand, by which also, as I said, you are saved unless you believed in vain.

"What I shared with you was what I also received: that Christ died for our sins according to the Scriptures, and that He was buried, and that He rose again the third day, and that He was seen by many, of whom most remain to the present, but some have died.

"After that He was seen by James, then by all the apostles. Then last of all He was seen by me also on the road to Damascus, as by one born out of due time. For I am the least of the apostles, not worthy to be called an apostle, because I persecuted the church of God. But by the grace of God I am what I am, and His grace toward me was not in vain; but I labor more than they all, but I know it is not I, but the grace of God in me.

"Now, I am telling you, Dr. Luke, that if you confess with your mouth the Lord Jesus and believe in your heart that God has raised Him from the dead, you will be saved."

"I do! How could I not?"

Paul smiled and held up a hand. "You see, it is with the heart one believes unto righteousness, and with the mouth confession is made unto salvation. For the Scripture says, 'Whoever believes on Him will not be put to shame.'"

"This is true for me as well as for you, Paul?"

"Oh, yes! For there is no distinction between Jew and Greek, for the same Lord over all is available to all who call upon Him. One of the main reasons Barnabas sent for me is to see Gentiles added to the number of believers in Antioch, for I have been uniquely called to reach these. Again, as the Scriptures say, 'Whoever calls on the name of the Lord shall be saved.'"

"What will this mean for me, Paul? It seems my very life will change."

"From what you told me, it needs to and you want it to. Did you not say you were a victim of your own inner desires, that while you wanted to do good—and often do—you question your own motives?"

"Yes, but I confess Stoicism has helped me some in that area. I believe in the brotherhood of man and want to do what will aid others."

"And that is good! Not every ideal of Stoicism is without merit or counter to the will of God. But now you will do these things because you will *want* to prefer others over yourself. You will want to serve mankind as an expression of gratefulness to God for your salvation, not as a way to earn it."

"Like the young man who was healed, I want to tell everyone!"

"And yet you have much to learn. As soon as you get back to Antioch, you must join the fellowship of believers and begin listening to the readings of the accounts written by eyewitnesses of Jesus. Barnabas has copies of these, and we delight in hearing portions of them read every Sunday."

"What else happens at these meetings?"

"We sing songs and psalms of praise to God. We pray for one another's needs. And someone teaches. Barnabas has been handling that for some time now, and I will enjoy helping."

"So if I come to the house meetings, you and Barnabas will be my teachers?"

"Yes, but where you live, Barnabas tells me this is more than a home meeting now. There are so many believers in Antioch that several of the small groups have joined together and now meet on the grounds of a believer who owns the stables not far from the Orontes."

"I know the area. Are they safe meeting there, so many?"

"I have urged them to be circumspect, but there will probably be little hiding the fact of a crowd that large every Sunday. Yet we will not be scared off. For now Rome allows the Jews to practice their faith, along with all the other various religions, as long as they do not threaten the empire. Until they begin to fear that we are revolutionaries or seek to overthrow the government, which is—of course—not our aim, we should enjoy the privileges the others enjoy. But you know me, Luke. No one will stop me from doing what I believe is right, regardless. No one said this would be safe or easy. We already have a host of martyrs to the new faith, and if I am to become one also, so be it."

Part Four

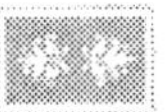

THE SCRIBE

TWENTY

Before Paul disembarked at Joppa to find passage back to Antioch, he prayed with Luke and encouraged him, urging him to pray frequently and plan his schedule so he could join the believers when he returned home. "The scholar in you will want to study all the written materials that have come from the new faith," Paul said. "When we can lend you scrolls, we will, but most of your exposure to these will come from your meeting with the brethren in Antioch. Barnabas traveled with many of the original disciples and often repeats their accounts orally. We all grow from these."

"I have never so longed to be home," Luke said. "I will see you the first Sunday I am back."

"When do you get in?"

"Next Friday, but I am already planning to trade clinic duty with one of my associates, as I must travel to Daphne."

"To talk with your former master."

"And current patron. He may abandon me over this."

"God will become your patron, Luke."

"Someone may need to. Not only is there no income from the clinic, but it also costs us unless we have sponsors. And Theophilus is by far our majority benefactor. Another might be tempted to keep this news from him, but I want him to know what's happened to me."

"Of course you do, and if he values you as much as you say, he should be thrilled for you. Maybe enough to become a believer himself."

"I'm not even hoping for that."

Paul's eyes bore into Luke's. "Don't ever say that again, friend. We not only hope to evangelize everyone, but we also pray for that and work toward it, believing God for everything. If He healed the young man on this ship—and you better than any knew how serious his wound was—and if He could save a sinner like me—"

"And me."

"Yes, and you, then who can shorten His arm? I will be praying and trusting for Theophilus's salvation. I will look forward to the day he becomes part of our assembly. You still look dubious."

"Well, I would like to hope for that too, Paul. I only wish I had your great faith."

"I have been given countless evidences to give me that faith, Luke, and already you have too. But growing faith comes by hearing the Word of God, and that is what you will enjoy in Antioch on Sundays."

"I will not want to miss even one week. I may have to change my schedule to ensure that."

"In due time I pray your associates will be part of us too."

THEOPHILUS BEGAN his usual meeting with Luke the way he always had, having someone meet the former slave at the gate, ushering him into the house, washing his feet, and offering him a snack of olives and grapes, which Luke always enjoyed and associated with his old home.

The master of the household always wanted to know the latest news, how things were going at the clinic, whether they needed anything more or different, and then brought Luke up to date on things around the estate.

Luke endured all this, eager to get to the real news. And he learned quickly that he could not hide this from Theophilus.

"Your knee is bouncing, Luke. What is on your mind?"

"Only the most monumental thing that could happen to a man, sir," he said.

"You have found a wife!"

Luke laughed. "It's been so long since I've even considered that, I have to say no, that is not my news. Life can be lonely, but my days are so full, I don't believe I would make a good husband."

"That's nonsense, but do tell me your news."

"Allow me to get right to it so you can respond with the shock I expect, and then we can discuss it."

"Oh, no, are you in trouble?"

"Perhaps in your mind. But in mine, my life has changed and will never be the same. I am happy and even believe I have found the way to conquer my passions."

"You don't say."

"I have become one of them, sir, a Christian, a believer in the resurrected Christ."

Theophilus seemed to freeze, staring.

"Say something," Luke said.

"I, I—well, it's just that you were the last person from whom I would ever have expected to hear this. Tell me everything."

And so Luke did.

Several minutes later Theophilus leaned forward. "So you were swayed by this silver-tongued orator, the one you used to complain about when you were at university."

"That's just it, sir. I was *not* swayed by him, though I should have been. He is brilliant and his arguments cogent, but I was so steeped in my own skepticism that nothing any human said could have penetrated my mind. But the healing I told you of, and the speaking of God to my heart and soul, entirely changed me."

"And you're certain this was not some trick, perhaps perpetrated by this Saul fellow. He couldn't have had the man fake the injury and the healing?"

"I thoroughly examined the damage before treating the man. He had suffered a gash from a hook line that sliced through his skin and inner tissue to where I could see the bone. This was no trick, sir. And neither was the healing. That hand looked whole, save for a thin pink scar that was as strong as if it had been there for months."

"Amazing."

"If you've ever believed in me, trusted me, valued me—"

"Don't even say that, Luke. You know I love you like a son."

"Then believe me. I wish I could remember everything Paul taught me, but I would not do it justice, and neither would I expect you to be persuaded without all the evidence. But I shall be joining the assembled brethren in Antioch on Sunday, and I would be honored if you could see your way clear to join me and at least investigate this."

Theophilus sat back. "I will ponder it. But I must tell you, it should come as no surprise that had anyone but you told me of this healing, I would have dismissed it out of hand. And the speaking to your inner man by God from heaven, well—"

"I know."

"But what reaches me and nearly persuades me to come is this idea of forgiveness of sin. If there is anything I have learned over a long lifetime, it is that I am weak in character, regardless of my best intentions and my reputation. I work and I try, but it is as if I am incapable of improving myself."

"Promise me you'll come Sunday. Stop by my apartment and we will go together."

LUKE WAS MORE THAN PLEASED when Theophilus agreed and followed through on his commitment. Luke felt conspicuous, arriving at the stables in an ornate coach, but Theophilus drove the horses himself, and Luke had to wonder when the last time was that this had happened.

The two were warmly welcomed by some and eyed warily by others until Paul hurried to embrace Luke and warmly greeted Theophilus. He introduced Barnabas, and while Luke and his former master were then free to find seats where they were largely unnoticed, it seemed the news traveled quickly among the two hundred or so that these were not interlopers but friends of the leadership.

Luke could only wonder what Theophilus thought of all of this. The two stood and hummed along to unfamiliar tunes and lyrics as the people worshiped and praised God. Then Barnabas asked if any had prayer requests, and from all over the room, one by one, people stood and told stories and asked for prayer.

One woman said she had talked of her faith in Christ to a woman she had met at the river every week for a year when they washed their clothes. "She seemed intrigued, but scared," she reported. "Please pray that God will allow me to use the right words and that she will come to faith."

Others asked prayer for ill or dying loved ones. Others for courage to be open about their faith, in spite of persecution. "We hear that leadership in Jerusalem is still in danger, so we worry."

Then Barnabas prayed, somehow remembering every request. When he finished, the people seemed to settle, as if knowing what was coming. Barnabas fished from a leather satchel two thick scrolls and spent the next half hour reading from each. The first was from Matthew, who, he reminded the faithful, had been a despised tax collector before becoming a disciple of Jesus. "Matthew is planning to write a complete history of his time with the Savior," Barnabas said. "These are some of his early memories."

Luke sat rapt, listening to accounts of Jesus' exploits in Judea and Samaria, preaching, telling stories, performing miracles.

Then Barnabas opened the other scroll, which he called the beginning of Mark's gospel, according to Peter. Luke could not remember ever being so eager to get his hands on a historical document, as rudimentary as these two might have been.

"And now," Barnabas said, handing the scrolls to an associate to be rerolled, "I know you are all as excited as I am to have in our midst today, and for the foreseeable future, the man whose letters and writings we have read aloud here for months. We need not read his scrolls today, for he is with us."

Luke could almost feel the genuine goodwill and affection this group seemed to emit toward their illustrious visitor. For his part, Paul immediately began praising God and Jesus. He prayed that God would give him utterance, and then launched into a message that made Luke wonder if he had planned it just for him and Theophilus. At one point Luke turned to glance at his mentor, and Theophilus looked no less than stricken at what he was hearing.

Paul said, "I want to speak to you today about the fact that those among you who have become believers in Jesus have also become dead to the law through the body of Christ, that you may become one with Him who was raised from the dead, that we should bear fruit to God. Like me, many of you were raised to study and love and live the law, but no more.

"For when we were in the flesh, the sinful passions which were aroused by the law were at work in our members to bear fruit to death. But now we have been delivered from the law, having died to what we were held by, so that we should serve in the newness of the Spirit and not in the oldness of the letter.

"What shall we say then? Is the law sin? Certainly not! On the contrary, I would not have known sin except through the law. For I would not have known covetousness unless the law had said, 'You shall not covet.' But sin produced in me all manner of evil desire. The very commandment against what I was doing, which was meant to bring life, I found to bring death.

"Has then what was meant for good—the law that made me aware of my sin—become death to me? Certainly not! But sin was producing death in me. The law showed me where I fell short, because I am carnal, sold under sin.

"Have you ever had the experience that you do not understand why you are doing what you are doing, because you know full well that it is wrong? That battle still rages in me. For what I will to do, that I do not practice; but what I hate, that I do. If, then, I do what I will not to do, I agree with the law that it is good.

"Now, hear me, I know that in me (that is, in my flesh) nothing good dwells; for to will is present with me, but how to perform what is good I do not find. For the good that I will to do, I do not do; but the evil I will not to do, that I practice. Now if I do what I will not to do, it is no longer I who do it, but sin that dwells in me.

"From this I can only conclude that evil is present with me, the one who wills to do good. For I delight in the law of God according to the inward man. But I see another law in my members, warring against the law of my mind, and bringing me into captivity to the law of sin, which is in my members. O wretched man that I am! Who will deliver me from this body of death? I thank God—through Jesus Christ our Lord!"

TWENTY-ONE

Luke had to wonder how long Theophilus's patience would last. He was a rich, successful man used to being served, getting his own way, and as kind as he was, he was not in the habit of having to wait—for anything. And as much as Luke wanted to get him together with Paul, dozens of others had already crowded around him and Barnabas.

They counseled some, prayed with others, and seemed to have all the time in the world for each. Luke could tell Theophilus was eager, but to his credit, he did not force the issue.

As they drew nearer to Paul, Luke heard a woman ask if he would baptize her. The evangelist turned to Barnabas. "Where do you conduct your baptisms?"

"In the Orontes when weather permits. And today is a fine day for a baptism."

"Then would you take this one and a few witnesses, and be sure to examine her to determine that she fully understands what she is doing."

"Oh, sir," the woman said, "I really wished that you would be involved."

"I appreciate your confidence, ma'am, but the Lord is impressing upon me that there is another here who has urgent need of my counsel, and I must follow that leading. And the rest of you," he said, gesturing to the dozen or so left, "if you would excuse me, I shall look forward to speaking personally with you either during the week as your schedules allow or next Sunday."

Luke thought no one seemed put out by this, except for perhaps Theophilus, who looked disappointed but resigned as he turned away.

Paul reached and touched his shoulder. "You, sir," he whispered. "The Lord would have me talk with you."

Theophilus appeared stunned but also amused. "Indeed?"

"If He is not impressing the same upon you, perhaps I am mistaken."

"No, to the contrary. I would love a few moments with you. I have many questions, though I confess I'm not sure I would know whether God is impressing anything upon me."

Paul laughed. "Oh, believe me, Theophilus, when God impresses something on a man, he knows it. So are your questions merely products of your curiosity, or did you feel some deep urgings as I was teaching?"

Theophilus blanched. "I confess, rabbi, that I did feel some definite stirring. You see, I—"

"Excuse me," Paul said, "but are you hungry?"

"Famished."

"Let us go somewhere where we might dine and talk, shall we? Dr. Luke, is there a convenient spot nearby?"

Luke suggested an open-air eatery a block from his clinic.

"And would we enjoy privacy?"

"We could actually eat at the clinic, Paul."

"Perfect."

LESS THAN HALF AN HOUR LATER, Paul, Luke, and Theophilus settled around a small table in the tiny clinic several blocks away, having ordered enough food for four and left directions for Barnabas.

In his usual direct manner, Paul took charge, praying over the food and beginning the conversation. "I have heard much about you, sir, and your kindness to my old friend. Tell me, what do you make of what has become of him?"

"Well," Theophilus said, looking less comfortable in the surroundings than Paul or Luke did, "that he has become a servant of people and gifted in medicine is no surprise to me."

"I am not talking about his profession, Theophilus. I speak of his newfound faith."

"I am not certain I know what to think of that."

"It must at least make you curious, for here you are."

"Here I am."

"No doubt you are a Stoic."

Theophilus nodded and seemed to stare with wonder at Paul, who, despite his education and background, spoke with his mouth full. "It's an interesting philosophy," Paul added, "which, as you know, Luke and I studied at university. Yet for all its good intentions and noble efforts, it results in the very dichotomy I spoke of this morning."

Theophilus shoved his plate aside and leaned forward, raising a palm. "If I may say, I found that most compelling. It was as if you knew me and my inner struggles. We Stoics pride ourselves in trying to serve mankind, but I wonder if any have really conquered their own selfish ambition. I am advancing in age, and yet I seem farther from that goal every day."

Paul wiped his mouth, then stood suddenly when Barnabas arrived. They embraced and Paul urged him to eat. As Barnabas looked on silently, Paul turned his attention back to Theophilus. "I venture to say, this may sound foreign to your ears, but hear me out. Those who live according to the flesh set their minds on the things of the flesh, but those who live according to the Spirit set their minds on the things of the Spirit. My aim here is not to criticize Stoicism but to tell you why it falls short of what you long for. For to be carnally minded is death, but to be spiritually minded is life and peace.

"The carnal mind is at enmity against God, for it is not subject to the law of God, nor indeed can it be. So, then, those who are in the flesh cannot please God, let alone their deepest inner desires for self-improvement. You follow?"

"Somewhat," Theophilus said. "But my intentions are pure. I have never even believed in God, let alone meant to be at enmity with him."

"Oh, I don't mean to impugn your motives, Theophilus. I'm saying that the reason Stoicism does not give you inner peace is that it does not acknowledge the Lord, your maker. Today you heard eyewitness accounts of some who walked with Jesus, the Son of God, when He spoke and performed miracles. You heard me expound on the gospel, how He came to seek and to save the lost. If you came to believe in Him, you would not be in the flesh but rather in the Spirit, if indeed the Spirit of God dwelt in you."

"Of course that can't happen to me until I can bring myself to believe."

Paul nodded. "Well said. And if anyone does not have the Spirit of Christ, he is not His. But if Christ were in you, despite that your body is dead because of sin, the Spirit would be alive because of His righteousness. If the Spirit of Him who raised Jesus from the dead dwelt in you, He who raised Christ from the dead would also give life to your mortal body through His Spirit.

"The fact is, Theophilus, that more than just giving you victory over yourself, the Spirit of God gives you life itself."

To Luke, Theophilus looked speechless. Luke had no idea how the man was responding to this, but if he had to guess, he would have said that Theophilus yearned for just what Paul was talking about.

"Let me say it this way," Paul said. "If you continue to live according to the flesh, you will die. But if you live by the Spirit of God, you put to death the deeds of the body, and you will live. As many as are led by the Spirit of God, these are sons of God."

"I have much to think about," Theophilus said, his voice raspy. "The very prospect of such a change in thinking scares me. And yet you seemed to move farther from your roots than you are asking me to do. You have risked your life for this."

"Oh, but I consider the sufferings of this present time not worthy to be compared with the glory that shall eventually be revealed. Creation itself will one day be delivered from the bondage of corruption into glorious liberty."

"I fear I am too weak for this endeavor," Theophilus said, "as attractive as it sounds."

"The Spirit helps in our weaknesses. For we do not know what we should pray for as we ought, but the Spirit Himself makes intercession for us with groanings that cannot be uttered. He searches our hearts and makes intercession for us according to the will of God."

"If only I knew this was the right course."

"One thing I know, sir, is that all things work together for good to those who love God, to those who are the called according to His purpose. For He conforms us to the image of His perfect Son, calling us, justifying us, and glorifying us."

"I am nearly persuaded, but I confess I worry that people will think me mad. Imagine the ridicule."

"You ask *me* to imagine the ridicule? Such is my daily portion from all sides. What do I say to these things? If God is for me, who can be against me? He who did not spare His own Son, but delivered Him up for us all, how shall He not with Him also freely give us all things? Who shall bring a charge against God's elect? It is God who justifies. Who is he who condemns? It is Christ who died, and furthermore is also risen, who is even at the right hand of God, who also makes intercession for us.

"Who shall separate us from the love of Christ? Shall tribulation, or distress, or persecution, or famine, or nakedness, or peril, or sword? As it is written:

For Your sake we are killed all day long;
We are accounted as sheep for the slaughter.

"Yet in all these things we are more than conquerors through Him who loved us."

"So you give yourself wholly to God," Theophilus said, "having faith His spirit will fill you, and you leave all your fears and worries behind?"

Paul nodded. "Theophilus, let me tell you that I am persuaded that neither death nor life, nor angels nor principalities nor powers, nor things present nor things to come, nor height nor depth, nor any other created thing, shall be able to separate me from the love of God, which is in Christ Jesus my Lord."

Theophilus stood and paced. "I feel so conflicted," he said softly.

Paul approached and put an arm around him. "The Lord is one God, maker of heaven and earth. He sent His Son, Jesus the Christ, to die on the cross for your sins. He was buried and raised again three days later and now sits on the right hand of God. If you believe this and confess it with your mouth, you will be saved and be indwelt with His Spirit. You will be imbued with power from on high so that you can serve Him and all men with a pure heart."

Theophilus moved away from Paul and stared out the window.

"Barnabas," Paul said, "let us leave these men to their thoughts. Should they have further need of us, they know where to find us."

TWENTY-TWO

Luke made a conscious decision to not put any pressure on his former master, but rather just to pray for him and let the man take his own counsel. Oh, Luke was curious, and many were the times over the next several weeks when he had to fight to keep himself from asking whether Theophilus had come to any conclusions. But he refrained.

As close as the conversation got to anything spiritual was late each week when the two got together over clinic business and Theophilus mentioned that he would pick up Luke for the Sunday assembly. Each week they sat together, Luke enthusiastically joining in the worship and learning more and more, Theophilus politely seeming to take it all in.

Finally came the Sunday when Luke asked Theophilus if he had the time and interest to stay after the meeting and witness his being baptized. Paul had taught that this instruction from Jesus was an expression of one's devotion to following in His steps.

"Not only would I be honored to be in attendance," Theophilus said, "but I would like to baptized too."

Luke stared at him. "You are confessing Christ?"

"I am. I believe Him to be the Son of God and trust Him for my salvation."

Luke wanted to leap and shout, but he simply said, "Come with me to inform Paul and Barnabas."

The two elders exulted and rejoiced with them, Paul leading them in prayer. Theophilus had a question. "It seems to me there should be, and there will be, no hiding this. I would ask that my entire household, slaves and all, be invited to witness this ceremony. That will give me the opportunity to make plain my commitment, and for you, Rabbi, to clearly preach the gospel to them."

DURING THE NEXT YEAR, Luke's life became one of frenetic activity. During the week he either manned the clinic or labored as ship's physician on a host of vessels plying their trade on the Mediterranean. Whenever possible, he arranged his schedule to be back in Antioch for Sundays, when Theophilus would bring many of his household and slaves via caravan to the stables for the assembling of believers. Hardly a month passed without someone in Theophilus's family or employ becoming a new believer.

Despite learning and growing in all areas of faith, Luke soon developed an obsession that nearly overwhelmed him. As more and more Greeks and Gentiles were added to the church's ranks, he found himself fascinated by people's personal stories. During his few spare minutes, which largely came only on Sundays before and after church, he took to interviewing new believers and carefully recording their histories and stories, probing for their feelings and emotions and documenting the dramatic changes in their lives. Luke asked Theophilus for larger supplies of papyrus and quills and ink, and found that his former master agreed that this was a worthy endeavor.

Nothing excited Luke more than when Paul and Barnabas called in favors from their friends and associates in Jerusalem and brought in guests who had personally known Jesus Christ. Luke realized he was just short of obnoxious, finagling and conniving and maneuvering for private time with these individuals, from the apostle John to Peter to any disciple who had become a traveling missionary. He feared he drove many of them to distraction, having to constantly apologize for asking them to go back and help him fill in chronologically exactly what happened, what was said, what the weather was like, where they were, what the landscape and the buildings looked like. He was determined to record every detail with meticulous accuracy, believing that the best history was that with the most specificity.

Luke's private pursuit became to piece together these various accounts in chronological fashion, making for himself the most complete outline and timeline of the three-year public ministry of Jesus.

When Paul and Barnabas had together been leading the Antiochian church for a year, they began to talk of venturing out on a missionary journey. A young man named John Mark came to Antioch to accompany the two elders on their trip, and the three set off. Luke missed Paul terribly and began dreaming of someday accompanying him on one of his sojourns to other churches and lands thus far unreached by the gospel.

During his own voyages as a ship's physician, Luke kept an eye out for messages from Paul, who wrote many letters to the church, detailing their adventures. He and Barnabas and Mark had sailed from Antioch to Seleucia and on to Cyprus, a large island about seventy miles off the coast of Syria. They went from there to Salamis and Paphos, where Paul wrote of a strange encounter with a sorcerer named Bar-Jesus.

Luke found fascinating Paul's account of the man he called a false prophet. Bar-Jesus was a Jew who was with the proconsul of Cyprus, Sergius Paulus, whom Paul referred to as an intelligent man. The latter had called for Barnabas and Paul, saying he wanted to hear the word of God.

But the sorcerer Bar-Jesus opposed them, seeking to turn the proconsul away from the faith. Paul's letter reported that, full of the Holy Spirit, he stared the man down and said, "O full of all deceit and all fraud, you son of the devil, you enemy of all righteousness, will you not cease perverting the straight ways of the Lord?

"And now, indeed, the hand of the Lord is upon you, and you shall be blind, not seeing the sun for a time." And immediately a dark mist fell on Bar-Jesus, and he went around seeking someone to lead him by the hand.

At that the proconsul believed, seeing what had happened and then being astonished at Paul and Barnabas's teaching of the Lord.

When they went to Perga in Pamphylia, there apparently was a falling out between Paul and Mark, and the young man left them to head back to Jerusalem.

Luke considered offering to fill in for Mark, but restrained himself. Already he was becoming busy in the Antioch church; he had become a teacher and an elder, along with Theophilus. Eventually he had to limit and finally eliminate ship doctoring from his schedule. His days were filled with clinic and church work, leaving time for only his writing of church history.

MOST CURIOUS ABOUT whatever rift had caused young John Mark to leave the missionary party, Luke wrote to Paul and asked. But when he finally received a reply, Paul chose to ignore the question and instead reported on their visit to another city called Antioch, this one in Pisidia.

"Luke, you will appreciate this, and perhaps it will find a place in your written history. Barnabas and I entered the synagogue here on the Sabbath day and sat down. After the reading of the Law and the Prophets, the rulers of the synagogue said to us, 'Men, if you have any word of exhortation for the people, say on.'

"As you can imagine, I needed little encouragement. I stood and motioned with my hand and said, 'Men of Israel, and you who fear God, listen: The God of this people Israel chose our fathers and exalted the people when they dwelt as strangers in the land of Egypt, and with an uplifted arm He brought them out of it. Now, for a time of about forty years He put up with their ways in the wilderness. And when He had destroyed seven nations in the land of Canaan, He distributed their land to them by allotment.

"'After that He gave them judges for about four hundred and fifty years, until Samuel the prophet. And afterward they asked for a king, so God gave them Saul the son of Kish, a man of the tribe of Benjamin, for forty years. And when He had removed him, He raised up for them David as king, to whom also He gave testimony and said, "I have found David the son of Jesse, a man after My own heart, who will do all My will."'

"I knew I had their attention, Luke, for I was clearly speaking as one who knew and shared their history. So I told them, 'From this man's seed, according to the promise, God raised up for Israel a Savior—Jesus—after John had first preached, before His coming, the baptism of repentance to all the people of Israel. And as John was finishing his mission and purpose, he said, "Who do you think I am? I am not He. But behold, there comes One after me, the sandals of whose feet I am not worthy to loose."

"'Men and brethren, sons of the family of Abraham, and those among you who fear God, to you the word of this salvation has been sent. For those who dwell in Jerusalem, and their rulers—because they did not know Him, nor even the voices of the Prophets, which are read every Sabbath—have fulfilled them in condemning Him. And though they found no cause for death in Him, they asked Pilate that He should be put to death.

"'Now when they had fulfilled all that was written concerning Him, they took Him down from the tree and laid Him in a tomb. But God raised Him from the dead. He was seen for many days by those who came up with Him from Galilee to Jerusalem, who are His witnesses to the people. And we declare to you glad tidings—that promise which was made to the fathers. God has fulfilled this for us their children, in that He has raised up Jesus. As it is also written in the second Psalm:

You are My Son,
Today I have begotten You.

"'And that He raised Him from the dead, no more to return to corruption, He has spoken thus:

I will give you the sure mercies of David.

"'Therefore He also says in another Psalm:

You will not allow Your Holy One to see corruption.

"'For David, after he had served his own generation by the will of God, died and was buried with his fathers, and saw corruption, but He whom God raised up saw no corruption. Therefore let it be known to you, brethren, that through this Man is preached to you the forgiveness of sins, and by Him everyone who believes is justified from all things from which you could not be justified by the law of Moses.

"'Beware therefore, lest what has been spoken in the Prophets come upon you:

Behold, you despisers,
Marvel and perish!
For I work a work in your days,
A work which you will by no means believe,
Though one were to declare it to you.

"Now, Luke, when the Jews left the synagogue, the Gentiles begged that these words might be preached to them the next Sabbath, and many of the Jews and devout proselytes followed us, so we persuaded them to continue in the grace of God.

"On the next Sabbath almost the whole city came together to hear the word of God. But when the Jews saw the multitudes, they were filled with envy. Contradicting and blaspheming, they opposed the things I preached. So Barnabas and I grew bold and said, 'It was necessary that the word of God should be spoken to you first; but since you reject it, and judge yourselves unworthy of everlasting life, behold, we turn to the Gentiles. For so the Lord has commanded us:

I have set you as a light to the Gentiles,
That you should be for salvation to the ends of the earth.

"Now when the Gentiles heard this, they were glad and glorified the word of the Lord. And as many as had been appointed to eternal life believed. And the word of the Lord was being spread throughout all the region. But the Jews stirred up the devout and prominent women and the chief men of the city, raised up persecution against Barnabas and me, and expelled us from their region.

"So we shook off the dust from our feet against them, and went on to Iconium, where we were filled with joy and with the Holy Spirit."

This report encouraged Luke and made him want all the more to one day travel with Paul and join him in ministry. But over the next few years, every time he suggested that to Paul, the evangelist wrote back that Luke must continue to grow in faith and in training by helping lead the church in Antioch. Paul expressed certainty that when he and Barnabas returned, even more Gentiles would be welcomed into the church at Syrian Antioch.

While Luke continued to write and labor in the clinic and in the church, he eagerly awaited Paul's letters. For a long time, Paul and Barnabas stayed in Iconium, preaching and teaching, and Luke heard nothing for months. Finally the report came that it happened in Iconium that they went together to the synagogue of the Jews, and so spoke that a great multitude both of the Jews and of the Greeks believed.

"But," Paul wrote, "the unbelieving Jews stirred up the Gentiles and poisoned their minds against us. We stayed there a long time, speaking boldly in the Lord, who was bearing witness to the word of His grace, granting signs and wonders done by our hands.

"But the multitude of the city was divided—part siding with the Jews, and part with us. And when both the Gentiles and Jews made a violent attempt, with their rulers, to abuse and stone us, we fled to Lystra and Derbe, cities of Lycaonia, and to the surrounding region.

"While we were preaching the gospel in Lystra, a certain man without strength in his feet was there, a cripple who had never walked. I observed him intently and saw that he had faith to be healed, so I said with a loud voice, 'Stand up straight on your feet!' And he leaped and walked!

"Now, when the people saw what I had done, they raised their voices, saying in their own language, 'The gods have come down to us in the likeness of men!' They called Barnabas Zeus and me Hermes.

"Then the priest of Zeus, whose temple was in front of their city, brought oxen and garlands to the gates, intending to sacrifice with the multitudes. But when we heard this, we tore our clothes and ran in among the multitude, crying out, 'Men, why are you doing these things? We also are men with the same nature as you, and preach to you that you should turn from these useless things to the living God, who made the heaven, the earth, the sea, and all things that are in them, who in bygone generations allowed all nations to walk in their own ways. Nevertheless He did not leave Himself without witness, in that He did good, gave us rain from heaven and fruitful seasons, filling our hearts with food and gladness.' But we could scarcely restrain the multitudes from sacrificing to us.

"Then Jews from Pisidian Antioch and Iconium arrived, and having persuaded the multitudes against us, they stoned me and dragged me out of the city, supposing me to be dead. When Barnabas and other disciples gathered around me, however, I rose up and went into the city. And the next day we departed for Derbe.

"When we had preached the gospel to that city and made many disciples, we returned to Lystra, Iconium, and Antioch, strengthening the souls of the disciples, exhorting them to continue in the faith, and saying, 'We must through many tribulations enter the kingdom of God.'

"So when we had appointed elders in every church, and prayed with fasting, we commended them to the Lord in whom they had believed. And after we had again passed through Pisidia, we came to Pamphylia, and when we had preached the word in Perga, we went down to Attalia. From here we will sail to Antioch, whence you and the brethren there commended us to the grace of God for the work that we have completed.

"With great anticipation, we long to be reunited with you in the Lord."

TWENTY-THREE

Syrian Antioch, A.D. *47*

Had Luke any doubt of the peril associated with his aligning himself with the new Christian movement, it had been dashed not only by the reports of Paul from his missionary travels, but also by news from Jerusalem. James, head of the church there, had been beheaded at the direction of King Herod, and Peter had been imprisoned. He had miraculously escaped, but there could no longer be any doubt that Christians remained the enemies of both the Romans and the Jews.

The assembly where Luke served had been spared much of the persecution because its members were not outspoken. While they proselytized friends and neighbors and associates, unlike Paul they did not challenge the existing authorities or argue in the synagogues.

When Paul and Barnabas returned, the church seemed revitalized by their oral memories and especially Paul's deep teaching about the ramifications of the Spirit-filled life. Luke soon gave up all outside activities, including his work at the clinic, and devoted his every waking hour to helping lead the church, tending to the medical needs of the body of believers, and his writing. Theophilus had encouraged this and agreed that his future held traveling as an aide to Paul on his missionary journeys.

Luke pleaded with the evangelist to be able to accompany him and Barnabas to Jerusalem for the council of leaders, but Paul said, "Do not be disappointed that I am declining your request, Doctor, but I have prayed about this and believe you are of more value here in our absence. I am, however, planning more trips in a few years and will be looking for just the right addition to our team."

LUKE LIVED ON THIS PROMISE for years but was bitterly disappointed when Paul returned from Jerusalem with a most engaging and spiritual man named Silas, who was clearly being groomed to be another traveling companion. And when Paul and Silas set out on Paul's second missionary journey in A.D. 51, again Luke remained in Antioch. Through much prayer and good counsel from Theophilus and other elders, he was able to accept this—with difficulty—as God's will and committed himself to remaining devoted to the work.

Night after night, however, he paced and prayed, beseeching the Lord for the reason He had planted such wanderlust in Luke's heart if he was to remain in Antioch. From all over the surrounding area came letters from Paul, recounting exploits in northern Syria, then Cilicia, Derbe, and Lystra again, where Timothy joined their company. They continued through Phrygia and Galatia, but Paul reported that they were "forbidden by the Spirit" to go to Asia.

When Luke's eyes fell on the next paragraph, he could not stanch his tears. "Our plan is to travel through Mysia to Troas. We have need of the beloved physician Luke to both tend to and encourage us as well as bringing his gifts to our work. Pray about sending him. We shall wait at Troas for him or word to the contrary."

Luke hired a horse-drawn wagon to race him to Daphne, where he gushed the news to Theophilus. The old man was as excited as he and immediately committed to sponsoring him for the trip. The rest of the elders soon agreed, and on Sunday a few days later, Luke was officially commissioned by the church body and sent.

NO SURPRISE TO LUKE, Paul immediately proved a difficult friend and traveling companion. But their friendship, tenuous as it had been in university years before, predated all Paul's other relationships and allowed Luke more understanding of the man.

Luke overlooked Paul's short temper—over which he always immediately apologized—and his indefatigable ability to argue and discuss a topic ad nauseam until their other mates fell asleep. Of Paul's devotion to Christ—not to mention his brilliance—Luke had no doubt. And while he was the one of the traveling party able to accept all Paul's foibles and not get crosswise with him, he believed the hatred focused on Paul was most egregious.

Everywhere they went, regardless of the great work and miraculous acts Paul performed, it wasn't long before he was labeled a rabble-rouser, a troublemaker who blasphemed and slandered and offended the very history of his own people, the Jews. To Paul's credit, of course, he was fearless, wading right into their temples to preach Christ as the promised Messiah. It was no wonder he was the object of ridicule and treachery and danger.

Often Paul and his little band of missionaries were hosted by local believers or stayed in small, inexpensive inns. Frequently they shared a room, lying within feet of one another with hardly room for two to move about at once.

One night, after Luke had tossed and turned for an hour, recounting the exciting adventures of the day and thanking God for the unspeakable privilege of getting to travel and witness these things firsthand, he finally fell into a deep sleep, only to be roughly shaken awake by Paul.

"I am so sorry to wake you," the evangelist said, "but the Lord has just now given me a vision."

The others roused and sat up. "What is it?" Silas said, as Barnabas lit a lamp.

Paul's eyes shone in the flickering light. "A man of Macedonia stood and pleaded with me, saying, 'Come over here and help us.' Brothers, we have no choice but to go. Plainly the Lord is calling us to preach the gospel to them."

At dawn they boarded a ship from Troas and ran a straight course to Samothrace, and the next day came to Neapolis. From there they proceeded to the colony of Philippi, the foremost city of that part of Macedonia. After several days there, on the Sabbath they left the city and went to the riverside where the locals customarily prayed. They sat and Paul spoke to several women who met there.

One woman, who introduced herself as Lydia, said she was a seller of purple from the city of Thyatira. "I worship God daily in the synagogue," she said. Paul immediately turned his attention to her and preached Christ as the foretold Messiah. Luke silently prayed and looked on in astonishment as it appeared God opened her heart to heed the things spoken by Paul. By the end of the day, she had become a believer, along with her whole family, and they were baptized.

Then she fell to her knees before Paul and said, "If you have judged me to be faithful to the Lord, come to my house and stay." So Paul and the others lodged there for several days as they ministered in the city.

One day a slave girl possessed with a spirit of divination—who brought her masters much profit by fortune-telling—began following them wherever they preached and taught and cried out, "These men are the servants of the Most High God, who proclaim to us the way of salvation."

At first Luke thought she was of God, but she did this for many days, and it was clear that Paul was greatly annoyed. Finally he turned and said to the spirit, "I command you in the name of Jesus Christ to come out of her." And she was delivered. But when her masters saw that their hope of profit was gone, they seized Paul and Silas and dragged them into the marketplace to the authorities.

Luke followed and watched as they told the magistrates, "These men, being Jews, exceedingly trouble our city. They teach customs not lawful for us, being Romans, to receive or observe."

Then the multitude rose up against Paul and Silas, and the magistrates tore off their clothes and commanded them to be beaten with rods. When they had laid many stripes on them, they threw them into prison, commanding the jailer to keep them securely. He put them into the inner prison and fastened their feet in stocks.

Paul told Luke the next day at Lydia's home that at midnight, as he and Silas were praying and singing hymns to God, the prisoners were listening. "And suddenly there was a great earthquake, so that the foundations of the prison were shaken, and immediately all the doors were opened and everyone's chains were loosed. And the keeper of the prison, awaking from sleep and seeing the prison doors open, supposing the prisoners had fled, drew his sword and was about to kill himself. But I called with a loud voice, 'Do yourself no harm, for we are all here!'

"The jailer called for a light and ran in, falling down trembling before us. Then he led us out and said, 'Sirs, what must I do to be saved?'

"Of course I told him, 'Believe on the Lord Jesus Christ, and you will be saved, you and your household.' Then we spoke the word of the Lord to him and to all who were in his house. And he took us that same hour and cleansed our wounds. And immediately he and all his family were baptized.

"Now when he had brought us into his house, he set food before us and rejoiced. When the sun rose, the jailer told me that the magistrates had sent officers, saying, 'Let those men go.' So he said, 'Now therefore depart, and go in peace.'"

"Praise God!" Luke said. "And that is why you are here."

"'No!' I told the jailer, 'They beat us openly, and we ourselves are uncondemned Romans, and threw us into prison. And now they want to put us out secretly? No indeed! Let them come themselves and get us out.'"

"Oh, Paul!" Luke said. "You said that?"

"I did, and the officers told these words to the magistrates, and they were afraid when they heard we were Romans. They came and pleaded with us to depart, so we finally did, and here we are."

As Paul and the others began packing to continue their journey, Luke begged permission to retire to a private room in Lydia's home, where he could record on papyrus all that he had heard. As he did this, it rekindled his passion to record all the miraculous events in the young history of the church, beginning from the time Jesus ministered among the people for three years.

But as he quickly wrote, he began to consider going back even further. Paul often spoke of John the Baptizer, who foretold of Jesus, his younger cousin. What intrigue must be in that story! Paul never knew John, of course, and he had come to a violent and ugly end. But this man had himself baptized the Son of God! How Luke longed to hear and record that account from someone who had been there.

When he finished his work and began packing his own satchel, he was eager to quiz Paul on who would be best to interview about the very origins of John and of Jesus and where he might find them. Surely not in the cities where Paul was traveling, but word was that the apostle John was lodging and caring for Jesus' mother, Mary, in the city of Ephesus, where there was a thriving church. Luke could not imagine a higher privilege than interviewing her.

As he made his way down to the loaded wagon, he noticed that Paul had a serious visage. He pulled Luke aside and, as usual, came directly to the point. "I am going to ask you to do something difficult. The brethren here have taken to you in an unusual way and have found you most compassionate and encouraging and knowledgeable. They have need of you here—now hear me out—and while I too have come to cherish your companionship, I am inclined to assign you here for a while."

"For how long?"

"The Lord has not indicated that to me, but I will make it back through here one day."

"In weeks, months, or years?"

"It could be years, Luke. Are you able to do as I believe the Lord would ask?"

"Of course, but—"

"You shall be the elder here, guiding and encouraging this flock, and also tending to their physical needs. I know it is a sacrifice, because your heart is with us. Selfishly, I would have you continue with me, but I believe God is asking this of both of us, so I am confident you will be blessed if you obey."

Luke could not argue, much as he wanted to, as he knew that Paul—over anyone else—knew the mind of the Lord. "I will want to continue my writing. Will you write me often, telling of your exploits?"

"Of course. And when I return, we shall again enjoy rich blessings in serving the Lord together."

Luke wept as he embraced Paul, then Barnabas and Silas.

TWENTY-FOUR

Philippi, A.D. *58*

Luke had enjoyed a wonderful season of life, though he terribly missed Theophilus and wrote him regularly. He also heard frequently from Paul and longed for the day when he might again join him in his travels. Meanwhile, various church leaders from Jerusalem and other elders from all over the world occasionally passed through Philippi and preached in the growing church. Luke, never interested in making a name for himself or putting himself above others, carefully led and managed behind the scenes, nurturing others into positions of leadership so the church would not forever be dependent on him.

Whenever anyone visited who was a personal friend of Jesus, like John or Peter or Matthew, Luke tried their patience by keeping them up until well after dark, plying them with questions and digging for every fact and detail they could remember.

While all fascinated him and added to his storehouse of knowledge, he was most impressed with the apostle John. "You should write your own gospel," he told the man as he was packing for his return to Ephesus after having ministered in Philippi for several days. Luke had interviewed him every day.

"Perhaps one day," John said. "I have much traveling to do, yet I dare not be away from Mary for too long a time. She has already lived many years past her contemporaries, and while her mind is still sharp, her vision, her hearing, and her limbs have grown weak from age. I have much help in caring for her from many of the women at Ephesus, but I fear she is not long for this world."

As Luke helped carry John's things down to the wagon, he said, "Is she too frail to reminisce about the birth of her Son?"

"Let me say it this way, young man," John said, making Luke feel good, for though he was not much younger than John, he was already well into his fifties. "If it were up to me, I would say don't go to the trouble to travel to Ephesus and stretch an old woman's strength to satisfy your own curiosity. But you know what she would say?" He chuckled. "She would welcome you with open arms, for there is nothing she would rather talk about. Of course it's a fascinating, miraculous story, and I have heard it many times. She has amazing recall, having pondered these things in her heart and rehearsed them for decades to anyone who would listen. Why, she even has a record of Jesus' genealogy, and it is not short."

"I would be welcome, then?"

"Only because I know it would warm her heart. Your earnestness has loosed my tongue. I can only imagine how it would be for a willing subject. Just don't wait too long, son."

Luke burned with desire to find the time and resources to make that trip.

Meanwhile, word came that Paul and many who traveled with him remained under constant persecution. After one uproar he departed again for Macedonia, where he encouraged the church with many words before going to Greece, where he stayed three months. When the local Jews plotted against him as he was about to sail to Syria, he decided to return through Macedonia. He wrote Luke, "Sopater of Berea, Aristarchus and Secundus of Thessalonica, Gaius of Derbe, Timothy, and Tychicus and Trophimus of Asia are all with me. As soon as you can, could you join us again in Troas, where first we ministered together years ago?"

Luke did not have to be asked twice. How wonderful it felt to be needed. He did not feel, however, that he should leave the church at Philippi until after the Days of Unleavened Bread, so five days later he sailed and joined Paul and his party in Troas, where they stayed seven days.

Thus began another exciting chapter in Luke's life, where he was an eyewitness to dramatic preaching from and miracles performed by Paul in many cities. Once while Paul was speaking in an upper room until after midnight, a young listener named Eutychus dozed off and fell three stories. Most—including Dr. Luke—thought he was dead, but Paul went down and embraced him and said, "Do not trouble yourselves, for his life is in him."

Presently the young man returned to the upper room, took nourishment, conversed till daybreak, and departed entirely healthy.

FROM THERE Paul, Luke, Timothy, and Paul's other disciples traversed many hundreds of miles to churches and bodies of believers all over the area. After many voyages, Paul decided to sail past Ephesus, so that he would not have to spend time in Asia, for he was hurrying to be at Jerusalem, if possible, on the Day of Pentecost. Luke made many inquiries about getting to Ephesus himself so he might interview Mary, but he could not make the arrangements work.

From Miletus, Paul sent a message to Ephesus calling for the elders of the church. When they reached him, he said, "You know, from the first day that I came to Asia, in what manner I always lived among you, serving the Lord with all humility, with many tears and trials that happened to me by the plotting of the Jews; how I kept back nothing that was helpful, but proclaimed it to you, and taught you publicly and from house to house, testifying to Jews, and also to Greeks, repentance toward God and faith toward our Lord Jesus Christ.

"And see, now I go bound in the spirit to Jerusalem, not knowing the things that will happen to me there, except that the Holy Spirit testifies in every city, saying that chains and tribulations await me. But none of these things move me; nor do I count my life dear to myself, so that I may finish my race with joy, and the ministry which I received from the Lord Jesus, to testify to the gospel of the grace of God.

"And indeed, now I know that you all, among whom I have gone preaching the kingdom of God, will see my face no more. Therefore I testify to you this day that I am innocent of the blood of all men. For I have not shunned to declare to you the whole counsel of God. Therefore take heed to yourselves and to all the flock, among which the Holy Spirit has made you overseers, to shepherd the church of God, which He purchased with His own blood. For I know this, that after my departure savage wolves will come in among you, not sparing the flock.

"Also from among yourselves men will rise up, speaking perverse things, to draw away the disciples after themselves. Therefore watch, and remember that for three years I did not cease to warn everyone night and day with tears.

"So now, brethren, I commend you to God and to the word of His grace, which is able to build you up and give you an inheritance among all those who are sanctified. I have coveted no one's silver or gold or apparel. Yes, you yourselves know that these hands have provided for my necessities, and for those who were with me. I have shown you in every way, by laboring like this, that you must support the weak. And remember the words of the Lord Jesus, that He said, 'It is more blessed to give than to receive.'"

Paul then knelt and prayed with them all, and they all wept freely and fell on his neck and kissed him, many expressing sorrow most of all for his prediction that they would see his face no more. They accompanied him and Luke to the ship, Luke wondering what the future held but taking courage from Paul's attitude.

For the next few weeks, Paul and Luke and the others made several stops and changed vessels, finding in many places believers they could encourage. In Tyre, well-meaning followers of Christ warned Paul through the Spirit not to go up to Jerusalem. And when Paul and his band departed, these men brought their wives and children and accompanied them until they were out of the city. Before boarding ship, Paul and his people knelt in the sand and prayed with these.

They voyaged to Ptolemais, where they greeted the brethren and stayed one day; then finally departed and came to Caesarea, where they were welcomed to the house of Philip the evangelist. Philip had four virgin daughters who prophesied and warned Paul against going on to Jerusalem. After many days, a prophet named Agabus came from Judea, took Paul's belt, bound his own hands and feet, and said, "Thus says the Holy Spirit, 'So shall the Jews at Jerusalem bind the man who owns this belt, and deliver him into the hands of the Gentiles.'"

Luke, like the others, had heard enough. How much more was needed to persuade Paul to end this suicidal mission? He and the other associates pleaded with Paul not to go up to Jerusalem.

Paul listened passively, and when they were finished, he said,

"What do you mean by weeping and breaking my heart? For I am ready not only to be bound, but also to die at Jerusalem for the name of the Lord Jesus."

Luke had to admit that none of the prophecies said the Spirit was telling Paul not to proceed. They merely foretold what would happen to him. So when he would not be persuaded, they ceased their pleading, saying, "The will of the Lord be done."

AFTER THOSE DAYS they packed and went to Jerusalem along with some of the disciples from Caesarea. The brethren of Jerusalem received them gladly, and Paul greeted them and told in detail those things that God had done among the Gentiles through his ministry. And when they heard it, they glorified the Lord. They said, "Many myriads of Jews have believed, and they are all zealous for the law; but they have been informed about you that you teach all the Jews who are among the Gentiles to forsake Moses, saying that they ought not to circumcise their children nor to walk according to the customs. What then? The assembly must certainly meet, for they will hear that you have come. Therefore do what we tell you: We have four men who have taken a vow. Take them and be purified with them, and pay their expenses so that they may shave their heads. In this way all may know that those things of which they were informed concerning you are nothing, but that you yourself also walk orderly and keep the law.

"But concerning the Gentiles who believe, we have written and decided that they should observe no such thing, except that they should keep themselves from things offered to idols, from blood, from things strangled, and from sexual immorality."

Paul did as they had said, and the next day, having been purified with the four men, entered the temple to announce the expiration of the days of purification, at which time an offering should be made for each one of them.

The Jews from Asia, seeing him in the temple, stirred up the whole crowd and laid hands on him, crying out, "Men of Israel, help! This is the man who teaches all men everywhere against the people, the law, and has defiled this holy place."

All the city was disturbed, and the people ran together, seized Paul, and dragged him out of the temple; and immediately the doors were shut. As they were seeking to kill him, news came to the commander of the garrison that all Jerusalem was in an uproar. He immediately took soldiers and centurions, and ran down to them. And when they saw the commander and the soldiers, they stopped beating Paul. Then the commander took him and commanded him to be bound with two chains, and he asked who he was and what he had done. Some among the multitude cried one thing and some another.

So when the commander could not ascertain the truth because of the tumult, he ordered him taken into the barracks. When Paul reached the stairs he had to be carried by the soldiers to keep him away from the mob, which cried out, "Away with him!"

As Paul was about to be led into the barracks, he said to the commander, "May I speak to you? I am a Jew from Tarsus, in Cilicia, a citizen of no mean city; and I implore you, permit me to speak to the people."

The commander gave him permission, so Paul stood on the stairs and motioned with his hand to the people. And when there was a great silence, he spoke in Hebrew, saying, "Brethren and fathers, hear my defense before you now. I am indeed a Jew, born in Tarsus of Cilicia, but brought up in this city at the feet of Gamaliel, taught according to the strictness of our fathers' law, and was zealous toward God as you all are today. I persecuted this Way to the death, binding and delivering into prisons both men and women, as also the high priest bears me witness, and all the council of the elders, from whom I also received letters to the brethren, and went to Damascus to bring in chains even those who were there to Jerusalem to be punished."

Luke was moved anew as he heard Paul recite again his own history of the account on the road to Damascus. He told of his blindness, of Ananias, of being told he was to be a witness of Christ to all men, even Gentiles.

Finally the mob raised their voices and said, "Away with such a fellow from the earth, for he is not fit to live!" As they cried out and tore off their clothes and threw dust into the air, the commander ordered Paul brought into the barracks, and said that he should be examined under scourging. As they bound him, Paul said to the centurion who stood by, "Is it lawful for you to scourge a man who is a Roman and uncondemned?"

The centurion went to the commander, saying, "Take care what you do, for this man is a Roman."

The commander said to Paul, "Tell me, are you a Roman?"

"Yes."

The commander said, "With a large sum I obtained my citizenship."

Paul said, "But I was born a citizen."

Immediately those who were about to examine him withdrew, and the commander was also afraid because he had bound a Roman citizen.

THE NEXT DAY, the commander released Paul from his bonds and set him before the chief priests and their council. Paul said, "Men and brethren, I have lived in all good conscience before God until this day."

The high priest commanded those who stood by him to strike him on the mouth. Paul said, "God will strike you, you whitewashed wall! For you sit to judge me according to the law, and do you command me to be struck contrary to the law?"

Those who stood by said, "Do you revile God's high priest?"

Paul said, "I did not know, brethren, that he was the high priest; for it is written, 'You shall not speak evil of a ruler of your people.'"

But Paul later told Luke he perceived some of the council were Sadducees and others Pharisees, so he cried out, "Men and brethren, I am a Pharisee, the son of a Pharisee; concerning the hope and resurrection of the dead I am being judged!"

Immediately, dissension arose between the Pharisees and the Sadducees, for Sadducees say that there is no resurrection—and no angel or spirit—but the Pharisees confess both. The scribes of the Pharisees arose and protested, "We find no evil in this man; but if a spirit or an angel has spoken to him, let us not fight against God."

The commander, fearing Paul might be pulled to pieces by the council, had soldiers take him by force from among them and bring him into the barracks. When Luke visited him that night, he was struck to find Paul dejected and in need of encouragement, so he prayed for him. Paul told him later that in the night the Lord stood by him and said, "Be of good cheer, Paul; for as you have testified for Me in Jerusalem, so you must also bear witness at Rome."

Luke had no idea what that meant, when they might go, or how long Paul might be restrained there. But taking heart from Paul, who had become his brave mentor in the faith, Luke decided he would remain with him regardless the danger.

TWENTY-FIVE

The next day more than forty of the Jews came to the chief priests and elders and said, "We have bound ourselves under a great oath that we will eat nothing until we have killed Paul. Now you, therefore, together with the council, suggest to the commander that he be brought down to you tomorrow, as though you were going to make further inquiries concerning him, but we are ready to kill him before he comes near."

When Paul's sister's son heard of their planned ambush, he went to the barracks and told Paul. Paul called one of the centurions and said, "Take this young man to the commander, for he has something to tell him."

When the commander, Claudius Lysias, heard of the plot, he told Paul's nephew, "Tell no one that you have revealed these things to me."

Then he called for two centurions, instructing them to prepare two hundred soldiers, seventy horsemen, and two hundred spearmen to accompany Paul to Caesarea at the third hour of the night and take Paul safely to Antonius Felix, the governor of Judea. Claudius Lysias wrote:

> *To the most excellent governor Felix:*
>
> *Greetings.*
>
> *This man was seized by the Jews and was about to be killed by them. Coming with the troops I rescued him, having learned that he was a Roman. And when I wanted to know the reason they accused him, I brought him before their council. I found out that he was accused concerning questions of their law, but had nothing charged against him deserving of death or chains. And when it was told me that the Jews lay in wait for the man, I sent him immediately to you, and also commanded his accusers to state before you the charges against him.*
>
> *Farewell.*

Then the soldiers, as they were commanded, took Paul by night to Antipatris. When they came to Caesarea and had delivered the letter to the governor, they presented Paul to him. And when the governor determined that Paul was from the province of Cilicia, he said, "I will hear you when your accusers also have come."

Paul was kept in Herod's Praetorium for five days until Ananias the high priest came down with the elders and an orator named Tertullus.

Tertullus flattered the governor, then began: "We have found this man a plague, a creator of dissension among all the Jews throughout the world, and a ringleader of the sect of the Nazarenes. He even tried to profane the temple, and we seized him, and wanted to judge him according to our law. But the commander Lysias with great violence took him out of our hands, commanding his accusers to come to you. By examining him yourself you may ascertain all these things of which we accuse him."

When Paul was allowed to speak, he said, "Inasmuch as I know that you have been for many years a judge of this nation, I do the more cheerfully answer for myself, because you may ascertain that it is no more than twelve days since I went up to Jerusalem to worship. And they neither found me in the temple disputing with anyone nor inciting the crowd, either in the synagogues or in the city. Nor can they prove the things of which they now accuse me. But this I confess to you, that according to The Way, which they call a sect, so I worship the God of my fathers, believing all things which are written in the Law and in the Prophets. I have hope in God, which they themselves also accept, that there will be a resurrection of the dead, both of the just and the unjust. This being so, I myself always strive to have a conscience without offense toward God and men.

"Now after many years I came to bring alms and offerings to my nation, in the midst of which some Jews from Asia found me purified in the temple, neither with a mob nor with tumult. They ought to have been here before you to object if they had anything against me. Or else let those who are here themselves say if they found any wrongdoing in me while I stood before the council, unless it is for this one statement which I cried out, standing among them, 'Concerning the resurrection of the dead I am being judged by you this day.'"

Governor Felix adjourned the proceedings, "When Lysias the commander comes down, I will make a decision on your case." He commanded the centurion to keep Paul but to let him have liberty, and told him not to forbid any of his friends to provide for or visit him. Luke spent every moment with Paul, encouraging him and praying with him.

Once Felix came with his wife, Drusilla, who was Jewish, and sent for Paul to hear him concerning the faith in Christ. As Paul reasoned about righteousness, self-control, and the judgment to come, Felix looked afraid and said, "Go away for now; when I have a convenient time I will call for you."

It became known that Felix hoped that Paul would come up with bribe money for his release, which caused the governor to send for him more often for "conversations." Paul never let on that he also understood what Felix really wanted, and all this did was to stall the proceedings for the next two years until Porcius Festus succeeded Felix as governor of Judea. The new governor, wanting to do the Jews a favor, would leave Paul bound for six more months until sending him to Rome.

The two and half years Paul was bound in Judea-Caesarea proved the most portentous and providential period of Luke's life. He spent the first several weeks meeting with Paul every day, bringing him news and encouragement and food to supplement the meager offerings he received from the Romans.

The rest of Paul's band gradually drifted away, some back to their hometowns and local churches, others on to missionary trips of their own. In letters Paul wrote to friends and bodies of believers during this time, he referred to Luke as the "beloved physician."

After a time, Paul sat with Luke and told him, "It is evident that you are distracted and preoccupied. What has God put on your heart?"

"That is the trouble, Paul. I feel compelled to keep you company and support you, but I also feel driven—and I do believe this is of the Lord—to write an orderly account of the life of Jesus. I know others have begun doing the same, and what I have heard and read of these efforts is thrilling and instructive. But as you have been called to preach Christ to Jew and Gentile alike, I would write to people like myself, slave and free, Greek and Gentile."

"And you are confident God has put this desire in you?"

"It burns within me. My interest, my education, my training—everything in my background has prepared me for this. I would start at the beginning, telling the events in chronological order from first-hand eyewitness accounts. As you know, over the years I have been able to compile countless details from Jesus' contemporaries, and this has given me a unique perspective of the Man."

"How so?"

"Well, I have been imagining my former master, Theophilus, as representative of my audience. He has, as you know, become a devoted elder and student of the things of Christ. I would write to him in as readable and understandable a manner as possible—"

"Employing your maddening penchant for accuracy and dating."

Luke chuckled. "You've noticed."

"You are more historian than physician, Luke, and you always have been."

"So perhaps the Lord uses even our obsessions."

"No doubt. Look at me. The same zeal that gets me locked up like this makes me an enthusiastic servant of God."

Luke nodded. "You know that Theophilus and the Greeks were raised to strive to become the ideal man, and yet, needless to say, no one has been able to accomplish such in his natural lifetime."

"Except the Lord Himself."

"Yes! And yet from all the accounts I have gathered, this Man was different in many other ways. Imagine you or me in His position. Would we also have been a friend to the poor and downtrodden, to women, to children, to the meek and lowly? He did not wear His position and privilege like royalty. In truth, He was a King with nowhere to lay His head."

"He made Himself lowly," Paul said.

"And He said He had come to seek and to save the lost. Many of his parables and stories taught this same truth. When we gather as believers, we are thrilled to hear of Jesus the Christ, but I am eager to make plain also His feelings and humanity. Oh, Paul, there is so much here that I must get to the writing. I want to portray Jesus as a friend to all whom society despises."

Paul seemed to study Luke. "Were He still on earth, I daresay he would have elevated women to revered status."

"The stories I've heard of Him include many women He clearly admired and trusted. If we are to advance His cause, we must do the same. My gospel would aim to do that."

"Then get to it, man! What holds you back?"

"You, Paul."

"Me?"

"I feel I have everything I need except the most important part, and that would take me to Ephesus."

"To speak with His mother."

Luke nodded. "And I dare not wait. She is elderly and frail."

"Then go!"

"But you will be left here alone."

"I am never really alone, Luke."

"Yet even you need companionship and encouragement. I know it."

"At the expense of your worthy project? I would never forgive myself if I kept you from it. Anyway, you don't plan to abandon me forever, do you? You will return and tell me all you have heard, and I will get to read your scrolls as you progress, no?"

"Of course!"

"Then off with you, and let me hear nothing to the contrary. I will pray for you and wish you Godspeed. Write me at every opportunity and return as soon as you can."

TWENTY-SIX

Of all the traveling Luke had done in his work and ministry, the journey from Caesarea to Ephesus was the longest, including several days on rough seas. He paid for his passage by offering his medical services on a huge cargo and passenger ship that carried more than three hundred souls, including crew. Fortunately the worst he had to deal with were minor injuries to mates and about a dozen cases of mild seasickness among new travelers.

During periods of high seas, which occurred mostly after dark, Luke took special care to protect his scrolls, quills, ink, and fresh papyrus that had been provided by Theophilus. He prayed the Lord would grant calm waters as they drew within a few days of the great port city, knowing that his excitement and anticipation alone would make sleep difficult.

When finally Luke disembarked just after midday on a Friday, he found his way ashore with two large wood crates—one bearing a makeshift collapsible desk he was pleased to discover had survived intact. He was grateful to be met by a middle-aged woman and two boys in their teens, the boys immediately relieving him of his burdens.

"Careful, lads," he said. "Precious cargo there."

The woman, a sturdy no-nonsense type who drove the horses with confidence and thick-fingered hands, introduced herself as Gregoriana, a servant of John's. She peered at Luke with dark eyes and said sternly, "So you know what that means."

"I'm not sure that I do," he said, smiling. "Does that make you a Daughter of Thunder?" Jesus Himself had called John and his brother James the Sons of Thunder because of their tempestuous tempers. Luke had found that John must have mellowed with age, though the old flames could be rekindled with just the right offense to his senses.

"I don't know about thunder," Gregoriana said. "But what it means to be a servant of Elder John is that I tend to the private residence of the mother of our Lord."

"Whom I am here to see."

"The entire church is well aware of that, Doctor. And you will enjoy a warm welcome, though John has instructed that your time not be presumed upon, as you are here for important work."

"That I am, and I appreciate it."

"In the elder's absence, sir, Mary's welfare is my responsibility."

"I assure you I will extend her every courtesy."

Gregoriana guided the horses through the crowded harbor traffic and onto the thoroughfare that led to the church. The boys in back held tight to Luke's crates, keeping them steady as the wagon jostled slowly along.

"In truth, sir, it is I who will ensure that you extend her every courtesy."

"I am at your disposal, ma'am. You tell me what her availability and limitations are."

"It happens that she is an early riser and a light eater, though I warn you she loves to lavish food on her guests."

"I am a careful eater myself," Luke said.

"Then go lightly at meals," she said, "as Mary will expect us to provide treats all the time you are with her."

"Is it best to see her in the mornings, then, or—?"

"That is the only time, sir. Unless you wish to come also very late, after dark, sometimes even in the midnight hours."

"Truly?"

The woman nodded. "She is at her best at dawn, after breakfast. But by midday she is ready for a nap, which sometimes lasts all afternoon. She rouses for a light evening meal then tries to retire early. But for the last year or so she has awakened in the middle of the evening and then likes to sit by the fire until falling asleep again, often hours later. Actually I shouldn't say she likes sitting up. No doubt she would prefer to sleep through the night. But she is not well, you know."

"Has any specific ailment been diagnosed?"

Gregoriana shook her head. "She is in her seventies, sir. I believe she is tired and worn-out and looks forward to the end. She has outlived her relatives and friends by many years and rarely even gets to the Sunday meetings. When she does, John prohibits the faithful from pressing her for attention. But as you can imagine, she is much beloved, and people so want to greet her and extend their best wishes. Daily she receives visitors mid-morning, and many bring gifts and food. John has announced that none are to visit her during your presence here, as you have much to accomplish."

"I appreciate that. And might he return before I leave in two weeks?"

Gregoriana shook her head. "My understanding is that he will be abroad for six weeks. He has visiting teachers lined up for some of those Sundays, and some of his own staff here for the others. He would like you to at least bring a greeting the day after tomorrow."

"Honored," Luke said. "Nonetheless, my top priority is interviewing Mary. Tell me, how lucid is she, and do you sense any misgivings on her part about the endeavor?"

Gregoriana, who had barely showed her teeth all this time, threw her head back and laughed loud. "Misgivings? Oh, Dr. Luke, we have not seen her with such energy for years! She has gathered materials and often regales us with stories she plans to tell you. You may not have to even ask questions."

"Might I be able to see her even today?"

"That is her hope," Gregoriana said, "but I'm afraid she failed in her resolve to stay awake, despite her excitement. She dozed just after a light repast late this morning, and we're all hoping she will remain asleep for the afternoon, as she was up late again last night. She asked that we wake her upon your arrival, but I hope you agree with us that we should decline."

"I would not want to counter the mother of Jesus," Luke said, smiling, "but I will trust your judgment."

"She will forgive us, sir. She knows we love her and put her health and strength ahead of all other considerations."

GREGORIANA PULLED INTO the main gate that led to a sprawling church compound, and servants seemed to come from every direction. Two young men helped the boys on the wagon take Luke's belongings to a tiny guest cottage within a short walk from Mary's residence. Luke had not known what to expect, but her place was only slightly larger and just as modest.

"I know what you're thinking," Gregoriana said as she led Luke into a welcoming parlor, where he would have his feet washed, be offered water, and await the official greeting of the elders. "There are those among us who would have prepared accommodations for her like those of royalty, but she refuses to be revered. You will find her refreshingly, disarmingly plain."

Gregoriana delivered Luke to the parlor and informed him that someone would help get him settled, then she would fetch him when Mary was awake and open to his visit. "It will probably be time for a light meal," she said.

"So I am to go easy on the food until then?" he said.

"Suit yourself," Gregoriana said, and she was gone.

Half a dozen eager elders welcomed Luke and supervised the hospitality. One said, "We promised John we would not impose upon your time, sir, but we did not expect that you would arrive when Mary was napping. Do you very much mind telling us of your project?"

As servants washed and dried his feet and gave him to drink, Luke enjoyed trading stories with the men. There was hardly an account he had heard that was not common among them, but they had heard them from different sources and enjoyed sharing the various perspectives. He told them his plan, to be meticulous and orderly and chronological, to use his knowledge of medicine, to emphasize Jesus' humanity and compassion, and to write primarily to the Greek mind.

One escorted him to the guest chambers and helped him uncrate his clothes and supplies. "There's hardly room to set up this desk here," the elder said.

"I was hoping I might use it while talking with Mary," he said.

"There *is* more room there. Let me consult with Gregoriana to see if you might leave it set up there during your stay."

"That would be wonderful. I get the sense that she guards the gate there, if you follow my meaning."

The elder smiled as he left. "You have assessed that accurately, Doctor."

A few minutes later he returned. "Gregoriana says setting up your desk in the visitors' parlor will be fine. You will get good sunlight much of the morning, and the room can be torch-lit and candlelit late in the evening." The elder took the desk to set it up in Mary's cottage.

Luke spent the next couple of hours poring over his various scrolls, and snacking from time to time on a bowl of figs, dates, and olives. Over the years he had interviewed dozens of eyewitnesses of Jesus, including shepherds in the Judean hills, elderly people who claimed they had been healed by Jesus, even many Romans who had looked on with skepticism and some who had come to believe in Him.

Luke had also exhaustively studied the history of Israel, so he knew which officials and leaders had been in charge during each phase of Jesus' life, from His birth to His death, burial, resurrection, and ascension. That would serve to add weight, he thought, to his narrative, but he was most interested in what he could learn from the most important woman in Jesus' life. Much of his time with Mary would be spent getting her perspective on stories he had heard from other sources, and he wanted to concentrate largely on the personal account only she could provide.

That it seemed she was eager to cooperate thrilled him. He didn't know what he would have done or how he would have proceeded if she had been resistant or refused to see him or, worse, was unable to communicate at such an advanced age.

Luke only hoped he could keep his excitement and reverence for her at bay so he could accomplish his work. He looked forward to the day when all the digging was over and he could settle somewhere and begin to pen his actual gospel account. Others were planning or already doing the same, he knew, but he trusted that the Lord had urged him to do this because of the unique direction his would take. While he did not have the advantage of being an eyewitness and knowing Jesus personally, his goal was to overcome that by constructing the most complete record possible, from the foretelling of Jesus by John the Baptist to the present.

As Luke was gazing out the window at the setting sun, his heart leapt as Gregoriana approached from next door.

"She is up and alert," the woman reported, "and only a little peeved with me for letting her sleep. Bring your writing materials."

TWENTY-SEVEN

Tiny, with clear eyes and a kind, close-mouthed smile, Mary stood under the arched doorway to her home. "Thank you, Gregoriana," she said, as the woman slipped inside.

Luke quickly set down his papyrus and writing instruments as Mary shyly reached for him. Her hands proved soft and supple as she clasped his hand and pulled him close. "Let these old eyes get a look at you, Dr. Luke. Welcome, welcome."

Luke could barely find his voice. "I'm deeply honored to have this privilege," he said finally.

"The honor is mine," she said, leading him in. "Are your accommodations adequate?"

"Perfect, thank you."

"And are you hungry?"

"If I wasn't, the aroma would make me so."

"You recognize it?"

"I couldn't name it specifically, but certainly fish."

"Local and fresh," she said, leading him to the table where Gregoriana and two others were delivering dishes and cups. "It seemed only appropriate to our conversation."

As Mary settled at the table, Gregoriana whispered to Luke, "She may need help rising."

Mary asked Luke to give thanks for the food, and while they conversed during the meal, he steered her away from anything that would have required he take notes. He didn't want to miss recording anything important.

As the sun set, he studied her in the candlelight and was struck at her crisp and strong voice, despite a face deeply lined by the years. When she led him into the parlor, where a wood stool had been set before his desk and her own scrolls had been placed next to a reclining bench, Luke felt as if he could burst at the possibilities before him.

And thus began a two-week adventure of daily visits, the first just after breakfast, and the second in time for an evening meal and a chat until Mary was clearly ready to doze. They took Sundays off, and on those days Luke was warmly welcomed by the body of believers.

Every moment with Mary, Luke scribbled as fast as his quill and ink would scratch over the papyrus. As Gregoriana had predicted, he barely had to ask questions except to direct the conversation where he thought it needed to go.

Once settled that first day, Luke felt Mary watching him spread his papyrus and dip his quill. She asked where he wanted to start, and he said, "From the beginning."

"I was hoping you'd say that," she said. "I must tell you, however, that I would rather not talk about myself and my upbringing, except to say that ours was a devout and godly family. The most wonderful gift in my young life, before we get to what you are here to discuss, of course, was my family's choice of my husband. Joseph would have been my choice too, had the decision been mine alone to make. My father sensed this, of course, and so I was deeply grateful to be betrothed to such a fine man."

It was obvious that Mary, as John had informed Luke, had told this story countless times before, but it was also clear that she had never been asked to dredge up so many details. "You must forgive me for interrupting so often," Luke said, "but I want every fact and detail you can remember."

"I don't mind at all, Doctor. I love to be reminded and am glad that you seem a careful scholar and historian."

"Well, it's just that many have taken in hand to set in order a narrative of these things, just as those who from the beginning were eyewitnesses and ministers of the word delivered accounts to us, and it seems good to me also to try to gain a perfect understanding of all things from the very first so I can write an orderly account."

"Well said."

"I particularly want those who fall under the hearing of this to know the certainty of the things of the Lord in which they have been instructed. Now, what can you relate to me about the foretelling of Jesus by His cousin?"

"Oh, yes, his parents were, of course my aunt and uncle, Elizabeth and Zacharias, a priest of the division of Abijah."

"Now, see, that's exactly the kind of detail I'm looking for. And this was during the reign of Herod, the king of Judea . . ."

"Yes, and you might be interested to know that my aunt was of the daughters of Aaron. She and my uncle were both righteous before God, walking blameless in all the commandments and ordinances of the Lord. But though they prayed for a child, she was barren, and at the time of my engagement to Joseph, they were both quite old—at least for childbearing. Even the possibility of Elizabeth having a child never crossed my mind. I would be shocked to learn of her pregnancy."

"And she told you when?"

"Oh, she didn't have to tell me! Just as I did not have to tell her when I became with child. God told each of us of the other."

"All right, let me get this just the way it occurred."

Mary shifted in her seat and sighed. "As you know, I lived in Nazareth . . ."

"The city in Galilee."

"Yes, and the archangel Gabriel appeared to me."

"And you and Joseph were by this time betrothed but not married. And Joseph was of the house of David."

"Correct. Now, Luke, you can imagine how I felt—well, perhaps you cannot."

"Of course I cannot!" Luke said, chuckling. "That's why I'm here."

"I was especially privileged as a young girl to be a student of the Scriptures, and I was well aware that there had been no appearances of angels to men and women of the earth for centuries."

"Please, ma'am, I want everything, just as you remember it."

"Do you think I could have forgotten even one word? This is exactly what he said: 'Rejoice, highly favored one, the Lord is with you; blessed are you among women!'

"I could barely believe my eyes, and, of course, I was terrified and speechless. But Gabriel said, 'Do not be afraid, Mary, for you have found favor with God. And behold, you will conceive in your womb and bring forth a Son, and shall call His name Jesus. He will be great, and will be called the Son of the Highest; and the Lord God will give Him the throne of His father David. And He will reign over the house of Jacob forever, and of His kingdom there will be no end.'"

Luke held up a hand to make her pause, then wrote as fast as he could. "And how did you respond?"

"Well, naturally, I was a virgin, and so I said, 'How can this be, since I do not know a man?'

"And the angel said, 'The Holy Spirit will come upon you, and the power of the Highest will overshadow you; therefore, also, that Holy One who is to be born will be called the Son of God.' Then, if that were not enough to make me think this was all a dream, he added, 'Now indeed, Elizabeth your relative has also conceived a son in her old age; and this is now the sixth month for her who was called barren. For with God nothing will be impossible.'"

Luke finished writing and looked up. Mary's face shone with the memory. Luke shook his head. "You must have been absolutely mystified. I mean—"

"Well, what could I say? I said, 'Behold the maidservant of the Lord! Let it be to me according to your word.' And the angel departed. Imagine my surprise that my elderly aunt was with child. I went with haste into the hill country, to a city of Judah, and entered my aunt and uncle's house and greeted Elizabeth.

"Elizabeth immediately covered her stomach with her hand and told me she had been filled with the Holy Spirit. She said with a loud voice, 'Blessed are you among women, and blessed is the fruit of your womb! But why is this granted to me, that the mother of my Lord should come to me? For indeed, as soon as your greeting sounded in my ears, the babe leaped in my womb for joy. Blessed is she who believed, for there will be a fulfillment of those things which were told her from the Lord.'"

"So she knew."

Mary nodded. "And while I was there she told me of how her own pregnancy came to be. Zacharias was in the temple in the order of his division, according to custom, when his lot fell to burn incense before the Lord. A multitude was praying outside at the hour of incense, and while he was inside an angel of the Lord appeared to him."

"Did he say exactly where?"

"Elizabeth told me he said the angel stood on the right side of the altar, and when Zacharias saw him, he was terrified. But the angel said, 'Do not be afraid, Zacharias, for your prayer is heard; and your wife Elizabeth will bear you a son, and you shall call his name John. And you will have joy and gladness, and many will rejoice at his birth. For he will be great in the sight of the Lord, and shall drink neither wine nor strong drink. He will also be filled with the Holy Spirit, even from his mother's womb. And he will turn many of the children of Israel to the Lord their God. He will also go before Him in the spirit and power of Elijah, *"to turn the hearts of the fathers to the children,"* and the disobedient to the wisdom of the just, to make ready a people prepared for the Lord.'"

"Did he understand what the angel was telling him?"

"Well, he doubted whether it could be true, of course. He said to the angel, 'How shall I know this? For I am an old man, and my wife is well advanced in years.'

"And the angel said, 'I am Gabriel, who stands in the presence of God, and was sent to speak to you and bring you these glad tidings. Behold, you will be mute and not able to speak until the day these things take place, because you did not believe my words which will be fulfilled in their own time.'

"Luke, you can imagine the people waiting for Zacharias marveled that he lingered so long in the temple. But when he came out, he could not speak, and they perceived that he had seen a vision in the temple, for he beckoned to them and remained speechless.

"As soon as the days of his service were completed, he went home.

Now, after Elizabeth conceived, she hid herself five months, saying, 'Thus the Lord has dealt with me, in the days when He looked on me, to take away my reproach among people.'"

"Mary, how did you respond to Elizabeth after she pronounced her blessing on you?"

Mary smiled. "I shall never forget. I have prayed this prayer thousands of times since. I said, 'My soul magnifies the Lord, and my spirit has rejoiced in God my Savior. For He has regarded the lowly state of His maidservant; for behold, henceforth all generations will call me blessed. For He who is mighty has done great things for me, and holy is His name. And His mercy is on those who fear Him from generation to generation.

"'He has shown strength with His arm; He has scattered the proud in the imagination of their hearts. He has put down the mighty from their thrones, and exalted the lowly. He has filled the hungry with good things, and the rich He has sent away empty. He has helped His servant Israel, in remembrance of His mercy, as He spoke to our fathers, to Abraham and to his seed forever.'"

Luke pressed his lips together as he transcribed, desperate to keep his tears at bay. When he finished, he whispered, "May I read it back to you to make sure I have gotten it exactly as you told me?" And in the reading of it, he was overcome anew.

"You rendered it perfectly," Mary said.

She told him she had remained with Elizabeth about three months, until just before John was born, before returning to her own home. "Elizabeth told me that when her full time came for her to be delivered, she brought forth a son. When her neighbors and relatives heard how the Lord had shown great mercy to her, they rejoiced with her.

"So it was, on the eighth day, that they came to circumcise the child; and they would have called him by the name of his father, Zacharias. But Aunt Elizabeth said, 'No, he shall be called John.'

"But they said, 'There is no one among your relatives who is called by this name.' So they made signs to Zacharias—as he must have lost his hearing as well as his speech—asking what he would have the child called.

"And he asked for a writing tablet, and wrote, 'His name is John.' So they all marveled. Immediately his mouth was opened and his tongue loosed, and he spoke, praising God.

"Then fear came on all who dwelt around them, and all these sayings were discussed throughout all the hill country of Judea. And all those who heard them kept them in their hearts, saying, 'What kind of child will this be?' And the hand of the Lord was with John.

"Zacharias was filled with the Holy Spirit, and prophesied, 'Blessed is the Lord God of Israel, for He has visited and redeemed His people, and has raised up a horn of salvation for us in the house of His servant David, as He spoke by the mouth of His holy prophets, who have been since the world began, that we should be saved from our enemies and from the hand of all who hate us, to perform the mercy promised to our fathers and to remember His holy covenant, the oath which He swore to our father Abraham: To grant us that we, being delivered from the hand of our enemies, might serve Him without fear, in holiness and righteousness before Him all the days of our life.

"'And you, child, will be called the prophet of the Highest; for you will go before the face of the Lord to prepare His ways, to give knowledge of salvation to His people by the remission of their sins, through the tender mercy of our God, with which the Dayspring from on high has visited us; to give light to those who sit in darkness and the shadow of death, to guide our feet into the way of peace.'"

Luke was further amazed. "How do you remember all this?"

"Oh, Doctor, anyone would have. These are such glorious utterances. I could not forget them if I wanted to."

TWENTY-EIGHT

Day after day and hour after hour, Luke cherished his time with the mother of Jesus. As Gregoriana had predicted, Mary was most lucid in the morning and seemed to fade by the time for her midday meal. Luke found that food reinvigorated him but did not seem to have the same effect on her, and so he took his leave and allowed her to rest. Most nights she sent for him when she couldn't sleep, and while the going was a little slower after dark, he still gained valuable information and insights. Most impressive, she had, as John had told him, a scroll that contained her husband's genealogy that would make a nice addition to Luke's gospel.

One day Luke was surprised to be roused from a sound sleep before dawn, Gregoriana telling him, "She's already up and has eaten and is eager to get to work. I brought you some warm bread, and you still have some fruit, correct?"

Luke thanked Gregoriana and asked her to tell Mary he would be there momentarily. He wolfed down the food, then trotted to a nearby stream where he plunged into the icy water, partly to cleanse himself but mostly to shock himself fully awake. It worked, and he showed up next door refreshed and dressed in clean garments.

"You said you wanted everything I could remember about the birth," she said, "and I awoke in the dark, my mind filled with the images."

"Yes, thank you. Start with why you were in Bethlehem."

"Well, a decree went out from Caesar Augustus that all the world should be registered, so we had to go to Bethlehem, the city of David, because of Joseph's lineage."

Luke's research had told him that this census took place while Quirinius was governor of Syria, but he chose not to interrupt Mary to determine whether she remembered that.

"So all went to be registered, everyone to his own city?"

She nodded. "It was a very difficult trip because I was nine months into the pregnancy. Joseph offered to let me stay behind, but I did not want to be apart from him when I was so close to delivering the baby. When we arrived, my time had come, but we could not find a room anywhere, not even in the inn. Joseph was frantic—and so was I, of course—but he found shelter in an animal pen, and when Jesus was born, we wrapped Him in swaddling cloths and laid Him in a manger.

"Now, I don't normally speak of such personal things, but it should come as no surprise to you as a physician that I was terribly sore and exhausted. Joseph was tending to the baby and I was trying to doze when suddenly we were visited by a band of shepherds. At first I could not fathom how they found us, but they told us they had been nearby in the fields, keeping watch over their flocks, when an angel of the Lord stood before them, and the glory of the Lord shone around them, and they were greatly afraid."

"Just as you had been."

"Of course. Then the angel said, 'Do not be afraid, for behold, I bring you good tidings of great joy which will be to all people. For there is born to you this day in the city of David a Savior, who is Christ the Lord. And this will be the sign to you: You will find a Babe wrapped in swaddling cloths, lying in a manger.'

"They said that then, suddenly, there was with the angel a multitude of the heavenly host praising God and saying, 'Glory to God in the highest, and on earth peace, goodwill toward men!'

"So when the angels had gone away from them into heaven, the shepherds told us that they said to one another, 'Let us now go to Bethlehem and see this thing that has come to pass, which the Lord has made known to us.' Oh, Luke, you should have seen the looks on their faces as they gazed at Jesus! It was plain they couldn't wait to tell everyone what had been told them concerning Him."

"I have talked with many in Judea who first heard of the Christ child from those shepherds," Luke said.

"Indeed?"

"And all those who heard it marveled at those things that were told them by the shepherds."

"None marveled as much as I, Doctor. I remembered all the details and have pondered them in my heart ever since."

"Does it ever leave your mind?"

"Not for long. I think of that night every day. Of course, there are other memories from Jesus' life I wish I could forget. But I remember every moment."

"We will have to revisit those too, I'm afraid."

"I know," she said. "But there is still much more to tell before the dark days arose. When Jesus was eight days old, we had Him circumcised and officially gave Him the name that the angel had told me before He was even conceived in the womb.

"And when the days of my purification—according to the law of

Moses—were completed, we took Him to Jerusalem to present Him to the Lord and to offer the required sacrifice.

"A man in Jerusalem named Simeon, who was just and devout, told us later he had been waiting for the Consolation of Israel and that it had been revealed to him by the Holy Spirit that he would not see death before he had seen the Lord's Christ. So the Spirit led him into the temple, and when we brought in the Child, to do for Him according to the custom of the law, Simeon took Him up in his arms and blessed God and said, 'Lord, now You are letting Your servant depart in peace, according to Your word; for my eyes have seen Your salvation which You have prepared before the face of all peoples, a light to bring revelation to the Gentiles, and the glory of Your people Israel.'

"As you can imagine, Luke, Joseph and I marveled at those things that were spoken of Jesus. Simeon blessed us and said to me, 'Behold, this Child is destined for the fall and rising of many in Israel, and for a sign which will be spoken against, that the thoughts of many hearts may be revealed.'"

"What did he mean about the sign?"

"He whispered to me, 'A sword will pierce through your own soul also.' Believe me, I eventually learned what that meant. But for now, if you don't mind, I prefer to dwell on the times of blessing.

"Anna, a prophetess, the daughter of Phanuel, of the tribe of Asher, was a widow of about eighty-four who did not depart from the temple, but served God with fastings and prayers night and day. And when she saw Jesus, she gave thanks to the Lord, and spoke of Him to all those who looked for redemption in Jerusalem.

"Once we had performed all things according to the law of the Lord, we returned to Nazareth." Mary lowered her head and gazed at the floor, a faraway look in her eyes. She struggled to stand, and Luke immediately left his stool to help her.

"I just want to see the sunrise," she said, her voice flat, as if she were somewhere else. Luke strained to hear her soft voice as she continued in a monotone with her back to him. "Jesus grew and became strong in spirit, filled with wisdom, and the grace of God was upon Him."

She fell silent and Luke waited, understanding that she had something on her mind and that he should not trouble her. She stood staring at the horizon until the sun appeared, then made her way back to her bench, where she reclined quietly for a time.

"Tell me a story from his childhood," Luke said.

"Hmm . . ." she said, pressing her fingers to her temples. "Well, we went to Jerusalem every year at Passover. When Jesus was twelve, we went, according to the custom of the feast. At the end of it we joined our caravan of relatives and acquaintances to journey back, not realizing that Jesus lingered behind. He had become quite independent by that time, and we never worried about Him. We supposed Him to be in the company for the entire first day's journey, and soon I realized I had not seen Him all day. I sought Him among our party.

"Naturally I was alarmed when we didn't find Him, so we made haste to return to Jerusalem. I worried myself sick for three days before we found Him in the temple, sitting in the midst of the teachers, both listening to them and asking them questions. I wanted to run to Him and scold Him and embrace Him, but I was as spellbound as the others. All who heard Him were astonished at His understanding and answers.

"Finally I interrupted and said, 'Son, why have You done this to us? Look, Your father and I have sought You anxiously.'"

Shaking her head, she said, "He asked why we had sought Him! He said, 'Did you not know that I must be about My Father's business?' Twelve years old, and he says this after having been apart from us four days!"

"Did you understand what He meant?"

"I confess we did not. Not then. Of course we then took Him home with us to Nazareth, and He was His usual obedient self. But again, I kept all these things in my heart. And Jesus increased in wisdom and stature, and in favor with God and men."

LUKE FEARED he had taxed Mary too much when she asked for a day free of talking. But when he finally returned to his desk in her home and she to her reclining bench, she was ready to pick up the story again.

"As was the custom in Nazareth, Jesus learned his father's trade and became a carpenter. He and Joseph worked closely together until His father's health began to fail. And just when Joseph could no longer take up his tools and it would have been natural for Jesus to take over the business, it became clear that He was to leave us. We had sensed this day was coming, for the Lord had foretold that He was destined for great things."

"He was how old now?"

"About thirty."

Luke nodded. His previous research had indicated that Jesus had begun His public ministry during the fifteenth year of the reign of Tiberius Caesar, when Pontius Pilate was the Roman governor of Judea, Herod Antipas being tetrarch of Galilee, his brother Philip tetrarch of Iturea and the region of Trachonitis, and Lysanias tetrarch of Abilene, while Annas and Caiaphas were high priests.

"This was when the word of God came to Jesus' cousin John in the wilderness. He went into all the region around the Jordan, preaching a baptism of repentance for the remission of sins, as was written in the words of Isaiah the prophet:

The voice of one crying in the wilderness:
"Prepare the way of the Lord:
Make His paths straight.
Every valley shall be filled
And every mountain and hill brought low;
The crooked places shall be made straight
And the rough ways smooth;
And all flesh shall see the salvation of God."

"I have talked to people who heard him preaching," Luke said. "Were you aware of what he was saying?"

"Oh, yes, word came to us that people were flocking to him to be baptized, but he did not soften his words. He called them a brood of vipers and asked who had warned them to flee the wrath to come."

Luke checked his scrolled notes. "Yes, some recall he demanded that they 'bear fruits worthy of repentance, and do not begin to say to yourselves, "We have Abraham as our father." For I say to you that God is able to raise up children to Abraham from these stones. And even now the ax is laid to the root of the trees. Therefore every tree which does not bear good fruit is cut down and thrown into the fire.'"

Mary smiled. "People asked him what should they then do, and he told them, 'He who has two tunics, let him give to him who has none; and he who has food, let him do likewise.' He told tax collectors to collect no more than what was appointed for them. He told soldiers to not intimidate anyone or accuse falsely, and to be content with their wages. People had never heard anything like this, and some thought *he* was the Christ. But he said, 'I indeed baptize you with water; but One mightier than I is coming, whose sandal strap I am not worthy to loose. He will baptize you with the Holy Spirit and fire. His winnowing fan is in His hand, and He will thoroughly clean out His threshing floor, and gather the wheat into His barn; but the chaff He will burn with unquenchable fire."

"I suppose it's no wonder," Luke said soberly, "that he came to a violent end."

Mary shook her head. "You must get more about John from other sources. All I know is that with many other exhortations he preached to the people, and rebuked Herod concerning his immorality with his brother's wife, not to mention all the other evils Herod had done. Eventually, of course, Herod threw John in prison."

Mary looked weary enough that Luke decided to wait another day before asking her to pick up the story. He had plenty of material on John the Baptizer—including when he baptized Jesus—and wanted to get to her memories of her Son's ministry.

TWENTY-NINE

Near the end of Luke's time with Mary, he began having trouble drawing her out about Jesus' last few years on earth.

"You must understand, Doctor," she said. "I was not witness to much of it. When He first left home, my time was taken tending to Joseph, who was not to linger long. There was a time after he had passed when I knew Jesus was in Capernaum and rumors were flying. I took His brothers and ventured out to find Him, partly to see what was really going on, but mostly to help if I could. But the crowd was so great, I could not even get near Him.

"I tell you, my pride in Him—a righteous one in hearing Him expound on God's kingdom—was offset by dread fear of the opposition."

"How did that manifest itself?"

"Well, soon He was hounded by Jewish leaders. If his cousin John had been forthright in his criticism of the king, Jesus criticized His own people's religious leaders and called them names. Worse, in their eyes, He claimed authority as God's Son, and He often did this in their own temples. Joseph and I had always known that great sorrow would come to us over His fate, but that didn't make it any easier for me when the time drew near."

"Did He know you had come to try to see Him?"

"Yes. We got word that someone had told Him His mother and brothers were outside and that He had responded that His mother and brothers were 'these who hear the word of God and do it.'"

"Oh, my! Did that offend you? Hurt you?"

"No, no. What hurt was realizing that He no longer belonged to me. I had known it down deep, of course, but that sealed it. I was one who heard the word of God and did it, so I know He wasn't excluding me. He belonged to the world now, and every believing soul had become His family. That is all He was saying."

"Did you ever get any time with Him? My records show that He visited Nazareth."

Mary furrowed her brow. "Yes," she said, pausing as if to let the memory fully return. "This was early in His ministry, and He spent an afternoon with me. How I cherished it. I merely let Him talk."

"And what did He say?"

"He asked my memories of his aunt and uncle and mentioned how instructive it was that Zacharias, though a priest, had still been found wanting for faith when the Lord had visited him. And that while he was punished for lack of it, God also used him."

"Did He tell you of any of His miracles or parables?"

"No, but of course I had heard about them all. The word spread throughout all Israel about Him. I worried after Him because He looked so thin and weak, and I asked whether He or the men he surrounded Himself with were taking care of Him.

"He told me He was still suffering the effects of a forty-day fast in the wilderness, where the Spirit had led Him so Satan could tempt Him. When He recounted that awful experience, it was as if my heart turned cold within me."

"Tell me about it."

"It had occurred some time even before I had tried to see Him in Capernaum. He said He had returned from the Jordan after being baptized by John when He was led alone into the wilderness and ate nothing for forty days. And when they had ended, naturally He was hungry. And the devil said to Him, 'If You are the Son of God, command this stone to become bread.'

"But Jesus answered, 'It is written, "*Man shall not live by bread alone, but by every word of God.*"'

"Then the devil, taking Him up on a high mountain, showed Him all the kingdoms of the world in a moment of time. And the devil said to Him, 'All this authority I will give You, and their glory; for this has been delivered to me, and I give it to whomever I wish. Therefore, if You will worship before me, all will be Yours.'

"And Jesus answered him, 'Get behind Me, Satan! For it is written, "*You shall worship the Lord your God, and Him only you shall serve.*"'

"Then Satan brought Him to Jerusalem, set Him on the pinnacle of the temple, and said, 'If You are the Son of God, throw Yourself down from here. For it is written:

He shall give His angels charge over you,
To keep you,

and,

In their hands they shall bear you up,
Lest you dash your foot against a stone.

"And Jesus said, 'It has been said, "*You shall not tempt the Lord your God.*"'

"Now, when the devil had ended every temptation, he departed from Him until an opportune time. Then Jesus returned in the power of the Spirit to Galilee, and news of Him went out through all the surrounding region. And He taught in their synagogues, being glorified by all.

"So He came to Nazareth, and as we talked, I asked if, as had become His custom, He would go into the synagogue on the Sabbath day and stand up to read. Well, of course He said yes, and so this was another of the few times I was able to see Him out among the people.

"In the temple He was handed the book of the prophet Isaiah. And when He had opened the book, He found the place where it was written:

The Spirit of the Lord is upon Me,
Because He has anointed Me
To preach the gospel to the poor;
He has sent Me to heal the brokenhearted,
To proclaim liberty to the captives
And recovery of sight to the blind,
To set at liberty those who are oppressed;
To proclaim the acceptable year of the Lord.

"Then He closed the book, and gave it back to the attendant and sat down. And the eyes of all who were in the synagogue were fixed on Him. And He began to say to them, 'Today this Scripture is fulfilled in your hearing.'

"So all bore witness to Him, and marveled at the gracious words that proceeded out of His mouth. And they said, 'Is this not Joseph's son?'

"He said, 'You will surely say this proverb to Me, "Physician, heal yourself! Whatever we have heard done in Capernaum, do also here in Your country." Assuredly, I say to you, no prophet is accepted in his own country. But I tell you truly, many widows were in Israel in the days of Elijah, when the heaven was shut up three years and six months, and there was a great famine throughout all the land; but to none of them was Elijah sent except to Zarephath, in the region of Sidon, to a woman who was a widow. And many lepers were in Israel in the time of Elisha the prophet, and none of them was cleansed except Naaman the Syrian.' "

"That could not have made them happy," Luke said.

"It certainly didn't. All those in the synagogue were filled with wrath, and rose up and thrust Him out of the city. They led Him to the brow of the hill on which our city was built, and I know they meant to throw Him over the cliff. I was so frightened, believing I had seen the last of Him, but He merely passed through the midst of them and went His way.

"From there I heard He went to Capernaum, where He again taught on the Sabbaths. And they were astonished at His teaching, for His word was with authority.

"Now, unfortunately, Dr. Luke, I was unable to follow Him until the very end, when He was despised."

Luke nodded. "I have countless reports of His travels and preaching and teaching and acts. But let me ask you, were you kept informed during this time?"

"I certainly was. I listened to every account and prayed constantly for Him."

"Some whom I've interviewed expressed surprise over how generously He treated women. To many men, women are considered little more than property."

"This is true," she said, "but to my knowledge He never favored men over women. In fact, I became aware of many women He revered and treated with great respect. He went through every city and village, preaching and bringing the glad tidings of the kingdom of God. And His twelve disciples were with Him, but also certain women who had been healed of evil spirits and infirmities—Mary called Magdalene, out of whom had come seven demons, and Joanna the wife of Chuza, Herod's steward, and Susanna, and many others who provided for Him from their substance.

"But, Luke, there were more than these, as well. No doubt in your research you have run across the names of Mary and Martha, the widow of Nain whose son He raised from the dead, Peter's mother-in-law, the woman whom He healed when she merely touched the hem of His garment, and many, many others. He taught that the kingdom of God was open to all, to women as equally as men, and many believed."

DURING LUKE'S LAST DAY with Mary, she told him she was going to eschew her customary afternoon nap or at least delay it until he was satisfied that they were finished.

"I do not want to weary you," he said, "but I do have two more questions if we may repair to the parlor."

He helped her up and walked her in to her reclining bench before taking his place at his desk.

"I know you have said that you were an eyewitness to little of Jesus' ministry, yet you seem to have heard an account of all His activities. What stands out to you as epitomizing His message to the world? Was there one act or one parable or one teaching that sums it all up in your mind?"

"Interesting you should ask, because I have always felt that the stories He used to explain the kingdom were most telling. I recall hearing someone tell of when He passed through Jericho. After He had called out the rich chief tax collector Zacchaeus— You know this story?"

"Yes, the man who was too short to see above the crowd and had to climb a tree to see Jesus."

"Correct. And Jesus honored him by going to his house. But Jesus was criticized by the people, even though Zacchaeus came to salvation. Yet what struck me about this event, Luke, was what Jesus said in announcing what had happened. He said, 'Today salvation has come to this house, because he also is a son of Abraham; for the Son of Man has come to seek and to save that which was lost.' That was His mission, His purpose.

"And later He told three parables about finding lost things and comparing the kingdom of God to these. Do you have those stories?"

"Yes, of the lost sheep, the lost coin, and the lost son. I plan to include them."

"Good, because I believe He intentionally emphasized what was most important."

"And you must do the same, ma'am, if you are up to it."

She looked away and spoke faintly. "The end, you mean."

"Yes."

Mary hung her head and rubbed her eyes. "No mother should ever have to endure that." And she told him all she remembered of seeing her Son put to death. Luke added this to all the accounts he had amassed, then rolled his scrolls, put away his quills and ink, and folded his desk.

He approached Mary and helped her stand. She embraced him and thanked him.

"I wasn't certain you would be grateful to be reminded of it all," he said.

"Make no mistake, Luke, it takes nothing to remind me of every bit of it. It is constantly with me. But so is my hope. You see, I know He arose, and I know He is my Savior too and that I will again see Him. I am most blessed to have been chosen of God to be used as a vessel to bring into the world His only Son, Immanuel, who saved His people from their sins."

THIRTY

Luke spent many days journeying on land and at sea, stopping in Antioch before heading back to Caesarea to rejoin Paul. While home for only a brief time, Luke invested many hours with Theophilus, who brought him up to date on what was happening in the Antiochian church. Mostly, however, they discussed Luke's gospel and how it was shaping up.

"My plan, sir, is to write it to you in the form of a letter," Luke said one afternoon as they sat in a small room behind the meeting place. "I don't know where I will be when I have completed it, but my goal is to be sure that Paul is content with it, and then I will have it copied before sending you the original."

"I will be honored to read it to the brothers and sisters here, and we will set about straightaway to have it copied many times for distribution to as many churches as possible all around the world. I shall be happy to cover the expense of this myself."

"You are too kind, master."

"I am no longer your master, Luke. But I am proud to have once been, and deeply grateful for your introducing me to faith in our Lord Christ."

A young deacon appeared at the door. "Sorry to interrupt, sirs," he said, a sealed scroll in his hand.

Theophilus waved him in. "What is it, son?"

"News from John for Dr. Luke, sir," the man said, leaving the scroll and departing.

Luke rose and stepped to where Theophilus could look on as he broke the seal and rolled back the papyrus,

> John, an apostle of Christ, to most excellent Luke and the elders of the church at Syrian Antioch:
>
> It is with great heaviness of heart that I have cut short my travels and am on my way back to Ephesus, as word has come to me of the passing of the mother of our Lord and Savior. Gregoriana reports that the blessed lady died quietly in her sleep during the afternoon a fortnight ago. News had also reached me of her great pleasure in meeting and working with you on your account, Luke, which makes me all the more eager to see the results.
>
> Pray for us as we honor this saint whom God chose as a vessel for His great gift. We shall grieve her and miss her terribly, yet we also rejoice in her blessed hope, which we share. Our eulogizing her will also be a celebration of her stellar life and all she has meant to the Ephesian church and to believing brothers and sisters everywhere.
>
> I understand that you are on your way back to our brother Paul, but if emissaries are available to be sent from Antioch for the funeral, be assured we will welcome them with all hospitality.
>
> And do greet Paul for me in the matchless name of our Re-

deemer and assure him of the prayers of all the saints aware of his dangerous plight.

Now blessed be the God and Father of our Lord Jesus Christ, who according to His abundant mercy has begotten us again to a living hope through the resurrection of Jesus Christ from the dead, to an inheritance incorruptible and undefiled and that does not fade away, reserved in heaven for you, who are kept by the power of God through faith for salvation ready to be revealed in the last time.

Greet one another with a kiss of love. Peace to you all who are in Christ Jesus. Amen.

Theophilus told Luke he would take two other elders and leave with dispatch for Ephesus to represent the church of Antioch at Mary's memorial.

"Greet all for me with much warmth, Theophilus," Luke said through tears. "They were most hospitable."

Luke slumped, suddenly aware of what a melancholy journey still lay ahead for him. Theophilus embraced him.

"What an unspeakable privilege," Luke managed, "to have had so much uninterrupted time with her before the end."

SEVERAL DAYS LATER, when Luke disembarked in Israel and made his way to Caesarea, he was stunned to find that Paul was already on his way to Rome. Luke was desperate that Paul not be alone during this trial, for despite the man's zeal, he was often in need of encouragement and companionship. He had redeemed the time while in protective custody in Judea by writing many letters to the churches he had started or encouraged over the years, but what would become of him in the capital of the empire?

Luke immediately booked passage on a ship bound for Rome, carefully protecting his precious documents and praying the entire time that nothing bad would come to Paul. The journey covered more than fourteen hundred miles, yet Luke was stunned to finally arrive in Rome unable to find where the government had incarcerated his friend.

For two days he searched and pleaded with any official he could find, finally learning that the ship bearing Paul and many other prisoners had wrecked off an island in the Mediterranean, and it had not yet been determined whether any had survived.

Luke sent word to all the churches to pray for Paul, and only working on his gospel account kept Luke from going mad with dread over the great missionary's fate. While he began his missive, as he had told Theophilus, as a letter to his former master, all the while he was writing he anticipated the thrill of reading it first to Paul.

The apologist for the faith would be the last person in the world to hesitate to criticize the work or its writer if he felt such was due. Luke did not look forward to that part of it—the wrangling over wording, turns of phrases, ideas, and doctrines with one of the most brilliant minds he had ever encountered. Yet the very prospect of it kept alive his hopes for Paul's welfare.

Oh, the man would wear him out if they disagreed, and Luke had to smile, imagining trying to hold his own for the sake of his work.

Joy overcame Luke just a short way into the final version when the area around the harbor came to life with rumors that a ship was arriving bearing survivors of a shipwreck off Malta. Luke raced to the shore, hoping to catch a glimpse of Paul. He would, like all the rest, be herded onto land and to the garrisons to be processed, but if Luke could only know the man had survived, he would be reinvigorated for his work.

It was just past noon when the Roman ship finally docked, and it took more than an hour to board soldiers who would help offload the assorted criminals and those—like Paul—who had been sent to Rome for trial.

It did not surprise Luke to find that Paul was the last to be escorted off the ship, personally guarded by a commander named Julius. Luke wanted to jump and cheer and praise God, but he forced himself to remain just one among the crowd. When Paul espied him, he slowed and the commander hesitated with him.

"I knew if any would be here for me, Luke," Paul said, "it would be you."

The commander informed Luke where Paul would be held and when he could see him, and Luke ran all the way back to his own quarters, eagerly getting his scrolls together so he could begin reading to his old friend.

Over the next two years, as Paul was allowed to rent his own chambers and enjoy occasional visits while the authorities tried to determine his disposition, Luke spent much time with him. They prayed and sang, and while Luke sought to encourage the man, he himself was emboldened just listening to Paul. While he was lonely and, naturally, worried over his own fate, still Paul wrote letters to the churches and shared these with Luke.

It warmed the doctor to see that Paul often told other believers that "only Luke is with me," and referred to him as "the beloved physician."

To Luke's great delight, Paul seemed to have no issues with his account of the history of Jesus. He urged Luke to keep on with it and begged him to bring him more and more of it. "It is as if the Holy Spirit Himself is giving you utterance through your pen," Paul said, making Luke all the more eager to stay at the task. Paul was most excited about Theophilus's generous offer to read the manuscript to the church at Antioch and to supervise its copying and distribution around the world.

"You know there is more for you to do, don't you, Luke, when this is finished?"

"More?"

"Much more. The story does not end with Jesus' ascension into heaven. Far from it. The beginning of the movement, the very founding of the church, the bravery of the disciples, the preaching of Peter—indeed, all the acts of the apostles—must be documented and recorded. How this will thrill the believers!"

"The Acts of the Apostles," Luke said. "I know much of the story already."

"And Peter and I can tell you the rest. I came along in the middle of it, of course, but when he arrives here, Peter will be a great source of information and inspiration for you."

"When he arrives?"

Paul smiled and showed Luke a scroll from Peter, announcing his intention to join them.

Luke was already full of anticipation. "I had wondered what I would do when my letter to Theophilus was complete. I would write this to him as well, telling him that after covering all that Jesus began both to do and teach until the day in which He was taken up, I would now tell of what He had commanded through the Holy Spirit to his chosen apostles, to whom He also presented Himself alive after His suffering by many infallible proofs, being seen by them during forty days and speaking of the things pertaining to the kingdom of God."

"Yes!" Paul said. "And Peter can tell you, as he has me, that being assembled together with them, Jesus commanded the disciples not to depart from Jerusalem, but to wait for the Promise of the Father, 'which,' He said, 'you have heard from Me; for John truly baptized with water, but you shall be baptized with the Holy Spirit not many days from now.'

"Then you can move right into His promise that they would receive power when the Holy Spirit had come upon them and that they would be witnesses to Him in Jerusalem, and in all Judea and Samaria, and to the end of the earth. Isn't it thrilling that we are privileged to be fulfilling that prophecy?"

"I can't wait to get to it," Luke said. "But I must keep it in abeyance until my gospel is finished. I'm very nearly to the end."

"Go and finish it, then, Doctor, then make haste to return to me and let me hear it."

Two years into Paul's imprisonment in Rome, Luke arrived early one morning with a carefully wrapped original of his scroll and a meticulously made copy.

"I have plenty of time to get this aboard the courier ship," he told Paul, "but you wanted to see me first?"

"Yes, my friend. I want to hear the very last portion one more time, and then I want to pray over it. This is only the beginning. Once your good sponsor Theophilus has this in hand, he will get it copied, and those copies will be copied, and as these make their way to the churches all over the world, copies will be made of copies until anyone who wants to hear this account will be able to. Meanwhile, you will be hard at work on your and Peter's Acts of the Apostles, which I believe will be every bit as anticipated and welcomed—perhaps more so because of this." He held the new scroll in both hands, as if cherishing it.

"Now, read to me of when the resurrected Jesus suddenly appeared to the eleven and those who were with them in the upper room."

Luke carefully unrolled the copied scroll and found the place. And he read:

"Jesus Himself stood in the midst of them, and said to them, 'Peace to you.' But they were terrified and frightened, and supposed they had seen a spirit. And He said to them, 'Why are you troubled? And why do doubts arise in your hearts? Behold My hands and My feet, that it is I Myself. Handle Me and see, for a spirit does not have flesh and bones as you see I have.'

"When He had said this, He showed them His hands and His feet. But while they still did not believe for joy, and marveled, He said to them, 'Have you any food here?' So they gave Him a piece of a broiled fish and some honeycomb. And He took it and ate in their presence.

"Then He said to them, 'These are the words which I spoke to you while I was still with you, that all things must be fulfilled which were written in the Law of Moses and the Prophets and the Psalms concerning Me.' And He opened their understanding, that they might comprehend the Scriptures.

"Then He said to them, 'Thus it is written, and thus it was necessary for the Christ to suffer and to rise from the dead the third day, and that repentance and remission of sins should be preached in His name to all nations, beginning at Jerusalem. And you are witnesses of these things. Behold, I send the Promise of My Father upon you; but tarry in the city of Jerusalem until you are endued with power from on high.'

"And He led them out as far as Bethany, and He lifted up His hands and blessed them. Now it came to pass, while He blessed them, that He was parted from them and carried up into heaven. And they worshiped Him, and returned to Jerusalem with great joy, and were continually in the temple praising and blessing God. Amen."

Luke had become overcome with emotion as he read, and when he finished, he looked up to see Paul with hands clasped and tears in his eyes. "Amen and amen," Paul said. "Come, my brother. Let us pray." With his hands on Luke's shoulders, he lifted his face and said, "God of all creation, I come to you in the name of Jesus Christ, our Lord and Savior, offering you thanks for the gift of salvation. And thank you too for my dear friend and brother, whom You have chosen to record this account of Jesus and His miraculous visit to this earth and then His return to the portals of heaven.

"As this gospel is sent forth, protect it by Your grace, and may all who come under its hearing or read it for themselves be quickened to their core with the truth and majesty of its message of grace.

"And now may the God of peace who brought up our Lord Jesus from the dead, that great Shepherd of the sheep, through the blood of the everlasting covenant, make us complete in every good work to do His will, working in us what is well pleasing in His sight, through Jesus Christ, to whom be glory forever and ever. Amen."

THE GOSPEL OF LUKE

LUKE

Dedication to Theophilus

1 Inasmuch as many have taken in hand to set in order a narrative of those things which have been fulfilled[a] among us, [2]just as those who from the beginning were eyewitnesses and ministers of the word delivered them to us, [3]it seemed good to me also, having had perfect understanding of all things from the very first, to write to you an orderly account, most excellent Theophilus, [4]that you may know the certainty of those things in which you were instructed.

John's Birth Announced to Zacharias

[5]There was in the days of Herod, the king of Judea, a certain priest named Zacharias, of the division of Abijah. His wife *was* of the daughters of Aaron, and her name *was* Elizabeth. [6]And they were both righteous before God, walking in all the commandments and ordinances of the Lord blameless. [7]But they had no child, because Elizabeth was barren, and they were both well advanced in years.

[8]So it was, that while he was serving as priest before God in the order of his division, [9]according to the custom of the priesthood, his lot fell to burn incense when he went into the temple of the Lord. [10]And the whole multitude of the people was praying outside at the hour of incense. [11]Then an angel of the Lord appeared

---

1:1 [a]Or *are most surely believed*

to him, standing on the right side of the altar of incense. [12]And when Zacharias saw *him,* he was troubled, and fear fell upon him.

[13]But the angel said to him, "Do not be afraid, Zacharias, for your prayer is heard; and your wife Elizabeth will bear you a son, and you shall call his name John. [14]And you will have joy and gladness, and many will rejoice at his birth. [15]For he will be great in the sight of the Lord, and shall drink neither wine nor strong drink. He will also be filled with the Holy Spirit, even from his mother's womb. [16]And he will turn many of the children of Israel to the Lord their God. [17]He will also go before Him in the spirit and power of Elijah, '*to turn the hearts of the fathers to the children,*'[a] and the disobedient to the wisdom of the just, to make ready a people prepared for the Lord."

[18]And Zacharias said to the angel, "How shall I know this? For I am an old man, and my wife is well advanced in years."

[19]And the angel answered and said to him, "I am Gabriel, who stands in the presence of God, and was sent to speak to you and bring you these glad tidings. [20]But behold, you will be mute and not able to speak until the day these things take place, because you did not believe my words which will be fulfilled in their own time."

[21]And the people waited for Zacharias, and marveled that he lingered so long in the temple. [22]But when he came out, he could not speak to them; and they perceived that he had seen a vision in the temple, for he beckoned to them and remained speechless.

[23]So it was, as soon as the days of his service were completed, that he departed to his own house. [24]Now after those days his wife Elizabeth conceived; and she hid herself five months, saying, [25]"Thus the Lord has dealt with me, in the days when He looked on *me,* to take away my reproach among people."

Christ's Birth Announced to Mary

[26]Now in the sixth month the angel Gabriel was sent by God to a city of Galilee named Nazareth, [27]to

1:17 [a]Malachi 4:5, 6

a virgin betrothed to a man whose
name was Joseph, of the house of
David. The virgin's name *was* Mary.
28And having come in, the angel said
to her, "Rejoice, highly favored *one*,
the Lord *is* with you; blessed *are* you
among women!"[a]

29But when she saw *him*,[a] she was
troubled at his saying, and considered
what manner of greeting this was.
30Then the angel said to her, "Do not
be afraid, Mary, for you have found
favor with God. 31And behold, you
will conceive in your womb and
bring forth a Son, and shall call His
name JESUS. 32He will be great, and
will be called the Son of the Highest;
and the Lord God will give Him the
throne of His father David. 33And He
will reign over the house of Jacob forever, and of His kingdom there will
be no end."

34Then Mary said to the angel,
"How can this be, since I do not know
a man?"

35And the angel answered and said
to her, "*The* Holy Spirit will come
upon you, and the power of the Highest will overshadow you; therefore,
also, that Holy One who is to be born
will be called the Son of God. 36Now
indeed, Elizabeth your relative has
also conceived a son in her old age;
and this is now the sixth month for
her who was called barren. 37For with
God nothing will be impossible."

38Then Mary said, "Behold the
maidservant of the Lord! Let it be to
me according to your word." And
the angel departed from her.

Mary Visits Elizabeth

39Now Mary arose in those days
and went into the hill country with
haste, to a city of Judah, 40and entered the house of Zacharias and
greeted Elizabeth. 41And it happened,
when Elizabeth heard the greeting of
Mary, that the babe leaped in her
womb; and Elizabeth was filled with
the Holy Spirit. 42Then she spoke out
with a loud voice and said, "Blessed
are you among women, and blessed *is*
the fruit of your womb! 43But why *is*
this *granted* to me, that the mother of
my Lord should come to me? 44For
indeed, as soon as the voice of your
greeting sounded in my ears, the babe
leaped in my womb for joy. 45Blessed
is she who believed, for there will be

1:28 [a]NU-Text omits *blessed are you among women.* **1:29** [a]NU-Text omits *when she saw him.*

a fulfillment of those things which were told her from the Lord."

The Song of Mary

46And Mary said:

"My soul magnifies the Lord,
47 And my spirit has rejoiced in God my Savior.
48 For He has regarded the lowly state of His maidservant;
For behold, henceforth all generations will call me blessed.
49 For He who is mighty has done great things for me,
And holy *is* His name.
50 And His mercy *is* on those who fear Him
From generation to generation.
51 He has shown strength with His arm;
He has scattered *the* proud in the imagination of their hearts.
52 He has put down the mighty from *their* thrones,
And exalted *the* lowly.
53 He has filled *the* hungry with good things,
And *the* rich He has sent away empty.
54 He has helped His servant Israel,
In remembrance of *His* mercy,
55 As He spoke to our fathers,
To Abraham and to his seed forever."

56And Mary remained with her about three months, and returned to her house.

Birth of John the Baptist

57Now Elizabeth's full time came
for her to be delivered, and she brought
forth a son. 58When her neighbors
and relatives heard how the Lord had shown great mercy to her, they rejoiced with her.

Circumcision of John the Baptist

59So it was, on the eighth day, that
they came to circumcise the child;
and they would have called him by
the name of his father, Zacharias.
60His mother answered and said, "No;
he shall be called John."

61But they said to her, "There is
no one among your relatives who is
called by this name." 62So they made
signs to his father—what he would have him called.

63 And he asked for a writing
tablet, and wrote, saying, "His name
is John." So they all marveled. 64 Immediately his mouth was opened and
his tongue *loosed,* and he spoke, praising God. 65 Then fear came on all who
dwelt around them; and all these
sayings were discussed throughout
all the hill country of Judea. 66 And all
those who heard *them* kept *them* in
their hearts, saying, "What kind of
child will this be?" And the hand of
the Lord was with him.

Zacharias' Prophecy

67 Now his father Zacharias was
filled with the Holy Spirit, and
prophesied, saying:

68 "Blessed *is* the Lord God of Israel,
For He has visited and
redeemed His people,
69 And has raised up a horn of
salvation for us
In the house of His servant
David,
70 As He spoke by the mouth of
His holy prophets,
Who *have been* since the world
began,
71 That we should be saved from
our enemies
And from the hand of all who
hate us,
72 To perform the mercy *promised*
to our fathers
And to remember His holy
covenant,
73 The oath which He swore to
our father Abraham:
74 To grant us that we,
Being delivered from the hand
of our enemies,
Might serve Him without fear,
75 In holiness and righteousness
before Him all the days of
our life.

76 "And you, child, will be called
the prophet of the Highest;
For you will go before the face
of the Lord to prepare His
ways,
77 To give knowledge of salvation
to His people
By the remission of their sins,
78 Through the tender mercy of
our God,
With which the Dayspring
from on high has visited[a] us;

1:78 [a]NU-Text reads *shall visit.*

79 To give light to those who sit in
darkness and the shadow of
death,
To guide our feet into the way
of peace."

80 So the child grew and became
strong in spirit, and was in the deserts
till the day of his manifestation to
Israel.

Christ Born of Mary

2 And it came to pass in those days
that a decree went out from Caesar
Augustus that all the world should
be registered. 2 This census first took
place while Quirinius was governing
Syria. 3 So all went to be registered,
everyone to his own city.

4 Joseph also went up from Galilee,
out of the city of Nazareth, into Judea,
to the city of David, which is called
Bethlehem, because he was of the
house and lineage of David, 5 to be
registered with Mary, his betrothed
wife,[a] who was with child. 6 So it was,
that while they were there, the days
were completed for her to be delivered.
7 And she brought forth her firstborn
Son, and wrapped Him in swaddling
cloths, and laid Him in a manger, because there was no room for them in
the inn.

Glory in the Highest

8 Now there were in the same
country shepherds living out in the
fields, keeping watch over their flock
by night. 9 And behold,[a] an angel of the
Lord stood before them, and the glory
of the Lord shone around them, and
they were greatly afraid. 10 Then the
angel said to them, "Do not be afraid,
for behold, I bring you good tidings of
great joy which will be to all people.
11 For there is born to you this day
in the city of David a Savior, who is
Christ the Lord. 12 And this *will be* the
sign to you: You will find a Babe
wrapped in swaddling cloths, lying in
a manger."

13 And suddenly there was with
the angel a multitude of the heavenly host praising God and saying:

14 "Glory to God in the highest,
And on earth peace, goodwill
toward men!"[a]

15 So it was, when the angels had
gone away from them into heaven,

2:5 [a]NU-Text omits *wife.* **2:9** [a]NU-Text omits *behold.* **2:14** [a]NU-Text reads *toward men of goodwill.*

that the shepherds said to one another,
"Let us now go to Bethlehem and see
this thing that has come to pass, which
the Lord has made known to us."
16And they came with haste and found
Mary and Joseph, and the Babe lying
in a manger. 17Now when they had
seen *Him,* they made widely[a] known
the saying which was told them concerning this Child. 18And all those who
heard *it* marveled at those things
which were told them by the shepherds. 19But Mary kept all these things
and pondered *them* in her heart. 20Then
the shepherds returned, glorifying
and praising God for all the things
that they had heard and seen, as it was
told them.

Circumcision of Jesus

21And when eight days were completed for the circumcision of the
Child,[a] His name was called JESUS, the
name given by the angel before He was
conceived in the womb.

Jesus Presented in the Temple

22Now when the days of her purification according to the law of
Moses were completed, they brought
Him to Jerusalem to present *Him* to
the Lord 23(as it is written in the law
of the Lord, *"Every male who opens
the womb shall be called holy to the
LORD"*),[a] 24and to offer a sacrifice according to what is said in the law of
the Lord, *"A pair of turtledoves or
two young pigeons."*[a]

Simeon Sees God's Salvation

25And behold, there was a man in
Jerusalem whose name *was* Simeon,
and this man *was* just and devout, waiting for the Consolation of Israel, and
the Holy Spirit was upon him. 26And it
had been revealed to him by the Holy
Spirit that he would not see death before he had seen the Lord's Christ. 27So
he came by the Spirit into the temple.
And when the parents brought in the
Child Jesus, to do for Him according
to the custom of the law, 28he took
Him up in his arms and blessed God
and said:

29 "Lord, now You are letting Your
servant depart in peace,
According to Your word;
30 For my eyes have seen Your
salvation

2:17 [a]NU-Text omits *widely.* 2:21 [a]NU-Text reads *for His circumcision.* 2:23 [a]Exodus 13:2, 12, 15 2:24 [a]Leviticus 12:8

31 Which You have prepared
before the face of all
peoples,
32 A light to *bring* revelation to the
Gentiles,
And the glory of Your people
Israel."

33 And Joseph and His mother[a]
marveled at those things which
were spoken of Him. 34 Then Simeon
blessed them, and said to Mary His
mother, "Behold, this *Child* is destined for the fall and rising of many
in Israel, and for a sign which will be
spoken against 35 (yes, a sword will
pierce through your own soul also),
that the thoughts of many hearts
may be revealed."

Anna Bears Witness to the Redeemer

36 Now there was one, Anna, a
prophetess, the daughter of Phanuel,
of the tribe of Asher. She was of a
great age, and had lived with a husband seven years from her virginity;
37 and this woman *was* a widow of
about eighty-four years,[a] who did not
depart from the temple, but served
God with fastings and prayers night
and day. 38 And coming in that instant
she gave thanks to the Lord,[a] and
spoke of Him to all those who looked
for redemption in Jerusalem.

The Family Returns to Nazareth

39 So when they had performed all
things according to the law of the
Lord, they returned to Galilee, to
their *own* city, Nazareth. 40 And the
Child grew and became strong in
spirit,[a] filled with wisdom; and the
grace of God was upon Him.

The Boy Jesus Amazes the Scholars

41 His parents went to Jerusalem
every year at the Feast of the
Passover. 42 And when He was twelve
years old, they went up to Jerusalem
according to the custom of the feast.
43 When they had finished the days, as
they returned, the Boy Jesus lingered
behind in Jerusalem. And Joseph and
His mother[a] did not know *it;* 44 but
supposing Him to have been in the
company, they went a day's journey,

2:33 [a]NU-Text reads *And His father and mother.* **2:37** [a]NU-Text reads *a widow until she was eighty-four.* **2:38** [a]NU-Text reads *to God.* **2:40** [a]NU-Text omits *in spirit.* **2:43** [a]NU-Text reads *And His parents.*

and sought Him among *their* relatives and acquaintances. 45 So when they did not find Him, they returned to Jerusalem, seeking Him. 46 Now so it was *that* after three days they found Him in the temple, sitting in the midst of the teachers, both listening to them and asking them questions. 47 And all who heard Him were astonished at His understanding and answers. 48 So when they saw Him, they were amazed; and His mother said to Him, "Son, why have You done this to us? Look, Your father and I have sought You anxiously."

49 And He said to them, "Why did you seek Me? Did you not know that I must be about My Father's business?" 50 But they did not understand the statement which He spoke to them.

Jesus Advances in Wisdom and Favor

51 Then He went down with them and came to Nazareth, and was subject to them, but His mother kept all these things in her heart. 52 And Jesus increased in wisdom and stature, and in favor with God and men.

John the Baptist Prepares the Way

3 Now in the fifteenth year of the reign of Tiberius Caesar, Pontius Pilate being governor of Judea, Herod being tetrarch of Galilee, his brother Philip tetrarch of Iturea and the region of Trachonitis, and Lysanias tetrarch of Abilene, 2 while Annas and Caiaphas were high priests,[a] the word of God came to John the son of Zacharias in the wilderness. 3 And he went into all the region around the Jordan, preaching a baptism of repentance for the remission of sins, 4 as it is written in the book of the words of Isaiah the prophet, saying:

"The voice of one crying in the
wilderness:
'Prepare the way of the L*ORD*;
Make His paths straight.
5 *Every valley shall be filled*
And every mountain and hill
brought low;
The crooked places shall be
made straight
And the rough ways smooth;

3:2 [a]NU-Text and M-Text read *in the high priesthood of Annas and Caiaphas.*

6 *And all flesh shall see the*
salvation of God.' "[a]

John Preaches to the People

7 Then he said to the multitudes that came out to be baptized by him, "Brood of vipers! Who warned you to flee from the wrath to come? 8 Therefore bear fruits worthy of repentance, and do not begin to say to yourselves, 'We have Abraham as *our* father.' For I say to you that God is able to raise up children to Abraham from these stones. 9 And even now the ax is laid to the root of the trees. Therefore every tree which does not bear good fruit is cut down and thrown into the fire."

10 So the people asked him, saying, "What shall we do then?"

11 He answered and said to them, "He who has two tunics, let him give to him who has none; and he who has food, let him do likewise."

12 Then tax collectors also came to be baptized, and said to him, "Teacher, what shall we do?"

13 And he said to them, "Collect no more than what is appointed for you."

14 Likewise the soldiers asked him, saying, "And what shall we do?"

So he said to them, "Do not intimidate anyone or accuse falsely, and be content with your wages."

15 Now as the people were in expectation, and all reasoned in their hearts about John, whether he was the Christ *or* not, 16 John answered, saying to all, "I indeed baptize you with water; but One mightier than I is coming, whose sandal strap I am not worthy to loose. He will baptize you with the Holy Spirit and fire. 17 His winnowing fan *is* in His hand, and He will thoroughly clean out His threshing floor, and gather the wheat into His barn; but the chaff He will burn with unquenchable fire."

18 And with many other exhortations he preached to the people. 19 But Herod the tetrarch, being rebuked by him concerning Herodias, his brother Philip's wife,[a] and for all the evils which Herod had done, 20 also added this, above all, that he shut John up in prison.

3:6 [a]Isaiah 40:3–5 **3:19** [a]NU-Text reads *his brother's wife.*

John Baptizes Jesus

21 When all the people were baptized, it came to pass that Jesus also
was baptized; and while He prayed,
the heaven was opened. 22 And the
Holy Spirit descended in bodily form
like a dove upon Him, and a voice
came from heaven which said, "You
are My beloved Son; in You I am well
pleased."

The Genealogy of Jesus Christ

23 Now Jesus Himself began *His
ministry at* about thirty years of age,
being (as was supposed) *the* son of
Joseph, *the son* of Heli, 24 *the son* of
Matthat,[a] *the son* of Levi, *the son*
of Melchi, *the son* of Janna, *the son* of Joseph, 25 *the son* of Mattathiah, *the son* of
Amos, *the son* of Nahum, *the son* of Esli,
the son of Naggai, 26 *the son* of Maath, *the
son* of Mattathiah, *the son* of Semei, *the
son* of Joseph, *the son* of Judah, 27 *the son*
of Joannas, *the son* of Rhesa, *the son* of
Zerubbabel, *the son* of Shealtiel, *the son*
of Neri, 28 *the son* of Melchi, *the son* of
Addi, *the son* of Cosam, *the son* of
Elmodam, *the son* of Er, 29 *the son* of
Jose, *the son* of Eliezer, *the son* of Jorim,
the son of Matthat, *the son* of Levi, 30 *the
son* of Simeon, *the son* of Judah, *the son* of
Joseph, *the son* of Jonan, *the son* of Eli-
akim, 31 *the son* of Melea, *the son* of
Menan, *the son* of Mattathah, *the son*
of Nathan, *the son* of David, 32 *the son* of
Jesse, *the son* of Obed, *the son* of Boaz,
the son of Salmon, *the son* of Nahshon,
33 *the son* of Amminadab, *the son* of Ram,
the son of Hezron, *the son* of Perez, *the
son* of Judah, 34 *the son* of Jacob, *the son*
of Isaac, *the son* of Abraham, *the son* of
Terah, *the son* of Nahor, 35 *the son* of
Serug, *the son* of Reu, *the son* of Peleg, *the
son* of Eber, *the son* of Shelah, 36 *the son*
of Cainan, *the son* of Arphaxad, *the son*
of Shem, *the son* of Noah, *the son* of
Lamech, 37 *the son* of Methuselah, *the son*
of Enoch, *the son* of Jared, *the son* of Ma-
halalel, *the son* of Cainan, 38 *the son* of
Enosh, *the son* of Seth, *the son* of Adam,
the son of God.

Satan Tempts Jesus

4 Then Jesus, being filled with the
Holy Spirit, returned from the

3:24 [a]This and several other names in the genealogy are spelled somewhat differently in the NU-Text. Since the New King James Version uses the Old Testament spelling for persons mentioned in the New Testament, these variations, which come from the Greek, have not been footnoted.

Jordan and was led by the Spirit into[a] the wilderness, 2 being tempted for forty days by the devil. And in those days He ate nothing, and afterward, when they had ended, He was hungry.

3 And the devil said to Him, "If You are the Son of God, command this stone to become bread."

4 But Jesus answered him, saying,[a] "It is written, *'Man shall not live by bread alone, but by every word of God.'* "[b]

5 Then the devil, taking Him up on a high mountain, showed Him[a] all the kingdoms of the world in a moment of time. 6 And the devil said to Him, "All this authority I will give You, and their glory; for *this* has been delivered to me, and I give it to whomever I wish. 7 Therefore, if You will worship before me, all will be Yours."

8 And Jesus answered and said to him, "Get behind Me, Satan![a] For[b] it is written, *'You shall worship the LORD your God, and Him only you shall serve.'* "[c]

9 Then he brought Him to Jerusalem, set Him on the pinnacle of the temple, and said to Him, "If You are the Son of God, throw Yourself down from here. 10 For it is written:

'He shall give His angels charge
over you,
To keep you,'

11 and,

'In their hands they shall bear
you up,
Lest you dash your foot against
a stone.' "[a]

12 And Jesus answered and said to him, "It has been said, *'You shall not tempt the LORD your God.'* "[a]

13 Now when the devil had ended every temptation, he departed from Him until an opportune time.

Jesus Begins His Galilean Ministry

14 Then Jesus returned in the power of the Spirit to Galilee, and news of Him went out through all the surrounding region. 15 And He

---

4:1 [a]NU-Text reads *in.* **4:4** [a]Deuteronomy 8:3 [b]NU-Text omits *but by every word of God.* **4:5** [a]NU-Text reads *And taking Him up, he showed Him.* **4:8** [a]NU-Text omits *Get behind Me, Satan.* [b]NU-Text and M-Text omit *For.* [c]Deuteronomy 6:13 **4:11** [a]Psalm 91:11, 12 **4:12** [a]Deuteronomy 6:16

taught in their synagogues, being
glorified by all.

Jesus Rejected at Nazareth

16 So He came to Nazareth, where
He had been brought up. And as His
custom was, He went into the synagogue on the Sabbath day, and stood
up to read. 17 And He was handed the
book of the prophet Isaiah. And
when He had opened the book, He
found the place where it was written:

18 *"The Spirit of the LORD is upon*
Me,
Because He has anointed Me
To preach the gospel to the poor;
He has sent Me to heal the
brokenhearted,[a]
To proclaim liberty to the
captives
And recovery of sight to the
blind,
To set at liberty those who are
oppressed;
19 *To proclaim the acceptable year*
of the LORD."[a]

20 Then He closed the book, and gave
it back to the attendant and sat
down. And the eyes of all who were
in the synagogue were fixed on Him.
21 And He began to say to them, "Today this Scripture is fulfilled in your
hearing." 22 So all bore witness to
Him, and marveled at the gracious
words which proceeded out of His
mouth. And they said, "Is this not
Joseph's son?"

23 He said to them, "You will
surely say this proverb to Me, 'Physician, heal yourself! Whatever we
have heard done in Capernaum,[a] do
also here in Your country.'" 24 Then
He said, "Assuredly, I say to you, no
prophet is accepted in his own
country. 25 But I tell you truly, many
widows were in Israel in the days of
Elijah, when the heaven was shut up
three years and six months, and
there was a great famine throughout all the land; 26 but to none of
them was Elijah sent except to
Zarephath,[a] *in the region* of Sidon, to
a woman *who was* a widow. 27 And
many lepers were in Israel in the
time of Elisha the prophet, and none
of them was cleansed except Naaman the Syrian."

4:18 [a]NU-Text omits *to heal the brokenhearted*. **4:19** [a]Isaiah 61:1, 2 **4:23** [a]Here and elsewhere the NU-Text spelling is *Capharnaum*. **4:26** [a]Greek *Sarepta*

[28]So all those in the synagogue, when they heard these things, were filled with wrath, [29]and rose up and thrust Him out of the city; and they led Him to the brow of the hill on which their city was built, that they might throw Him down over the cliff. [30]Then passing through the midst of them, He went His way.

Jesus Casts Out an Unclean Spirit

[31]Then He went down to Capernaum, a city of Galilee, and was teaching them on the Sabbaths. [32]And they were astonished at His teaching, for His word was with authority. [33]Now in the synagogue there was a man who had a spirit of an unclean demon. And he cried out with a loud voice, [34]saying, "Let *us* alone! What have we to do with You, Jesus of Nazareth? Did You come to destroy us? I know who You are—the Holy One of God!"

[35]But Jesus rebuked him, saying, "Be quiet, and come out of him!" And when the demon had thrown him in *their* midst, it came out of him and did not hurt him. [36]Then they were all amazed and spoke among themselves, saying, "What a word this *is!* For with authority and power He commands the unclean spirits, and they come out." [37]And the report about Him went out into every place in the surrounding region.

Peter's Mother-in-Law Healed

[38]Now He arose from the synagogue and entered Simon's house. But Simon's wife's mother was sick with a high fever, and they made request of Him concerning her. [39]So He stood over her and rebuked the fever, and it left her. And immediately she arose and served them.

Many Healed After Sabbath Sunset

[40]When the sun was setting, all those who had any that were sick with various diseases brought them to Him; and He laid His hands on every one of them and healed them. [41]And demons also came out of many, crying out and saying, "You are the Christ,[a] the Son of God!"

And He, rebuking *them,* did not

4:41 [a]NU-Text omits *the Christ.*

allow them to speak, for they knew that He was the Christ.

Jesus Preaches in Galilee

42 Now when it was day, He departed and went into a deserted place. And the crowd sought Him and came to Him, and tried to keep Him from leaving them; 43 but He said to them, "I must preach the kingdom of God to the other cities also, because for this purpose I have been sent." 44 And He was preaching in the synagogues of Galilee.[a]

Four Fishermen Called as Disciples

5 So it was, as the multitude pressed about Him to hear the word of God, that He stood by the Lake of Gennesaret, 2 and saw two boats standing by the lake; but the fishermen had gone from them and were washing *their* nets. 3 Then He got into one of the boats, which was Simon's, and asked him to put out a little from the land. And He sat down and taught the multitudes from the boat.

4 When He had stopped speaking, He said to Simon, "Launch out into the deep and let down your nets for a catch."

5 But Simon answered and said to Him, "Master, we have toiled all night and caught nothing; nevertheless at Your word I will let down the net." 6 And when they had done this, they caught a great number of fish, and their net was breaking. 7 So they signaled to *their* partners in the other boat to come and help them. And they came and filled both the boats, so that they began to sink. 8 When Simon Peter saw *it,* he fell down at Jesus' knees, saying, "Depart from me, for I am a sinful man, O Lord!"

9 For he and all who were with him were astonished at the catch of fish which they had taken; 10 and so also *were* James and John, the sons of Zebedee, who were partners with Simon. And Jesus said to Simon, "Do not be afraid. From now on you will catch men." 11 So when they had brought their boats to land, they forsook all and followed Him.

Jesus Cleanses a Leper

12 And it happened when He was in a certain city, that behold, a man

---

4:44 [a]NU-Text reads *Judea.*

who was full of leprosy saw Jesus; and he fell on *his* face and implored Him, saying, "Lord, if You are willing, You can make me clean."

13 Then He put out *His* hand and touched him, saying, "I am willing; be cleansed." Immediately the leprosy left him. 14 And He charged him to tell no one, "But go and show yourself to the priest, and make an offering for your cleansing, as a testimony to them, just as Moses commanded."

15 However, the report went around concerning Him all the more; and great multitudes came together to hear, and to be healed by Him of their infirmities. 16 So He Himself *often* withdrew into the wilderness and prayed.

Jesus Forgives and Heals a Paralytic

17 Now it happened on a certain day, as He was teaching, that there were Pharisees and teachers of the law sitting by, who had come out of every town of Galilee, Judea, and Jerusalem. And the power of the Lord was *present* to heal them.[a] 18 Then behold, men brought on a bed a man who was paralyzed, whom they sought to bring in and lay before Him. 19 And when they could not find how they might bring him in, because of the crowd, they went up on the housetop and let him down with *his* bed through the tiling into the midst before Jesus.

20 When He saw their faith, He said to him, "Man, your sins are forgiven you."

21 And the scribes and the Pharisees began to reason, saying, "Who is this who speaks blasphemies? Who can forgive sins but God alone?"

22 But when Jesus perceived their thoughts, He answered and said to them, "Why are you reasoning in your hearts? 23 Which is easier, to say, 'Your sins are forgiven you,' or to say, 'Rise up and walk'? 24 But that you may know that the Son of Man has power on earth to forgive sins"—He said to the man who was paralyzed, "I say to you, arise, take up your bed, and go to your house."

25 Immediately he rose up before them, took up what he had been

---

5:17 [a] NU-Text reads *present with Him to heal.*

lying on, and departed to his own
house, glorifying God. 26And they
were all amazed, and they glorified
God and were filled with fear, saying, "We have seen strange things
today!"

Matthew the Tax Collector

27After these things He went out
and saw a tax collector named Levi,
sitting at the tax office. And He said
to him, "Follow Me." 28So he left all,
rose up, and followed Him.

29Then Levi gave Him a great feast
in his own house. And there were a
great number of tax collectors and
others who sat down with them.
30And their scribes and the Pharisees[a]
complained against His disciples, saying, "Why do You eat and drink with
tax collectors and sinners?"

31Jesus answered and said to
them, "Those who are well have
no need of a physician, but those
who are sick. 32I have not come to
call *the* righteous, but sinners, to repentance."

Jesus Is Questioned About Fasting

33Then they said to Him, "Why
do[a] the disciples of John fast often
and make prayers, and likewise those
of the Pharisees, but Yours eat and
drink?"

34And He said to them, "Can you
make the friends of the bridegroom
fast while the bridegroom is with
them? 35But the days will come when
the bridegroom will be taken away
from them; then they will fast in
those days."

36Then He spoke a parable to
them: "No one puts a piece from a
new garment on an old one;[a] otherwise the new makes a tear, and also
the piece that was *taken* out of the new
does not match the old. 37And no
one puts new wine into old wineskins; or else the new wine will burst
the wineskins and be spilled, and
the wineskins will be ruined. 38But
new wine must be put into new
wineskins, and both are preserved.[a]
39And no one, having drunk old *wine,*

5:30 [a]NU-Text reads *But the Pharisees and their scribes.* **5:33** [a]NU-Text omits *Why do,* making the verse a statement.
5:36 [a]NU-Text reads *No one tears a piece from a new garment and puts it on an old one.* **5:38** [a]NU-Text omits *and both are preserved.*

immediately[a] desires new; for he says,
'The old is better.'"[b]

Jesus Is Lord of the Sabbath

6 Now it happened on the second
Sabbath after the first[a] that He
went through the grainfields. And
His disciples plucked the heads of
grain and ate *them,* rubbing *them* in
their hands. 2 And some of the Pharisees said to them, "Why are you
doing what is not lawful to do on the
Sabbath?"

3 But Jesus answering them said,
"Have you not even read this, what
David did when he was hungry, he
and those who were with him:
4 how he went into the house of God,
took and ate the showbread, and
also gave some to those with him,
which is not lawful for any but the
priests to eat?" 5 And He said to them,
"The Son of Man is also Lord of the
Sabbath."

Healing on the Sabbath

6 Now it happened on another
Sabbath, also, that He entered the
synagogue and taught. And a man
was there whose right hand was
withered. 7 So the scribes and Pharisees watched Him closely, whether
He would heal on the Sabbath, that
they might find an accusation against
Him. 8 But He knew their thoughts,
and said to the man who had the
withered hand, "Arise and stand
here." And he arose and stood. 9 Then
Jesus said to them, "I will ask you one
thing: Is it lawful on the Sabbath to
do good or to do evil, to save life or to
destroy?"[a] 10 And when He had looked
around at them all, He said to the
man,[a] "Stretch out your hand." And
he did so, and his hand was restored
as whole as the other.[b] 11 But they
were filled with rage, and discussed
with one another what they might
do to Jesus.

The Twelve Apostles

12 Now it came to pass in those
days that He went out to the mountain to pray, and continued all night
in prayer to God. 13 And when it
was day, He called His disciples to
Himself; and from them He chose
twelve whom He also named apos-

5:39 [a]NU-Text omits *immediately.* [b]NU-Text reads *good.* **6:1** [a]NU-Text reads *on a Sabbath.* **6:9** [a]M-Text reads *to kill.* **6:10** [a]NU-Text and M-Text read *to him.* [b]NU-Text omits *as whole as the other.*

tles: [14]Simon, whom He also named
Peter, and Andrew his brother; James
and John; Philip and Bartholomew;
[15]Matthew and Thomas; James the
son of Alphaeus, and Simon called
the Zealot; [16]Judas *the son* of James,
and Judas Iscariot who also became a
traitor.

Jesus Heals a Great Multitude

[17]And He came down with them
and stood on a level place with a
crowd of His disciples and a great
multitude of people from all Judea
and Jerusalem, and from the seacoast
of Tyre and Sidon, who came to hear
Him and be healed of their diseases,
[18]as well as those who were tormented with unclean spirits. And
they were healed. [19]And the whole
multitude sought to touch Him, for
power went out from Him and
healed *them* all.

The Beatitudes

[20]Then He lifted up His eyes toward His disciples, and said:

"Blessed *are you* poor,
For yours is the kingdom of God.

21 Blessed *are you* who hunger now,
For you shall be filled.
Blessed *are you* who weep now,
For you shall laugh.

22 Blessed are you when men hate you,
And when they exclude you,
And revile *you*, and cast out your name as evil,
For the Son of Man's sake.

23 Rejoice in that day and leap for joy!
For indeed your reward *is* great in heaven,
For in like manner their fathers did to the prophets.

Jesus Pronounces Woes

24 "But woe to you who are rich,
For you have received your consolation.

25 Woe to you who are full,
For you shall hunger.
Woe to you who laugh now,
For you shall mourn and weep.

26 Woe to you[a] when all[b] men speak well of you,
For so did their fathers to the false prophets.

6:26 [a]NU-Text and M-Text omit *to you*. [b]M-Text omits *all*.

Love Your Enemies

27“But I say to you who hear: Love
your enemies, do good to those who
hate you, 28bless those who curse
you, and pray for those who spite-
fully use you. 29To him who strikes
you on the *one* cheek, offer the other
also. And from him who takes away
your cloak, do not withhold *your*
tunic either. 30Give to everyone who
asks of you. And from him who takes
away your goods do not ask *them* back.
31And just as you want men to do to
you, you also do to them likewise.

32“But if you love those who love
you, what credit is that to you? For
even sinners love those who love
them. 33And if you do good to those
who do good to you, what credit is
that to you? For even sinners do the
same. 34And if you lend *to those* from
whom you hope to receive back,
what credit is that to you? For even
sinners lend to sinners to receive as
much back. 35But love your enemies,
do good, and lend, hoping for nothing in return; and your reward will
be great, and you will be sons of the
Most High. For He is kind to the
unthankful and evil. 36Therefore be
merciful, just as your Father also is
merciful.

Do Not Judge

37“Judge not, and you shall not be
judged. Condemn not, and you shall
not be condemned. Forgive, and you
will be forgiven. 38Give, and it will be
given to you: good measure, pressed
down, shaken together, and running
over will be put into your bosom. For
with the same measure that you use,
it will be measured back to you.”

39And He spoke a parable to them:
“Can the blind lead the blind? Will
they not both fall into the ditch? 40A
disciple is not above his teacher, but
everyone who is perfectly trained will
be like his teacher. 41And why do you
look at the speck in your brother’s
eye, but do not perceive the plank in
your own eye? 42Or how can you say to
your brother, ‘Brother, let me remove
the speck that *is* in your eye,’ when
you yourself do not see the plank that
is in your own eye? Hypocrite! First
remove the plank from your own eye,
and then you will see clearly to remove the speck that is in your
brother’s eye.

A Tree Is Known by Its Fruit

43"For a good tree does not bear bad fruit, nor does a bad tree bear good fruit. 44For every tree is known by its own fruit. For *men* do not gather figs from thorns, nor do they gather grapes from a bramble bush. 45A good man out of the good treasure of his heart brings forth good; and an evil man out of the evil treasure of his heart[a] brings forth evil. For out of the abundance of the heart his mouth speaks.

Build on the Rock

46"But why do you call Me 'Lord, Lord,' and not do the things which I say? 47Whoever comes to Me, and hears My sayings and does them, I will show you whom he is like: 48He is like a man building a house, who dug deep and laid the foundation on the rock. And when the flood arose, the stream beat vehemently against that house, and could not shake it, for it was founded on the rock.[a] 49But he who heard and did nothing is like a man who built a house on the earth without a foundation, against which the stream beat vehemently; and immediately it fell.[a] And the ruin of that house was great."

Jesus Heals a Centurion's Servant

7 Now when He concluded all His sayings in the hearing of the people, He entered Capernaum. 2And a certain centurion's servant, who was dear to him, was sick and ready to die. 3So when he heard about Jesus, he sent elders of the Jews to Him, pleading with Him to come and heal his servant. 4And when they came to Jesus, they begged Him earnestly, saying that the one for whom He should do this was deserving, 5"for he loves our nation, and has built us a synagogue."

6Then Jesus went with them. And when He was already not far from the house, the centurion sent friends to Him, saying to Him, "Lord, do not trouble Yourself, for I am not worthy that You should enter under my roof. 7Therefore I did not even think myself worthy to come to You. But say

---

6:45 [a]NU-Text omits *treasure of his heart.* **6:48** [a]NU-Text reads *for it was well built.* **6:49** [a]NU-Text reads *collapsed.*

the word, and my servant will be
healed. 8 For I also am a man placed
under authority, having soldiers
under me. And I say to one, 'Go,' and
he goes; and to another, 'Come,' and
he comes; and to my servant, 'Do this,'
and he does *it*."
9 When Jesus heard these things,
He marveled at him, and turned
around and said to the crowd that
followed Him, "I say to you, I have
not found such great faith, not even
in Israel!" 10 And those who were sent,
returning to the house, found the
servant well who had been sick.[a]

Jesus Raises the Son of the Widow of Nain

11 Now it happened, the day after,
that He went into a city called Nain;
and many of His disciples went with
Him, and a large crowd. 12 And when
He came near the gate of the city,
behold, a dead man was being carried out, the only son of his mother;
and she was a widow. And a large
crowd from the city was with her.
13 When the Lord saw her, He had compassion on her and said to her, "Do not
weep." 14 Then He came and touched
the open coffin, and those who carried
him stood still. And He said, "Young
man, I say to you, arise." 15 So he who
was dead sat up and began to speak.
And He presented him to his mother.
16 Then fear came upon all, and
they glorified God, saying, "A great
prophet has risen up among us"; and,
"God has visited His people." 17 And
this report about Him went throughout all Judea and all the surrounding
region.

John the Baptist Sends Messengers to Jesus

18 Then the disciples of John reported to him concerning all these
things. 19 And John, calling two of his
disciples to *him*, sent *them* to Jesus,[a]
saying, "Are You the Coming One, or
do we look for another?"
20 When the men had come to
Him, they said, "John the Baptist has
sent us to You, saying, 'Are You the
Coming One, or do we look for another?'" 21 And that very hour He
cured many of infirmities, afflictions,
and evil spirits; and to many blind He
gave sight.
22 Jesus answered and said to

7:10 [a]NU-Text omits *who had been sick*. **7:19** [a]NU-Text reads *the Lord*.

them, "Go and tell John the things you have seen and heard: that *the* blind see, *the* lame walk, *the* lepers are cleansed, *the* deaf hear, *the* dead are raised, *the* poor have the gospel preached to them. **23**And blessed is *he* who is not offended because of Me."

24When the messengers of John had departed, He began to speak to the multitudes concerning John: "What did you go out into the wilderness to see? A reed shaken by the wind? **25**But what did you go out to see? A man clothed in soft garments? Indeed those who are gorgeously appareled and live in luxury are in kings' courts. **26**But what did you go out to see? A prophet? Yes, I say to you, and more than a prophet. **27**This is *he* of whom it is written:

> '*Behold, I send My messenger*
> *before Your face,*
> *Who will prepare Your way*
> *before You.*'[a]

28For I say to you, among those born of women there is not a greater prophet than John the Baptist;[a] but he who is least in the kingdom of God is greater than he."

29And when all the people heard *Him,* even the tax collectors justified God, having been baptized with the baptism of John. **30**But the Pharisees and lawyers rejected the will of God for themselves, not having been baptized by him.

31And the Lord said,[a] "To what then shall I liken the men of this generation, and what are they like? **32**They are like children sitting in the marketplace and calling to one another, saying:

> 'We played the flute for you,
> And you did not dance;
> We mourned to you,
> And you did not weep.'

33For John the Baptist came neither eating bread nor drinking wine, and you say, 'He has a demon.' **34**The Son of Man has come eating and drinking, and you say, 'Look, a glutton and a winebibber, a friend of tax collectors and sinners!' **35**But wisdom is justified by all her children."

7:27 [a]Malachi 3:1 **7:28** [a]NU-Text reads *there is none greater than John.* **7:31** [a]NU-Text and M-Text omit *And the Lord said.*

A Sinful Woman Forgiven

36 Then one of the Pharisees asked
Him to eat with him. And He went to
the Pharisee's house, and sat down
to eat. 37 And behold, a woman in
the city who was a sinner, when she
knew that *Jesus* sat at the table in the
Pharisee's house, brought an alabaster
flask of fragrant oil, 38 and stood at
His feet behind *Him* weeping; and
she began to wash His feet with her
tears, and wiped *them* with the hair of
her head; and she kissed His feet
and anointed *them* with the fragrant
oil. 39 Now when the Pharisee who
had invited Him saw *this,* he spoke
to himself, saying, "This Man, if He
were a prophet, would know who
and what manner of woman *this is*
who is touching Him, for she is a
sinner."

40 And Jesus answered and said to
him, "Simon, I have something to say
to you."

So he said, "Teacher, say it."

41 "There was a certain creditor
who had two debtors. One owed five
hundred denarii, and the other fifty.
42 And when they had nothing with
which to repay, he freely forgave
them both. Tell Me, therefore, which
of them will love him more?"

43 Simon answered and said, "I
suppose the *one* whom he forgave
more."

And He said to him, "You have
rightly judged." 44 Then He turned to
the woman and said to Simon, "Do
you see this woman? I entered your
house; you gave Me no water for My
feet, but she has washed My feet with
her tears and wiped *them* with the hair
of her head. 45 You gave Me no kiss,
but this woman has not ceased to kiss
My feet since the time I came in.
46 You did not anoint My head with
oil, but this woman has anointed My
feet with fragrant oil. 47 Therefore I
say to you, her sins, which *are* many,
are forgiven, for she loved much. But
to whom little is forgiven, *the same*
loves little."

48 Then He said to her, "Your sins
are forgiven."

49 And those who sat at the table
with Him began to say to themselves, "Who is this who even forgives
sins?"

50 Then He said to the woman,
"Your faith has saved you. Go in
peace."

Many Women Minister to Jesus

8 Now it came to pass, afterward,
that He went through every city
and village, preaching and bringing the glad tidings of the kingdom
of God. And the twelve *were* with
Him, 2 and certain women who had
been healed of evil spirits and infirmities—Mary called Magdalene, out
of whom had come seven demons,
3 and Joanna the wife of Chuza,
Herod's steward, and Susanna, and
many others who provided for Him[a]
from their substance.

The Parable of the Sower

4 And when a great multitude had
gathered, and they had come to Him
from every city, He spoke by a parable: 5 "A sower went out to sow his
seed. And as he sowed, some fell by
the wayside; and it was trampled
down, and the birds of the air devoured it. 6 Some fell on rock; and as
soon as it sprang up, it withered away
because it lacked moisture. 7 And
some fell among thorns, and the
thorns sprang up with it and choked
it. 8 But others fell on good ground,
sprang up, and yielded a crop a hun-
dredfold." When He had said these
things He cried, "He who has ears to
hear, let him hear!"

The Purpose of Parables

9 Then His disciples asked Him,
saying, "What does this parable
mean?"

10 And He said, "To you it has been
given to know the mysteries of the
kingdom of God, but to the rest *it is
given* in parables, that

'Seeing they may not see,
And hearing they may not
understand.'[a]

The Parable of the Sower Explained

11 "Now the parable is this: The
seed is the word of God. 12 Those
by the wayside are the ones who hear;
then the devil comes and takes away
the word out of their hearts, lest they
should believe and be saved. 13 But the
ones on the rock *are those* who, when
they hear, receive the word with joy;
and these have no root, who believe
for a while and in time of temptation

8:3 [a]NU-Text and M-Text read *them*. **8:10** [a]Isaiah 6:9

fall away. 14 Now the ones *that* fell among thorns are those who, when they have heard, go out and are choked with cares, riches, and pleasures of life, and bring no fruit to maturity. 15 But the ones *that* fell on the good ground are those who, having heard the word with a noble and good heart, keep *it* and bear fruit with patience.

The Parable of the Revealed Light

16 "No one, when he has lit a lamp, covers it with a vessel or puts *it* under a bed, but sets *it* on a lampstand, that those who enter may see the light. 17 For nothing is secret that will not be revealed, nor *anything* hidden that will not be known and come to light. 18 Therefore take heed how you hear. For whoever has, to him *more* will be given; and whoever does not have, even what he seems to have will be taken from him."

Jesus' Mother and Brothers Come to Him

19 Then His mother and brothers came to Him, and could not approach Him because of the crowd. 20 And it was told Him *by some,* who said, "Your mother and Your brothers are standing outside, desiring to see You."

21 But He answered and said to them, "My mother and My brothers are these who hear the word of God and do it."

Wind and Wave Obey Jesus

22 Now it happened, on a certain day, that He got into a boat with His disciples. And He said to them, "Let us cross over to the other side of the lake." And they launched out. 23 But as they sailed He fell asleep. And a windstorm came down on the lake, and they were filling *with water,* and were in jeopardy. 24 And they came to Him and awoke Him, saying, "Master, Master, we are perishing!"

Then He arose and rebuked the wind and the raging of the water. And they ceased, and there was a calm. 25 But He said to them, "Where is your faith?"

And they were afraid, and marveled, saying to one another, "Who can this be? For He commands even the winds and water, and they obey Him!"

A Demon-Possessed Man Healed

26 Then they sailed to the country of the Gadarenes,[a] which is opposite Galilee. 27 And when He stepped out on the land, there met Him a certain man from the city who had demons for a long time. And he wore no clothes,[a] nor did he live in a house but in the tombs. 28 When he saw Jesus, he cried out, fell down before Him, and with a loud voice said, "What have I to do with You, Jesus, Son of the Most High God? I beg You, do not torment me!" 29 For He had commanded the unclean spirit to come out of the man. For it had often seized him, and he was kept under guard, bound with chains and shackles; and he broke the bonds and was driven by the demon into the wilderness.

30 Jesus asked him, saying, "What is your name?"

And he said, "Legion," because many demons had entered him. 31 And they begged Him that He would not command them to go out into the abyss.

32 Now a herd of many swine was feeding there on the mountain. So they begged Him that He would permit them to enter them. And He permitted them. 33 Then the demons went out of the man and entered the swine, and the herd ran violently down the steep place into the lake and drowned.

34 When those who fed *them* saw what had happened, they fled and told *it* in the city and in the country. 35 Then they went out to see what had happened, and came to Jesus, and found the man from whom the demons had departed, sitting at the feet of Jesus, clothed and in his right mind. And they were afraid. 36 They also who had seen *it* told them by what means he who had been demon-possessed was healed. 37 Then the whole multitude of the surrounding region of the Gadarenes[a] asked Him to depart from them, for they were seized with great fear. And He got into the boat and returned.

38 Now the man from whom the demons had departed begged Him that he might be with Him. But Jesus

---

8:26 [a]NU-Text reads *Gerasenes.* **8:27** [a]NU-Text reads *who had demons and for a long time wore no clothes.* **8:37** [a]NU-Text reads *Gerasenes.*

sent him away, saying, 39 "Return to
your own house, and tell what great
things God has done for you." And
he went his way and proclaimed
throughout the whole city what
great things Jesus had done for him.

A Girl Restored to Life and a Woman Healed

40 So it was, when Jesus returned,
that the multitude welcomed Him, for
they were all waiting for Him. 41 And
behold, there came a man named
Jairus, and he was a ruler of the synagogue. And he fell down at Jesus' feet
and begged Him to come to his house,
42 for he had an only daughter about
twelve years of age, and she was dying.

But as He went, the multitudes
thronged Him. 43 Now a woman, having a flow of blood for twelve years,
who had spent all her livelihood
on physicians and could not be
healed by any, 44 came from behind
and touched the border of His garment. And immediately her flow of
blood stopped.

45 And Jesus said, "Who touched
Me?"

When all denied it, Peter and
those with him[a] said, "Master, the
multitudes throng and press You, and
You say, 'Who touched Me?' "[b]

46 But Jesus said, "Somebody
touched Me, for I perceived power
going out from Me." 47 Now when the
woman saw that she was not hidden,
she came trembling; and falling
down before Him, she declared to
Him in the presence of all the people
the reason she had touched Him and
how she was healed immediately.

48 And He said to her, "Daughter,
be of good cheer;[a] your faith has
made you well. Go in peace."

49 While He was still speaking,
someone came from the ruler of the
synagogue's *house,* saying to him,
"Your daughter is dead. Do not trouble the Teacher."[a]

50 But when Jesus heard *it,* He answered him, saying, "Do not be afraid;
only believe, and she will be made
well." 51 When He came into the house,
He permitted no one to go in[a] except
Peter, James, and John,[b] and the father
and mother of the girl. 52 Now all wept
and mourned for her; but He said, "Do

8:45 [a]NU-Text omits *and those with him.* [b]NU-Text omits *and You say, 'Who touched Me?'* **8:48** [a]NU-Text omits *be of good cheer.* **8:49** [a]NU-Text adds *anymore.* **8:51** [a]NU-Text adds *with Him.* [b]NU-Text and M-Text read *Peter, John, and James.*

not weep; she is not dead, but sleeping." 53And they ridiculed Him, knowing that she was dead.

54But He put them all outside,[a] took her by the hand and called, saying, "Little girl, arise." 55Then her spirit returned, and she arose immediately. And He commanded that she be given *something* to eat. 56And her parents were astonished, but He charged them to tell no one what had happened.

Sending Out the Twelve

9 Then He called His twelve disciples together and gave them power and authority over all demons, and to cure diseases. 2He sent them to preach the kingdom of God and to heal the sick. 3And He said to them, "Take nothing for the journey, neither staffs nor bag nor bread nor money; and do not have two tunics apiece.

4"Whatever house you enter, stay there, and from there depart. 5And whoever will not receive you, when you go out of that city, shake off the very dust from your feet as a testimony against them."

6So they departed and went through the towns, preaching the gospel and healing everywhere.

Herod Seeks to See Jesus

7Now Herod the tetrarch heard of all that was done by Him; and he was perplexed, because it was said by some that John had risen from the dead, 8and by some that Elijah had appeared, and by others that one of the old prophets had risen again. 9Herod said, "John I have beheaded, but who is this of whom I hear such things?" So he sought to see Him.

Feeding the Five Thousand

10And the apostles, when they had returned, told Him all that they had done. Then He took them and went aside privately into a deserted place belonging to the city called Bethsaida. 11But when the multitudes knew *it,* they followed Him; and He received them and spoke to them about the kingdom of God, and healed those who had need of healing. 12When the day began to wear away, the twelve came and said to Him, "Send the mul-

---

8:54 [a]NU-Text omits *put them all outside.*

titude away, that they may go into the
surrounding towns and country, and
lodge and get provisions; for we are in
a deserted place here."
[13]But He said to them, "You give
them something to eat."
And they said, "We have no more
than five loaves and two fish, unless
we go and buy food for all these people." [14]For there were about five
thousand men.
Then He said to His disciples,
"Make them sit down in groups of
fifty." [15]And they did so, and made
them all sit down.
[16]Then He took the five loaves
and the two fish, and looking up to
heaven, He blessed and broke them,
and gave *them* to the disciples to set before the multitude. [17]So they all ate
and were filled, and twelve baskets of
the leftover fragments were taken up
by them.

Peter Confesses Jesus as the Christ

[18]And it happened, as He was
alone praying, *that* His disciples joined
Him, and He asked them, saying,
"Who do the crowds say that I am?"
[19]So they answered and said,
"John the Baptist, but some *say* Elijah; and others *say* that one of the old
prophets has risen again."
[20]He said to them, "But who do
you say that I am?"
Peter answered and said, "The
Christ of God."

Jesus Predicts His Death and Resurrection

[21]And He strictly warned and
commanded them to tell this to no
one, [22]saying, "The Son of Man must
suffer many things, and be rejected
by the elders and chief priests and
scribes, and be killed, and be raised the
third day."

Take Up the Cross and Follow Him

[23]Then He said to *them* all, "If anyone desires to come after Me, let
him deny himself, and take up his
cross daily,[a] and follow Me. [24]For whoever desires to save his life will lose it,
but whoever loses his life for My sake
will save it. [25]For what profit is it to
a man if he gains the whole world,
and is himself destroyed or lost? [26]For

9:23 [a]M-Text omits *daily*.

whoever is ashamed of Me and My words, of him the Son of Man will be ashamed when He comes in His *own* glory, and *in His* Father's, and of the holy angels. 27But I tell you truly, there are some standing here who shall not taste death till they see the kingdom of God."

Jesus Transfigured on the Mount

28Now it came to pass, about eight days after these sayings, that He took Peter, John, and James and went up on the mountain to pray. 29As He prayed, the appearance of His face was altered, and His robe *became* white *and* glistening. 30And behold, two men talked with Him, who were Moses and Elijah, 31who appeared in glory and spoke of His decease which He was about to accomplish at Jerusalem. 32But Peter and those with him were heavy with sleep; and when they were fully awake, they saw His glory and the two men who stood with Him. 33Then it happened, as they were parting from Him, *that* Peter said to Jesus, "Master, it is good for us to be here; and let us make three tabernacles: one for You, one for Moses, and one for Elijah"—not knowing what he said.

34While he was saying this, a cloud came and overshadowed them; and they were fearful as they entered the cloud. 35And a voice came out of the cloud, saying, "This is My beloved Son.[a] Hear Him!" 36When the voice had ceased, Jesus was found alone. But they kept quiet, and told no one in those days any of the things they had seen.

A Boy Is Healed

37Now it happened on the next day, when they had come down from the mountain, that a great multitude met Him. 38Suddenly a man from the multitude cried out, saying, "Teacher, I implore You, look on my son, for he is my only child. 39And behold, a spirit seizes him, and he suddenly cries out; it convulses him so that he foams *at the mouth;* and it departs from him with great difficulty, bruising him. 40So I implored Your disciples to cast it out, but they could not."

9:35 [a]NU-Text reads *This is My Son, the Chosen One.*

41Then Jesus answered and said, "O faithless and perverse generation, how long shall I be with you and bear with you? Bring your son here." 42And as he was still coming, the demon threw him down and convulsed *him*. Then Jesus rebuked the unclean spirit, healed the child, and gave him back to his father.

Jesus Again Predicts His Death

43And they were all amazed at the majesty of God.

But while everyone marveled at all the things which Jesus did, He said to His disciples, 44"Let these words sink down into your ears, for the Son of Man is about to be betrayed into the hands of men." 45But they did not understand this saying, and it was hidden from them so that they did not perceive it; and they were afraid to ask Him about this saying.

Who Is the Greatest?

46Then a dispute arose among them as to which of them would be greatest. 47And Jesus, perceiving the thought of their heart, took a little child and set him by Him, 48and said to them, "Whoever receives this little child in My name receives Me; and whoever receives Me receives Him who sent Me. For he who is least among you all will be great."

Jesus Forbids Sectarianism

49Now John answered and said, "Master, we saw someone casting out demons in Your name, and we forbade him because he does not follow with us."

50But Jesus said to him, "Do not forbid *him*, for he who is not against us[a] is on our[b] side."

A Samaritan Village Rejects the Savior

51Now it came to pass, when the time had come for Him to be received up, that He steadfastly set His face to go to Jerusalem, 52and sent messengers before His face. And as they went, they entered a village of the Samaritans, to prepare for Him. 53But they did not receive Him, because His face was *set* for the journey to Jerusalem. 54And when His disci-

---

9:50 [a]NU-Text reads *you*. [b]NU-Text reads *your*.

ples James and John saw *this,* they
said, "Lord, do You want us to command fire to come down from
heaven and consume them, just as
Elijah did?"[a]
55 But He turned and rebuked
them,[a] and said, "You do not know
what manner of spirit you are of.
56 For the Son of Man did not come to
destroy men's lives but to save *them.*"[a]
And they went to another village.

The Cost of Discipleship

57 Now it happened as they journeyed on the road, *that* someone said
to Him, "Lord, I will follow You
wherever You go."
58 And Jesus said to him, "Foxes
have holes and birds of the air *have*
nests, but the Son of Man has
nowhere to lay *His* head."
59 Then He said to another, "Follow Me."
But he said, "Lord, let me first go
and bury my father."
60 Jesus said to him, "Let the dead
bury their own dead, but you go and
preach the kingdom of God."
61 And another also said, "Lord, I
will follow You, but let me first go *and*
bid them farewell who are at my
house."
62 But Jesus said to him, "No one,
having put his hand to the plow, and
looking back, is fit for the kingdom
of God."

The Seventy Sent Out

10 After these things the Lord appointed seventy others also,[a]
and sent them two by two before
His face into every city and place
where He Himself was about to go.
2 Then He said to them, "The harvest
truly *is* great, but the laborers *are*
few; therefore pray the Lord of the
harvest to send out laborers into His
harvest. 3 Go your way; behold, I send
you out as lambs among wolves.
4 Carry neither money bag, knapsack,
nor sandals; and greet no one along
the road. 5 But whatever house you
enter, first say, 'Peace to this house.'
6 And if a son of peace is there, your
peace will rest on it; if not, it will return to you. 7 And remain in the same
house, eating and drinking such
things as they give, for the laborer is

9:54 [a]NU-Text omits *just as Elijah did.* **9:55** [a]NU-Text omits the rest of this verse. **9:56** [a]NU-Text omits the first sentence of this verse. **10:1** [a]NU-Text reads *seventy-two others.*

worthy of his wages. Do not go from
house to house. 8Whatever city you
enter, and they receive you, eat such
things as are set before you. 9And heal
the sick there, and say to them, 'The
kingdom of God has come near to
you.' 10But whatever city you enter,
and they do not receive you, go out
into its streets and say, 11'The very
dust of your city which clings to us[a]
we wipe off against you. Nevertheless
know this, that the kingdom of God
has come near you.' 12But[a] I say to
you that it will be more tolerable in
that Day for Sodom than for that city.

Woe to the Impenitent Cities

13"Woe to you, Chorazin! Woe to
you, Bethsaida! For if the mighty
works which were done in you had
been done in Tyre and Sidon, they
would have repented long ago, sitting in sackcloth and ashes. 14But it
will be more tolerable for Tyre and
Sidon at the judgment than for you.
15And you, Capernaum, who are exalted to heaven, will be brought
down to Hades.[a] 16He who hears
you hears Me, he who rejects you
rejects Me, and he who rejects Me rejects Him who sent Me."

The Seventy Return with Joy

17Then the seventy[a] returned with
joy, saying, "Lord, even the demons
are subject to us in Your name."
18And He said to them, "I saw Satan fall like lightning from heaven.
19Behold, I give you the authority to
trample on serpents and scorpions,
and over all the power of the enemy,
and nothing shall by any means hurt
you. 20Nevertheless do not rejoice in
this, that the spirits are subject to
you, but rather[a] rejoice because your
names are written in heaven."

Jesus Rejoices in the Spirit

21In that hour Jesus rejoiced in
the Spirit and said, "I thank You, Father, Lord of heaven and earth, that
You have hidden these things from
the wise and prudent and revealed
them to babes. Even so, Father, for
so it seemed good in Your sight.
22All[a] things have been delivered to
Me by My Father, and no one knows
who the Son is except the Father,

10:11 [a]NU-Text reads *our feet.* **10:12** [a]NU-Text and M-Text omit *But.* **10:15** [a]NU-Text reads *will you be exalted to heaven? You will be thrust down to Hades!* **10:17** [a]NU-Text reads *seventy-two.* **10:20** [a]NU-Text and M-Text omit *rather.* **10:22** [a]M-Text reads *And turning to the disciples He said, "All . . .*

and who the Father is except the
Son, and *the one* to whom the Son
wills to reveal *Him*."

23 Then He turned to *His* disciples
and said privately, "Blessed *are* the
eyes which see the things you see;
24 for I tell you that many prophets
and kings have desired to see what
you see, and have not seen *it*, and to
hear what you hear, and have not
heard *it*."

The Parable of the Good Samaritan

25 And behold, a certain lawyer
stood up and tested Him, saying,
"Teacher, what shall I do to inherit
eternal life?"

26 He said to him, "What is written in the law? What is your reading
of it?"

27 So he answered and said, "'*You
shall love the* L*ORD your God with
all your heart, with all your soul,
with all your strength, and with all
your mind*,'[a] and '*your neighbor as
yourself*.'"[b]

28 And He said to him, "You have
answered rightly; do this and you will
live."

29 But he, wanting to justify himself, said to Jesus, "And who is my
neighbor?"

30 Then Jesus answered and said:
"A certain *man* went down from Jerusalem to Jericho, and fell among
thieves, who stripped him of his
clothing, wounded *him*, and departed,
leaving *him* half dead. 31 Now by
chance a certain priest came down
that road. And when he saw him, he
passed by on the other side. 32 Likewise a Levite, when he arrived at the
place, came and looked, and passed
by on the other side. 33 But a certain
Samaritan, as he journeyed, came
where he was. And when he saw him,
he had compassion. 34 So he went to
him and bandaged his wounds, pour-
ing on oil and wine; and he set him
on his own animal, brought him to
an inn, and took care of him. 35 On
the next day, when he departed,[a]
he took out two denarii, gave *them* to
the innkeeper, and said to him, 'Take
care of him; and whatever more you
spend, when I come again, I will
repay you.' 36 So which of these three
do you think was neighbor to him
who fell among the thieves?"

10:27 [a]Deuteronomy 6:5 [b]Leviticus 19:18 **10:35** [a]NU-Text omits *when he departed*.

37 And he said, "He who showed mercy on him."

Then Jesus said to him, "Go and do likewise."

Mary and Martha Worship and Serve

38 Now it happened as they went that He entered a certain village; and a certain woman named Martha welcomed Him into her house. 39 And she had a sister called Mary, who also sat at Jesus'[a] feet and heard His word. 40 But Martha was distracted with much serving, and she approached Him and said, "Lord, do You not care that my sister has left me to serve alone? Therefore tell her to help me."

41 And Jesus[a] answered and said to her, "Martha, Martha, you are worried and troubled about many things. 42 But one thing is needed, and Mary has chosen that good part, which will not be taken away from her."

The Model Prayer

11 Now it came to pass, as He was praying in a certain place, when He ceased, *that* one of His disciples said to Him, "Lord, teach us to pray, as John also taught his disciples."

2 So He said to them, "When you pray, say:

Our Father in heaven,[a]
Hallowed be Your name.
Your kingdom come.[b]
Your will be done
On earth as *it is* in heaven.
3 Give us day by day our daily
bread.
4 And forgive us our sins,
For we also forgive everyone
who is indebted to us.
And do not lead us into
temptation,
But deliver us from the evil
one." [a]

A Friend Comes at Midnight

5 And He said to them, "Which of you shall have a friend, and go to him at midnight and say to him, 'Friend, lend me three loaves; 6 for a friend of mine has come to me on his journey, and I have nothing to set before him'; 7 and he will answer from within and say, 'Do not trouble me; the door is

---

10:39 [a]NU-Text reads *the Lord's*. **10:41** [a]NU-Text reads *the Lord*. **11:2** [a]NU-Text omits *Our* and *in heaven*. [b]NU-Text omits the rest of this verse. **11:4** [a]NU-Text omits *But deliver us from the evil one*.

now shut, and my children are with me in bed; I cannot rise and give to you'? 8I say to you, though he will not rise and give to him because he is his friend, yet because of his persistence he will rise and give him as many as he needs.

Keep Asking, Seeking, Knocking

9"So I say to you, ask, and it will be given to you; seek, and you will find; knock, and it will be opened to you. 10For everyone who asks receives, and he who seeks finds, and to him who knocks it will be opened. 11If a son asks for bread[a] from any father among you, will he give him a stone? Or if *he asks* for a fish, will he give him a serpent instead of a fish? 12Or if he asks for an egg, will he offer him a scorpion? 13If you then, being evil, know how to give good gifts to your children, how much more will *your* heavenly Father give the Holy Spirit to those who ask Him!"

A House Divided Cannot Stand

14And He was casting out a demon, and it was mute. So it was, when the demon had gone out, that the mute spoke; and the multitudes marveled. 15But some of them said, "He casts out demons by Beelzebub,[a] the ruler of the demons."

16Others, testing *Him,* sought from Him a sign from heaven. 17But He, knowing their thoughts, said to them: "Every kingdom divided against itself is brought to desolation, and a house *divided* against a house falls. 18If Satan also is divided against himself, how will his kingdom stand? Because you say I cast out demons by Beelzebub. 19And if I cast out demons by Beelzebub, by whom do your sons cast *them* out? Therefore they will be your judges. 20But if I cast out demons with the finger of God, surely the kingdom of God has come upon you. 21When a strong man, fully armed, guards his own palace, his goods are in peace. 22But when a stronger than he comes upon him and overcomes him, he takes from him all his armor in which he trusted, and divides his spoils. 23He who is not with Me is against Me, and he who does not gather with Me scatters.

11:11 [a]NU-Text omits the words from *bread* through *for* in the next sentence. **11:15** [a]NU-Text and M-Text read *Beelzebul.*

An Unclean Spirit Returns

24“When an unclean spirit goes out of a man, he goes through dry places, seeking rest; and finding none, he says, ‘I will return to my house from which I came.’ 25And when he comes, he finds *it* swept and put in order. 26Then he goes and takes with *him* seven other spirits more wicked than himself, and they enter and dwell there; and the last *state* of that man is worse than the first.”

Keeping the Word

27And it happened, as He spoke these things, that a certain woman from the crowd raised her voice and said to Him, “Blessed *is* the womb that bore You, and *the* breasts which nursed You!”

28But He said, “More than that, blessed *are* those who hear the word of God and keep it!”

Seeking a Sign

29And while the crowds were thickly gathered together, He began to say, “This is an evil generation. It seeks a sign, and no sign will be given to it except the sign of Jonah the prophet.[a] 30For as Jonah became a sign to the Ninevites, so also the Son of Man will be to this generation. 31The queen of the South will rise up in the judgment with the men of this generation and condemn them, for she came from the ends of the earth to hear the wisdom of Solomon; and indeed a greater than Solomon *is* here. 32The men of Nineveh will rise up in the judgment with this generation and condemn it, for they repented at the preaching of Jonah; and indeed a greater than Jonah *is* here.

The Lamp of the Body

33“No one, when he has lit a lamp, puts *it* in a secret place or under a basket, but on a lampstand, that those who come in may see the light. 34The lamp of the body is the eye. Therefore, when your eye is good, your whole body also is full of light. But when *your eye* is bad, your body also *is* full of darkness. 35Therefore take heed that the light which is in you is not darkness. 36If then your whole body *is* full of light, having no

---

11:29 [a]NU-Text omits *the prophet.*

part dark, *the* whole *body* will be full of light, as when the bright shining of a lamp gives you light."

Woe to the Pharisees and Lawyers

37 And as He spoke, a certain Pharisee asked Him to dine with him. So He went in and sat down to eat. 38 When the Pharisee saw *it,* he marveled that He had not first washed before dinner.

39 Then the Lord said to him, "Now you Pharisees make the outside of the cup and dish clean, but your inward part is full of greed and wickedness. 40 Foolish ones! Did not He who made the outside make the inside also? 41 But rather give alms of such things as you have; then indeed all things are clean to you.

42 "But woe to you Pharisees! For you tithe mint and rue and all manner of herbs, and pass by justice and the love of God. These you ought to have done, without leaving the others undone. 43 Woe to you Pharisees! For you love the best seats in the synagogues and greetings in the marketplaces. 44 Woe to you, scribes and Pharisees, hypocrites![a] For you are like graves which are not seen, and the men who walk over *them* are not aware *of them.*"

45 Then one of the lawyers answered and said to Him, "Teacher, by saying these things You reproach us also."

46 And He said, "Woe to you also, lawyers! For you load men with burdens hard to bear, and you yourselves do not touch the burdens with one of your fingers. 47 Woe to you! For you build the tombs of the prophets, and your fathers killed them. 48 In fact, you bear witness that you approve the deeds of your fathers; for they indeed killed them, and you build their tombs. 49 Therefore the wisdom of God also said, 'I will send them prophets and apostles, and *some* of them they will kill and persecute,' 50 that the blood of all the prophets which was shed from the foundation of the world may be required of this generation, 51 from the blood of Abel to the blood of Zechariah who perished between the altar and the temple. Yes, I say to you, it shall be required of this generation.

11:44 [a]NU-Text omits *scribes and Pharisees, hypocrites.*

52"Woe to you lawyers! For you
have taken away the key of knowledge. You did not enter in yourselves,
and those who were entering in you
hindered."

53And as He said these things to
them,[a] the scribes and the Pharisees
began to assail *Him* vehemently, and to
cross-examine Him about many things,
54lying in wait for Him, and seeking to
catch Him in something He might say,
that they might accuse Him.[a]

Beware of Hypocrisy

12 In the meantime, when an innumerable multitude of people had gathered together, so that
they trampled one another, He began
to say to His disciples first *of all,* "Beware of the leaven of the Pharisees,
which is hypocrisy. 2For there is
nothing covered that will not be revealed, nor hidden that will not be
known. 3Therefore whatever you
have spoken in the dark will be heard
in the light, and what you have spoken in the ear in inner rooms will be
proclaimed on the housetops.

Jesus Teaches the Fear of God

4"And I say to you, My friends, do
not be afraid of those who kill the
body, and after that have no more
that they can do. 5But I will show
you whom you should fear: Fear
Him who, after He has killed, has
power to cast into hell; yes, I say to
you, fear Him!

6"Are not five sparrows sold for
two copper coins?[a] And not one of
them is forgotten before God. 7But
the very hairs of your head are all
numbered. Do not fear therefore;
you are of more value than many
sparrows.

Confess Christ Before Men

8"Also I say to you, whoever confesses Me before men, him the Son of
Man also will confess before the angels of God. 9But he who denies Me
before men will be denied before the
angels of God.

10"And anyone who speaks a
word against the Son of Man, it will
be forgiven him; but to him who

11:53 [a]NU-Text reads *And when He left there.* **11:54** [a]NU-Text omits *and seeking* and *that they might accuse Him.* **12:6** [a]Greek *assarion,* a coin of very small value

blasphemes against the Holy Spirit, it
will not be forgiven.

11"Now when they bring you to
the synagogues and magistrates and
authorities, do not worry about how
or what you should answer, or what
you should say. 12For the Holy Spirit
will teach you in that very hour what
you ought to say."

The Parable of the Rich Fool

13Then one from the crowd said
to Him, "Teacher, tell my brother to
divide the inheritance with me."

14But He said to him, "Man, who
made Me a judge or an arbitrator over
you?" 15And He said to them, "Take
heed and beware of covetousness,[a] for
one's life does not consist in the abundance of the things he possesses."

16Then He spoke a parable to
them, saying: "The ground of a certain rich man yielded plentifully.
17And he thought within himself, saying, 'What shall I do, since I have no
room to store my crops?' 18So he said,
'I will do this: I will pull down my
barns and build greater, and there I
will store all my crops and my goods.
19And I will say to my soul, "Soul, you
have many goods laid up for many
years; take your ease; eat, drink, *and*
be merry."' 20But God said to him,
'Fool! This night your soul will be required of you; then whose will those
things be which you have provided?'

21"So *is* he who lays up treasure
for himself, and is not rich toward
God."

Do Not Worry

22Then He said to His disciples,
"Therefore I say to you, do not worry
about your life, what you will eat; nor
about the body, what you will put on.
23Life is more than food, and the body
is more than clothing. 24Consider the
ravens, for they neither sow nor reap,
which have neither storehouse nor
barn; and God feeds them. Of how
much more value are you than the
birds? 25And which of you by worrying can add one cubit to his stature?
26If you then are not able to do *the*
least, why are you anxious for the
rest? 27Consider the lilies, how they
grow: they neither toil nor spin; and
yet I say to you, even Solomon in all

12:15 [a]NU-Text reads *all covetousness.*

his glory was not arrayed like one of
these. 28If then God so clothes the
grass, which today is in the field and
tomorrow is thrown into the oven,
how much more *will He clothe* you, O
you of little faith?

29"And do not seek what you
should eat or what you should
drink, nor have an anxious mind.
30For all these things the nations of
the world seek after, and your Father
knows that you need these things.
31But seek the kingdom of God,
and all these things[a] shall be added
to you.

32"Do not fear, little flock, for it is
your Father's good pleasure to give
you the kingdom. 33Sell what you
have and give alms; provide yourselves money bags which do not grow
old, a treasure in the heavens that
does not fail, where no thief ap-
proaches nor moth destroys. 34For
where your treasure is, there your
heart will be also.

The Faithful Servant and the Evil Servant

35"Let your waist be girded and
your lamps burning; 36and you yourselves be like men who wait for their
master, when he will return from the
wedding, that when he comes and
knocks they may open to him immediately. 37Blessed *are* those servants
whom the master, when he comes,
will find watching. Assuredly, I say to
you that he will gird himself and
have them sit down *to eat,* and will
come and serve them. 38And if he
should come in the second watch, or
come in the third watch, and find
them so, blessed are those servants.
39But know this, that if the master
of the house had known what hour
the thief would come, he would have
watched and[a] not allowed his house
to be broken into. 40Therefore you
also be ready, for the Son of Man is
coming at an hour you do not expect."

41Then Peter said to Him, "Lord,
do You speak this parable *only* to us, or
to all *people?*"

42And the Lord said, "Who then
is that faithful and wise steward,
whom *his* master will make ruler
over his household, to give *them their*
portion of food in due season?
43Blessed *is* that servant whom his

12:31 [a]NU-Text reads *His kingdom, and these things.* **12:39** [a]NU-Text reads *he would not have allowed.*

master will find so doing when he comes. 44Truly, I say to you that he will make him ruler over all that he has. 45But if that servant says in his heart, 'My master is delaying his coming,' and begins to beat the male and female servants, and to eat and drink and be drunk, 46the master of that servant will come on a day when he is not looking for *him,* and at an hour when he is not aware, and will cut him in two and appoint *him* his portion with the unbelievers. 47And that servant who knew his master's will, and did not prepare *himself* or do according to his will, shall be beaten with many *stripes.* 48But he who did not know, yet committed things deserving of stripes, shall be beaten with few. For everyone to whom much is given, from him much will be required; and to whom much has been committed, of him they will ask the more.

Christ Brings Division

49"I came to send fire on the earth, and how I wish it were already kindled! 50But I have a baptism to be baptized with, and how distressed I am till it is accomplished! 51Do *you* suppose that I came to give peace on earth? I tell you, not at all, but rather division. 52For from now on five in one house will be divided: three against two, and two against three. 53Father will be divided against son and son against father, mother against daughter and daughter against mother, mother-in-law against her daughter-in-law and daughter-in-law against her mother-in-law."

Discern the Time

54Then He also said to the multitudes, "Whenever you see a cloud rising out of the west, immediately you say, 'A shower is coming'; and so it is. 55And when *you see* the south wind blow, you say, 'There will be hot weather'; and there is. 56Hypocrites! You can discern the face of the sky and of the earth, but how *is it* you do not discern this time?

Make Peace with Your Adversary

57"Yes, and why, even of yourselves, do you not judge what is right? 58When you go with your adversary to the magistrate, make every effort along the way to settle with him, lest he drag you to the judge, the judge

deliver you to the officer, and the officer throw you into prison. 59 I tell
you, you shall not depart from there
till you have paid the very last mite."

Repent or Perish

13 There were present at that
season some who told Him
about the Galileans whose blood Pilate had mingled with their sacrifices.
2 And Jesus answered and said to
them, "Do you suppose that these
Galileans were worse sinners than all
other Galileans, because they suffered
such things? 3 I tell you, no; but unless
you repent you will all likewise perish. 4 Or those eighteen on whom the
tower in Siloam fell and killed them,
do you think that they were worse
sinners than all *other* men who dwelt
in Jerusalem? 5 I tell you, no; but unless you repent you will all likewise
perish."

The Parable of the Barren Fig Tree

6 He also spoke this parable: "A
certain *man* had a fig tree planted in
his vineyard, and he came seeking
fruit on it and found none. 7 Then he
said to the keeper of his vineyard,
'Look, for three years I have come
seeking fruit on this fig tree and find
none. Cut it down; why does it use
up the ground?' 8 But he answered
and said to him, 'Sir, let it alone this
year also, until I dig around it and
fertilize *it*. 9 And if it bears fruit, *well*.
But if not, after that[a] you can cut it
down.'"

A Spirit of Infirmity

10 Now He was teaching in one of
the synagogues on the Sabbath.
11 And behold, there was a woman
who had a spirit of infirmity eighteen years, and was bent over and
could in no way raise *herself* up. 12 But
when Jesus saw her, He called *her* to
Him and said to her, "Woman, you
are loosed from your infirmity."
13 And He laid *His* hands on her, and
immediately she was made straight,
and glorified God.

14 But the ruler of the synagogue
answered with indignation, because
Jesus had healed on the Sabbath; and
he said to the crowd, "There are six

13:9 [a] NU-Text reads *And if it bears fruit after that, well. But if not, you can cut it down.*

days on which men ought to work;
therefore come and be healed on
them, and not on the Sabbath day."
15The Lord then answered him
and said, "Hypocrite![a] Does not each
one of you on the Sabbath loose his ox
or donkey from the stall, and lead *it*
away to water it? 16So ought not this
woman, being a daughter of Abraham, whom Satan has bound—think
of it—for eighteen years, be loosed
from this bond on the Sabbath?" 17And
when He said these things, all His adversaries were put to shame; and all
the multitude rejoiced for all the glorious things that were done by Him.

The Parable of the Mustard Seed

18Then He said, "What is the kingdom of God like? And to what shall I
compare it? 19It is like a mustard seed,
which a man took and put in his garden; and it grew and became a large[a]
tree, and the birds of the air nested in
its branches."

The Parable of the Leaven

20And again He said, "To what
shall I liken the kingdom of God? 21It
is like leaven, which a woman took
and hid in three measures[a] of meal
till it was all leavened."

The Narrow Way

22And He went through the cities
and villages, teaching, and journeying toward Jerusalem. 23Then one
said to Him, "Lord, are there few who
are saved?"

And He said to them, 24"Strive to
enter through the narrow gate, for
many, I say to you, will seek to enter
and will not be able. 25When once the
Master of the house has risen up and
shut the door, and you begin to stand
outside and knock at the door, saying, 'Lord, Lord, open for us,' and He
will answer and say to you, 'I do not
know you, where you are from,'
26then you will begin to say, 'We ate
and drank in Your presence, and You
taught in our streets.' 27But He will
say, 'I tell you I do not know you,
where you are from. Depart from
Me, all you workers of iniquity.'
28There will be weeping and gnashing of teeth, when you see Abraham
and Isaac and Jacob and all the proph-

13:15 [a]NU-Text and M-Text read *Hypocrites.* 13:19 [a]NU-Text omits *large.* 13:21 [a]Greek *sata,* approximately two pecks in all

ets in the kingdom of God, and yourselves thrust out. 29They will come from the east and the west, from the north and the south, and sit down in the kingdom of God. 30And indeed there are last who will be first, and there are first who will be last."

31On that very day[a] some Pharisees came, saying to Him, "Get out and depart from here, for Herod wants to kill You."

32And He said to them, "Go, tell that fox, 'Behold, I cast out demons and perform cures today and tomorrow, and the third *day* I shall be perfected.' 33Nevertheless I must journey today, tomorrow, and the *day* following; for it cannot be that a prophet should perish outside of Jerusalem.

Jesus Laments over Jerusalem

34"O Jerusalem, Jerusalem, the one who kills the prophets and stones those who are sent to her! How often I wanted to gather your children together, as a hen *gathers* her brood under *her* wings, but you were not willing! 35See! Your house is left to you desolate; and assuredly,[a] I say to you, you shall not see Me until *the time* comes when you say, *'Blessed is He who comes in the name of the LORD!'* "[b]

A Man with Dropsy Healed on the Sabbath

14 Now it happened, as He went into the house of one of the rulers of the Pharisees to eat bread on the Sabbath, that they watched Him closely. 2And behold, there was a certain man before Him who had dropsy. 3And Jesus, answering, spoke to the lawyers and Pharisees, saying, "Is it lawful to heal on the Sabbath?"[a]

4But they kept silent. And He took *him* and healed him, and let him go. 5Then He answered them, saying, "Which of you, having a donkey[a] or an ox that has fallen into a pit, will not immediately pull him out on the Sabbath day?" 6And they could not answer Him regarding these things.

Take the Lowly Place

7So He told a parable to those who were invited, when He noted how they chose the best places, say-

13:31 [a]NU-Text reads *In that very hour.* 13:35 [a]NU-Text and M-Text omit *assuredly.* [b]Psalm 118:26 14:3 [a]NU-Text adds *or not.* 14:5 [a]NU-Text and M-Text read *son.*

ing to them: 8"When you are invited by anyone to a wedding feast, do not sit down in the best place, lest one more honorable than you be invited by him; 9and he who invited you and him come and say to you, 'Give place to this man,' and then you begin with shame to take the lowest place. 10But when you are invited, go and sit down in the lowest place, so that when he who invited you comes he may say to you, 'Friend, go up higher.' Then you will have glory in the presence of those who sit at the table with you. 11For whoever exalts himself will be humbled, and he who humbles himself will be exalted."

12Then He also said to him who invited Him, "When you give a dinner or a supper, do not ask your friends, your brothers, your relatives, nor rich neighbors, lest they also invite you back, and you be repaid. 13But when you give a feast, invite *the* poor, *the* maimed, *the* lame, *the* blind. 14And you will be blessed, because they cannot repay you; for you shall be repaid at the resurrection of the just."

The Parable of the Great Supper

15Now when one of those who sat at the table with Him heard these things, he said to Him, "Blessed *is* he who shall eat bread[a] in the kingdom of God!"

16Then He said to him, "A certain man gave a great supper and invited many, 17and sent his servant at supper time to say to those who were invited, 'Come, for all things are now ready.' 18But they all with one *accord* began to make excuses. The first said to him, 'I have bought a piece of ground, and I must go and see it. I ask you to have me excused.' 19And another said, 'I have bought five yoke of oxen, and I am going to test them. I ask you to have me excused.' 20Still another said, 'I have married a wife, and therefore I cannot come.' 21So that servant came and reported these things to his master. Then the master of the house, being angry, said to his servant, 'Go out quickly into the streets and lanes of the city, and bring in here *the* poor and *the* maimed and *the* lame and *the* blind.' 22And the servant said,

14:15 [a]M-Text reads *dinner*.

'Master, it is done as you commanded, and still there is room.' 23 Then the master said to the servant, 'Go out into the highways and hedges, and compel *them* to come in, that my house may be filled. 24 For I say to you that none of those men who were invited shall taste my supper.' "

Leaving All to Follow Christ

25 Now great multitudes went with Him. And He turned and said to them, 26 "If anyone comes to Me and does not hate his father and mother, wife and children, brothers and sisters, yes, and his own life also, he cannot be My disciple. 27 And whoever does not bear his cross and come after Me cannot be My disciple. 28 For which of you, intending to build a tower, does not sit down first and count the cost, whether he has *enough* to finish *it*— 29 lest, after he has laid the foundation, and is not able to finish, all who see *it* begin to mock him, 30 saying, 'This man began to build and was not able to finish.' 31 Or what king, going to make war against another king, does not sit down first and consider whether he is able with ten thousand to meet him who comes against him with twenty thousand? 32 Or else, while the other is still a great way off, he sends a delegation and asks conditions of peace. 33 So likewise, whoever of you does not forsake all that he has cannot be My disciple.

Tasteless Salt Is Worthless

34 "Salt *is* good; but if the salt has lost its flavor, how shall it be seasoned? 35 It is neither fit for the land nor for the dunghill, *but* men throw it out. He who has ears to hear, let him hear!"

The Parable of the Lost Sheep

15 Then all the tax collectors and the sinners drew near to Him to hear Him. 2 And the Pharisees and scribes complained, saying, "This Man receives sinners and eats with them." 3 So He spoke this parable to them, saying:

4 "What man of you, having a hundred sheep, if he loses one of them, does not leave the ninety-nine in the wilderness, and go after the one which is lost until he finds it? 5 And when he has found *it*, he lays *it* on his shoulders, rejoicing. 6 And when he comes home, he calls to-

gether *his* friends and neighbors, saying to them, 'Rejoice with me, for I have found my sheep which was lost!' 7I say to you that likewise there will be more joy in heaven over one sinner who repents than over ninety-nine just persons who need no repentance.

The Parable of the Lost Coin

8"Or what woman, having ten silver coins,[a] if she loses one coin, does not light a lamp, sweep the house, and search carefully until she finds *it?* 9And when she has found *it,* she calls *her* friends and neighbors together, saying, 'Rejoice with me, for I have found the piece which I lost!' 10Likewise, I say to you, there is joy in the presence of the angels of God over one sinner who repents."

The Parable of the Lost Son

11Then He said: "A certain man had two sons. 12And the younger of them said to *his* father, 'Father, give me the portion of goods that falls *to me.*' So he divided to them *his* livelihood. 13And not many days after, the younger son gathered all together, journeyed to a far country, and there wasted his possessions with prodigal living. 14But when he had spent all, there arose a severe famine in that land, and he began to be in want. 15Then he went and joined himself to a citizen of that country, and he sent him into his fields to feed swine. 16And he would gladly have filled his stomach with the pods that the swine ate, and no one gave him *anything.*

17"But when he came to himself, he said, 'How many of my father's hired servants have bread enough and to spare, and I perish with hunger! 18I will arise and go to my father, and will say to him, "Father, I have sinned against heaven and before you, 19and I am no longer worthy to be called your son. Make me like one of your hired servants."'

20"And he arose and came to his father. But when he was still a great way off, his father saw him and had compassion, and ran and fell on his neck and kissed him. 21And the son said to him, 'Father, I have sinned against heaven and in your sight, and am no longer worthy to be called your son.'

15:8 [a]Greek *drachma,* a valuable coin often worn in a ten-piece garland by married women

22"But the father said to his servants, 'Bring[a] out the best robe and put
it on him, and put a ring on his hand
and sandals on *his* feet. 23And bring the
fatted calf here and kill *it*, and let us eat
and be merry; 24for this my son was
dead and is alive again; he was lost and
is found.' And they began to be merry.

25"Now his older son was in the
field. And as he came and drew near
to the house, he heard music and
dancing. 26So he called one of the servants and asked what these things
meant. 27And he said to him, 'Your
brother has come, and because he has
received him safe and sound, your father has killed the fatted calf.'

28"But he was angry and would
not go in. Therefore his father came
out and pleaded with him. 29So he
answered and said to *his* father, 'Lo,
these many years I have been serving
you; I never transgressed your commandment at any time; and yet you
never gave me a young goat, that I
might make merry with my friends.
30But as soon as this son of yours
came, who has devoured your livelihood with harlots, you killed the fatted calf for him.'

31"And he said to him, 'Son, you
are always with me, and all that I
have is yours. 32It was right that we
should make merry and be glad, for
your brother was dead and is alive
again, and was lost and is found.'"

The Parable of the Unjust Steward

16 He also said to His disciples:
"There was a certain rich man
who had a steward, and an accusation was brought to him that this
man was wasting his goods. 2So he
called him and said to him, 'What is
this I hear about you? Give an account of your stewardship, for you
can no longer be steward.'

3"Then the steward said within
himself, 'What shall I do? For my master is taking the stewardship away
from me. I cannot dig; I am ashamed
to beg. 4I have resolved what to do,
that when I am put out of the stewardship, they may receive me into
their houses.'

5"So he called every one of his
master's debtors to *him*, and said to
the first, 'How much do you owe my
master?' 6And he said, 'A hundred

15:22 [a]NU-Text reads *Quickly bring*.

measures[a] of oil.' So he said to him, 'Take your bill, and sit down quickly and write fifty.' 7 Then he said to another, 'And how much do you owe?' So he said, 'A hundred measures[a] of wheat.' And he said to him, 'Take your bill, and write eighty.' 8 So the master commended the unjust steward because he had dealt shrewdly. For the sons of this world are more shrewd in their generation than the sons of light.

9 "And I say to you, make friends for yourselves by unrighteous mammon, that when you fail,[a] they may receive you into an everlasting home. 10 He who *is* faithful in *what is* least is faithful also in much; and he who is unjust in *what is* least is unjust also in much. 11 Therefore if you have not been faithful in the unrighteous mammon, who will commit to your trust the true *riches?* 12 And if you have not been faithful in what is another man's, who will give you what is your own?

13 "No servant can serve two masters; for either he will hate the one and love the other, or else he will be loyal to the one and despise the other. You cannot serve God and mammon."

The Law, the Prophets, and the Kingdom

14 Now the Pharisees, who were lovers of money, also heard all these things, and they derided Him. 15 And He said to them, "You are those who justify yourselves before men, but God knows your hearts. For what is highly esteemed among men is an abomination in the sight of God.

16 "The law and the prophets *were* until John. Since that time the kingdom of God has been preached, and everyone is pressing into it. 17 And it is easier for heaven and earth to pass away than for one tittle of the law to fail.

18 "Whoever divorces his wife and marries another commits adultery; and whoever marries her who is divorced from *her* husband commits adultery.

The Rich Man and Lazarus

19 "There was a certain rich man who was clothed in purple and fine

---

16:6 [a]Greek *batos,* eight or nine gallons each (Old Testament *bath*) **16:7** [a]Greek *koros,* ten or twelve bushels each (Old Testament *kor*) **16:9** [a]NU-Text reads *it fails.*

linen and fared sumptuously every
day. 20 But there was a certain beggar
named Lazarus, full of sores, who was
laid at his gate, 21 desiring to be fed
with the crumbs which fell[a] from the
rich man's table. Moreover the dogs
came and licked his sores. 22 So it was
that the beggar died, and was carried
by the angels to Abraham's bosom.
The rich man also died and was
buried. 23 And being in torments in
Hades, he lifted up his eyes and saw
Abraham afar off, and Lazarus in his
bosom.

24 "Then he cried and said, 'Father
Abraham, have mercy on me, and
send Lazarus that he may dip the tip
of his finger in water and cool my
tongue; for I am tormented in this
flame.' 25 But Abraham said, 'Son, remember that in your lifetime you
received your good things, and likewise Lazarus evil things; but now he is
comforted and you are tormented.
26 And besides all this, between us and
you there is a great gulf fixed, so that
those who want to pass from here to
you cannot, nor can those from
there pass to us.'

27 "Then he said, 'I beg you therefore, father, that you would send him
to my father's house, 28 for I have five
brothers, that he may testify to them,
lest they also come to this place of torment.' 29 Abraham said to him, 'They
have Moses and the prophets; let
them hear them.' 30 And he said, 'No,
father Abraham; but if one goes to
them from the dead, they will repent.'
31 But he said to him, 'If they do not
hear Moses and the prophets, neither
will they be persuaded though one rise
from the dead.' "

Jesus Warns of Offenses

17 Then He said to the disciples,
"It is impossible that no offenses should come, but woe *to him*
through whom they do come! 2 It
would be better for him if a millstone
were hung around his neck, and he
were thrown into the sea, than that
he should offend one of these little
ones. 3 Take heed to yourselves. If your
brother sins against you,[a] rebuke him;
and if he repents, forgive him. 4 And if
he sins against you seven times in a
day, and seven times in a day returns
to you,[a] saying, 'I repent,' you shall
forgive him."

16:21 [a]NU-Text reads *with what fell.* **17:3** [a]NU-Text omits *against you.* **17:4** [a]M-Text omits *to you.*

Faith and Duty

5 And the apostles said to the
Lord, "Increase our faith."

6 So the Lord said, "If you have
faith as a mustard seed, you can say to
this mulberry tree, 'Be pulled up by
the roots and be planted in the sea,'
and it would obey you. 7 And which of
you, having a servant plowing or
tending sheep, will say to him when
he has come in from the field, 'Come
at once and sit down to eat'? 8 But will
he not rather say to him, 'Prepare
something for my supper, and gird
yourself and serve me till I have eaten
and drunk, and afterward you will
eat and drink'? 9 Does he thank that
servant because he did the things that
were commanded him? I think not.[a]
10 So likewise you, when you have
done all those things which you are
commanded, say, 'We are unprofit-
able servants. We have done what was
our duty to do.'"

Ten Lepers Cleansed

11 Now it happened as He went to
Jerusalem that He passed through the
midst of Samaria and Galilee. 12 Then
as He entered a certain village, there
met Him ten men who were lepers,
who stood afar off. 13 And they lifted
up *their* voices and said, "Jesus, Master,
have mercy on us!"

14 So when He saw *them,* He said to
them, "Go, show yourselves to the
priests." And so it was that as they
went, they were cleansed.

15 And one of them, when he saw
that he was healed, returned, and
with a loud voice glorified God,
16 and fell down on *his* face at His
feet, giving Him thanks. And he was
a Samaritan.

17 So Jesus answered and said,
"Were there not ten cleansed? But
where *are* the nine? 18 Were there not
any found who returned to give
glory to God except this foreigner?"
19 And He said to him, "Arise, go your
way. Your faith has made you well."

The Coming of the Kingdom

20 Now when He was asked by the
Pharisees when the kingdom of God
would come, He answered them and
said, "The kingdom of God does not
come with observation; 21 nor will
they say, 'See here!' or 'See there!'[a]

17:9 [a] NU-Text ends verse with *commanded;* M-Text omits *him.*

17:21 [a] NU-Text reverses *here* and *there.*

For indeed, the kingdom of God is
within you."

22 Then He said to the disciples,
"The days will come when you will
desire to see one of the days of the
Son of Man, and you will not see *it*.
23 And they will say to you, 'Look
here!' or 'Look there!'[a] Do not go
after *them* or follow *them*. 24 For as the
lightning that flashes out of one
part under heaven shines to the other
part under heaven, so also the Son of
Man will be in His day. 25 But first He
must suffer many things and be rejected by this generation. 26 And as it
was in the days of Noah, so it will be
also in the days of the Son of Man:
27 They ate, they drank, they married
wives, they were given in marriage,
until the day that Noah entered the
ark, and the flood came and destroyed them all. 28 Likewise as it was
also in the days of Lot: They ate, they
drank, they bought, they sold, they
planted, they built; 29 but on the day
that Lot went out of Sodom it rained
fire and brimstone from heaven and
destroyed *them* all. 30 Even so will it
be in the day when the Son of Man is
revealed.

31 "In that day, he who is on the
housetop, and his goods *are* in the
house, let him not come down to
take them away. And likewise the
one who is in the field, let him not
turn back. 32 Remember Lot's wife.
33 Whoever seeks to save his life will
lose it, and whoever loses his life will
preserve it. 34 I tell you, in that night
there will be two *men* in one bed: the
one will be taken and the other will
be left. 35 Two *women* will be grinding
together: the one will be taken and
the other left. 36 Two *men* will be in the
field: the one will be taken and the
other left."[a]

37 And they answered and said to
Him, "Where, Lord?"

So He said to them, "Wherever
the body is, there the eagles will be
gathered together."

The Parable of the Persistent Widow

18 Then He spoke a parable to
them, that men always
ought to pray and not lose heart,
2 saying: "There was in a certain city
a judge who did not fear God nor regard man. 3 Now there was a widow

---

17:23 [a]NU-Text reverses *here* and *there*. **17:36** [a]NU-Text and M-Text omit verse 36.

in that city; and she came to him,
saying, 'Get justice for me from my
adversary.' 4And he would not for a
while; but afterward he said within
himself, 'Though I do not fear God
nor regard man, 5yet because this
widow troubles me I will avenge her,
lest by her continual coming she
weary me.' "

6Then the Lord said, "Hear what
the unjust judge said. 7And shall God
not avenge His own elect who cry out
day and night to Him, though He
bears long with them? 8I tell you that
He will avenge them speedily. Nevertheless, when the Son of Man comes,
will He really find faith on the earth?"

The Parable of the Pharisee and the Tax Collector

9Also He spoke this parable to
some who trusted in themselves that
they were righteous, and despised
others: 10"Two men went up to the
temple to pray, one a Pharisee and
the other a tax collector. 11The Pharisee stood and prayed thus with himself, 'God, I thank You that I am not
like other men—extortioners, unjust, adulterers, or even as this tax
collector. 12I fast twice a week; I give
tithes of all that I possess.' 13And the
tax collector, standing afar off, would
not so much as raise *his* eyes to
heaven, but beat his breast, saying,
'God, be merciful to me a sinner!' 14I
tell you, this man went down to his
house justified *rather* than the other;
for everyone who exalts himself will
be humbled, and he who humbles
himself will be exalted."

Jesus Blesses Little Children

15Then they also brought infants
to Him that He might touch them;
but when the disciples saw *it*, they rebuked them. 16But Jesus called them
to *Him* and said, "Let the little children
come to Me, and do not forbid
them; for of such is the kingdom of
God. 17Assuredly, I say to you, whoever does not receive the kingdom of
God as a little child will by no means
enter it."

Jesus Counsels the Rich Young Ruler

18Now a certain ruler asked Him,
saying, "Good Teacher, what shall I
do to inherit eternal life?"

19So Jesus said to him, "Why do
you call Me good? No one *is* good but

One, *that is,* God. 20 You know the commandments: *'Do not commit adultery,' 'Do not murder,' 'Do not steal,' 'Do not bear false witness,' 'Honor your father and your mother.'* "[a]

21 And he said, "All these things I have kept from my youth."

22 So when Jesus heard these things, He said to him, "You still lack one thing. Sell all that you have and distribute to the poor, and you will have treasure in heaven; and come, follow Me."

23 But when he heard this, he became very sorrowful, for he was very rich.

With God All Things Are Possible

24 And when Jesus saw that he became very sorrowful, He said, "How hard it is for those who have riches to enter the kingdom of God! 25 For it is easier for a camel to go through the eye of a needle than for a rich man to enter the kingdom of God."

26 And those who heard it said, "Who then can be saved?"

27 But He said, "The things which are impossible with men are possible with God."

28 Then Peter said, "See, we have left all[a] and followed You."

29 So He said to them, "Assuredly, I say to you, there is no one who has left house or parents or brothers or wife or children, for the sake of the kingdom of God, 30 who shall not receive many times more in this present time, and in the age to come eternal life."

Jesus a Third Time Predicts His Death and Resurrection

31 Then He took the twelve aside and said to them, "Behold, we are going up to Jerusalem, and all things that are written by the prophets concerning the Son of Man will be accomplished. 32 For He will be delivered to the Gentiles and will be mocked and insulted and spit upon. 33 They will scourge *Him* and kill Him. And the third day He will rise again."

34 But they understood none of these things; this saying was hidden from them, and they did not know the things which were spoken.

18:20 [a]Exodus 20:12–16; Deuteronomy 5:16–20 **18:28** [a]NU-Text reads *our own.*

A Blind Man Receives His Sight

35 Then it happened, as He was
coming near Jericho, that a certain
blind man sat by the road begging.
36 And hearing a multitude passing
by, he asked what it meant. 37 So they
told him that Jesus of Nazareth was
passing by. 38 And he cried out, saying, "Jesus, Son of David, have mercy
on me!"

39 Then those who went before
warned him that he should be quiet;
but he cried out all the more, "Son of
David, have mercy on me!"

40 So Jesus stood still and commanded him to be brought to Him.
And when he had come near, He
asked him, 41 saying, "What do you
want Me to do for you?"

He said, "Lord, that I may receive
my sight."

42 Then Jesus said to him, "Receive
your sight; your faith has made you
well." 43 And immediately he received
his sight, and followed Him, glorifying God. And all the people, when
they saw *it,* gave praise to God.

Jesus Comes to Zacchaeus' House

19 Then *Jesus* entered and passed
through Jericho. 2 Now be-
hold, *there was* a man named Zacchaeus who was a chief tax collector, and
he was rich. 3 And he sought to see
who Jesus was, but could not because
of the crowd, for he was of short
stature. 4 So he ran ahead and climbed
up into a sycamore tree to see Him,
for He was going to pass that *way.*
5 And when Jesus came to the place,
He looked up and saw him,[a] and said
to him, "Zacchaeus, make haste and
come down, for today I must stay at
your house." 6 So he made haste and
came down, and received Him joy-
fully. 7 But when they saw *it,* they all
complained, saying, "He has gone
to be a guest with a man who is a
sinner."

8 Then Zacchaeus stood and said
to the Lord, "Look, Lord, I give half of
my goods to the poor; and if I have
taken anything from anyone by false
accusation, I restore fourfold."

9 And Jesus said to him, "Today

19:5 [a]NU-Text omits *and saw him.*

salvation has come to this house, because he also is a son of Abraham; [10]for the Son of Man has come to seek and to save that which was lost."

The Parable of the Minas

[11]Now as they heard these things, He spoke another parable, because He was near Jerusalem and because they thought the kingdom of God would appear immediately. [12]Therefore He said: "A certain nobleman went into a far country to receive for himself a kingdom and to return. [13]So he called ten of his servants, delivered to them ten minas,[a] and said to them, 'Do business till I come.' [14]But his citizens hated him, and sent a delegation after him, saying, 'We will not have this *man* to reign over us.'

[15]"And so it was that when he returned, having received the kingdom, he then commanded these servants, to whom he had given the money, to be called to him, that he might know how much every man had gained by trading. [16]Then came the first, saying, 'Master, your mina has earned ten minas.' [17]And he said to him, 'Well *done,* good servant; because you were faithful in a very little, have authority over ten cities.' [18]And the second came, saying, 'Master, your mina has earned five minas.' [19]Likewise he said to him, 'You also be over five cities.'

[20]"Then another came, saying, 'Master, here is your mina, which I have kept put away in a handkerchief. [21]For I feared you, because you are an austere man. You collect what you did not deposit, and reap what you did not sow.' [22]And he said to him, 'Out of your own mouth I will judge you, *you* wicked servant. You knew that I was an austere man, collecting what I did not deposit and reaping what I did not sow. [23]Why then did you not put my money in the bank, that at my coming I might have collected it with interest?'

[24]"And he said to those who stood by, 'Take the mina from him, and give *it* to him who has ten minas.' [25](But they said to him, 'Master, he has ten minas.') [26]'For I say to you, that to everyone who has will be given; and from him who does not

---

19:13 [a]The *mina* (Greek *mna,* Hebrew *minah*) was worth about three months' salary.

have, even what he has will be taken
away from him. 27But bring here
those enemies of mine, who did not
want me to reign over them, and slay
them before me.'"

The Triumphal Entry

28When He had said this, He went
on ahead, going up to Jerusalem.
29And it came to pass, when He drew
near to Bethphage[a] and Bethany, at
the mountain called Olivet, *that* He
sent two of His disciples, 30saying,
"Go into the village opposite *you,*
where as you enter you will find a
colt tied, on which no one has ever
sat. Loose it and bring *it here.* 31And
if anyone asks you, 'Why are you
loosing *it?*' thus you shall say to him,
'Because the Lord has need of it.'"

32So those who were sent went
their way and found *it* just as He had
said to them. 33But as they were loosing the colt, the owners of it said
to them, "Why are you loosing the
colt?"

34And they said, "The Lord has
need of him." 35Then they brought
him to Jesus. And they threw their
own clothes on the colt, and they set
Jesus on him. 36And as He went, *many*
spread their clothes on the road.

37Then, as He was now drawing
near the descent of the Mount of
Olives, the whole multitude of
the disciples began to rejoice and
praise God with a loud voice for all
the mighty works they had seen,
38saying:

"'*Blessed is the King who comes*
in the name of the LORD!'[a]
Peace in heaven and glory in
the highest!"

39And some of the Pharisees
called to Him from the crowd,
"Teacher, rebuke Your disciples."

40But He answered and said to
them, "I tell you that if these should
keep silent, the stones would immediately cry out."

Jesus Weeps over Jerusalem

41Now as He drew near, He saw
the city and wept over it, 42saying, "If
you had known, even you, especially
in this your day, the things *that make*
for your peace! But now they are

19:29 [a]M-Text reads *Bethsphage.* **19:38** [a]Psalm 118:26

hidden from your eyes. **43**For days will come upon you when your enemies will build an embankment around you, surround you and close you in on every side, **44**and level you, and your children within you, to the ground; and they will not leave in you one stone upon another, because you did not know the time of your visitation."

Jesus Cleanses the Temple

45Then He went into the temple and began to drive out those who bought and sold in it,[a] **46**saying to them, "It is written, *'My house is*[a] *a house of prayer,'*[b] but you have made it a *'den of thieves.'* "[c]

47And He was teaching daily in the temple. But the chief priests, the scribes, and the leaders of the people sought to destroy Him, **48**and were unable to do anything; for all the people were very attentive to hear Him.

Jesus' Authority Questioned

20 Now it happened on one of those days, as He taught the people in the temple and preached the gospel, *that* the chief priests and the scribes, together with the elders, confronted *Him* **2**and spoke to Him, saying, "Tell us, by what authority are You doing these things? Or who is he who gave You this authority?"

3But He answered and said to them, "I also will ask you one thing, and answer Me: **4**The baptism of John—was it from heaven or from men?"

5And they reasoned among themselves, saying, "If we say, 'From heaven,' He will say, 'Why then[a] did you not believe him?' **6**But if we say, 'From men,' all the people will stone us, for they are persuaded that John was a prophet." **7**So they answered that they did not know where *it was* from.

8And Jesus said to them, "Neither will I tell you by what authority I do these things."

The Parable of the Wicked Vinedressers

9Then He began to tell the people this parable: "A certain man planted a vineyard, leased it to vinedressers, and went into a far country

---

19:45 [a]NU-Text reads *those who were selling.* **19:46** [a]NU-Text reads *shall be.* [b]Isaiah 56:7 [c]Jeremiah 7:11 **20:5** [a]NU-Text and M-Text omit *then.*

for a long time. **10**Now at vintage-
time he sent a servant to the vinedressers, that they might give him
some of the fruit of the vineyard. But
the vinedressers beat him and sent
him away empty-handed. **11**Again he
sent another servant; and they beat
him also, treated *him* shamefully, and
sent *him* away empty-handed. **12**And
again he sent a third; and they
wounded him also and cast *him* out.

13"Then the owner of the vineyard said, 'What shall I do? I will send
my beloved son. Probably they will
respect *him* when they see him.' **14**But
when the vinedressers saw him, they
reasoned among themselves, saying,
'This is the heir. Come, let us kill
him, that the inheritance may be
ours.' **15**So they cast him out of the
vineyard and killed *him*. Therefore
what will the owner of the vineyard
do to them? **16**He will come and destroy those vinedressers and give the
vineyard to others."

And when they heard *it* they said, "Certainly not!"

17Then He looked at them
and said, "What then is this that is
written:

'The stone which the builders
rejected
Has become the chief
cornerstone'?[a]

18Whoever falls on that stone will be
broken; but on whomever it falls, it
will grind him to powder."

19And the chief priests and the
scribes that very hour sought to lay
hands on Him, but they feared the
people[a]—for they knew He had spoken this parable against them.

The Pharisees: Is It Lawful to Pay Taxes to Caesar?

20So they watched *Him*, and sent
spies who pretended to be righteous,
that they might seize on His words,
in order to deliver Him to the power
and the authority of the governor.

21Then they asked Him, saying,
"Teacher, we know that You say and
teach rightly, and You do not show
personal favoritism, but teach the
way of God in truth: **22**Is it lawful for
us to pay taxes to Caesar or not?"

23But He perceived their crafti-
ness, and said to them, "Why do you
test Me?[a] **24**Show Me a denarius.

20:17 [a]Psalm 118:22 **20:19** [a]M-Text reads *but they were afraid*. **20:23** [a]NU-Text omits *Why do you test Me?*

Whose image and inscription does
it have?"

They answered and said, "Caesar's."

25 And He said to them, "Render
therefore to Caesar the things that
are Caesar's, and to God the things
that are God's."

26 But they could not catch Him
in His words in the presence of the
people. And they marveled at His answer and kept silent.

The Sadducees: What About the Resurrection?

27 Then some of the Sadducees,
who deny that there is a resurrection,
came to *Him* and asked Him, 28 saying:
"Teacher, Moses wrote to us *that* if a
man's brother dies, having a wife, and
he dies without children, his brother
should take his wife and raise up offspring for his brother. 29 Now there
were seven brothers. And the first
took a wife, and died without children. 30 And the second[a] took her as
wife, and he died childless. 31 Then
the third took her, and in like manner the seven also; and they left no
children,[a] and died. 32 Last of all the
woman died also. 33 Therefore, in the
resurrection, whose wife does she become? For all seven had her as wife."

34 Jesus answered and said to them,
"The sons of this age marry and are
given in marriage. 35 But those who
are counted worthy to attain that age,
and the resurrection from the dead,
neither marry nor are given in marriage; 36 nor can they die anymore, for
they are equal to the angels and are
sons of God, being sons of the resurrection. 37 But even Moses showed in
the *burning* bush *passage* that the dead
are raised, when he called the Lord
'*the God of Abraham, the God of
Isaac, and the God of Jacob.*'[a] 38 For He
is not the God of the dead but of the
living, for all live to Him."

39 Then some of the scribes answered and said, "Teacher, You have
spoken well." 40 But after that they
dared not question Him anymore.

Jesus: How Can David Call His Descendant Lord?

41 And He said to them, "How can
they say that the Christ is the Son of

20:30 [a]NU-Text ends verse 30 here. **20:31** [a]NU-Text and M-Text read *the seven also left no children.* **20:37** [a]Exodus 3:6, 15

David? 42 Now David himself said in
the Book of Psalms:

'The LORD *said to my Lord,*
"Sit at My right hand,
43 *Till I make Your enemies Your*
footstool."'[a]

44 Therefore David calls Him *'Lord'*;
how is He then his Son?"

Beware of the Scribes

45 Then, in the hearing of all the
people, He said to His disciples, 46 "Beware of the scribes, who desire to go
around in long robes, love greetings
in the marketplaces, the best seats in
the synagogues, and the best places
at feasts, 47 who devour widows'
houses, and for a pretense make long
prayers. These will receive greater
condemnation."

The Widow's Two Mites

21 And He looked up and saw
the rich putting their gifts
into the treasury, 2 and He saw also
a certain poor widow putting in
two mites. 3 So He said, "Truly I say
to you that this poor widow has put
in more than all; 4 for all these out
of their abundance have put in offerings for God,[a] but she out of her
poverty put in all the livelihood that
she had."

Jesus Predicts the Destruction of the Temple

5 Then, as some spoke of the temple, how it was adorned with beautiful
stones and donations, He said, 6 "These
things which you see—the days will
come in which not *one* stone shall be
left upon another that shall not be
thrown down."

The Signs of the Times and the End of the Age

7 So they asked Him, saying,
"Teacher, but when will these things
be? And what sign *will there be* when
these things are about to take place?"
8 And He said: "Take heed that you
not be deceived. For many will come
in My name, saying, 'I am *He*,' and,
'The time has drawn near.' Therefore[a]
do not go after them. 9 But when you
hear of wars and commotions, do not
be terrified; for these things must

20:43 [a]Psalm 110:1 **21:4** [a]NU-Text omits *for God.* **21:8** [a]NU-Text omits *Therefore.*

come to pass first, but the end *will* not *come* immediately."

10Then He said to them, "Nation will rise against nation, and kingdom against kingdom. 11And there will be great earthquakes in various places, and famines and pestilences; and there will be fearful sights and great signs from heaven. 12But before all these things, they will lay their hands on you and persecute *you,* delivering *you* up to the synagogues and prisons. You will be brought before kings and rulers for My name's sake. 13But it will turn out for you as an occasion for testimony. 14Therefore settle *it* in your hearts not to meditate beforehand on what you will answer; 15for I will give you a mouth and wisdom which all your adversaries will not be able to contradict or resist. 16You will be betrayed even by parents and brothers, relatives and friends; and they will put *some* of you to death. 17And you will be hated by all for My name's sake. 18But not a hair of your head shall be lost. 19By your patience possess your souls.

The Destruction of Jerusalem

20"But when you see Jerusalem surrounded by armies, then know that its desolation is near. 21Then let those who are in Judea flee to the mountains, let those who are in the midst of her depart, and let not those who are in the country enter her. 22For these are the days of vengeance, that all things which are written may be fulfilled. 23But woe to those who are pregnant and to those who are nursing babies in those days! For there will be great distress in the land and wrath upon this people. 24And they will fall by the edge of the sword, and be led away captive into all nations. And Jerusalem will be trampled by Gentiles until the times of the Gentiles are fulfilled.

The Coming of the Son of Man

25"And there will be signs in the sun, in the moon, and in the stars; and on the earth distress of nations, with perplexity, the sea and the waves roaring; 26men's hearts failing them from fear and the expectation of those things which are coming on the earth, for the powers of the heavens will be shaken. 27Then they will see the Son of Man coming in a cloud with power and great glory. 28Now when these things begin to happen, look up and lift up your heads, because your redemption draws near."

The Parable of the Fig Tree

29 Then He spoke to them a parable: "Look at the fig tree, and all the trees. 30 When they are already budding, you see and know for yourselves that summer is now near. 31 So you also, when you see these things happening, know that the kingdom of God is near. 32 Assuredly, I say to you, this generation will by no means pass away till all things take place. 33 Heaven and earth will pass away, but My words will by no means pass away.

The Importance of Watching

34 "But take heed to yourselves, lest your hearts be weighed down with carousing, drunkenness, and cares of this life, and that Day come on you unexpectedly. 35 For it will come as a snare on all those who dwell on the face of the whole earth. 36 Watch therefore, and pray always that you may be counted worthy[a] to escape all these things that will come to pass, and to stand before the Son of Man."

37 And in the daytime He was teaching in the temple, but at night He went out and stayed on the mountain called Olivet. 38 Then early in the morning all the people came to Him in the temple to hear Him.

The Plot to Kill Jesus

22 Now the Feast of Unleavened Bread drew near, which is called Passover. 2 And the chief priests and the scribes sought how they might kill Him, for they feared the people.

3 Then Satan entered Judas, surnamed Iscariot, who was numbered among the twelve. 4 So he went his way and conferred with the chief priests and captains, how he might betray Him to them. 5 And they were glad, and agreed to give him money. 6 So he promised and sought opportunity to betray Him to them in the absence of the multitude.

Jesus and His Disciples Prepare the Passover

7 Then came the Day of Unleavened Bread, when the Passover must be killed. 8 And He sent Peter and

---

21:36 [a]NU-Text reads *may have strength.*

John, saying, "Go and prepare the Passover for us, that we may eat."

9So they said to Him, "Where do You want us to prepare?"

10And He said to them, "Behold, when you have entered the city, a man will meet you carrying a pitcher of water; follow him into the house which he enters. 11Then you shall say to the master of the house, 'The Teacher says to you, "Where is the guest room where I may eat the Passover with My disciples?"' 12Then he will show you a large, furnished upper room; there make ready."

13So they went and found it just as He had said to them, and they prepared the Passover.

Jesus Institutes the Lord's Supper

14When the hour had come, He sat down, and the twelve[a] apostles with Him. 15Then He said to them, "With *fervent* desire I have desired to eat this Passover with you before I suffer; 16for I say to you, I will no longer eat of it until it is fulfilled in the kingdom of God."

17Then He took the cup, and gave thanks, and said, "Take this and divide *it* among yourselves; 18for I say to you,[a] I will not drink of the fruit of the vine until the kingdom of God comes."

19And He took bread, gave thanks and broke *it*, and gave *it* to them, saying, "This is My body which is given for you; do this in remembrance of Me."

20Likewise He also *took* the cup after supper, saying, "This cup *is* the new covenant in My blood, which is shed for you. 21But behold, the hand of My betrayer *is* with Me on the table. 22And truly the Son of Man goes as it has been determined, but woe to that man by whom He is betrayed!"

23Then they began to question among themselves, which of them it was who would do this thing.

The Disciples Argue About Greatness

24Now there was also a dispute among them, as to which of them should be considered the greatest. 25And He said to them, "The kings of the Gentiles exercise lordship over

---

22:14 [a]NU-Text omits *twelve*. **22:18** [a]NU-Text adds *from now on*.

them, and those who exercise authority over them are called 'benefactors.' 26But not so *among* you; on the contrary, he who is greatest among you, let him be as the younger, and he who governs as he who serves. 27For who *is* greater, he who sits at the table, or he who serves? *Is* it not he who sits at the table? Yet I am among you as the One who serves.

28"But you are those who have continued with Me in My trials. 29And I bestow upon you a kingdom, just as My Father bestowed *one* upon Me, 30that you may eat and drink at My table in My kingdom, and sit on thrones judging the twelve tribes of Israel."

Jesus Predicts Peter's Denial

31And the Lord said,[a] "Simon, Simon! Indeed, Satan has asked for you, that he may sift *you* as wheat. 32But I have prayed for you, that your faith should not fail; and when you have returned to *Me*, strengthen your brethren."

33But he said to Him, "Lord, I am ready to go with You, both to prison and to death."

34Then He said, "I tell you, Peter, the rooster shall not crow this day before you will deny three times that you know Me."

Supplies for the Road

35And He said to them, "When I sent you without money bag, knapsack, and sandals, did you lack anything?"

So they said, "Nothing."

36Then He said to them, "But now, he who has a money bag, let him take *it*, and likewise a knapsack; and he who has no sword, let him sell his garment and buy one. 37For I say to you that this which is written must still be accomplished in Me: *'And He was numbered with the transgressors.'*[a] For the things concerning Me have an end."

38So they said, "Lord, look, here *are* two swords."

And He said to them, "It is enough."

The Prayer in the Garden

39Coming out, He went to the Mount of Olives, as He was accustomed, and His disciples also

---

22:31 [a]NU-Text omits *And the Lord said.* **22:37** [a]Isaiah 53:12.

followed Him. 40 When He came to
the place, He said to them, "Pray
that you may not enter into temptation."

41 And He was withdrawn from
them about a stone's throw, and He
knelt down and prayed, 42 saying, "Father, if it is Your will, take this cup
away from Me; nevertheless not My
will, but Yours, be done." 43 Then an
angel appeared to Him from heaven,
strengthening Him. 44 And being in
agony, He prayed more earnestly.
Then His sweat became like great
drops of blood falling down to the
ground.[a]

45 When He rose up from prayer,
and had come to His disciples, He
found them sleeping from sorrow.
46 Then He said to them, "Why do you
sleep? Rise and pray, lest you enter
into temptation."

Betrayal and Arrest in Gethsemane

47 And while He was still speaking,
behold, a multitude; and he who was
called Judas, one of the twelve, went
before them and drew near to Jesus
to kiss Him. 48 But Jesus said to him,
"Judas, are you betraying the Son of
Man with a kiss?"

49 When those around Him saw
what was going to happen, they said
to Him, "Lord, shall we strike with
the sword?" 50 And one of them
struck the servant of the high priest
and cut off his right ear.

51 But Jesus answered and said,
"Permit even this." And He touched
his ear and healed him.

52 Then Jesus said to the chief
priests, captains of the temple, and the
elders who had come to Him, "Have
you come out, as against a robber,
with swords and clubs? 53 When I was
with you daily in the temple, you did
not try to seize Me. But this is your
hour, and the power of darkness."

Peter Denies Jesus, and Weeps Bitterly

54 Having arrested Him, they led
Him and brought Him into the high
priest's house. But Peter followed at a
distance. 55 Now when they had kindled a fire in the midst of the courtyard and sat down together, Peter sat
among them. 56 And a certain servant
girl, seeing him as he sat by the fire,

22:44 [a]NU-Text brackets verses 43 and 44 as not in the original text.

looked intently at him and said, "This
man was also with Him."
57 But he denied Him,[a] saying,
"Woman, I do not know Him."
58 And after a little while another
saw him and said, "You also are of
them."
But Peter said, "Man, I am not!"
59 Then after about an hour had
passed, another confidently affirmed,
saying, "Surely this *fellow* also was
with Him, for he is a Galilean."
60 But Peter said, "Man, I do not
know what you are saying!"
Immediately, while he was still
speaking, the rooster[a] crowed. 61 And
the Lord turned and looked at Peter.
Then Peter remembered the word of
the Lord, how He had said to him,
"Before the rooster crows,[a] you will
deny Me three times." 62 So Peter
went out and wept bitterly.

Jesus Mocked and Beaten

63 Now the men who held Jesus
mocked Him and beat Him. 64 And
having blindfolded Him, they struck
Him on the face and asked Him,[a] saying, "Prophesy! Who is the one who
struck You?" 65 And many other
things they blasphemously spoke
against Him.

Jesus Faces the Sanhedrin

66 As soon as it was day, the elders
of the people, both chief priests and
scribes, came together and led Him
into their council, saying, 67 "If You
are the Christ, tell us."
But He said to them, "If I tell you,
you will by no means believe. 68 And
if I also ask *you*, you will by no means
answer Me or let *Me* go.[a] 69 Hereafter
the Son of Man will sit on the right
hand of the power of God."
70 Then they all said, "Are You
then the Son of God?"
So He said to them, "You *rightly*
say that I am."
71 And they said, "What further
testimony do we need? For we have
heard it ourselves from His own
mouth."

Jesus Handed Over to Pontius Pilate

23 Then the whole multitude
of them arose and led Him to

22:57 [a]NU-Text reads *denied it.* **22:60** [a]NU-Text and M-Text read *a rooster.* **22:61** [a]NU-Text adds *today.*
22:64 [a]NU-Text reads *And having blindfolded Him, they asked Him.* **22:68** [a]NU-Text omits *also* and *Me or let Me go.*

Pilate. [2]And they began to accuse
Him, saying, "We found this *fellow*
perverting the[a] nation, and forbidding to pay taxes to Caesar, saying
that He Himself is Christ, a King."

[3]Then Pilate asked Him, saying,
"Are You the King of the Jews?"

He answered him and said, "*It is as*
you say."

[4]So Pilate said to the chief priests
and the crowd, "I find no fault in this
Man."

[5]But they were the more fierce,
saying, "He stirs up the people, teaching throughout all Judea, beginning
from Galilee to this place."

Jesus Faces Herod

[6]When Pilate heard of Galilee,[a] he
asked if the Man were a Galilean.
[7]And as soon as he knew that He belonged to Herod's jurisdiction, he sent
Him to Herod, who was also in Jerusalem at that time. [8]Now when Herod
saw Jesus, he was exceedingly glad; for
he had desired for a long *time* to see
Him, because he had heard many
things about Him, and he hoped to
see some miracle done by Him. [9]Then
he questioned Him with many words,
but He answered him nothing. [10]And
the chief priests and scribes stood and
vehemently accused Him. [11]Then
Herod, with his men of war, treated
Him with contempt and mocked *Him*,
arrayed Him in a gorgeous robe, and
sent Him back to Pilate. [12]That very
day Pilate and Herod became friends
with each other, for previously they
had been at enmity with each other.

Taking the Place of Barabbas

[13]Then Pilate, when he had called
together the chief priests, the rulers,
and the people, [14]said to them, "You
have brought this Man to me, as one
who misleads the people. And indeed,
having examined *Him* in your presence, I have found no fault in this
Man concerning those things of
which you accuse Him; [15]no, neither
did Herod, for I sent you back to him;[a]
and indeed nothing deserving of
death has been done by Him. [16]I will
therefore chastise Him and release
Him" [17](for it was necessary for him
to release one to them at the feast).[a]

[18]And they all cried out at once,

23:2 [a]NU-Text reads *our*. **23:6** [a]NU-Text omits *of Galilee*. **23:15** [a]NU-Text reads *for he sent Him back to us*.
23:17 [a]NU-Text omits verse 17.

saying, "Away with this *Man,* and release to us Barabbas"— [19]who had been thrown into prison for a certain rebellion made in the city, and for murder.

[20]Pilate, therefore, wishing to release Jesus, again called out to them. [21]But they shouted, saying, "Crucify *Him,* crucify Him!"

[22]Then he said to them the third time, "Why, what evil has He done? I have found no reason for death in Him. I will therefore chastise Him and let *Him* go."

[23]But they were insistent, demanding with loud voices that He be crucified. And the voices of these men and of the chief priests prevailed.[a] [24]So Pilate gave sentence that it should be as they requested. [25]And he released to them[a] the one they requested, who for rebellion and murder had been thrown into prison; but he delivered Jesus to their will.

The King on a Cross

[26]Now as they led Him away, they laid hold of a certain man, Simon a Cyrenian, who was coming from the country, and on him they laid the cross that he might bear *it* after Jesus.

[27]And a great multitude of the people followed Him, and women who also mourned and lamented Him. [28]But Jesus, turning to them, said, "Daughters of Jerusalem, do not weep for Me, but weep for yourselves and for your children. [29]For indeed the days are coming in which they will say, 'Blessed *are* the barren, wombs that never bore, and breasts which never nursed!' [30]Then they will begin *'to say to the mountains, "Fall on us!" and to the hills, "Cover us!"'*[a] [31]For if they do these things in the green wood, what will be done in the dry?"

[32]There were also two others, criminals, led with Him to be put to death. [33]And when they had come to the place called Calvary, there they crucified Him, and the criminals, one on the right hand and the other on the left. [34]Then Jesus said, "Father, forgive them, for they do not know what they do."[a]

And they divided His garments and cast lots. [35]And the people stood looking on. But even the rulers with

---

23:23 [a]NU-Text omits *and of the chief priests.* **23:25** [a]NU-Text and M-Text omit *to them.* **23:30** [a]Hosea 10:8
23:34 [a]NU-Text brackets the first sentence as a later addition.

them sneered, saying, "He saved others; let Him save Himself if He is the Christ, the chosen of God."

36The soldiers also mocked Him, coming and offering Him sour wine, 37and saying, "If You are the King of the Jews, save Yourself."

38And an inscription also was written over Him in letters of Greek, Latin, and Hebrew:[a]

THIS IS THE KING OF THE JEWS.

39Then one of the criminals who were hanged blasphemed Him, saying, "If You are the Christ,[a] save Yourself and us."

40But the other, answering, rebuked him, saying, "Do you not even fear God, seeing you are under the same condemnation? 41And we indeed justly, for we receive the due reward of our deeds; but this Man has done nothing wrong." 42Then he said to Jesus, "Lord,[a] remember me when You come into Your kingdom."

43And Jesus said to him, "Assuredly, I say to you, today you will be with Me in Paradise."

Jesus Dies on the Cross

44Now it was[a] about the sixth hour, and there was darkness over all the earth until the ninth hour. 45Then the sun was darkened,[a] and the veil of the temple was torn in two. 46And when Jesus had cried out with a loud voice, He said, "Father, *'into Your hands I commit My spirit.'*"[a] Having said this, He breathed His last.

47So when the centurion saw what had happened, he glorified God, saying, "Certainly this was a righteous Man!"

48And the whole crowd who came together to that sight, seeing what had been done, beat their breasts and returned. 49But all His acquaintances, and the women who followed Him from Galilee, stood at a distance, watching these things.

Jesus Buried in Joseph's Tomb

50Now behold, *there was* a man named Joseph, a council member, a good and just man. 51He had not consented to their decision and deed.

23:38 [a]NU-Text omits *written* and *in letters of Greek, Latin, and Hebrew.* **23:39** [a]NU-Text reads *Are You not the Christ?* **23:42** [a]NU-Text reads *And he said, "Jesus, remember me.* **23:44** [a]NU-Text adds *already.* **23:45** [a]NU-Text reads *obscured.* **23:46** [a]Psalm 31:5.

He was from Arimathea, a city of the Jews, who himself was also waiting[a] for the kingdom of God. **52**This man went to Pilate and asked for the body of Jesus. **53**Then he took it down, wrapped it in linen, and laid it in a tomb *that was* hewn out of the rock, where no one had ever lain before. **54**That day was the Preparation, and the Sabbath drew near.

55And the women who had come with Him from Galilee followed after, and they observed the tomb and how His body was laid. **56**Then they returned and prepared spices and fragrant oils. And they rested on the Sabbath according to the commandment.

He Is Risen

24 Now on the first *day* of the week, very early in the morning, they, and certain *other women* with them,[a] came to the tomb bringing the spices which they had prepared. **2**But they found the stone rolled away from the tomb. **3**Then they went in and did not find the body of the Lord Jesus. **4**And it happened, as they were greatly[a] perplexed about this, that behold, two men stood by them in shining garments. **5**Then, as they were afraid and bowed *their* faces to the earth, they said to them, "Why do you seek the living among the dead? **6**He is not here, but is risen! Remember how He spoke to you when He was still in Galilee, **7**saying, 'The Son of Man must be delivered into the hands of sinful men, and be crucified, and the third day rise again.'"

8And they remembered His words. **9**Then they returned from the tomb and told all these things to the eleven and to all the rest. **10**It was Mary Magdalene, Joanna, Mary *the mother* of James, and the other *women* with them, who told these things to the apostles. **11**And their words seemed to them like idle tales, and they did not believe them. **12**But Peter arose and ran to the tomb; and stooping down, he saw the linen cloths lying[a] by themselves; and he departed, marveling to himself at what had happened.

23:51 [a]NU-Text reads *who was waiting* **24:1** [a]NU-Text omits *and certain other women with them.* **24:4** [a]NU-Text omits *greatly.* **24:12** [a]NU-Text omits *lying.*

The Road to Emmaus

13 Now behold, two of them were traveling that same day to a village called Emmaus, which was seven miles[a] from Jerusalem. 14 And they talked together of all these things which had happened. 15 So it was, while they conversed and reasoned, that Jesus Himself drew near and went with them. 16 But their eyes were restrained, so that they did not know Him.

17 And He said to them, "What kind of conversation *is* this that you have with one another as you walk and are sad?"[a]

18 Then the one whose name was Cleopas answered and said to Him, "Are You the only stranger in Jerusalem, and have You not known the things which happened there in these days?"

19 And He said to them, "What things?"

So they said to Him, "The things concerning Jesus of Nazareth, who was a Prophet mighty in deed and word before God and all the people, 20 and how the chief priests and our rulers delivered Him to be condemned to death, and crucified Him. 21 But we were hoping that it was He who was going to redeem Israel. Indeed, besides all this, today is the third day since these things happened. 22 Yes, and certain women of our company, who arrived at the tomb early, astonished us. 23 When they did not find His body, they came saying that they had also seen a vision of angels who said He was alive. 24 And certain of those *who were* with us went to the tomb and found *it* just as the women had said; but Him they did not see."

25 Then He said to them, "O foolish ones, and slow of heart to believe in all that the prophets have spoken! 26 Ought not the Christ to have suffered these things and to enter into His glory?" 27 And beginning at Moses and all the Prophets, He expounded to them in all the Scriptures the things concerning Himself.

The Disciples' Eyes Opened

28 Then they drew near to the village where they were going, and He indicated that He would have gone

---

24:13 [a]Literally *sixty stadia* **24:17** [a]NU-Text reads *as you walk? And they stood still, looking sad.*

farther. 29 But they constrained Him, saying, "Abide with us, for it is toward evening, and the day is far spent." And He went in to stay with them.

30 Now it came to pass, as He sat at the table with them, that He took bread, blessed and broke *it,* and gave it to them. 31 Then their eyes were opened and they knew Him; and He vanished from their sight.

32 And they said to one another, "Did not our heart burn within us while He talked with us on the road, and while He opened the Scriptures to us?" 33 So they rose up that very hour and returned to Jerusalem, and found the eleven and those *who were* with them gathered together, 34 saying, "The Lord is risen indeed, and has appeared to Simon!" 35 And they told about the things *that had happened* on the road, and how He was known to them in the breaking of bread.

Jesus Appears to His Disciples

36 Now as they said these things, Jesus Himself stood in the midst of them, and said to them, "Peace to you." 37 But they were terrified and frightened, and supposed they had seen a spirit. 38 And He said to them, "Why are you troubled? And why do doubts arise in your hearts? 39 Behold My hands and My feet, that it is I Myself. Handle Me and see, for a spirit does not have flesh and bones as you see I have."

40 When He had said this, He showed them His hands and His feet.[a] 41 But while they still did not believe for joy, and marveled, He said to them, "Have you any food here?" 42 So they gave Him a piece of a broiled fish and some honeycomb.[a] 43 And He took *it* and ate in their presence.

The Scriptures Opened

44 Then He said to them, "These *are* the words which I spoke to you while I was still with you, that all things must be fulfilled which were written in the Law of Moses and *the* Prophets and *the* Psalms concerning Me." 45 And He opened their understanding, that they might comprehend the Scriptures.

24:40 [a]Some printed New Testaments omit this verse. It is found in nearly all Greek manuscripts.

24:42 [a]NU-Text omits *and some honeycomb.*

46 Then He said to them, "Thus it is written, and thus it was necessary for the Christ to suffer and to rise[a] from the dead the third day, 47 and that repentance and remission of sins should be preached in His name to all nations, beginning at Jerusalem. 48 And you are witnesses of these things. 49 Behold, I send the Promise of My Father upon you; but tarry in the city of Jerusalem[a] until you are endued with power from on high."

The Ascension

50 And He led them out as far as Bethany, and He lifted up His hands and blessed them. 51 Now it came to pass, while He blessed them, that He was parted from them and carried up into heaven. 52 And they worshiped Him, and returned to Jerusalem with great joy, 53 and were continually in the temple praising and[a] blessing God. Amen.[b]

24:46 [a]NU-Text reads *written, that the Christ should suffer and rise.* **24:49** [a]NU-Text omits *of Jerusalem.* **24:53** [a]NU-Text omits *praising and.* [b]NU-Text omits *Amen.*

ACTS OF THE APOSTLES

Prologue

1 The former account I made,
O Theophilus, of all that Jesus
began both to do and teach, 2until
the day in which He was taken up,
after He through the Holy Spirit had
given commandments to the apostles whom He had chosen, 3to whom
He also presented Himself alive after
His suffering by many infallible
proofs, being seen by them during
forty days and speaking of the things
pertaining to the kingdom of God.

The Holy Spirit Promised

4And being assembled together
with *them,* He commanded them not
to depart from Jerusalem, but to
wait for the Promise of the Father,
"which," *He said,* "you have heard
from Me; 5for John truly baptized
with water, but you shall be baptized
with the Holy Spirit not many days
from now." 6Therefore, when they
had come together, they asked Him,
saying, "Lord, will You at this time restore the kingdom to Israel?" 7And

He said to them, "It is not for you to know times or seasons which the Father has put in His own authority. [8]But you shall receive power when the Holy Spirit has come upon you; and you shall be witnesses to Me[a] in Jerusalem, and in all Judea and Samaria, and to the end of the earth."

Jesus Ascends to Heaven

[9]Now when He had spoken these things, while they watched, He was taken up, and a cloud received Him out of their sight. [10]And while they looked steadfastly toward heaven as He went up, behold, two men stood by them in white apparel, [11]who also said, "Men of Galilee, why do you stand gazing up into heaven? This *same* Jesus, who was taken up from you into heaven, will so come in like manner as you saw Him go into heaven."

The Upper Room Prayer Meeting

[12]Then they returned to Jerusalem from the mount called Olivet, which is near Jerusalem, a Sabbath day's journey. [13]And when they had entered, they went up into the upper room where they were staying: Peter, James, John, and Andrew; Philip and Thomas; Bartholomew and Matthew; James *the son* of Alphaeus and Simon the Zealot; and Judas *the son* of James. [14]These all continued with one accord in prayer and supplication,[a] with the women and Mary the mother of Jesus, and with His brothers.

Matthias Chosen

[15]And in those days Peter stood up in the midst of the disciples[a] (altogether the number of names was about a hundred and twenty), and said, [16]"Men *and* brethren, this Scripture had to be fulfilled, which the Holy Spirit spoke before by the mouth of David concerning Judas, who became a guide to those who arrested Jesus; [17]for he was numbered with us and obtained a part in this ministry."

[18](Now this man purchased a field with the wages of iniquity; and falling headlong, he burst open in the middle and all his entrails gushed out. [19]And it became known to all those dwelling in Jerusalem; so that field is called in their own language, Akel Dama, that is, Field of Blood.)

1:8 [a]NU-Text reads *My witnesses.* **1:14** [a]NU-Text omits *and supplication.* **1:15** [a]NU-Text reads *brethren.*

20 “For it is written in the Book of Psalms:

‘Let his dwelling place be
desolate,
And let no one live in it’;[a]

and,

‘Let[b] *another take his office.’*[c]

21 “Therefore, of these men who have accompanied us all the time that the Lord Jesus went in and out among us, 22 beginning from the baptism of John to that day when He was taken up from us, one of these must become a witness with us of His resurrection.”

23 And they proposed two: Joseph called Barsabas, who was surnamed Justus, and Matthias. 24 And they prayed and said, “You, O Lord, who know the hearts of all, show which of these two You have chosen 25 to take part in this ministry and apostleship from which Judas by transgression fell, that he might go to his own place.” 26 And they cast their lots, and the lot fell on Matthias. And he was numbered with the eleven apostles.

Coming of the Holy Spirit

2 When the Day of Pentecost had fully come, they were all with one accord[a] in one place. 2 And suddenly there came a sound from heaven, as of a rushing mighty wind, and it filled the whole house where they were sitting. 3 Then there appeared to them divided tongues, as of fire, and *one* sat upon each of them. 4 And they were all filled with the Holy Spirit and began to speak with other tongues, as the Spirit gave them utterance.

The Crowd’s Response

5 And there were dwelling in Jerusalem Jews, devout men, from every nation under heaven. 6 And when this sound occurred, the multitude came together, and were confused, because everyone heard them speak in his own language. 7 Then they were all amazed and marveled, saying to one another, “Look, are not all these who speak Galileans? 8 And how *is it that* we hear, each in our own language in which we were born? 9 Parthians and Medes and Elamites, those dwelling in Mesopotamia, Judea and Cappadocia, Pon-

1:20 [a]Psalm 69:25 [b]Psalm 109:8 [c]Greek *episkopen*, position of overseer **2:1** [a]NU-Text reads *together*.

tus and Asia, [10]Phrygia and Pamphylia,
Egypt and the parts of Libya adjoining
Cyrene, visitors from Rome, both Jews
and proselytes, [11]Cretans and Arabs—
we hear them speaking in our own
tongues the wonderful works of God."
[12]So they were all amazed and perplexed, saying to one another, "Whatever could this mean?"

[13]Others mocking said, "They are
full of new wine."

Peter's Sermon

[14]But Peter, standing up with the
eleven, raised his voice and said to
them, "Men of Judea and all who
dwell in Jerusalem, let this be known
to you, and heed my words. [15]For
these are not drunk, as you suppose,
since it is *only* the third hour of the
day. [16]But this is what was spoken by
the prophet Joel:

17 *'And it shall come to pass in the last days, says God,*
That I will pour out of My Spirit on all flesh;
Your sons and your daughters shall prophesy,
Your young men shall see visions,
Your old men shall dream dreams.
18 *And on My menservants and on My maidservants*
I will pour out My Spirit in those days;
And they shall prophesy.
19 *I will show wonders in heaven above*
And signs in the earth beneath:
Blood and fire and vapor of smoke.
20 *The sun shall be turned into darkness,*
And the moon into blood,
Before the coming of the great and awesome day of the LORD.
21 *And it shall come to pass*
That whoever calls on the name of the LORD
Shall be saved.'[a]

[22]"Men of Israel, hear these words:
Jesus of Nazareth, a Man attested by
God to you by miracles, wonders, and

2:21 [a]Joel 2:28–32.

signs which God did through Him in
your midst, as you yourselves also
know— 23 Him, being delivered by
the determined purpose and fore-
knowledge of God, you have taken[a] by
lawless hands, have crucified, and put
to death; 24 whom God raised up, having loosed the pains of death, because
it was not possible that He should be
held by it. 25 For David says concerning Him:

'I foresaw the LORD always
before my face,
For He is at my right hand, that
I may not be shaken.
26 *Therefore my heart rejoiced,*
and my tongue was glad;
Moreover my flesh also will
rest in hope.
27 *For You will not leave my soul*
in Hades,
Nor will You allow Your Holy
One to see corruption.
28 *You have made known to me*
the ways of life;
You will make me full of joy in
Your presence.'[a]

29 "Men *and* brethren, let *me* speak
freely to you of the patriarch David,
that he is both dead and buried, and
his tomb is with us to this day.
30 Therefore, being a prophet, and
knowing that God had sworn with
an oath to him that of the fruit of his
body, according to the flesh, He
would raise up the Christ to sit on his
throne,[a] 31 he, foreseeing this, spoke
concerning the resurrection of the
Christ, that His soul was not left in
Hades, nor did His flesh see corruption. 32 This Jesus God has raised
up, of which we are all witnesses.
33 Therefore being exalted to the right
hand of God, and having received
from the Father the promise of the
Holy Spirit, He poured out this which
you now see and hear.

34 "For David did not ascend into
the heavens, but he says himself:

'The LORD said to my Lord,
"Sit at My right hand,
35 *Till I make Your enemies Your*
footstool."'[a]

2:23 [a]NU-Text omits *have taken.* **2:28** [a]Psalm 16:8–11 **2:30** [a]NU-Text omits *according to the flesh, He would raise up the Christ* and completes the verse with *He would seat one on his throne.* **2:35** [a]Psalm 110:1

36"Therefore let all the house of
Israel know assuredly that God has
made this Jesus, whom you crucified,
both Lord and Christ."

37Now when they heard *this,* they
were cut to the heart, and said to Peter and the rest of the apostles, "Men
and brethren, what shall we do?"

38Then Peter said to them, "Repent, and let every one of you be baptized in the name of Jesus Christ for
the remission of sins; and you shall
receive the gift of the Holy Spirit.
39For the promise is to you and to
your children, and to all who are afar
off, as many as the Lord our God will
call."

A Vital Church Grows

40And with many other words he
testified and exhorted them, saying,
"Be saved from this perverse generation." 41Then those who gladly[a]
received his word were baptized; and
that day about three thousand souls
were added *to them.* 42And they continued steadfastly in the apostles' doctrine and fellowship, in the breaking
of bread, and in prayers. 43Then fear
came upon every soul, and many
wonders and signs were done
through the apostles. 44Now all who
believed were together, and had all
things in common, 45and sold their
possessions and goods, and divided
them among all, as anyone had need.

46So continuing daily with one
accord in the temple, and breaking
bread from house to house, they ate
their food with gladness and simplic-
ity of heart, 47praising God and having favor with all the people. And the
Lord added to the church[a] daily those
who were being saved.

A Lame Man Healed

3 Now Peter and John went up together to the temple at the hour
of prayer, the ninth *hour.* 2And a certain man lame from his mother's
womb was carried, whom they laid
daily at the gate of the temple which
is called Beautiful, to ask alms from
those who entered the temple; 3who,
seeing Peter and John about to go
into the temple, asked for alms. 4And
fixing his eyes on him, with John, Peter said, "Look at us." 5So he gave
them his attention, expecting to receive something from them. 6Then

---

2:41 [a]NU-Text omits *gladly.* **2:47** [a]NU-Text omits *to the church.*

Peter said, "Silver and gold I do not have, but what I do have I give you: In the name of Jesus Christ of Nazareth, rise up and walk." 7 And he took him by the right hand and lifted *him* up, and immediately his feet and ankle bones received strength. 8 So he, leaping up, stood and walked and entered the temple with them—walking, leaping, and praising God. 9 And all the people saw him walking and praising God. 10 Then they knew that it was he who sat begging alms at the Beautiful Gate of the temple; and they were filled with wonder and amazement at what had happened to him.

Preaching in Solomon's Portico

11 Now as the lame man who was healed held on to Peter and John, all the people ran together to them in the porch which is called Solomon's, greatly amazed. 12 So when Peter saw *it,* he responded to the people: "Men of Israel, why do you marvel at this? Or why look so intently at us, as though by our own power or godliness we had made this man walk? 13 The God of Abraham, Isaac, and Jacob, the God of our fathers, glorified His Servant Jesus, whom you delivered up and denied in the presence of Pilate, when he was determined to let *Him* go. 14 But you denied the Holy One and the Just, and asked for a murderer to be granted to you, 15 and killed the Prince of life, whom God raised from the dead, of which we are witnesses. 16 And His name, through faith in His name, has made this man strong, whom you see and know. Yes, the faith which *comes* through Him has given him this perfect soundness in the presence of you all.

17 "Yet now, brethren, I know that you did *it* in ignorance, as *did* also your rulers. 18 But those things which God foretold by the mouth of all His prophets, that the Christ would suffer, He has thus fulfilled. 19 Repent therefore and be converted, that your sins may be blotted out, so that times of refreshing may come from the presence of the Lord, 20 and that He may send Jesus Christ, who was preached to you before,[a] 21 whom heaven must receive until the times of restoration of all things, which God has spoken by the mouth of all

---

3:20 [a] NU-Text and M-Text read *Christ Jesus, who was ordained for you before.*

His holy prophets since the world began. 22For Moses truly said to the fathers, '*The* LORD *your God will raise up for you a Prophet like me from your brethren. Him you shall hear in all things, whatever He says to you.* 23*And it shall be* that *every soul who will not hear that Prophet shall be utterly destroyed from among the people.*'[a] 24Yes, and all the prophets, from Samuel and those who follow, as many as have spoken, have also foretold[a] these days. 25You are sons of the prophets, and of the covenant which God made with our fathers, saying to Abraham, '*And in your seed all the families of the earth shall be blessed.*'[a] 26To you first, God, having raised up His Servant Jesus, sent Him to bless you, in turning away every one *of you* from your iniquities."

Peter and John Arrested

4 Now as they spoke to the people, the priests, the captain of the temple, and the Sadducees came upon them, 2being greatly disturbed that they taught the people and preached in Jesus the resurrection from the dead. 3And they laid hands on them, and put *them* in custody until the next day, for it was already evening. 4However, many of those who heard the word believed; and the number of the men came to be about five thousand.

Addressing the Sanhedrin

5And it came to pass, on the next day, that their rulers, elders, and scribes, 6as well as Annas the high priest, Caiaphas, John, and Alexander, and as many as were of the family of the high priest, were gathered together at Jerusalem. 7And when they had set them in the midst, they asked, "By what power or by what name have you done this?"

8Then Peter, filled with the Holy Spirit, said to them, "Rulers of the people and elders of Israel: 9If we this day are judged for a good deed *done* to a helpless man, by what means he has been made well, 10let it be known to you all, and to all the people of Israel, that by the name of Jesus Christ of Nazareth, whom you crucified, whom God raised from the dead, by Him this man stands here before you whole. 11This is the '*stone which was*

3:23 [a]Deuteronomy 18:15, 18, 19 **3:24** [a]NU-Text and M-Text read *proclaimed*. **3:25** [a]Genesis 22:18; 26:4; 28:14

rejected by you builders, which has
become the chief cornerstone.'[a] 12Nor
is there salvation in any other, for
there is no other name under heaven
given among men by which we must
be saved."

The Name of Jesus Forbidden

13Now when they saw the boldness of Peter and John, and perceived that they were uneducated
and untrained men, they marveled.
And they realized that they had been
with Jesus. 14And seeing the man
who had been healed standing with
them, they could say nothing against
it. 15But when they had commanded
them to go aside out of the council,
they conferred among themselves,
16saying, "What shall we do to these
men? For, indeed, that a notable miracle has been done through them *is*
evident to all who dwell in Jerusalem,
and we cannot deny *it.* 17But so that
it spreads no further among the people, let us severely threaten them,
that from now on they speak to no
man in this name."

18So they called them and commanded them not to speak at all nor
teach in the name of Jesus. 19But
Peter and John answered and said to
them, "Whether it is right in the sight
of God to listen to you more than to
God, you judge. 20For we cannot but
speak the things which we have seen
and heard." 21So when they had further threatened them, they let them
go, finding no way of punishing
them, because of the people, since
they all glorified God for what had
been done. 22For the man was over
forty years old on whom this miracle
of healing had been performed.

Prayer for Boldness

23And being let go, they went to
their own *companions* and reported all
that the chief priests and elders
had said to them. 24So when they
heard that, they raised their voice to
God with one accord and said: "Lord,
You *are* God, who made heaven and
earth and the sea, and all that is in
them, 25who by the mouth of Your
servant David[a] have said:

'Why did the nations rage,
And the people plot vain
things?

4:11 [a]Psalm 118:22. **4:25** [a]NU-Text reads *who through the Holy Spirit, by the mouth of our father, Your servant David.*

26 *The kings of the earth took*
their stand,
And the rulers were gathered
together
Against the LORD *and against*
His Christ.'[a]

27 "For truly against Your holy
Servant Jesus, whom You anointed,
both Herod and Pontius Pilate, with
the Gentiles and the people of Israel,
were gathered together 28 to do whatever Your hand and Your purpose
determined before to be done. 29 Now,
Lord, look on their threats, and grant
to Your servants that with all boldness they may speak Your word, 30 by
stretching out Your hand to heal, and
that signs and wonders may be done
through the name of Your holy Servant Jesus."

31 And when they had prayed, the
place where they were assembled together was shaken; and they were
all filled with the Holy Spirit, and they
spoke the word of God with boldness.

Sharing in All Things

32 Now the multitude of those
who believed were of one heart and
one soul; neither did anyone say that
any of the things he possessed was his
own, but they had all things in common. 33 And with great power the
apostles gave witness to the resurrection of the Lord Jesus. And great
grace was upon them all. 34 Nor was
there anyone among them who
lacked; for all who were possessors of
lands or houses sold them, and
brought the proceeds of the things
that were sold, 35 and laid *them* at the
apostles' feet; and they distributed to
each as anyone had need.

36 And Joses,[a] who was also named
Barnabas by the apostles (which is
translated Son of Encouragement), a
Levite of the country of Cyprus,
37 having land, sold *it,* and brought
the money and laid *it* at the apostles'
feet.

Lying to the Holy Spirit

5 But a certain man named Ananias, with Sapphira his wife, sold
a possession. 2 And he kept back *part*
of the proceeds, his wife also being
aware *of it,* and brought a certain
part and laid *it* at the apostles' feet.
3 But Peter said, "Ananias, why has

4:26 [a]Psalm 2:1, 2 **4:36** [a]NU-Text reads *Joseph.*

Satan filled your heart to lie to the
Holy Spirit and keep back *part* of the
price of the land for yourself? 4 While
it remained, was it not your own?
And after it was sold, was it not
in your own control? Why have
you conceived this thing in your
heart? You have not lied to men but
to God."

5 Then Ananias, hearing these
words, fell down and breathed his
last. So great fear came upon all those
who heard these things. 6 And the
young men arose and wrapped him
up, carried *him* out, and buried *him*.

7 Now it was about three hours
later when his wife came in, not
knowing what had happened. 8 And
Peter answered her, "Tell me
whether you sold the land for so
much?"

She said, "Yes, for so much."

9 Then Peter said to her, "How is
it that you have agreed together to
test the Spirit of the Lord? Look, the
feet of those who have buried your
husband *are* at the door, and they will
carry you out." 10 Then immediately
she fell down at his feet and breathed
her last. And the young men came
in and found her dead, and carrying
her out, buried *her* by her husband.
11 So great fear came upon all the
church and upon all who heard these
things.

Continuing Power in the Church

12 And through the hands of the
apostles many signs and wonders
were done among the people. And
they were all with one accord in
Solomon's Porch. 13 Yet none of the
rest dared join them, but the people
esteemed them highly. 14 And believers were increasingly added to the
Lord, multitudes of both men and
women, 15 so that they brought the
sick out into the streets and laid *them*
on beds and couches, that at least the
shadow of Peter passing by might fall
on some of them. 16 Also a multitude
gathered from the surrounding cities
to Jerusalem, bringing sick people
and those who were tormented by
unclean spirits, and they were all
healed.

Imprisoned Apostles Freed

17 Then the high priest rose up,
and all those who *were* with him
(which is the sect of the Sadducees),
and they were filled with indignation,
18 and laid their hands on the apostles

and put them in the common prison.
19 But at night an angel of the Lord
opened the prison doors and brought
them out, and said, 20 "Go, stand in
the temple and speak to the people
all the words of this life."

21 And when they heard *that,* they
entered the temple early in the
morning and taught. But the high
priest and those with him came and
called the council together, with all
the elders of the children of Israel,
and sent to the prison to have them
brought.

Apostles on Trial Again

22 But when the officers came and
did not find them in the prison, they
returned and reported, 23 saying, "Indeed we found the prison shut securely, and the guards standing
outside[a] before the doors; but when
we opened them, we found no one
inside!" 24 Now when the high priest,[a]
the captain of the temple, and the
chief priests heard these things, they
wondered what the outcome would
be. 25 So one came and told them, saying,[a] "Look, the men whom you put
in prison are standing in the temple
and teaching the people!"

26 Then the captain went with the
officers and brought them without violence, for they feared the people, lest
they should be stoned. 27 And when
they had brought them, they set *them*
before the council. And the high priest
asked them, 28 saying, "Did we not
strictly command you not to teach in
this name? And look, you have filled
Jerusalem with your doctrine, and intend to bring this Man's blood on us!"

29 But Peter and the *other* apostles
answered and said: "We ought to
obey God rather than men. 30 The
God of our fathers raised up Jesus
whom you murdered by hanging on
a tree. 31 Him God has exalted to His
right hand *to be* Prince and Savior, to
give repentance to Israel and forgiveness of sins. 32 And we are His witnesses to these things, and *so* also *is*
the Holy Spirit whom God has given
to those who obey Him."

Gamaliel's Advice

33 When they heard *this,* they were
furious and plotted to kill them.

5:23 [a]NU-Text and M-Text omit *outside.* **5:24** [a]NU-Text omits *the high priest.* **5:25** [a]NU-Text and M-Text omit *saying.*

34 Then one in the council stood up, a
Pharisee named Gamaliel, a teacher
of the law held in respect by all the
people, and commanded them to
put the apostles outside for a little
while. 35 And he said to them: "Men
of Israel, take heed to yourselves
what you intend to do regarding
these men. 36 For some time ago
Theudas rose up, claiming to be
somebody. A number of men, about
four hundred, joined him. He was
slain, and all who obeyed him were
scattered and came to nothing. 37 After this man, Judas of Galilee rose up
in the days of the census, and drew
away many people after him. He also
perished, and all who obeyed him
were dispersed. 38 And now I say to
you, keep away from these men and
let them alone; for if this plan or this
work is of men, it will come to nothing; 39 but if it is of God, you cannot
overthrow it—lest you even be
found to fight against God."

40 And they agreed with him, and
when they had called for the apostles and beaten *them,* they commanded that they should not speak
in the name of Jesus, and let them go.
41 So they departed from the presence
of the council, rejoicing that they
were counted worthy to suffer shame
for His[a] name. 42 And daily in the
temple, and in every house, they did
not cease teaching and preaching Jesus *as* the Christ.

Seven Chosen to Serve

6 Now in those days, when *the number of* the disciples was multiply-
ing, there arose a complaint against
the Hebrews by the Hellenists,[a] because their widows were neglected in
the daily distribution. 2 Then the
twelve summoned the multitude
of the disciples and said, "It is not de-
sirable that we should leave the word
of God and serve tables. 3 Therefore,
brethren, seek out from among you
seven men of *good* reputation, full of
the Holy Spirit and wisdom, whom
we may appoint over this business;
4 but we will give ourselves continually to prayer and to the ministry of
the word."

5 And the saying pleased the
whole multitude. And they chose
Stephen, a man full of faith and
the Holy Spirit, and Philip, Procho-

5:41 [a]NU-Text reads *the name;* M-Text reads *the name of Jesus.* **6:1** [a]That is, Greek-speaking Jews

rus, Nicanor, Timon, Parmenas, and
Nicolas, a proselyte from Antioch,
6 whom they set before the apostles;
and when they had prayed, they laid
hands on them.

7 Then the word of God spread,
and the number of the disciples multiplied greatly in Jerusalem, and a
great many of the priests were obedient to the faith.

Stephen Accused of Blasphemy

8 And Stephen, full of faith[a] and
power, did great wonders and signs
among the people. 9 Then there arose
some from what is called the Synagogue of the Freedmen (Cyrenians,
Alexandrians, and those from Cilicia
and Asia), disputing with Stephen.
10 And they were not able to resist the
wisdom and the Spirit by which he
spoke. 11 Then they secretly induced
men to say, "We have heard him
speak blasphemous words against
Moses and God." 12 And they stirred
up the people, the elders, and the
scribes; and they came upon *him*,
seized him, and brought *him* to the
council. 13 They also set up false witnesses who said, "This man does not
cease to speak blasphemous[a] words
against this holy place and the law;
14 for we have heard him say that this
Jesus of Nazareth will destroy this
place and change the customs which
Moses delivered to us." 15 And all who
sat in the council, looking steadfastly
at him, saw his face as the face of an
angel.

Stephen's Address: The Call of Abraham

7 Then the high priest said, "Are
these things so?"

2 And he said, "Brethren and fathers, listen: The God of glory appeared to our father Abraham when
he was in Mesopotamia, before he
dwelt in Haran, 3 and said to him, *'Get
out of your country and from your
relatives, and come to a land that I
will show you.'*[a] 4 Then he came out
of the land of the Chaldeans and
dwelt in Haran. And from there,
when his father was dead, He moved
him to this land in which you now
dwell. 5 And *God* gave him no inheritance in it, not even *enough* to set his
foot on. But even when *Abraham* had
no child, He promised to give it to

6:8 [a]NU-Text reads *grace*. **6:13** [a]NU-Text omits *blasphemous*. **7:3** [a]Genesis 12:1

him for a possession, and to his descendants after him. 6But God spoke in this way: that his descendants would dwell in a foreign land, and that they would bring them into bondage and oppress *them* four hundred years. 7'*And the nation to whom they will be in bondage I will judge*,'[a] said God, '*and after that they shall come out and serve Me in this place*.'[b] 8Then He gave him the covenant of circumcision; and so *Abraham* begot Isaac and circumcised him on the eighth day; and Isaac *begot* Jacob, and Jacob *begot* the twelve patriarchs.

The Patriarchs in Egypt

9"And the patriarchs, becoming envious, sold Joseph into Egypt. But God was with him 10and delivered him out of all his troubles, and gave him favor and wisdom in the presence of Pharaoh, king of Egypt; and he made him governor over Egypt and all his house. 11Now a famine and great trouble came over all the land of Egypt and Canaan, and our fathers found no sustenance. 12But when Jacob heard that there was grain in Egypt, he sent out our fathers first. 13And the second *time* Joseph was made known to his brothers, and Joseph's family became known to the Pharaoh. 14Then Joseph sent and called his father Jacob and all his relatives to *him*, seventy-five[a] people. 15So Jacob went down to Egypt; and he died, he and our fathers. 16And they were carried back to Shechem and laid in the tomb that Abraham bought for a sum of money from the sons of Hamor, *the father* of Shechem.

God Delivers Israel by Moses

17"But when the time of the promise drew near which God had sworn to Abraham, the people grew and multiplied in Egypt 18till another king arose who did not know Joseph. 19This man dealt treacherously with our people, and oppressed our forefathers, making them expose their babies, so that they might not live. 20At this time Moses was born, and was well pleasing to God; and he was brought up in his father's house for three months. 21But when he was set out, Pharaoh's daughter took him away and brought him up as her own son. 22And Moses was learned in all

7:7 [a]Genesis 15:14 [b]Exodus 3:12 **7:14** [a]Or *seventy* (compare Exodus 1:5)

the wisdom of the Egyptians, and was
mighty in words and deeds.

23 "Now when he was forty years
old, it came into his heart to visit
his brethren, the children of Israel.
24 And seeing one of *them* suffer wrong,
he defended and avenged him who
was oppressed, and struck down the
Egyptian. 25 For he supposed that his
brethren would have understood
that God would deliver them by his
hand, but they did not understand.
26 And the next day he appeared to *two*
of them as they were fighting, and
tried to reconcile them, saying, 'Men,
you are brethren; why do you wrong
one another?' 27 But he who did his
neighbor wrong pushed him away,
saying, '*Who made you a ruler and a*
judge over us? 28 *Do you want to kill*
me as you did the Egyptian yester-
day?'[a] 29 Then, at this saying, Moses
fled and became a dweller in the land
of Midian, where he had two sons.

30 "And when forty years had
passed, an Angel of the Lord[a] appeared to him in a flame of fire in a
bush, in the wilderness of Mount Sinai. 31 When Moses saw *it*, he marveled at the sight; and as he drew
near to observe, the voice of the Lord
came to him, 32 saying, '*I am the God*
of your fathers—the God of Abra-
ham, the God of Isaac, and the God of
Jacob.'[a] And Moses trembled and
dared not look. 33 '*Then the* LORD *said*
to him, "Take your sandals off your
feet, for the place where you stand is
holy ground. 34 *I have surely seen the*
oppression of My people who are in
Egypt; I have heard their groaning
and have come down to deliver
them. And now come, I will send you
to Egypt." '[a]

35 "This Moses, whom they rejected, saying, '*Who made you a ruler*
and a judge?'[a] is the one God sent *to be*
a ruler and a deliverer by the hand of
the Angel who appeared to him in
the bush. 36 He brought them out,
after he had shown wonders and
signs in the land of Egypt, and in the
Red Sea, and in the wilderness forty
years.

Israel Rebels Against God

37 "This is that Moses who said to
the children of Israel,[a] '*The* LORD

7:28 [a]Exodus 2:14 **7:30** [a]NU-Text omits *of the Lord.* **7:32** [a]Exodus 3:6, 15 **7:34** [a]Exodus 3:5, 7, 8, 10
7:35 [a]Exodus 2:14 **7:37** [a]Deuteronomy 18:15

your God will raise up for you a
Prophet like me from your brethren.
Him you shall hear.'[b]

38"This is he who was in the congregation in the wilderness with the
Angel who spoke to him on Mount
Sinai, and *with* our fathers, the one
who received the living oracles to give
to us, 39whom our fathers would not
obey, but rejected. And in their hearts
they turned back to Egypt, 40saying to
Aaron, '*Make us gods to go before us;*
as for this Moses who brought us out of
the land of Egypt, we do not know
what has become of him.'[a] 41And they
made a calf in those days, offered sacrifices to the idol, and rejoiced in the
works of their own hands. 42Then
God turned and gave them up to
worship the host of heaven, as it is
written in the book of the Prophets:

'*Did you offer Me slaughtered*
animals and sacrifices during
forty years in the wilderness,
O house of Israel?
43 *You also took up the tabernacle*
of Moloch,
And the star of your god
Remphan,
Images which you made to
worship;
And I will carry you away
beyond Babylon.'[a]

God's True Tabernacle

44"Our fathers had the tabernacle
of witness in the wilderness, as He appointed, instructing Moses to make it
according to the pattern that he had
seen, 45which our fathers, having received it in turn, also brought with
Joshua into the land possessed by the
Gentiles, whom God drove out before the face of our fathers until the
days of David, 46who found favor before God and asked to find a dwelling
for the God of Jacob. 47But Solomon
built Him a house.

48"However, the Most High does
not dwell in temples made with
hands, as the prophet says:

49 '*Heaven is My throne,*
And earth is My footstool.
What house will you build for
Me? says the LORD,
Or what is the place of My rest?
50 *Has My hand not made all*
these things?'[a]

7:37 [b]NU-Text and M-Text omit *Him you shall hear.* 7:40 [a]Exodus 32:1, 23 7:43 [a]Amos 5:25–27 7:50 [a]Isaiah 66:1, 2

Israel Resists the Holy Spirit

51"*You* stiff-necked and uncircumcised in heart and ears! You always
resist the Holy Spirit; as your fathers
did, so *do* you. 52Which of the prophets did your fathers not persecute?
And they killed those who foretold
the coming of the Just One, of whom
you now have become the betrayers
and murderers, 53who have received
the law by the direction of angels and
have not kept *it*."

Stephen the Martyr

54When they heard these things
they were cut to the heart, and they
gnashed at him with *their* teeth. 55But
he, being full of the Holy Spirit, gazed
into heaven and saw the glory of
God, and Jesus standing at the right
hand of God, 56and said, "Look! I see
the heavens opened and the Son of
Man standing at the right hand
of God!"

57Then they cried out with a loud
voice, stopped their ears, and ran at
him with one accord; 58and they cast
him out of the city and stoned *him*.
And the witnesses laid down their
clothes at the feet of a young man
named Saul. 59And they stoned
Stephen as he was calling on *God* and
saying, "Lord Jesus, receive my spirit."
60Then he knelt down and cried out
with a loud voice, "Lord, do not
charge them with this sin." And
when he had said this, he fell asleep.

Saul Persecutes the Church

8 Now Saul was consenting to his
death.

At that time a great persecution
arose against the church which was
at Jerusalem; and they were all scattered throughout the regions of
Judea and Samaria, except the apostles. 2And devout men carried
Stephen *to his burial*, and made great
lamentation over him.

3As for Saul, he made havoc of
the church, entering every house,
and dragging off men and women,
committing *them* to prison.

Christ Is Preached in Samaria

4Therefore those who were scattered went everywhere preaching the
word. 5Then Philip went down to
the[a] city of Samaria and preached

8:5 [a]Or *a*

Christ to them. 6And the multitudes with one accord heeded the things spoken by Philip, hearing and seeing the miracles which he did. 7For unclean spirits, crying with a loud voice, came out of many who were possessed; and many who were paralyzed and lame were healed. 8And there was great joy in that city.

The Sorcerer's Profession of Faith

9But there was a certain man called Simon, who previously practiced sorcery in the city and astonished the people of Samaria, claiming that he was someone great, 10to whom they all gave heed, from the least to the greatest, saying, "This man is the great power of God." 11And they heeded him because he had astonished them with his sorceries for a long time. 12But when they believed Philip as he preached the things concerning the kingdom of God and the name of Jesus Christ, both men and women were baptized. 13Then Simon himself also believed; and when he was baptized he continued with Philip, and was amazed, seeing the miracles and signs which were done.

The Sorcerer's Sin

14Now when the apostles who were at Jerusalem heard that Samaria had received the word of God, they sent Peter and John to them, 15who, when they had come down, prayed for them that they might receive the Holy Spirit. 16For as yet He had fallen upon none of them. They had only been baptized in the name of the Lord Jesus. 17Then they laid hands on them, and they received the Holy Spirit.

18And when Simon saw that through the laying on of the apostles' hands the Holy Spirit was given, he offered them money, 19saying, "Give me this power also, that anyone on whom I lay hands may receive the Holy Spirit."

20But Peter said to him, "Your money perishes with you, because you thought that the gift of God could be purchased with money! 21You have neither part nor portion in this matter, for your heart is not right in the sight of God. 22Repent therefore of this your wickedness, and pray God if perhaps the thought of your heart may be forgiven you. 23For I see that you are poi-

soned by bitterness and bound by
iniquity."
24 Then Simon answered and said,
"Pray to the Lord for me, that none
of the things which you have spoken
may come upon me."
25 So when they had testified and
preached the word of the Lord, they
returned to Jerusalem, preaching
the gospel in many villages of the
Samaritans.

Christ Is Preached to an Ethiopian

26 Now an angel of the Lord spoke
to Philip, saying, "Arise and go toward the south along the road which
goes down from Jerusalem to Gaza."
This is desert. 27 So he arose and went.
And behold, a man of Ethiopia, a
eunuch of great authority under
Candace the queen of the Ethio-
pians, who had charge of all her
treasury, and had come to Jerusalem to worship, 28 was returning. And
sitting in his chariot, he was reading
Isaiah the prophet. 29 Then the Spirit
said to Philip, "Go near and overtake
this chariot."
30 So Philip ran to him, and heard
him reading the prophet Isaiah, and
said, "Do you understand what you
are reading?"
31 And he said, "How can I, unless
someone guides me?" And he asked
Philip to come up and sit with him.
32 The place in the Scripture which he
read was this:

"He was led as a sheep to the
slaughter;
And as a lamb before its shearer
is silent,
So He opened not His mouth.
33 *In His humiliation His justice*
was taken away,
And who will declare His
generation?
For His life is taken from the
earth."[a]

34 So the eunuch answered Philip
and said, "I ask you, of whom does
the prophet say this, of himself or of
some other man?" 35 Then Philip
opened his mouth, and beginning
at this Scripture, preached Jesus to
him. 36 Now as they went down the
road, they came to some water.

8:33 [a]Isaiah 53:7, 8

And the eunuch said, "See, *here is*
water. What hinders me from being
baptized?"

37 Then Philip said, "If you believe
with all your heart, you may."

And he answered and said, "I
believe that Jesus Christ is the Son
of God."[a]

38 So he commanded the chariot
to stand still. And both Philip and the
eunuch went down into the water,
and he baptized him. 39 Now when
they came up out of the water, the
Spirit of the Lord caught Philip away,
so that the eunuch saw him no
more; and he went on his way rejoicing. 40 But Philip was found at Azotus.
And passing through, he preached in
all the cities till he came to Caesarea.

The Damascus Road: Saul Converted

9 Then Saul, still breathing threats
and murder against the disciples
of the Lord, went to the high priest
2 and asked letters from him to the
synagogues of Damascus, so that if he
found any who were of the Way,
whether men or women, he might
bring them bound to Jerusalem.

3 As he journeyed he came near
Damascus, and suddenly a light
shone around him from heaven.
4 Then he fell to the ground, and
heard a voice saying to him, "Saul,
Saul, why are you persecuting Me?"

5 And he said, "Who are You,
Lord?"

Then the Lord said, "I am Jesus,
whom you are persecuting.[a] It *is* hard
for you to kick against the goads."

6 So he, trembling and astonished,
said, "Lord, what do You want me
to do?"

Then the Lord *said* to him, "Arise
and go into the city, and you will be
told what you must do."

7 And the men who journeyed
with him stood speechless, hearing a
voice but seeing no one. 8 Then Saul
arose from the ground, and when his
eyes were opened he saw no one. But
they led him by the hand and
brought *him* into Damascus. 9 And he
was three days without sight, and
neither ate nor drank.

8:37 [a]NU-Text and M-Text omit this verse. It is found in Western texts, including the Latin tradition. **9:5** [a]NU-Text and M-Text omit the last sentence of verse 5 and begin verse 6 with *But arise and go.*

Ananias Baptizes Saul

10Now there was a certain disciple at Damascus named Ananias; and
to him the Lord said in a vision,
"Ananias."

And he said, "Here I am, Lord."

11So the Lord *said* to him, "Arise
and go to the street called Straight,
and inquire at the house of Judas for
one called Saul of Tarsus, for behold,
he is praying. **12**And in a vision he has
seen a man named Ananias coming
in and putting *his* hand on him, so
that he might receive his sight."

13Then Ananias answered, "Lord, I
have heard from many about this
man, how much harm he has done to
Your saints in Jerusalem. **14**And here
he has authority from the chief priests
to bind all who call on Your name."

15But the Lord said to him, "Go,
for he is a chosen vessel of Mine to
bear My name before Gentiles, kings,
and the children of Israel. **16**For I will
show him how many things he must
suffer for My name's sake."

17And Ananias went his way and
entered the house; and laying his
hands on him he said, "Brother Saul,
the Lord Jesus,[a] who appeared to you
on the road as you came, has sent me
that you may receive your sight and
be filled with the Holy Spirit." **18**Immediately there fell from his eyes
something like scales, and he received
his sight at once; and he arose and
was baptized.

19So when he had received food,
he was strengthened. Then Saul
spent some days with the disciples at
Damascus.

Saul Preaches Christ

20Immediately he preached the
Christ[a] in the synagogues, that He is
the Son of God.

21Then all who heard were
amazed, and said, "Is this not he who
destroyed those who called on this
name in Jerusalem, and has come
here for that purpose, so that he
might bring them bound to the chief
priests?"

22But Saul increased all the more
in strength, and confounded the Jews
who dwelt in Damascus, proving that
this *Jesus* is the Christ.

9:17 [a]M-Text omits *Jesus.* **9:20** [a]NU-Text reads *Jesus.*

Saul Escapes Death

23Now after many days were past, the Jews plotted to kill him. 24But their plot became known to Saul. And they watched the gates day and night, to kill him. 25Then the disciples took him by night and let *him* down through the wall in a large basket.

Saul at Jerusalem

26And when Saul had come to Jerusalem, he tried to join the disciples; but they were all afraid of him, and did not believe that he was a disciple. 27But Barnabas took him and brought *him* to the apostles. And he declared to them how he had seen the Lord on the road, and that He had spoken to him, and how he had preached boldly at Damascus in the name of Jesus. 28So he was with them at Jerusalem, coming in and going out. 29And he spoke boldly in the name of the Lord Jesus and disputed against the Hellenists, but they attempted to kill him. 30When the brethren found out, they brought him down to Caesarea and sent him out to Tarsus.

The Church Prospers

31Then the churches[a] throughout all Judea, Galilee, and Samaria had peace and were edified. And walking in the fear of the Lord and in the comfort of the Holy Spirit, they were multiplied.

Aeneas Healed

32Now it came to pass, as Peter went through all *parts of the country*, that he also came down to the saints who dwelt in Lydda. 33There he found a certain man named Aeneas, who had been bedridden eight years and was paralyzed. 34And Peter said to him, "Aeneas, Jesus the Christ heals you. Arise and make your bed." Then he arose immediately. 35So all who dwelt at Lydda and Sharon saw him and turned to the Lord.

Dorcas Restored to Life

36At Joppa there was a certain disciple named Tabitha, which is translated Dorcas. This woman was full of good works and charitable deeds which she did. 37But it happened in those days that she became sick and

---

9:31 [a]NU-Text reads *church . . . was edified.*

died. When they had washed her, they laid *her* in an upper room. 38And since Lydda was near Joppa, and the disciples had heard that Peter was there, they sent two men to him, imploring *him* not to delay in coming to them. 39Then Peter arose and went with them. When he had come, they brought *him* to the upper room. And all the widows stood by him weeping, showing the tunics and garments which Dorcas had made while she was with them. 40But Peter put them all out, and knelt down and prayed. And turning to the body he said, "Tabitha, arise." And she opened her eyes, and when she saw Peter she sat up. 41Then he gave her *his* hand and lifted her up; and when he had called the saints and widows, he presented her alive. 42And it became known throughout all Joppa, and many believed on the Lord. 43So it was that he stayed many days in Joppa with Simon, a tanner.

Cornelius Sends a Delegation

10 There was a certain man in Caesarea called Cornelius, a centurion of what was called the Italian Regiment, 2a devout *man* and one who feared God with all his household, who gave alms generously to the people, and prayed to God always. 3About the ninth hour of the day he saw clearly in a vision an angel of God coming in and saying to him, "Cornelius!"

4And when he observed him, he was afraid, and said, "What is it, Lord?"

So he said to him, "Your prayers and your alms have come up for a memorial before God. 5Now send men to Joppa, and send for Simon whose surname is Peter. 6He is lodging with Simon, a tanner, whose house is by the sea.[a] He will tell you what you must do." 7And when the angel who spoke to him had departed, Cornelius called two of his household servants and a devout soldier from among those who waited on him continually. 8So when he had explained all *these* things to them, he sent them to Joppa.

Peter's Vision

9The next day, as they went on their journey and drew near the city,

---

10:6 [a]NU-Text and M-Text omit the last sentence of this verse.

Peter went up on the housetop to pray, about the sixth hour. 10 Then he became very hungry and wanted to eat; but while they made ready, he fell into a trance 11 and saw heaven opened and an object like a great sheet bound at the four corners, descending to him and let down to the earth. 12 In it were all kinds of four-footed animals of the earth, wild beasts, creeping things, and birds of the air. 13 And a voice came to him, "Rise, Peter; kill and eat."

14 But Peter said, "Not so, Lord! For I have never eaten anything common or unclean."

15 And a voice *spoke* to him again the second time, "What God has cleansed you must not call common." 16 This was done three times. And the object was taken up into heaven again.

Summoned to Caesarea

17 Now while Peter wondered within himself what this vision which he had seen meant, behold, the men who had been sent from Cornelius had made inquiry for Simon's house, and stood before the gate. 18 And they called and asked whether Simon, whose surname was Peter, was lodging there.

19 While Peter thought about the vision, the Spirit said to him, "Behold, three men are seeking you. 20 Arise therefore, go down and go with them, doubting nothing; for I have sent them."

21 Then Peter went down to the men who had been sent to him from Cornelius,[a] and said, "Yes, I am he whom you seek. For what reason have you come?"

22 And they said, "Cornelius *the* centurion, a just man, one who fears God and has a good reputation among all the nation of the Jews, was divinely instructed by a holy angel to summon you to his house, and to hear words from you." 23 Then he invited them in and lodged *them.*

On the next day Peter went away with them, and some brethren from Joppa accompanied him.

Peter Meets Cornelius

24 And the following day they entered Caesarea. Now Cornelius was waiting for them, and had called to-

---

10:21 [a]NU-Text and M-Text omit *who had been sent to him from Cornelius.*

gether his relatives and close friends. [25]As Peter was coming in, Cornelius met him and fell down at his feet and worshiped *him.* [26]But Peter lifted him up, saying, "Stand up; I myself am also a man." [27]And as he talked with him, he went in and found many who had come together. [28]Then he said to them, "You know how unlawful it is for a Jewish man to keep company with or go to one of another nation. But God has shown me that I should not call any man common or unclean. [29]Therefore I came without objection as soon as I was sent for. I ask, then, for what reason have you sent for me?"

[30]So Cornelius said, "Four days ago I was fasting until this hour; and at the ninth hour[a] I prayed in my house, and behold, a man stood before me in bright clothing, [31]and said, 'Cornelius, your prayer has been heard, and your alms are remembered in the sight of God. [32]Send therefore to Joppa and call Simon here, whose surname is Peter. He is lodging in the house of Simon, a tanner, by the sea.[a] When he comes, he will speak to you.' [33]So I sent to you immediately, and you have done well to come. Now therefore, we are all present before God, to hear all the things commanded you by God."

Preaching to Cornelius' Household

[34]Then Peter opened *his* mouth and said: "In truth I perceive that God shows no partiality. [35]But in every nation whoever fears Him and works righteousness is accepted by Him. [36]The word which *God* sent to the children of Israel, preaching peace through Jesus Christ—He is Lord of all— [37]that word you know, which was proclaimed throughout all Judea, and began from Galilee after the baptism which John preached: [38]how God anointed Jesus of Nazareth with the Holy Spirit and with power, who went about doing good and healing all who were oppressed by the devil, for God was with Him. [39]And we are witnesses of all things which He did both in the land of the Jews and in Jerusalem, whom they[a] killed by hanging on a

---

10:30 [a]NU-Text reads *Four days ago to this hour, at the ninth hour.* **10:32** [a]NU-Text omits the last sentence of this verse.
10:39 [a]NU-Text and M-Text add *also.*

tree. [40]Him God raised up on the
third day, and showed Him openly,
[41]not to all the people, but to witnesses chosen before by God, *even*
to us who ate and drank with Him
after He arose from the dead.
[42]And He commanded us to preach
to the people, and to testify that it
is He who was ordained by God *to*
be Judge of the living and the dead.
[43]To Him all the prophets witness
that, through His name, whoever
believes in Him will receive remission
of sins."

The Holy Spirit Falls on the Gentiles

[44]While Peter was still speaking
these words, the Holy Spirit fell upon
all those who heard the word. [45]And
those of the circumcision who believed were astonished, as many as
came with Peter, because the gift of
the Holy Spirit had been poured out
on the Gentiles also. [46]For they heard
them speak with tongues and mag-
nify God.

Then Peter answered, [47]"Can
anyone forbid water, that these
should not be baptized who have received the Holy Spirit just as we *have*?"
[48]And he commanded them to be
baptized in the name of the Lord.
Then they asked him to stay a few
days.

Peter Defends God's Grace

11 Now the apostles and brethren who were in Judea heard
that the Gentiles had also received
the word of God. [2]And when Peter
came up to Jerusalem, those of the
circumcision contended with him,
[3]saying, "You went in to uncircumcised men and ate with them!"

[4]But Peter explained *it* to them
in order from the beginning, saying:
[5]"I was in the city of Joppa praying;
and in a trance I saw a vision, an
object descending like a great sheet,
let down from heaven by four
corners; and it came to me. [6]When I
observed it intently and considered,
I saw four-footed animals of the
earth, wild beasts, creeping things,
and birds of the air. [7]And I heard
a voice saying to me, 'Rise, Peter;
kill and eat.' [8]But I said, 'Not so,
Lord! For nothing common or
unclean has at any time entered my
mouth.' [9]But the voice answered me
again from heaven, 'What God has
cleansed you must not call common.' [10]Now this was done three

times, and all were drawn up again
into heaven. 11 At that very moment,
three men stood before the house
where I was, having been sent to me
from Caesarea. 12 Then the Spirit told
me to go with them, doubting nothing. Moreover these six brethren
accompanied me, and we entered
the man's house. 13 And he told us
how he had seen an angel standing
in his house, who said to him, 'Send
men to Joppa, and call for Simon
whose surname is Peter, 14 who will
tell you words by which you and
all your household will be saved.'
15 And as I began to speak, the Holy
Spirit fell upon them, as upon us at
the beginning. 16 Then I remembered
the word of the Lord, how He said,
'John indeed baptized with water,
but you shall be baptized with the
Holy Spirit.' 17 If therefore God gave
them the same gift as *He gave* us
when we believed on the Lord Jesus
Christ, who was I that I could with-
stand God?"

18 When they heard these things
they became silent; and they glorified
God, saying, "Then God has also
granted to the Gentiles repentance
to life."

Barnabas and Saul at Antioch

19 Now those who were scattered
after the persecution that arose over
Stephen traveled as far as Phoenicia,
Cyprus, and Antioch, preaching the
word to no one but the Jews only.
20 But some of them were men from
Cyprus and Cyrene, who, when they
had come to Antioch, spoke to the
Hellenists, preaching the Lord Jesus.
21 And the hand of the Lord was with
them, and a great number believed
and turned to the Lord.

22 Then news of these things came
to the ears of the church in Jerusalem, and they sent out Barnabas to
go as far as Antioch. 23 When he came
and had seen the grace of God, he
was glad, and encouraged them all
that with purpose of heart they
should continue with the Lord. 24 For
he was a good man, full of the Holy
Spirit and of faith. And a great many
people were added to the Lord.

25 Then Barnabas departed for
Tarsus to seek Saul. 26 And when he
had found him, he brought him to
Antioch. So it was that for a whole
year they assembled with the church
and taught a great many people. And

the disciples were first called Christians in Antioch.

Relief to Judea

[27]And in these days prophets came from Jerusalem to Antioch. [28]Then one of them, named Agabus, stood up and showed by the Spirit that there was going to be a great famine throughout all the world, which also happened in the days of Claudius Caesar. [29]Then the disciples, each according to his ability, determined to send relief to the brethren dwelling in Judea. [30]This they also did, and sent it to the elders by the hands of Barnabas and Saul.

Herod's Violence to the Church

12 Now about that time Herod the king stretched out *his* hand to harass some from the church. [2]Then he killed James the brother of John with the sword. [3]And because he saw that it pleased the Jews, he proceeded further to seize Peter also. Now it was *during* the Days of Unleavened Bread. [4]So when he had arrested him, he put *him* in prison, and delivered *him* to four squads of soldiers to keep him, intending to bring him before the people after Passover.

Peter Freed from Prison

[5]Peter was therefore kept in prison, but constant[a] prayer was offered to God for him by the church. [6]And when Herod was about to bring him out, that night Peter was sleeping, bound with two chains between two soldiers; and the guards before the door were keeping the prison. [7]Now behold, an angel of the Lord stood by *him*, and a light shone in the prison; and he struck Peter on the side and raised him up, saying, "Arise quickly!" And his chains fell off *his* hands. [8]Then the angel said to him, "Gird yourself and tie on your sandals"; and so he did. And he said to him, "Put on your garment and follow me." [9]So he went out and followed him, and did not know that what was done by the angel was real, but thought he was seeing a vision. [10]When they were past the first and

---

12:5 [a]NU-Text reads *constantly* (or *earnestly*).

the second guard posts, they came to
the iron gate that leads to the city,
which opened to them of its own accord; and they went out and went
down one street, and immediately
the angel departed from him.

11 And when Peter had come to
himself, he said, "Now I know for
certain that the Lord has sent His
angel, and has delivered me from the
hand of Herod and *from* all the expectation of the Jewish people."

12 So, when he had considered *this,*
he came to the house of Mary, the
mother of John whose surname was
Mark, where many were gathered together praying. 13 And as Peter knocked
at the door of the gate, a girl named
Rhoda came to answer. 14 When she
recognized Peter's voice, because of *her*
gladness she did not open the gate, but
ran in and announced that Peter stood
before the gate. 15 But they said to her,
"You are beside yourself!" Yet she kept
insisting that it was so. So they said, "It
is his angel."

16 Now Peter continued knocking;
and when they opened *the door* and
saw him, they were astonished. 17 But
motioning to them with his hand to
keep silent, he declared to them how
the Lord had brought him out of the
prison. And he said, "Go, tell these
things to James and to the brethren."
And he departed and went to another place.

18 Then, as soon as it was day, there
was no small stir among the soldiers
about what had become of Peter.
19 But when Herod had searched for
him and not found him, he examined
the guards and commanded that *they*
should be put to death.

And he went down from Judea to
Caesarea, and stayed *there.*

Herod's Violent Death

20 Now Herod had been very
angry with the people of Tyre and
Sidon; but they came to him with
one accord, and having made Blastus
the king's personal aide their friend,
they asked for peace, because their
country was supplied with food by
the king's *country.*

21 So on a set day Herod, arrayed
in royal apparel, sat on his throne
and gave an oration to them. 22 And
the people kept shouting, "The voice
of a god and not of a man!" 23 Then
immediately an angel of the Lord
struck him, because he did not give
glory to God. And he was eaten by
worms and died.

24 But the word of God grew and multiplied.

Barnabas and Saul Appointed

25 And Barnabas and Saul returned from[a] Jerusalem when they had fulfilled *their* ministry, and they also took with them John whose surname was Mark.

13 Now in the church that was at Antioch there were certain prophets and teachers: Barnabas, Simeon who was called Niger, Lucius of Cyrene, Manaen who had been brought up with Herod the tetrarch, and Saul. 2 As they ministered to the Lord and fasted, the Holy Spirit said, "Now separate to Me Barnabas and Saul for the work to which I have called them." 3 Then, having fasted and prayed, and laid hands on them, they sent *them* away.

Preaching in Cyprus

4 So, being sent out by the Holy Spirit, they went down to Seleucia, and from there they sailed to Cyprus. 5 And when they arrived in Salamis, they preached the word of God in the synagogues of the Jews. They also had John as *their* assistant.

6 Now when they had gone through the island[a] to Paphos, they found a certain sorcerer, a false prophet, a Jew whose name *was* Bar-Jesus, 7 who was with the proconsul, Sergius Paulus, an intelligent man. This man called for Barnabas and Saul and sought to hear the word of God. 8 But Elymas the sorcerer (for so his name is translated) withstood them, seeking to turn the proconsul away from the faith. 9 Then Saul, who also *is called* Paul, filled with the Holy Spirit, looked intently at him 10 and said, "O full of all deceit and all fraud, *you* son of the devil, *you* enemy of all righteousness, will you not cease perverting the straight ways of the Lord? 11 And now, indeed, the hand of the Lord *is* upon you, and you shall be blind, not seeing the sun for a time."

And immediately a dark mist fell on him, and he went around seeking someone to lead him by the hand. 12 Then the proconsul believed, when he saw what had been done, being astonished at the teaching of the Lord.

12:25 [a]NU-Text and M-Text read *to.* **13:6** [a]NU-Text reads *the whole island.*

At Antioch in Pisidia

13 Now when Paul and his party set sail from Paphos, they came to Perga in Pamphylia; and John, departing from them, returned to Jerusalem. 14 But when they departed from Perga, they came to Antioch in Pisidia, and went into the synagogue on the Sabbath day and sat down. 15 And after the reading of the Law and the Prophets, the rulers of the synagogue sent to them, saying, "Men *and* brethren, if you have any word of exhortation for the people, say on."

16 Then Paul stood up, and motioning with *his* hand said, "Men of Israel, and you who fear God, listen: 17 The God of this people Israel[a] chose our fathers, and exalted the people when they dwelt as strangers in the land of Egypt, and with an uplifted arm He brought them out of it. 18 Now for a time of about forty years He put up with their ways in the wilderness. 19 And when He had destroyed seven nations in the land of Canaan, He distributed their land to them by allotment.

20 "After that He gave *them* judges for about four hundred and fifty years, until Samuel the prophet. 21 And afterward they asked for a king; so God gave them Saul the son of Kish, a man of the tribe of Benjamin, for forty years. 22 And when He had removed him, He raised up for them David as king, to whom also He gave testimony and said, *'I have found David*[a] the *son* of Jesse, *a man after My own heart, who will do all My will.'*[b] 23 From this man's seed, according to *the* promise, God raised up for Israel a Savior—Jesus—[a] 24 after John had first preached, before His coming, the baptism of repentance to all the people of Israel. 25 And as John was finishing his course, he said, 'Who do you think I am? I am not *He*. But behold, there comes One after me, the sandals of whose feet I am not worthy to loose.'

26 "Men *and* brethren, sons of the family of Abraham, and those among you who fear God, to you the word of this salvation has been sent. 27 For those who dwell in Jerusalem, and their rulers, because they did not know Him, nor even the voices of the Prophets which are read every Sab-

---

13:17 [a]M-Text omits *Israel.* **13:22** [a]Psalm 89:20 [b]1 Samuel 13:14 **13:23** [a]M-Text reads *for Israel salvation.*

bath, have fulfilled *them* in condemning *Him.* 28And though they found no
cause for death *in Him,* they asked Pilate that He should be put to death.
29Now when they had fulfilled all that
was written concerning Him, they
took *Him* down from the tree and laid
Him in a tomb. 30But God raised Him
from the dead. 31He was seen for
many days by those who came up
with Him from Galilee to Jerusalem,
who are His witnesses to the people. 32And we declare to you glad
tidings—that promise which was
made to the fathers. 33God has fulfilled this for us their children, in that
He has raised up Jesus. As it is also
written in the second Psalm:

> *'You are My Son,*
> *Today I have begotten You.'*[a]

34And that He raised Him from the
dead, no more to return to corruption, He has spoken thus:

> *'I will give you the sure mercies*
> *of David.'*[a]

35Therefore He also says in another
Psalm:

> *'You will not allow Your Holy*
> *One to see corruption.'*[a]

36"For David, after he had served
his own generation by the will of
God, fell asleep, was buried with his
fathers, and saw corruption; 37but He
whom God raised up saw no corruption. 38Therefore let it be known to
you, brethren, that through this Man
is preached to you the forgiveness of
sins; 39and by Him everyone who believes is justified from all things from
which you could not be justified by
the law of Moses. 40Beware therefore,
lest what has been spoken in the
prophets come upon you:

41 *'Behold, you despisers,*
> *Marvel and perish!*
> *For I work a work in your days,*
> *A work which you will by no*
> *means believe,*
> *Though one were to declare it*
> *to you.'"*[a]

Blessing and Conflict at Antioch

42So when the Jews went out
of the synagogue,[a] the Gentiles begged
that these words might be preached

13:33 [a]Psalm 2:7 13:34 [a]Isaiah 55:3 13:35 [a]Psalm 16:10 13:41 [a]Habakkuk 1:5 13:42 [a]Or *And when they went out of the synagogue of the Jews;* NU-Text reads *And when they went out, they begged.*

to them the next Sabbath. 43Now
when the congregation had broken
up, many of the Jews and devout
proselytes followed Paul and Barnabas, who, speaking to them, persuaded them to continue in the grace
of God.

44On the next Sabbath almost
the whole city came together to hear
the word of God. 45But when the
Jews saw the multitudes, they were
filled with envy; and contradicting
and blaspheming, they opposed the
things spoken by Paul. 46Then Paul
and Barnabas grew bold and said,
"It was necessary that the word of
God should be spoken to you first;
but since you reject it, and judge
yourselves unworthy of everlasting
life, behold, we turn to the Gentiles. 47For so the Lord has commanded us:

'I have set you as a light to the
Gentiles,
That you should be for
salvation to the ends of the
earth.'"[a]

48Now when the Gentiles heard
this, they were glad and glorified the
word of the Lord. And as many as
had been appointed to eternal life
believed.

49And the word of the Lord was
being spread throughout all the region. 50But the Jews stirred up the
devout and prominent women and
the chief men of the city, raised up
persecution against Paul and Barnabas, and expelled them from their
region. 51But they shook off the dust
from their feet against them, and
came to Iconium. 52And the disciples
were filled with joy and with the
Holy Spirit.

At Iconium

14 Now it happened in Iconium
that they went together to
the synagogue of the Jews, and so
spoke that a great multitude both of
the Jews and of the Greeks believed.
2But the unbelieving Jews stirred up
the Gentiles and poisoned their
minds against the brethren. 3There-
fore they stayed there a long time,
speaking boldly in the Lord, who was
bearing witness to the word of His
grace, granting signs and wonders to
be done by their hands.

13:47 [a]Isaiah 49:6

4But the multitude of the city was divided: part sided with the Jews, and part with the apostles. 5And when a violent attempt was made by both the Gentiles and Jews, with their rulers, to abuse and stone them, 6they became aware of it and fled to Lystra and Derbe, cities of Lycaonia, and to the surrounding region. 7And they were preaching the gospel there.

Idolatry at Lystra

8And in Lystra a certain man without strength in his feet was sitting, a cripple from his mother's womb, who had never walked. 9*This* man heard Paul speaking. Paul, observing him intently and seeing that he had faith to be healed, 10said with a loud voice, "Stand up straight on your feet!" And he leaped and walked. 11Now when the people saw what Paul had done, they raised their voices, saying in the Lycaonian *language,* "The gods have come down to us in the likeness of men!" 12And Barnabas they called Zeus, and Paul, Hermes, because he was the chief speaker. 13Then the priest of Zeus, whose temple was in front of their city, brought oxen and garlands to the gates, intending to sacrifice with the multitudes.

14But when the apostles Barnabas and Paul heard this, they tore their clothes and ran in among the multitude, crying out 15and saying, "Men, why are you doing these things? We also are men with the same nature as you, and preach to you that you should turn from these useless things to the living God, who made the heaven, the earth, the sea, and all things that are in them, 16who in bygone generations allowed all nations to walk in their own ways. 17Nevertheless He did not leave Himself without witness, in that He did good, gave us rain from heaven and fruitful seasons, filling our hearts with food and gladness." 18And with these sayings they could scarcely restrain the multitudes from sacrificing to them.

Stoning, Escape to Derbe

19Then Jews from Antioch and Iconium came there; and having persuaded the multitudes, they stoned Paul *and* dragged *him* out of the city, supposing him to be dead. 20However, when the disciples gathered around him, he rose up and

went into the city. And the next
day he departed with Barnabas to
Derbe.

Strengthening the Converts

21 And when they had preached
the gospel to that city and made many
disciples, they returned to Lystra, Iconium, and Antioch, 22 strengthening
the souls of the disciples, exhorting
them to continue in the faith, and
saying, "We must through many tribulations enter the kingdom of God."
23 So when they had appointed elders
in every church, and prayed with
fasting, they commended them to
the Lord in whom they had believed.
24 And after they had passed through
Pisidia, they came to Pamphylia. 25 Now
when they had preached the word in
Perga, they went down to Attalia.
26 From there they sailed to Antioch,
where they had been commended to
the grace of God for the work which
they had completed.

27 Now when they had come and
gathered the church together, they
reported all that God had done with
them, and that He had opened the
door of faith to the Gentiles. 28 So
they stayed there a long time with
the disciples.

Conflict over Circumcision

15 And certain *men* came down
from Judea and taught the
brethren, "Unless you are circumcised according to the custom of
Moses, you cannot be saved." 2 Therefore, when Paul and Barnabas had no
small dissension and dispute with
them, they determined that Paul
and Barnabas and certain others of
them should go up to Jerusalem, to
the apostles and elders, about this
question.

3 So, being sent on their way by
the church, they passed through
Phoenicia and Samaria, describing
the conversion of the Gentiles; and
they caused great joy to all the
brethren. 4 And when they had come
to Jerusalem, they were received by
the church and the apostles and the
elders; and they reported all things
that God had done with them. 5 But
some of the sect of the Pharisees who
believed rose up, saying, "It is necessary to circumcise them, and to command *them* to keep the law of Moses."

The Jerusalem Council

6 Now the apostles and elders
came together to consider this mat-

ter. **7**And when there had been much dispute, Peter rose up *and* said to them: "Men *and* brethren, you know that a good while ago God chose among us, that by my mouth the Gentiles should hear the word of the gospel and believe. **8**So God, who knows the heart, acknowledged them by giving them the Holy Spirit, just as *He did* to us, **9**and made no distinction between us and them, purifying their hearts by faith. **10**Now therefore, why do you test God by putting a yoke on the neck of the disciples which neither our fathers nor we were able to bear? **11**But we believe that through the grace of the Lord Jesus Christ[a] we shall be saved in the same manner as they."

12Then all the multitude kept silent and listened to Barnabas and Paul declaring how many miracles and wonders God had worked through them among the Gentiles. **13**And after they had become silent, James answered, saying, "Men *and* brethren, listen to me: **14**Simon has declared how God at the first visited the Gentiles to take out of them a people for His name. **15**And with this the words of the prophets agree, just as it is written:

16 *'After this I will return*
And will rebuild the tabernacle
of David, which has fallen
down;
I will rebuild its ruins,
And I will set it up;
17 *So that the rest of mankind*
may seek the LORD,
Even all the Gentiles who are
called by My name,
Says the LORD who does all
these things.'[a]

18"Known to God from eternity are all His works.[a] **19**Therefore I judge that we should not trouble those from among the Gentiles who are turning to God, **20**but that we write to them to abstain from things polluted by idols, *from* sexual immorality,[a] *from* things strangled, and *from* blood. **21**For Moses has had throughout many generations those who preach him in every city, being read in the synagogues every Sabbath."

15:11 [a]NU-Text and M-Text omit *Christ*. **15:17** [a]Amos 9:11, 12 **15:18** [a]NU-Text (combining with verse 17) reads *Says the Lord, who makes these things known from eternity (of old)*. **15:20** [a]Or *fornication*

The Jerusalem Decree

[22]Then it pleased the apostles and elders, with the whole church, to send chosen men of their own company to Antioch with Paul and Barnabas, *namely,* Judas who was also named Barsabas,[a] and Silas, leading men among the brethren.

[23]They wrote this, *letter* by them:

The apostles, the elders, and the brethren,

To the brethren who are of the Gentiles in Antioch, Syria, and Cilicia:

Greetings.

[24]Since we have heard that some who went out from us have troubled you with words, unsettling your souls, saying, "*You must* be circumcised and keep the law"[a]—to whom we gave no *such* commandment—[25]it seemed good to us, being assembled with one accord, to send chosen men to you with our beloved Barnabas and Paul, [26]men who have risked their lives for the name of our Lord Jesus Christ. [27]We have therefore sent Judas and Silas, who will also report the same things by word of mouth. [28]For it seemed good to the Holy Spirit, and to us, to lay upon you no greater burden than these necessary things: [29]that you abstain from things offered to idols, from blood, from things strangled, and from sexual immorality.[a] If you keep yourselves from these, you will do well.

Farewell.

Continuing Ministry in Syria

[30]So when they were sent off, they came to Antioch; and when they had gathered the multitude together, they delivered the letter. [31]When they had read it, they rejoiced over its encouragement. [32]Now Judas and Silas, themselves being prophets also, exhorted and strengthened the brethren with many words. [33]And after they had stayed *there* for a time, they were sent back with greetings from the brethren to the apostles.[a]

[34]However, it seemed good to Silas to remain there.[a] [35]Paul and Barnabas also remained in Antioch,

---

15:22 [a]NU-Text and M-Text read *Barsabbas.* **15:24** [a]NU-Text omits *saying, "You must be circumcised and keep the law."* **15:29** [a]Or *fornication.* **15:33** [a]NU-Text reads *to those who had sent them.* **15:34** [a]NU-Text and M-Text omit this verse.

teaching and preaching the word of
the Lord, with many others also.

Division over John Mark

36 Then after some days Paul said
to Barnabas, "Let us now go back and
visit our brethren in every city where
we have preached the word of the
Lord, *and see* how they are doing."
37 Now Barnabas was determined to
take with them John called Mark.
38 But Paul insisted that they should
not take with them the one who had
departed from them in Pamphylia,
and had not gone with them to the
work. 39 Then the contention became so sharp that they parted from
one another. And so Barnabas took
Mark and sailed to Cyprus; 40 but Paul
chose Silas and departed, being commended by the brethren to the grace
of God. 41 And he went through
Syria and Cilicia, strengthening the
churches.

Timothy Joins Paul and Silas

16 Then he came to Derbe and
Lystra. And behold, a certain
disciple was there, named Timothy,
the son of a certain Jewish woman
who believed, but his father *was*
Greek. 2 He was well spoken of by the
brethren who were at Lystra and Iconium. 3 Paul wanted to have him go
on with him. And he took *him* and
circumcised him because of the Jews
who were in that region, for they all
knew that his father was Greek. 4 And
as they went through the cities, they
delivered to them the decrees to
keep, which were determined by the
apostles and elders at Jerusalem. 5 So
the churches were strengthened in
the faith, and increased in number
daily.

The Macedonian Call

6 Now when they had gone
through Phrygia and the region of
Galatia, they were forbidden by the
Holy Spirit to preach the word in
Asia. 7 After they had come to Mysia,
they tried to go into Bithynia, but the
Spirit[a] did not permit them. 8 So passing by Mysia, they came down to
Troas. 9 And a vision appeared to Paul
in the night. A man of Macedonia
stood and pleaded with him, saying,
"Come over to Macedonia and help
us." 10 Now after he had seen the vi-

16:7 [a]NU-Text adds *of Jesus.*

sion, immediately we sought to go to Macedonia, concluding that the Lord had called us to preach the gospel to them.

Lydia Baptized at Philippi

11Therefore, sailing from Troas, we ran a straight course to Samothrace, and the next *day* came to Neapolis, 12and from there to Philippi, which is the foremost city of that part of Macedonia, a colony. And we were staying in that city for some days. 13And on the Sabbath day we went out of the city to the riverside, where prayer was customarily made; and we sat down and spoke to the women who met *there.* 14Now a certain woman named Lydia heard *us.* She was a seller of purple from the city of Thyatira, who worshiped God. The Lord opened her heart to heed the things spoken by Paul. 15And when she and her household were baptized, she begged *us,* saying, "If you have judged me to be faithful to the Lord, come to my house and stay." So she persuaded us.

Paul and Silas Imprisoned

16Now it happened, as we went to prayer, that a certain slave girl possessed with a spirit of divination met us, who brought her masters much profit by fortune-telling. 17This girl followed Paul and us, and cried out, saying, "These men are the servants of the Most High God, who proclaim to us the way of salvation." 18And this she did for many days.

But Paul, greatly annoyed, turned and said to the spirit, "I command you in the name of Jesus Christ to come out of her." And he came out that very hour. 19But when her masters saw that their hope of profit was gone, they seized Paul and Silas and dragged *them* into the marketplace to the authorities.

20And they brought them to the magistrates, and said, "These men, being Jews, exceedingly trouble our city; 21and they teach customs which are not lawful for us, being Romans, to receive or observe." 22Then the multitude rose up together against them; and the magistrates tore off their clothes and commanded *them* to be beaten with rods. 23And when they had laid many stripes on them, they threw *them* into prison, commanding the jailer to keep them securely. 24Having received such a charge, he put them into the inner

prison and fastened their feet in the
stocks.

The Philippian Jailer Saved

25But at midnight Paul and Silas
were praying and singing hymns to
God, and the prisoners were listening
to them. 26Suddenly there was a great
earthquake, so that the foundations
of the prison were shaken; and immediately all the doors were opened
and everyone's chains were loosed.
27And the keeper of the prison, awaking from sleep and seeing the prison
doors open, supposing the prisoners
had fled, drew his sword and was
about to kill himself. 28But Paul called
with a loud voice, saying, "Do yourself no harm, for we are all here."

29Then he called for a light, ran
in, and fell down trembling before
Paul and Silas. 30And he brought
them out and said, "Sirs, what must
I do to be saved?"

31So they said, "Believe on the
Lord Jesus Christ, and you will be
saved, you and your household."
32Then they spoke the word of the
Lord to him and to all who were in
his house. 33And he took them the
same hour of the night and washed
their stripes. And immediately he and
all his *family* were baptized. 34Now
when he had brought them into his
house, he set food before them; and
he rejoiced, having believed in God
with all his household.

Paul Refuses to Depart Secretly

35And when it was day, the magistrates sent the officers, saying, "Let
those men go."

36So the keeper of the prison reported these words to Paul, saying,
"The magistrates have sent to let you
go. Now therefore depart, and go in
peace."

37But Paul said to them, "They
have beaten us openly, uncondemned
Romans, *and* have thrown *us* into
prison. And now do they put us out
secretly? No indeed! Let them come
themselves and get us out."

38And the officers told these
words to the magistrates, and they
were afraid when they heard that
they were Romans. 39Then they
came and pleaded with them and
brought *them* out, and asked *them* to
depart from the city. 40So they went
out of the prison and entered *the house*
of Lydia; and when they had seen the
brethren, they encouraged them and
departed.

Preaching Christ at Thessalonica

17 Now when they had passed through Amphipolis and Apollonia, they came to Thessalonica, where there was a synagogue of the Jews. 2 Then Paul, as his custom was, went in to them, and for three Sabbaths reasoned with them from the Scriptures, 3 explaining and demonstrating that the Christ had to suffer and rise again from the dead, and *saying,* "This Jesus whom I preach to you is the Christ." 4 And some of them were persuaded; and a great multitude of the devout Greeks, and not a few of the leading women, joined Paul and Silas.

Assault on Jason's House

5 But the Jews who were not persuaded, becoming envious,[a] took some of the evil men from the marketplace, and gathering a mob, set all the city in an uproar and attacked the house of Jason, and sought to bring them out to the people. 6 But when they did not find them, they dragged Jason and some brethren to the rulers of the city, crying out, "These who have turned the world upside down have come here too. 7 Jason has harbored them, and these are all acting contrary to the decrees of Caesar, saying there is another king—Jesus." 8 And they troubled the crowd and the rulers of the city when they heard these things. 9 So when they had taken security from Jason and the rest, they let them go.

Ministering at Berea

10 Then the brethren immediately sent Paul and Silas away by night to Berea. When they arrived, they went into the synagogue of the Jews. 11 These were more fair-minded than those in Thessalonica, in that they received the word with all readiness, and searched the Scriptures daily *to find out* whether these things were so. 12 Therefore many of them believed, and also not a few of the Greeks, prominent women as well as men. 13 But when the Jews from Thessalonica learned that the word of God was preached by Paul at Berea, they came there also and stirred up the crowds. 14 Then immediately the

---

17:5 [a] NU-Text omits *who were not persuaded;* M-Text omits *becoming envious.*

brethren sent Paul away, to go to the sea; but both Silas and Timothy remained there. 15 So those who conducted Paul brought him to Athens; and receiving a command for Silas and Timothy to come to him with all speed, they departed.

The Philosophers at Athens

16 Now while Paul waited for them at Athens, his spirit was provoked within him when he saw that the city was given over to idols. 17 Therefore he reasoned in the synagogue with the Jews and with the *Gentile* worshipers, and in the marketplace daily with those who happened to be there. 18 Then[a] certain Epicurean and Stoic philosophers encountered him. And some said, "What does this babbler want to say?"

Others said, "He seems to be a proclaimer of foreign gods," because he preached to them Jesus and the resurrection.

19 And they took him and brought him to the Areopagus, saying, "May we know what this new doctrine *is* of which you speak? 20 For you are bringing some strange things to our ears. Therefore we want to know what these things mean." 21 For all the Athenians and the foreigners who were there spent their time in nothing else but either to tell or to hear some new thing.

Addressing the Areopagus

22 Then Paul stood in the midst of the Areopagus and said, "Men of Athens, I perceive that in all things you are very religious; 23 for as I was passing through and considering the objects of your worship, I even found an altar with this inscription:

TO THE UNKNOWN GOD.

Therefore, the One whom you worship without knowing, Him I proclaim to you: 24 God, who made the world and everything in it, since He is Lord of heaven and earth, does not dwell in temples made with hands. 25 Nor is He worshiped with men's hands, as though He needed anything, since He gives to all life, breath, and all things. 26 And He has made from one blood[a] every nation of men to dwell on all the face of the earth, and has determined their

---

17:18 [a]NU-Text and M-Text add *also.* **17:26** [a]NU-Text omits *blood.*

preappointed times and the boundaries of their dwellings, [27]so that they should seek the Lord, in the hope that they might grope for Him and find Him, though He is not far from each one of us; [28]for in Him we live and move and have our being, as also some of your own poets have said, 'For we are also His offspring.' [29]Therefore, since we are the offspring of God, we ought not to think that the Divine Nature is like gold or silver or stone, something shaped by art and man's devising. [30]Truly, these times of ignorance God overlooked, but now commands all men everywhere to repent, [31]because He has appointed a day on which He will judge the world in righteousness by the Man whom He has ordained. He has given assurance of this to all by raising Him from the dead."

[32]And when they heard of the resurrection of the dead, some mocked, while others said, "We will hear you again on this *matter.*" [33]So Paul departed from among them. [34]However, some men joined him and believed, among them Dionysius the Areopagite, a woman named Damaris, and others with them.

Ministering at Corinth

18 After these things Paul departed from Athens and went to Corinth. [2]And he found a certain Jew named Aquila, born in Pontus, who had recently come from Italy with his wife Priscilla (because Claudius had commanded all the Jews to depart from Rome); and he came to them. [3]So, because he was of the same trade, he stayed with them and worked; for by occupation they were tentmakers. [4]And he reasoned in the synagogue every Sabbath, and persuaded both Jews and Greeks.

[5]When Silas and Timothy had come from Macedonia, Paul was compelled by the Spirit, and testified to the Jews *that* Jesus *is* the Christ. [6]But when they opposed him and blasphemed, he shook *his* garments and said to them, "Your blood *be* upon your *own* heads; I *am* clean. From now on I will go to the Gentiles." [7]And he departed from there and entered the house of a certain *man* named Justus,[a]

18:7 [a]NU-Text reads *Titius Justus.*

one who worshiped God, whose house
was next door to the synagogue.
8 Then Crispus, the ruler of the synagogue, believed on the Lord with all
his household. And many of the
Corinthians, hearing, believed and
were baptized.

9 Now the Lord spoke to Paul in
the night by a vision, "Do not be
afraid, but speak, and do not keep
silent; 10 for I am with you, and no
one will attack you to hurt you; for I
have many people in this city." 11 And
he continued *there* a year and six
months, teaching the word of God
among them.

12 When Gallio was proconsul of
Achaia, the Jews with one accord rose
up against Paul and brought him to
the judgment seat, 13 saying, "This *fellow* persuades men to worship God
contrary to the law."

14 And when Paul was about to
open *his* mouth, Gallio said to the
Jews, "If it were a matter of wrongdoing or wicked crimes, O Jews, there
would be reason why I should bear
with you. 15 But if it is a question
of words and names and your own
law, look *to it* yourselves; for I do not
want to be a judge of such *matters*."
16 And he drove them from the judgment seat. 17 Then all the Greeks[a]
took Sosthenes, the ruler of the synagogue, and beat *him* before the judgment seat. But Gallio took no notice
of these things.

Paul Returns to Antioch

18 So Paul still remained a good
while. Then he took leave of the
brethren and sailed for Syria, and
Priscilla and Aquila *were* with him. He
had *his* hair cut off at Cenchrea, for
he had taken a vow. 19 And he came
to Ephesus, and left them there; but
he himself entered the synagogue
and reasoned with the Jews. 20 When
they asked *him* to stay a longer time
with them, he did not consent, 21 but
took leave of them, saying, "I must
by all means keep this coming feast in
Jerusalem;[a] but I will return again to
you, God willing." And he sailed
from Ephesus.

22 And when he had landed at Caesarea, and gone up and greeted the
church, he went down to Antioch.
23 After he had spent some time *there*,
he departed and went over the region

18:17 [a]NU-Text reads *they all*. **18:21** [a]NU-Text omits *I must* through *Jerusalem*.

of Galatia and Phrygia in order,
strengthening all the disciples.

Ministry of Apollos

24Now a certain Jew named Apol-
los, born at Alexandria, an eloquent
man *and* mighty in the Scriptures,
came to Ephesus. 25This man had
been instructed in the way of the
Lord; and being fervent in spirit,
he spoke and taught accurately the
things of the Lord, though he knew
only the baptism of John. 26So he
began to speak boldly in the synagogue. When Aquila and Priscilla
heard him, they took him aside and
explained to him the way of God
more accurately. 27And when he desired to cross to Achaia, the brethren
wrote, exhorting the disciples to
receive him; and when he arrived,
he greatly helped those who had
believed through grace; 28for he vigorously refuted the Jews publicly,
showing from the Scriptures that
Jesus is the Christ.

Paul at Ephesus

19 And it happened, while Apol-
los was at Corinth, that Paul,
having passed through the upper
regions, came to Ephesus. And finding some disciples 2he said to them,
"Did you receive the Holy Spirit
when you believed?"

So they said to him, "We have not
so much as heard whether there is a
Holy Spirit."

3And he said to them, "Into what
then were you baptized?"

So they said, "Into John's baptism."

4Then Paul said, "John indeed
baptized with a baptism of repentance, saying to the people that they
should believe on Him who would
come after him, that is, on Christ
Jesus."

5When they heard *this,* they were
baptized in the name of the Lord Jesus. 6And when Paul had laid hands
on them, the Holy Spirit came upon
them, and they spoke with tongues
and prophesied. 7Now the men were
about twelve in all.

8And he went into the synagogue
and spoke boldly for three months,
reasoning and persuading concerning the things of the kingdom of
God. 9But when some were hardened
and did not believe, but spoke evil of
the Way before the multitude, he departed from them and withdrew the
disciples, reasoning daily in the

school of Tyrannus. [10]And this continued for two years, so that all who
dwelt in Asia heard the word of the
Lord Jesus, both Jews and Greeks.

Miracles Glorify Christ

[11]Now God worked unusual miracles by the hands of Paul, [12]so that
even handkerchiefs or aprons were
brought from his body to the sick,
and the diseases left them and the evil
spirits went out of them. [13]Then
some of the itinerant Jewish exorcists
took it upon themselves to call the
name of the Lord Jesus over those
who had evil spirits, saying, "We[a] ex-
orcise you by the Jesus whom Paul
preaches." [14]Also there were seven
sons of Sceva, a Jewish chief priest,
who did so.

[15]And the evil spirit answered and
said, "Jesus I know, and Paul I know;
but who are you?"

[16]Then the man in whom the evil
spirit was leaped on them, overpowered[a] them, and prevailed against
them,[b] so that they fled out of that
house naked and wounded. [17]This became known both to all Jews and
Greeks dwelling in Ephesus; and fear
fell on them all, and the name of
the Lord Jesus was magnified. [18]And
many who had believed came confessing and telling their deeds. [19]Also,
many of those who had practiced
magic brought their books together
and burned *them* in the sight of
all. And they counted up the value of
them, and *it* totaled fifty thousand
pieces of silver. [20]So the word of
the Lord grew mightily and prevailed.

The Riot at Ephesus

[21]When these things were accomplished, Paul purposed in the
Spirit, when he had passed through
Macedonia and Achaia, to go to Jerusalem, saying, "After I have been
there, I must also see Rome." [22]So he
sent into Macedonia two of those
who ministered to him, Timothy and
Erastus, but he himself stayed in Asia
for a time.

[23]And about that time there arose
a great commotion about the Way.
[24]For a certain man named Demetrius, a silversmith, who made silver
shrines of Diana,[a] brought no small
profit to the craftsmen. [25]He called
them together with the workers of

19:13 [a]NU-Text reads *I.* **19:16** [a]M-Text reads *and they overpowered.* [b]NU-Text reads *both of them.* **19:24** [a]Greek *Artemis.*

similar occupation, and said: "Men, you know that we have our prosperity by this trade. [26]Moreover you see and hear that not only at Ephesus, but throughout almost all Asia, this Paul has persuaded and turned away many people, saying that they are not gods which are made with hands. [27]So not only is this trade of ours in danger of falling into disrepute, but also the temple of the great goddess Diana may be despised and her magnificence destroyed,[a] whom all Asia and the world worship."

[28]Now when they heard *this,* they were full of wrath and cried out, saying, "Great *is* Diana of the Ephesians!" [29]So the whole city was filled with confusion, and rushed into the theater with one accord, having seized Gaius and Aristarchus, Macedonians, Paul's travel companions. [30]And when Paul wanted to go in to the people, the disciples would not allow him. [31]Then some of the officials of Asia, who were his friends, sent to him pleading that he would not venture into the theater. [32]Some therefore cried one thing and some another, for the assembly was confused, and most of them did not know why they had come together. [33]And they drew Alexander out of the multitude, the Jews putting him forward. And Alexander motioned with his hand, and wanted to make his defense to the people. [34]But when they found out that he was a Jew, all with one voice cried out for about two hours, "Great *is* Diana of the Ephesians!"

[35]And when the city clerk had quieted the crowd, he said: "Men of Ephesus, what man is there who does not know that the city of the Ephesians is temple guardian of the great goddess Diana, and of the *image* which fell down from Zeus? [36]Therefore, since these things cannot be denied, you ought to be quiet and do nothing rashly. [37]For you have brought these men here who are neither robbers of temples nor blasphemers of your[a] goddess. [38]Therefore, if Demetrius and his fellow craftsmen have a case against anyone, the courts are open and there are proconsuls. Let them bring charges against one another. [39]But if you have any other inquiry to make,

---

19:27 [a]NU-Text reads *she be deposed from her magnificence.* **19:37** [a]NU-Text reads *our.*

it shall be determined in the lawful
assembly. 40For we are in danger of
being called in question for today's
uproar, there being no reason which
we may give to account for this disor-
derly gathering." 41And when he had
said these things, he dismissed the
assembly.

Journeys in Greece

20 After the uproar had ceased,
Paul called the disciples to
himself, embraced *them,* and departed to
go to Macedonia. 2Now when he had
gone over that region and encouraged
them with many words, he came to
Greece 3and stayed three months.
And when the Jews plotted against
him as he was about to sail to Syria, he
decided to return through Macedonia. 4And Sopater of Berea accompanied him to Asia—also Aristarchus
and Secundus of the Thessalonians,
and Gaius of Derbe, and Timothy, and
Tychicus and Trophimus of Asia.
5These men, going ahead, waited for
us at Troas. 6But we sailed away from
Philippi after the Days of Unleavened
Bread, and in five days joined them at
Troas, where we stayed seven days.

Ministering at Troas

7Now on the first *day* of the week,
when the disciples came together to
break bread, Paul, ready to depart the
next day, spoke to them and continued his message until midnight.
8There were many lamps in the
upper room where they[a] were gathered together. 9And in a window sat
a certain young man named Eutychus, who was sinking into a deep
sleep. He was overcome by sleep; and
as Paul continued speaking, he fell
down from the third story and was
taken up dead. 10But Paul went
down, fell on him, and embracing
him said, "Do not trouble yourselves,
for his life is in him." 11Now when
he had come up, had broken bread
and eaten, and talked a long while,
even till daybreak, he departed.
12And they brought the young man
in alive, and they were not a little
comforted.

From Troas to Miletus

13Then we went ahead to the
ship and sailed to Assos, there intending to take Paul on board; for

---

20:8 [a]NU-Text and M-Text read *we.*

so he had given orders, intending himself to go on foot. [14]And when he met us at Assos, we took him on board and came to Mitylene. [15]We sailed from there, and the next *day* came opposite Chios. The following *day* we arrived at Samos and stayed at Trogyllium. The next *day* we came to Miletus. [16]For Paul had decided to sail past Ephesus, so that he would not have to spend time in Asia; for he was hurrying to be at Jerusalem, if possible, on the Day of Pentecost.

The Ephesian Elders Exhorted

[17]From Miletus he sent to Ephesus and called for the elders of the church. [18]And when they had come to him, he said to them: "You know, from the first day that I came to Asia, in what manner I always lived among you, [19]serving the Lord with all humility, with many tears and trials which happened to me by the plotting of the Jews; [20]how I kept back nothing that was helpful, but proclaimed it to you, and taught you publicly and from house to house, [21]testifying to Jews, and also to Greeks, repentance toward God and faith toward our Lord Jesus Christ. [22]And see, now I go bound in the spirit to Jerusalem, not knowing the things that will happen to me there, [23]except that the Holy Spirit testifies in every city, saying that chains and tribulations await me. [24]But none of these things move me; nor do I count my life dear to myself,[a] so that I may finish my race with joy, and the ministry which I received from the Lord Jesus, to testify to the gospel of the grace of God.

[25]"And indeed, now I know that you all, among whom I have gone preaching the kingdom of God, will see my face no more. [26]Therefore I testify to you this day that I *am* innocent of the blood of all *men.* [27]For I have not shunned to declare to you the whole counsel of God. [28]Therefore take heed to yourselves and to all the flock, among which the Holy Spirit has made you overseers, to shepherd the church of God[a] which He purchased with His own blood. [29]For I know this, that after my departure savage wolves will come in among you, not sparing the flock.

20:24 [a]NU-Text reads *But I do not count my life of any value or dear to myself.* **20:28** [a]M-Text reads *of the Lord and God.*

30 Also from among yourselves men will rise up, speaking perverse things, to draw away the disciples after themselves. 31 Therefore watch, and remember that for three years I did not cease to warn everyone night and day with tears.

32 "So now, brethren, I commend you to God and to the word of His grace, which is able to build you up and give you an inheritance among all those who are sanctified. 33 I have coveted no one's silver or gold or apparel. 34 Yes,[a] you yourselves know that these hands have provided for my necessities, and for those who were with me. 35 I have shown you in every way, by laboring like this, that you must support the weak. And remember the words of the Lord Jesus, that He said, 'It is more blessed to give than to receive.'"

36 And when he had said these things, he knelt down and prayed with them all. 37 Then they all wept freely, and fell on Paul's neck and kissed him, 38 sorrowing most of all for the words which he spoke, that they would see his face no more. And they accompanied him to the ship.

Warnings on the Journey to Jerusalem

21 Now it came to pass, that when we had departed from them and set sail, running a straight course we came to Cos, the following *day* to Rhodes, and from there to Patara. 2 And finding a ship sailing over to Phoenicia, we went aboard and set sail. 3 When we had sighted Cyprus, we passed it on the left, sailed to Syria, and landed at Tyre; for there the ship was to unload her cargo. 4 And finding disciples,[a] we stayed there seven days. They told Paul through the Spirit not to go up to Jerusalem. 5 When we had come to the end of those days, we departed and went on our way; and they all accompanied us, with wives and children, till *we were* out of the city. And we knelt down on the shore and prayed. 6 When we had taken our leave of one another, we boarded the ship, and they returned home.

7 And when we had finished *our* voyage from Tyre, we came to Ptolemais, greeted the brethren, and stayed with them one day. 8 On the

20:34 [a]NU-Text and M-Text omit *Yes.* **21:4** [a]NU-Text reads *the disciples.*

next *day* we who were Paul's companions[a] departed and came to Caesarea, and entered the house of Philip
the evangelist, who was *one* of the
seven, and stayed with him. 9Now
this man had four virgin daughters
who prophesied. 10And as we stayed
many days, a certain prophet named
Agabus came down from Judea.
11When he had come to us, he took
Paul's belt, bound his *own* hands and
feet, and said, "Thus says the Holy
Spirit, 'So shall the Jews at Jerusalem
bind the man who owns this belt,
and deliver *him* into the hands of the
Gentiles.'"

12Now when we heard these
things, both we and those from that
place pleaded with him not to go up
to Jerusalem. 13Then Paul answered,
"What do you mean by weeping and
breaking my heart? For I am ready
not only to be bound, but also to die
at Jerusalem for the name of the Lord
Jesus."

14So when he would not be persuaded, we ceased, saying, "The will
of the Lord be done."

Paul Urged to Make Peace

15And after those days we packed
and went up to Jerusalem. 16Also
some of the disciples from Caesarea
went with us and brought with them
a certain Mnason of Cyprus, an early
disciple, with whom we were to
lodge.

17And when we had come to Jerusalem, the brethren received us
gladly. 18On the following *day* Paul
went in with us to James, and all the
elders were present. 19When he had
greeted them, he told in detail those
things which God had done among
the Gentiles through his ministry.
20And when they heard *it,* they
glorified the Lord. And they said to
him, "You see, brother, how many
myriads of Jews there are who have
believed, and they are all zealous for
the law; 21but they have been informed about you that you teach all
the Jews who are among the Gentiles
to forsake Moses, saying that they
ought not to circumcise *their* children
nor to walk according to the cus-

21:8 [a]NU-Text omits *who were Paul's companions.*

toms. 22What then? The assembly must certainly meet, for they will[a] hear that you have come. 23Therefore do what we tell you: We have four men who have taken a vow. 24Take them and be purified with them, and pay their expenses so that they may shave *their* heads, and that all may know that those things of which they were informed concerning you are nothing, but *that* you yourself also walk orderly and keep the law. 25But concerning the Gentiles who believe, we have written *and* decided that they should observe no such thing, except[a] that they should keep themselves from *things* offered to idols, from blood, from things strangled, and from sexual immorality."

Arrested in the Temple

26Then Paul took the men, and the next day, having been purified with them, entered the temple to announce the expiration of the days of purification, at which time an offering should be made for each one of them.

27Now when the seven days were almost ended, the Jews from Asia, seeing him in the temple, stirred up the whole crowd and laid hands on him, 28crying out, "Men of Israel, help! This is the man who teaches all *men* everywhere against the people, the law, and this place; and furthermore he also brought Greeks into the temple and has defiled this holy place." 29(For they had previously[a] seen Trophimus the Ephesian with him in the city, whom they supposed that Paul had brought into the temple.)

30And all the city was disturbed; and the people ran together, seized Paul, and dragged him out of the temple; and immediately the doors were shut. 31Now as they were seeking to kill him, news came to the commander of the garrison that all Jerusalem was in an uproar. 32He immediately took soldiers and centurions, and ran down to them. And when they saw the commander and the soldiers, they stopped beating Paul. 33Then the commander came

---

21:22 [a]NU-Text reads *What then is to be done? They will certainly.* **21:25** [a]NU-Text omits *that they should observe no such thing, except.* **21:29** [a]M-Text omits *previously.*

near and took him, and commanded
him to be bound with two chains;
and he asked who he was and what
he had done. 34 And some among the
multitude cried one thing and some
another.

So when he could not ascertain
the truth because of the tumult, he
commanded him to be taken into
the barracks. 35 When he reached the
stairs, he had to be carried by the soldiers because of the violence of the
mob. 36 For the multitude of the people followed after, crying out, "Away
with him!"

Addressing the Jerusalem Mob

37 Then as Paul was about to be led
into the barracks, he said to the commander, "May I speak to you?"

He replied, "Can you speak
Greek? 38 Are you not the Egyptian
who some time ago stirred up a rebellion and led the four thousand as-
sassins out into the wilderness?"

39 But Paul said, "I am a Jew from
Tarsus, in Cilicia, a citizen of no mean
city; and I implore you, permit me to
speak to the people."

40 So when he had given him permission, Paul stood on the stairs and
motioned with his hand to the people. And when there was a great silence, he spoke to *them* in the Hebrew
language, saying,

22 "Brethren and fathers, hear
my defense before you now."
2 And when they heard that he spoke
to them in the Hebrew language,
they kept all the more silent.

Then he said: 3 "I am indeed a Jew,
born in Tarsus of Cilicia, but brought
up in this city at the feet of Gamaliel,
taught according to the strictness
of our fathers' law, and was zealous
toward God as you all are today. 4 I
persecuted this Way to the death,
binding and delivering into prisons
both men and women, 5 as also the
high priest bears me witness, and all
the council of the elders, from whom
I also received letters to the brethren,
and went to Damascus to bring in
chains even those who were there to
Jerusalem to be punished.

6 "Now it happened, as I journeyed and came near Damascus at
about noon, suddenly a great light
from heaven shone around me. 7 And
I fell to the ground and heard a voice
saying to me, 'Saul, Saul, why are you

persecuting Me?' 8So I answered,
'Who are You, Lord?' And He said to
me, 'I am Jesus of Nazareth, whom
you are persecuting.'

9"And those who were with me
indeed saw the light and were afraid,[a]
but they did not hear the voice of
Him who spoke to me. 10So I said,
'What shall I do, Lord?' And the Lord
said to me, 'Arise and go into Damascus, and there you will be told all
things which are appointed for you
to do.' 11And since I could not see
for the glory of that light, being led
by the hand of those who were with
me, I came into Damascus.

12"Then a certain Ananias, a devout man according to the law, having a good testimony with all the
Jews who dwelt *there,* 13came to me;
and he stood and said to me, 'Brother
Saul, receive your sight.' And at that
same hour I looked up at him.
14Then he said, 'The God of our fathers has chosen you that you should
know His will, and see the Just One,
and hear the voice of His mouth.
15For you will be His witness to all
men of what you have seen and
heard. 16And now why are you waiting? Arise and be baptized, and wash
away your sins, calling on the name
of the Lord.'

17"Now it happened, when I
returned to Jerusalem and was praying in the temple, that I was in a
trance 18and saw Him saying to me,
'Make haste and get out of Jerusalem
quickly, for they will not receive your
testimony concerning Me.' 19So I said,
'Lord, they know that in every synagogue I imprisoned and beat those
who believe on You. 20And when the
blood of Your martyr Stephen was
shed, I also was standing by consenting to his death,[a] and guarding the
clothes of those who were killing
him.' 21Then He said to me, 'Depart,
for I will send you far from here to
the Gentiles.'"

Paul's Roman Citizenship

22And they listened to him until
this word, and *then* they raised their
voices and said, "Away with such a *fellow* from the earth, for he is not fit to
live!" 23Then, as they cried out and
tore off *their* clothes and threw dust

22:9 [a]NU-Text omits *and were afraid.* **22:20** [a]NU-Text omits *to his death.*

into the air, 24the commander ordered him to be brought into the barracks, and said that he should be examined under scourging, so that he might know why they shouted so against him. 25And as they bound him with thongs, Paul said to the centurion who stood by, "Is it lawful for you to scourge a man who is a Roman, and uncondemned?"

26When the centurion heard *that,* he went and told the commander, saying, "Take care what you do, for this man is a Roman."

27Then the commander came and said to him, "Tell me, are you a Roman?"

He said, "Yes."

28The commander answered, "With a large sum I obtained this citizenship."

And Paul said, "But I was born *a citizen.*"

29Then immediately those who were about to examine him withdrew from him; and the commander was also afraid after he found out that he was a Roman, and because he had bound him.

The Sanhedrin Divided

30The next day, because he wanted to know for certain why he was accused by the Jews, he released him from *his* bonds, and commanded the chief priests and all their council to appear, and brought Paul down and set him before them.

23 Then Paul, looking earnestly at the council, said, "Men *and* brethren, I have lived in all good conscience before God until this day." 2And the high priest Ananias commanded those who stood by him to strike him on the mouth. 3Then Paul said to him, "God will strike you, *you* whitewashed wall! For you sit to judge me according to the law, and do you command me to be struck contrary to the law?"

4And those who stood by said, "Do you revile God's high priest?"

5Then Paul said, "I did not know, brethren, that he was the high priest; for it is written, *'You shall not speak evil of a ruler of your people.'*"[a]

6But when Paul perceived that

23:5 [a]Exodus 22:28

one part were Sadducees and the
other Pharisees, he cried out in the
council, "Men *and* brethren, I am a
Pharisee, the son of a Pharisee; concerning the hope and resurrection of
the dead I am being judged!"

7 And when he had said this, a
dissension arose between the Pharisees
and the Sadducees; and the assembly
was divided. 8 For Sadducees say that
there is no resurrection—and no
angel or spirit; but the Pharisees confess both. 9 Then there arose a loud
outcry. And the scribes of the Pharisees' party arose and protested, saying, "We find no evil in this man; but
if a spirit or an angel has spoken to
him, let us not fight against God."[a]

10 Now when there arose a great
dissension, the commander, fearing
lest Paul might be pulled to pieces by
them, commanded the soldiers to go
down and take him by force from
among them, and bring *him* into the
barracks.

The Plot Against Paul

11 But the following night the
Lord stood by him and said, "Be of
good cheer, Paul; for as you have testified for Me in Jerusalem, so you
must also bear witness at Rome."

12 And when it was day, some of
the Jews banded together and bound
themselves under an oath, saying
that they would neither eat nor
drink till they had killed Paul. 13 Now
there were more than forty who
had formed this conspiracy. 14 They
came to the chief priests and elders,
and said, "We have bound ourselves
under a great oath that we will eat
nothing until we have killed Paul.
15 Now you, therefore, together with
the council, suggest to the commander that he be brought down to
you tomorrow,[a] as though you were
going to make further inquiries concerning him; but we are ready to kill
him before he comes near."

16 So when Paul's sister's son heard
of their ambush, he went and entered
the barracks and told Paul. 17 Then
Paul called one of the centurions to
him and said, "Take this young man
to the commander, for he has something to tell him." 18 So he took him
and brought *him* to the commander
and said, "Paul the prisoner called me
to *him* and asked *me* to bring this

23:9 [a]NU-Text omits last clause and reads *what if a spirit or an angel has spoken to him?* **23:15** [a]NU-Text omits *tomorrow.*

young man to you. He has something to say to you."

19 Then the commander took him
by the hand, went aside, and asked
privately, "What is it that you have to
tell me?"

20 And he said, "The Jews have
agreed to ask that you bring Paul
down to the council tomorrow, as
though they were going to inquire
more fully about him. 21 But do not
yield to them, for more than forty of
them lie in wait for him, men who
have bound themselves by an oath
that they will neither eat nor drink
till they have killed him; and now
they are ready, waiting for the promise from you."

22 So the commander let the
young man depart, and commanded
him, "Tell no one that you have revealed these things to me."

Sent to Felix

23 And he called for two centurions, saying, "Prepare two hundred
soldiers, seventy horsemen, and two
hundred spearmen to go to Caesarea
at the third hour of the night; 24 and
provide mounts to set Paul on, and
bring *him* safely to Felix the governor." 25 He wrote a letter in the following manner:

26 Claudius Lysias,

To the most excellent governor Felix:

Greetings.

27 This man was seized by the Jews and
was about to be killed by them. Coming with the troops I rescued him,
having learned that he was a Roman.
28 And when I wanted to know the reason they accused him, I brought him
before their council. 29 I found out that
he was accused concerning questions
of their law, but had nothing charged
against him deserving of death or
chains. 30 And when it was told me
that the Jews lay in wait for the man,[a]
I sent him immediately to you, and
also commanded his accusers to state
before you the charges against him.

Farewell.

31 Then the soldiers, as they were
commanded, took Paul and brought

23:30 [a]NU-Text reads *there would be a plot against the man.*

him by night to Antipatris. 32The next day they left the horsemen to go on with him, and returned to the barracks. 33When they came to Caesarea and had delivered the letter to the governor, they also presented Paul to him. 34And when the governor had read *it,* he asked what province he was from. And when he understood that *he was* from Cilicia, 35he said, "I will hear you when your accusers also have come." And he commanded him to be kept in Herod's Praetorium.

Accused of Sedition

24 Now after five days Ananias the high priest came down with the elders and a certain orator *named* Tertullus. These gave evidence to the governor against Paul.

2And when he was called upon, Tertullus began his accusation, saying: "Seeing that through you we enjoy great peace, and prosperity is being brought to this nation by your foresight, 3we accept *it* always and in all places, most noble Felix, with all thankfulness. 4Nevertheless, not to be tedious to you any further, I beg you to hear, by your courtesy, a few words from us. 5For we have found this man a plague, a creator of dissension among all the Jews throughout the world, and a ringleader of the sect of the Nazarenes. 6He even tried to profane the temple, and we seized him,[a] and wanted to judge him according to our law. 7But the commander Lysias came by and with great violence took *him* out of our hands, 8commanding his accusers to come to you. By examining him yourself you may ascertain all these things of which we accuse him." 9And the Jews also assented,[a] maintaining that these things were so.

The Defense Before Felix

10Then Paul, after the governor had nodded to him to speak, answered: "Inasmuch as I know that you have been for many years a judge of this nation, I do the more cheerfully answer for myself, 11because you may ascertain that it is no more than twelve days since I went up to Jerusalem to worship. 12And they neither

---

24:6 [a]NU-Text ends the sentence here and omits the rest of verse 6, all of verse 7, and the first clause of verse 8.
24:9 [a]NU-Text and M-Text read *joined the attack.*

found me in the temple disputing
with anyone nor inciting the crowd,
either in the synagogues or in the city.
13 Nor can they prove the things of
which they now accuse me. 14 But this
I confess to you, that according to the
Way which they call a sect, so I worship the God of my fathers, believing
all things which are written in the
Law and in the Prophets. 15 I have hope
in God, which they themselves also
accept, that there will be a resurrection of *the* dead,[a] both of *the* just and *the*
unjust. 16 This *being* so, I myself always
strive to have a conscience without
offense toward God and men.

17 "Now after many years I came
to bring alms and offerings to my nation, 18 in the midst of which some
Jews from Asia found me purified in
the temple, neither with a mob nor
with tumult. 19 They ought to have
been here before you to object if they
had anything against me. 20 Or else let
those who are *here* themselves say if
they found any wrongdoing[a] in me
while I stood before the council,
21 unless *it is* for this one statement
which I cried out, standing among
them, 'Concerning the resurrection
of the dead I am being judged by you
this day.' "

Felix Procrastinates

22 But when Felix heard these
things, having more accurate knowledge of *the* Way, he adjourned the
proceedings and said, "When Lysias
the commander comes down, I will
make a decision on your case." 23 So
he commanded the centurion to
keep Paul and to let *him* have liberty,
and told him not to forbid any of his
friends to provide for or visit him.

24 And after some days, when Felix
came with his wife Drusilla, who was
Jewish, he sent for Paul and heard
him concerning the faith in Christ.
25 Now as he reasoned about righteousness, self-control, and the judgment to come, Felix was afraid and
answered, "Go away for now; when I
have a convenient time I will call for
you." 26 Meanwhile he also hoped
that money would be given him by
Paul, that he might release him.[a]
Therefore he sent for him more often
and conversed with him.

24:15 [a]NU-Text omits *of the dead.* **24:20** [a]NU-Text and M-Text read *say what wrongdoing they found.* **24:26** [a]NU-Text omits *that he might release him.*

27But after two years Porcius Festus succeeded Felix; and Felix, wanting to do the Jews a favor, left Paul bound.

Paul Appeals to Caesar

25 Now when Festus had come to the province, after three days he went up from Caesarea to Jerusalem. 2Then the high priest[a] and the chief men of the Jews informed him against Paul; and they petitioned him, 3asking a favor against him, that he would summon him to Jerusalem—while *they* lay in ambush along the road to kill him. 4But Festus answered that Paul should be kept at Caesarea, and that he himself was going *there* shortly. 5"Therefore," he said, "let those who have authority among you go down with *me* and accuse this man, to see if there is any fault in him."

6And when he had remained among them more than ten days, he went down to Caesarea. And the next day, sitting on the judgment seat, he commanded Paul to be brought. 7When he had come, the Jews who had come down from Jerusalem stood about and laid many serious complaints against Paul, which they could not prove, 8while he answered for himself, "Neither against the law of the Jews, nor against the temple, nor against Caesar have I offended in anything at all."

9But Festus, wanting to do the Jews a favor, answered Paul and said, "Are you willing to go up to Jerusalem and there be judged before me concerning these things?"

10So Paul said, "I stand at Caesar's judgment seat, where I ought to be judged. To the Jews I have done no wrong, as you very well know. 11For if I am an offender, or have committed anything deserving of death, I do not object to dying; but if there is nothing in these things of which these men accuse me, no one can deliver me to them. I appeal to Caesar."

12Then Festus, when he had conferred with the council, answered, "You have appealed to Caesar? To Caesar you shall go!"

Paul Before Agrippa

13And after some days King Agrippa and Bernice came to Cae-

25:2 [a]NU-Text reads *chief priests.*

sarea to greet Festus. 14When they
had been there many days, Festus laid
Paul's case before the king, saying:
"There is a certain man left a prisoner
by Felix, 15about whom the chief
priests and the elders of the Jews informed *me,* when I was in Jerusalem,
asking for a judgment against him.
16To them I answered, 'It is not the
custom of the Romans to deliver any
man to destruction[a] before the accused meets the accusers face to
face, and has opportunity to answer
for himself concerning the charge
against him.' 17Therefore when they
had come together, without any
delay, the next day I sat on the
judgment seat and commanded
the man to be brought in. 18When
the accusers stood up, they brought
no accusation against him of such
things as I supposed, 19but had some
questions against him about their
own religion and about a certain Jesus, who had died, whom Paul affirmed to be alive. 20And because I
was uncertain of such questions, I
asked whether he was willing to go to
Jerusalem and there be judged concerning these matters. 21But when
Paul appealed to be reserved for the
decision of Augustus, I commanded
him to be kept till I could send him
to Caesar."

22Then Agrippa said to Festus, "I
also would like to hear the man
myself."

"Tomorrow," he said, "you shall
hear him."

23So the next day, when Agrippa
and Bernice had come with great
pomp, and had entered the audito-
rium with the commanders and the
prominent men of the city, at Festus'
command Paul was brought in.
24And Festus said: "King Agrippa and
all the men who are here present
with us, you see this man about
whom the whole assembly of the
Jews petitioned me, both at Jerusalem and here, crying out that he was
not fit to live any longer. 25But when
I found that he had committed nothing deserving of death, and that he
himself had appealed to Augustus, I
decided to send him. 26I have nothing
certain to write to my lord concerning him. Therefore I have brought
him out before you, and especially
before you, King Agrippa, so that

25:16 [a]NU-Text omits *to destruction,* although it is implied.

after the examination has taken place
I may have something to write. 27For
it seems to me unreasonable to send
a prisoner and not to specify the
charges against him."

Paul's Early Life

26 Then Agrippa said to Paul,
"You are permitted to speak
for yourself."

So Paul stretched out his hand
and answered for himself: 2"I think
myself happy, King Agrippa, because
today I shall answer for myself before
you concerning all the things of
which I am accused by the Jews, 3es-
pecially because you are expert in all
customs and questions which have to
do with the Jews. Therefore I beg you
to hear me patiently.

4"My manner of life from my
youth, which was spent from the
beginning among my own nation at
Jerusalem, all the Jews know. 5They
knew me from the first, if they were
willing to testify, that according to
the strictest sect of our religion I
lived a Pharisee. 6And now I stand
and am judged for the hope of the
promise made by God to our fathers.
7To this *promise* our twelve tribes,
earnestly serving *God* night and day,
hope to attain. For this hope's sake,
King Agrippa, I am accused by the
Jews. 8Why should it be thought in-
credible by you that God raises the
dead?

9"Indeed, I myself thought I must
do many things contrary to the
name of Jesus of Nazareth. 10This I
also did in Jerusalem, and many of
the saints I shut up in prison, having
received authority from the chief
priests; and when they were put to
death, I cast my vote against *them.*
11And I punished them often in every
synagogue and compelled *them* to
blaspheme; and being exceedingly
enraged against them, I persecuted
them even to foreign cities.

Paul Recounts His Conversion

12"While thus occupied, as I journeyed to Damascus with authority
and commission from the chief
priests, 13at midday, O king, along the
road I saw a light from heaven,
brighter than the sun, shining
around me and those who journeyed
with me. 14And when we all had
fallen to the ground, I heard a voice
speaking to me and saying in the Hebrew language, 'Saul, Saul, why are
you persecuting Me? *It is* hard for you

to kick against the goads.' 15 So I said,
'Who are You, Lord?' And He said, 'I
am Jesus, whom you are persecuting.
16 But rise and stand on your feet;
for I have appeared to you for this
purpose, to make you a minister
and a witness both of the things
which you have seen and of the
things which I will yet reveal to
you. 17 I will deliver you from the *Jew-*
ish people, as well as *from* the Gentiles,
to whom I now[a] send you, 18 to open
their eyes, *in order* to turn *them* from
darkness to light, and *from* the power
of Satan to God, that they may receive forgiveness of sins and an inheritance among those who are
sanctified by faith in Me.'

Paul's Post-Conversion Life

19 "Therefore, King Agrippa, I was
not disobedient to the heavenly vision, 20 but declared first to those in
Damascus and in Jerusalem, and
throughout all the region of Judea,
and *then* to the Gentiles, that they
should repent, turn to God, and do
works befitting repentance. 21 For these
reasons the Jews seized me in the temple and tried to kill *me*. 22 Therefore,
having obtained help from God, to
this day I stand, witnessing both to
small and great, saying no other
things than those which the prophets
and Moses said would come— 23 that
the Christ would suffer, that He
would be the first to rise from the
dead, and would proclaim light to the
Jewish people and to the Gentiles."

Agrippa Parries Paul's Challenge

24 Now as he thus made his defense, Festus said with a loud voice,
"Paul, you are beside yourself! Much
learning is driving you mad!"

25 But he said, "I am not mad,
most noble Festus, but speak the
words of truth and reason. 26 For the
king, before whom I also speak freely,
knows these things; for I am convinced that none of these things
escapes his attention, since this
thing was not done in a corner. 27 King
Agrippa, do you believe the prophets?
I know that you do believe."

28 Then Agrippa said to Paul, "You
almost persuade me to become a
Christian."

29 And Paul said, "I would to God
that not only you, but also all who

26:17 [a]NU-Text and M-Text omit *now*.

hear me today, might become both
almost and altogether such as I am,
except for these chains."
30When he had said these things,
the king stood up, as well as the
governor and Bernice and those who
sat with them; 31and when they
had gone aside, they talked among
themselves, saying, "This man is
doing nothing deserving of death or
chains."
32Then Agrippa said to Festus,
"This man might have been set free if
he had not appealed to Caesar."

The Voyage to Rome Begins

27And when it was decided that
we should sail to Italy, they
delivered Paul and some other prisoners to *one* named Julius, a centurion of the Augustan Regiment. 2So,
entering a ship of Adramyttium, we
put to sea, meaning to sail along the
coasts of Asia. Aristarchus, a Mac-
edonian of Thessalonica, was with us.
3And the next *day* we landed at Sidon.
And Julius treated Paul kindly and
gave *him* liberty to go to his friends
and receive care. 4When we had put
to sea from there, we sailed under *the
shelter of* Cyprus, because the winds
were contrary. 5And when we had
sailed over the sea which is off Cilicia
and Pamphylia, we came to Myra, *a
city* of Lycia. 6There the centurion
found an Alexandrian ship sailing to
Italy, and he put us on board.
7When we had sailed slowly many
days, and arrived with difficulty off
Cnidus, the wind not permitting us
to proceed, we sailed under *the shelter
of* Crete off Salmone. 8Passing it with
difficulty, we came to a place called
Fair Havens, near the city *of* Lasea.

Paul's Warning Ignored

9Now when much time had been
spent, and sailing was now dangerous
because the Fast was already over,
Paul advised them, 10saying, "Men, I
perceive that this voyage will end
with disaster and much loss, not only
of the cargo and ship, but also our
lives." 11Nevertheless the centurion
was more persuaded by the helms-
man and the owner of the ship than
by the things spoken by Paul. 12And
because the harbor was not suitable
to winter in, the majority advised to
set sail from there also, if by any
means they could reach Phoenix, a
harbor of Crete opening toward the
southwest and northwest, *and* winter
there.

In the Tempest

13 When the south wind blew softly, supposing that they had obtained *their* desire, putting out to sea, they sailed close by Crete. 14 But not long after, a tempestuous head wind arose, called Euroclydon.[a] 15 So when the ship was caught, and could not head into the wind, we let *her* drive. 16 And running under *the shelter of* an island called Clauda,[a] we secured the skiff with difficulty. 17 When they had taken it on board, they used cables to undergird the ship; and fearing lest they should run aground on the Syrtis[a] *Sands,* they struck sail and so were driven. 18 And because we were exceedingly tempest-tossed, the next *day* they lightened the ship. 19 On the third *day* we threw the ship's tackle overboard with our own hands. 20 Now when neither sun nor stars appeared for many days, and no small tempest beat on *us,* all hope that we would be saved was finally given up.

21 But after long abstinence from food, then Paul stood in the midst of them and said, "Men, you should have listened to me, and not have sailed from Crete and incurred this disaster and loss. 22 And now I urge you to take heart, for there will be no loss of life among you, but only of the ship. 23 For there stood by me this night an angel of the God to whom I belong and whom I serve, 24 saying, 'Do not be afraid, Paul; you must be brought before Caesar; and indeed God has granted you all those who sail with you.' 25 Therefore take heart, men, for I believe God that it will be just as it was told me. 26 However, we must run aground on a certain island."

27 Now when the fourteenth night had come, as we were driven up and down in the Adriatic *Sea,* about midnight the sailors sensed that they were drawing near some land. 28 And they took soundings and found *it* to be twenty fathoms; and when they had gone a little farther, they took soundings again and found *it* to be fifteen fathoms. 29 Then, fearing lest we should run aground on the rocks, they dropped four anchors

---

27:14 [a]NU-Text reads *Euraquilon.* **27:16** [a]NU-Text reads *Cauda.* **27:17** [a]M-Text reads *Syrtes* **28:19** [a]That is, the ruling authorities.

from the stern, and prayed for day to
come. 30And as the sailors were seeking to escape from the ship, when
they had let down the skiff into the
sea, under pretense of putting out
anchors from the prow, 31Paul said to
the centurion and the soldiers, "Unless these men stay in the ship, you
cannot be saved." 32Then the soldiers
cut away the ropes of the skiff and let
it fall off.

33And as day was about to dawn,
Paul implored *them* all to take food,
saying, "Today is the fourteenth day
you have waited and continued
without food, and eaten nothing.
34Therefore I urge you to take nourishment, for this is for your survival,
since not a hair will fall from the
head of any of you." 35And when he
had said these things, he took bread
and gave thanks to God in the presence of them all; and when he had
broken *it* he began to eat. 36Then they
were all encouraged, and also took
food themselves. 37And in all we were
two hundred and seventy-six persons
on the ship. 38So when they had
eaten enough, they lightened the
ship and threw out the wheat into
the sea.

Shipwrecked on Malta

39When it was day, they did not
recognize the land; but they observed
a bay with a beach, onto which they
planned to run the ship if possible.
40And they let go the anchors and left
them in the sea, meanwhile loosing
the rudder ropes; and they hoisted
the mainsail to the wind and made
for shore. 41But striking a place
where two seas met, they ran the
ship aground; and the prow stuck fast
and remained immovable, but the
stern was being broken up by the violence of the waves.

42And the soldiers' plan was to
kill the prisoners, lest any of them
should swim away and escape. 43But
the centurion, wanting to save Paul,
kept them from *their* purpose, and
commanded that those who could
swim should jump *overboard* first and
get to land, 44and the rest, some on
boards and some on *parts* of the ship.
And so it was that they all escaped
safely to land.

Paul's Ministry on Malta

28 Now when they had escaped,
they then found out that the
island was called Malta. 2And the na-

tives showed us unusual kindness; for they kindled a fire and made us all welcome, because of the rain that was falling and because of the cold. [3]But when Paul had gathered a bundle of sticks and laid *them* on the fire, a viper came out because of the heat, and fastened on his hand. [4]So when the natives saw the creature hanging from his hand, they said to one another, "No doubt this man is a murderer, whom, though he has escaped the sea, yet justice does not allow to live." [5]But he shook off the creature into the fire and suffered no harm. [6]However, they were expecting that he would swell up or suddenly fall down dead. But after they had looked for a long time and saw no harm come to him, they changed their minds and said that he was a god.

[7]In that region there was an estate of the leading citizen of the island, whose name was Publius, who received us and entertained us courteously for three days. [8]And it happened that the father of Publius lay sick of a fever and dysentery. Paul went in to him and prayed, and he laid his hands on him and healed him. [9]So when this was done, the rest of those on the island who had diseases also came and were healed. [10]They also honored us in many ways; and when we departed, they provided such things as were necessary.

Arrival at Rome

[11]After three months we sailed in an Alexandrian ship whose figurehead was the Twin Brothers, which had wintered at the island. [12]And landing at Syracuse, we stayed three days. [13]From there we circled round and reached Rhegium. And after one day the south wind blew; and the next day we came to Puteoli, [14]where we found brethren, and were invited to stay with them seven days. And so we went toward Rome. [15]And from there, when the brethren heard about us, they came to meet us as far as Appii Forum and Three Inns. When Paul saw them, he thanked God and took courage.

[16]Now when we came to Rome, the centurion delivered the prisoners to the captain of the guard; but Paul was permitted to dwell by himself with the soldier who guarded him.

Paul's Ministry at Rome

[17]And it came to pass after three days that Paul called the leaders of the

Jews together. So when they had
come together, he said to them: "Men
and brethren, though I have done
nothing against our people or the customs of our fathers, yet I was delivered as a prisoner from Jerusalem into
the hands of the Romans, **18**who,
when they had examined me, wanted
to let *me* go, because there was no
cause for putting me to death. **19**But
when the Jews[a] spoke against *it,* I was
compelled to appeal to Caesar, not
that I had anything of which to accuse
my nation. **20**For this reason therefore
I have called for you, to see *you* and
speak with *you,* because for the hope of
Israel I am bound with this chain."

21Then they said to him, "We neither received letters from Judea concerning you, nor have any of the
brethren who came reported or spoken any evil of you. **22**But we desire to
hear from you what you think; for
concerning this sect, we know that it
is spoken against everywhere."

23So when they had appointed him
a day, many came to him at *his* lodging,
to whom he explained and solemnly
testified of the kingdom of God, persuading them concerning Jesus from
both the Law of Moses and the Prophets, from morning till evening. **24**And
some were persuaded by the things
which were spoken, and some disbe-
lieved. **25**So when they did not agree
among themselves, they departed after
Paul had said one word: "The Holy
Spirit spoke rightly through Isaiah the
prophet to our[a] fathers, **26**saying,

'Go to this people and say:
"Hearing you will hear, and shall
not understand;
And seeing you will see, and
not perceive;
27 *For the hearts of this people*
have grown dull.
Their ears are hard of hearing,
And their eyes they have closed,
Lest they should see with their
eyes and hear with their
ears,
Lest they should understand
with their hearts and turn,
So that I should heal them."'[a]

28"Therefore let it be known to
you that the salvation of God has
been sent to the Gentiles, and they
will hear it!" **29**And when he had

28:25 [a]NU-Text reads *your.* **28:27** [a]Isaiah 6:9, 10

said these words, the Jews departed
and had a great dispute among themselves.[a]

30 Then Paul dwelt two whole
years in his own rented house, and
received all who came to him,
31 preaching the kingdom of God and
teaching the things which concern
the Lord Jesus Christ with all confidence, no one forbidding him.

28:29 [a]NU-Text omits this verse.

Following is a special selection from

MATTHEW'S STORY

BY

TIM LAHAYE

and

JERRY B. JENKINS

Coming soon in hardcover from Putnam Praise
Published by G. P. Putnam's Sons

The Palace of Herod the Great, Jerusalem

The king toddled like a baby in the wee hours of the morning, gingerly favoring hips and knees worn from more than seven decades of service. Shuffling across vast marble floors, he drew his robe tight around his neck and settled heavily on the portico steps.

Herod's chief aide maintained an appropriate distance.

"Ariel, come," the king said, sighing. "Sit with me."

Ariel hastened to the stairs, bowed, and sat two steps below the king.

"You can tell I am vexed," Herod said. "Can you not?"

"Of course, Majesty. Allow me to send for some wine perhaps. Ale? Water?"

With a dismissive wave, Herod shook his head and looked away, gazing out over his expansive gardens, lit by the dancing flames of torches. "The stargazers," he muttered. "What did you make of them?"

Ariel shrugged. "I made of them what you made of them, Sire."

"And you know my assessment?"

"Of course. For all their finery and diplomacy and scholarship, they made a grave error. Asking the King of the Jews for news of the birth of the King of the Jews—verily!"

Herod stood and tottered down the steps, and Ariel immediately began to rise. "Stay put," the king said. "I am going nowhere." He placed a hand against a column and stared at the floor. "The Roman Senate themselves made me King of Judea! My subjects can call me half a Jew all they want—don't look at me as if you are unaware. You are surprised that I know?"

"Somewhat."

"You should know better by now. I know all. Has it been too long since Marc Antony and Octavian themselves walked me from the meeting in Rome and allowed me to sacrifice to their gods?"

Ariel nodded. "I daresay many have no knowledge of it, except what they've heard from their elders. You were a young man."

"Thirty. But it's history, man! To be taught from birth! When Octavian defeated Antony and became Augustus, I confessed that I had been loyal to his foe. I hid nothing! I pledged myself to him thenceforth, and he himself told me Judea was too small for a man like me."

"And everyone knows he added territories to your kingdom, Highness."

"Then how is it that the so-called wise men did not seem to know?"

"They showed you great deference, sir."

Herod sat again. "You said yourself, they asked me—*me!*—about the newborn King of the Jews!"

"And may I say, Highness, your response was priceless."

"It was, wasn't it?"

"Persuading them to bring you news of him so you yourself could worship him!"

Herod had to laugh, though he convulsed into a spasm of coughs. "Could they have been blinded by the splendor of my kingdom and thus unaware of my determination?"

"That is all I can surmise. Though your passion is not secret . . ."

Herod held up a hand. "Please, don't speak of it. My brother-in-law, three of my sons, my mother-in-law . . ."

"Their demises at your hand merely confirm your resolve to preserve your power, Sire."

"Could these men not know that I spared not even my own beloved?"

"They must, sir."

"I miss her."

"After all this time? You've had nine others."

Herod nodded miserably. "It is not guilt, Ariel. Just melancholy. I love her still."

"But you could countenance no threat to your throne."

Herod sat in silence, staring into the heavens. "And I am not about to start now."

"Are you not tired, Majesty?"

"Of course. But how can I sleep? You know this child is the prophesied Messiah."

"So the scribes say."

Herod shifted his eyes to the arched ceiling. "The priests confirm it! The child the seers seek is to be the Christ."

Ariel leaned back and stretched. "Born in Bethlehem."

"So the prophets write," Herod whispered.

"And when the men from the East bring you news of him?"

"I will invite him here, of course!"

Ariel laughed. "And worship him . . ."

"No doubt! I'll worship him with a sword."

Ariel eventually persuaded the elderly king to fill his belly with wine. "It always makes you drowsy."

Herod slept fitfully nonetheless, and after a morning bath in one of his magnificent pools, he summoned his aide again. "What news of the magi?"

"None, Sire."

"Bethlehem is but a village. Surely they are conspicuous."

"I'll send scouts."

"I want those foreigners here with news—if not with the infant himself—by nightfall. They have had more than enough time to find him and report back to me."

ONE

Bet Guvrin, twenty miles southwest of Bethlehem

Levi loved being the older brother, but at nearly eight years old, he was not allowed to carry little Chavivi, who had just learned to walk. The toddler provided no end of delight to Levi, who followed him about, calling his name, and trying everything he could to amuse the boy. To hear a giggle or to see a flash of those few tiny teeth was all Levi was after. How he wished he could hold the baby the way his parents did.

"You are lithe and lanky," his mother said. "And you will one day be tall and strong. But Chavivi is fragile, understand?"

Levi nodded, but that didn't keep him from pleading his case to his father when he returned from his day's work at the tannery just beyond the village market. Levi sat on his father's lap, smelling the pungent leather on the man and tracing his orange tinted hands with his own fingers.

"But I'm strong, Father, and I won't drop him."

"You know the rules," Alphaeus said. "When your mother and I are present, you may hold the lad."

"Even now?"

"Of course. Bring him to me."

Levi ran off to get his brother, his father calling after him, "Remember, don't try to lift him until you get him in here!"

Chavivi sat on the ground near where his mother was checking the risen barley dough, preparing to bake it. "Come!" Levi called out, and the little one leaped to his feet with a smile and scampered away. "No! We're not playing chase! Come see Father!"

But the boy was headed for the goat pen, where he held his nose and looked back at Levi. The older son overtook him and grabbed his hand, making him laugh. He pulled Chavivi to the side of the house where his father was washing up.

"Cha-cha!" Alphaeus roared, quickly drying his hands and squatting, opening his arms. Chavivi ran to him and jumped, and his father swung him in the air. "Now let Levi hold you."

Levi reached for the boy, but his father made him sit on the ground first. Yet when he was settled, Chavivi wriggled to stay with his father, laughing when he plopped him into Levi's lap. Soon he seemed to have had enough of that and ran off again to find his mother.

"Keep him from the fire," Alphaeus said, as Levi rose to follow. He would never allow his little brother to be hurt, though once he had neglected him for only a few seconds and was startled by his cries. The boy had tripped over donkey dung and landed atop the pile. Levi's mother made him wash Chavivi, then she checked the baby over carefully, sniffing his whole body before dressing him afresh.

Now as the family lit the candelabrum and sat for dinner, Levi asked if they were still planning on a trip to Jerusalem the next day. Once each month his father picked up raw hides at a trading center near the Holy City. Twice a year he took the family along.

Alphaeus nodded. "Tomorrow is Wednesday, when the Damascus traders arrive with their goods. Mary, rumor has it they will have silk from the East."

Levi's mother smiled. "You know as well as I that I can only look. We can't afford such . . ."

"I know," Alphaeus said. "But you can dream. And perhaps they'll have trinkets for Chavivi again."

She smiled. "Trinkets I can afford." She turned to the child and broke off a small piece of bread, tucking it into his mouth. "You want a toy, little one? Do you?"

Chavivi's eyes widened and he smiled, the bread slipping from his mouth. Mary pressed it back in and drew her finger across his cheek, causing the baby to grin again, the bread to reappear, and the family to laugh. Levi couldn't wait until the next morning. On their last trip, Chavivi slept on the long wagon ride into Jerusalem, but that had been half a year ago. He would be more alert now, and it would be fun to see his face when he saw the bustle of the city and especially the pageantry at the Temple.

Levi had learned to read at a young age, and at five years old began the daily reading of the Torah, looking forward to the day he could join his older friends at the synagogue school to study the Oral Law—commentaries from sages on biblical passages. His parents sat with him, huddled over a lamp, helping him sound out all the words and then explaining them to him. It was as if he could feel himself becoming smarter every day.

He knew friends who dreaded the daily readings and did not look forward to turning ten and starting to really study at the synagogue.

But that was not true with Levi. He took pride in his name and his future, especially in his parents' expectations for him. Often they had talked about how he would not have to break his back farming or tanning or shaping pottery. He would be a priest, called out, separated for the service of the Lord God Almighty. "You will never have riches," his mother would say, "but you will be richly blessed in the service of the one true God."

Levi dreamed of someday taking his place in the Levite choir that sang at the daily sacrificial service at the Holy Temple in Jerusalem. On the few occasions when his parents had taken him there, he was fascinated by the signal for the choir to begin—the dropping of the rake used to clean the altar. Lyres, harps, cymbals, and trumpets accompanied the dozen or so singers, who had a different song for each day. Levi's father explained that each song represented one day of the creation week.

The last time Levi had heard the choir had been on a Friday, when they commemorated the crowning completion of creation by singing Psalm 93:

The Lord reigns, He is clothed with majesty;
The Lord is clothed,
He has girded Himself with strength.
Surely the world is established, so that it cannot be moved.
Your throne is established from of old;
You are from everlasting.
The floods have lifted up, O Lord,
The floods have lifted up their voice;
The floods lift up their waves.
The Lord on high is mightier
Than the noise of many waters,

Than the mighty waves of the sea.
Your testimonies are very sure;
Holiness adorns Your house,
O Lord, forever.

Levi had asked his father if the Lord was clothed with majesty the same as King Herod was, not realizing until he saw his father's face cloud over that he had apparently made a grave mistake.

"You are young, son, and so can be forgiven for mentioning the name of our evil king in the same breath with that of our great Lord and the God of our fathers Abraham, Isaac, and Jacob."

"I'm sorry, Father."

"The song refers not to God's clothes but to His majesty. Today, the sixth day, was the day man was created, and of all God's handiworks, only man is able to recognize God's true greatness and become His subject."

Levi felt bad because he had clearly displeased his father, though his question had been innocent. He had hoped to suggest that the family complete that visit to Jerusalem with a walk past Herod's palace inside the city's southern walls, but in light of his father's reprimand, that was clearly out of the question. Still, although his parents despised the king, it had not stopped them from gazing at the palace before.

Tomorrow's visit would be better. He would know not to compare Herod with God. Plus, Levi had never been to the Holy Temple on a Wednesday. "What will the choir sing tomorrow, Father?"

Alphaeus glanced at his wife, his brow furrowed. "Hmm. The fourth day is Psalm Ninety-four, Mary, is it not?"

Levi's mother nodded. "Son," she said, "keep Chavivi occupied while I tidy up, then I want to hear your prayer, as you will not be doing your reading in the morning."

Levi was amused by the baby. Chavivi always grew sleepy after eating, especially in the evening. Now he sat on the floor, staring. His eyelids drooped, leading to long, slow blinks. He nodded like a man who had imbibed too much wine, and Levi laughed, rousing the boy, but he started to nod off again a few seconds later.

"He's falling asleep, Mother!"

"Prepare his mat and put him down then, but be careful."

Sometimes the baby fought being put to bed, but not tonight. He appeared to be trying to stay awake, staring wide-eyed at Levi and then at his mother as she bustled about. Finally he turned and shut his eyes. Levi draped a small blanket over him.

"Sing him your prayer, Levi," his mother said.

"Yes," his father said. "And do it perfectly, every word. I have two prutahs here that will afford you a dessert of pears and honey from the vendors tomorrow."

"Oh, Alphaeus," his mother said. "He should do it for its own sake."

"I will!" Levi said. "But I will enjoy the treat too."

He cleared his throat and chanted softly, "Hear, O Israel: The Lord our God, the Lord is one! You shall love the Lord your God with all your heart, with all your soul, and with all your strength. And it shall be that if you earnestly obey My commandments which I command you today, to love the Lord your God and serve Him with all your heart and with all your soul, then I will give you the rain for your land in its season, the early rain and the latter rain, that you may gather in your grain, your new wine, and your oil. And I will send grass in your fields for your livestock, that you may eat and be filled.

"Take heed to yourselves, lest your heart be deceived, and you turn aside and serve other gods and worship them, lest the Lord's anger be aroused against you, and He shut up the heavens so that there be no rain, and the land yield no produce, and you perish quickly from the good land which the Lord is giving you.

"Therefore you shall lay up these words of mine in your heart and in your soul, and bind them as a sign on your hand, and they shall be as frontlets between your eyes. You shall teach them to your children, speaking of them when you sit in your house, when you walk by the way, when you lie down, and when you rise up. And you shall write them on the doorposts of your house and on your gates, that your days and the days of your children may be multiplied in the land of which the Lord swore to your fathers to give them, like the days of the heavens above the earth."

"Excellent!" his father announced, proffering the coins.

Levi helped him pull the table to the wall and move the chairs. He then laid out his parents' and his own mats, not far from the baby's. With the setting of the sun the air grew cold, and his father brought fresh charcoal for the brazier. That was Levi's favorite way to sleep—a cool night with the air stealing in around the shutters on one side, the fire warming him on the other.

Printed in the United States
by Baker & Taylor Publisher Services